About the author

With more than a million copies of her books in print,
LaVyrle Spencer is an award-winning, critically
acclaimed author of ten romance novels. Her devotion
to her craft, her love for people and her appreciation
of the drama in day-to-day living help to make her
a master storyteller. A joy to read, LaVyrle's writing
is distinctive for its witty earthiness, sensitivity and
innovative plots. She is not afraid to explore the most
serious or even risqué territory, and she delights
readers by having fun with her characters and seeing
the lighter side of any situation. The women in her
books are strong and resourceful, much like the
author herself.

Along with her husband and two daughters, LaVyrle
lives in Minneapolis, Minnesota. Respected and
admired by her peers and colleagues, she won the
Romance Writers of America award for Best Historical
Novel for her book *The Endearment*.

Harlequin is proud to present *Sweet Memories*, a story
of courage that will make you laugh and make you
cry–a story you won't soon forget.

Books by LaVyrle Spencer

SWEET MEMORIES

HARLEQUIN TEMPTATION
1—SPRING FANCY

These books may be available at your local bookseller.

For a list of all titles currently available,
send your name and address to:

Harlequin Reader Service
P.O. Box 52040, Phoenix, AZ 85072-2040
Canadian address: P.O. Box 2800, Postal Station A,
5170 Yonge St., Willowdale, Ont. M2N 5T5

LAVYRLE SPENCER
SWEET MEMORIES

WORLDWIDE

TORONTO · NEW YORK · LONDON · PARIS
AMSTERDAM · STOCKHOLM · HAMBURG
ATHENS · MILAN · TOKYO · SYDNEY

First edition May 1984
ISBN 0-373-97008-0

With love to
the Huebners:
Jeannie
George
Jason
Tracy
and
Duke
And for my "other daughter"
Theresa Schaeffer

Chapter One

AT LAST, Jeff was coming home, but he wasn't alone. Watching the big-bellied jet taxiing to a stop, Theresa Brubaker felt two conflicting emotions—excitement that her "baby brother" would be here for two whole weeks, and annoyance that he'd dragged along some stranger to interfere with their family holiday. Theresa never liked meeting strangers, and at the thought of meeting one now, especially a *man*, a nervous ache grabbed her between the shoulder blades. She worked her head in a circle, flexed her shoulders and tried to shrug away the annoyance.

Through the soles of her knee-high snow boots she felt the shudder and rumble of the engines as they wheezed a last inflated breath, then whistled through a dying decrescendo and sighed into silence. The accordion pleats of the jetway eased forward, its mouth molded against the curve of the plane, and Theresa riveted her eyes on the doorway set in the wall of glass. As the first footsteps of disembarking passengers thudded down the tunnel, she self-consciously glanced down and made sure her heavy gray wool coat was buttoned up completely. She clutched a small black leather purse against her left side in a way that partially concealed her breast and gave her reason to cross her arms.

Her heart tripped out a staccato beat of anticipation—*Jeff. My crazy clown of a brother, the life of the family, coming home to make Christmas what all the songs said it should be. Oh, there's no place like home for the holidays.* Jeff—how she'd missed him. She bit her lower lip and trained her eyes on the door as the first passengers debarked: a young mother carrying a squalling baby, a businessman with a topcoat and briefcase, a bearded, blue-jeaned ski bum hefting a blue satchel boasting the word Vail, two long-legged military men clad in dress blues and garrison caps with visors set squarely across their eyebrows. *Two long-legged military men!*

"Jeff!" Her arm flew up joyously.

He caught sight of Theresa at the same moment she saw his lips form her name. But sister and brother were separated by a fifteen-foot-long ramp and handrail, and what seemed to be one-quarter of the population of Minneapolis greeting incoming arrivals. Jeff pointed her out while she read his lips again—"There she is"—and shouldered through the crowd toward the crown of the ramp.

She was scarcely conscious of her brother's companion as she flew into Jeff's arms, lifting her own around his neck while he scooped her off the floor and whirled her in a circle. His shoulders were broad and hard, his neck smelled of lime, and her eyes were suddenly swimming with tears while he laughed against her temple.

He plopped her onto her feet, smiled down into her joyous face and said gruffly, "Hiya, Treat."

"Hiya, snot-nose," she choked, then tried to laugh, but it came out a chugging gulp before she abashedly buried her face against him again, suddenly conscious of the other man looking on. Beside her ear, she heard the smile in Jeff's voice as he spoke to his friend.

"Didn't I tell you?"

"Yup, you did," came the stranger's voice, rich and deep.

She backed up. "Tell him what?"

Jeff grinned down teasingly. "That you're a sentimental fool. Look at you, tears flooding everything, and all over my dress blues." He examined his crisp lapel where a dark blotch showed.

"Oh, I'm sorry," she wailed, "I'm just so glad to see you." She dabbed at the tear spot on his jacket while he touched her just beneath an eye.

"You'd be sorrier if you could see how those tears make the freckles you hate so much stand out like new pennies."

She slapped his finger away and dabbed at her eyes self-consciously.

"Don't worry about it, Theresa. Come on, meet Brian." Jeff clapped an arm around her shoulders and turned her to face his friend. "This is the light o' my life, who never let me chase women, smoke pot or drive when I drank." At this last, Jeff winked broadly. "So let's not tell her what we did last night, okay, Scanlon?" He squeezed her shoulder, grinned down fondly while his teasing did absolutely nothing to disguise the deeper note of pride in his voice. "My big sister, Theresa. Theresa, this is Brian Scanlon."

She saw his hand first, with long, tapered fingers, extended in greeting. But she was afraid to look up and see where his eyes rested. Thankfully, the way Jeff had commandeered her shoulders, she was able to half hide behind him with one arm about his waist while extending her own hand.

"Hello, Theresa."

She could no longer avoid it. She raised her eyes to

his face, but he looked straight into her eyes, smiling.
And what a smile!

"Hello, Brian."

"I've heard a lot about you."

I've heard a lot about you, too, she thought, but
answered gaily, "I'll just bet you have. My brother
could never keep anything to himself."

Brian Scanlon laughed—a pleasant baritone rumble like a soft roll on a tympani—and held her hand
in a hard grip, smiling at her from beneath the horizontal visor of his military hat that made her suddenly understand why some women shamelessly chase
soldiers.

"Don't worry, he only told me the nice stuff."

Her glance fluttered away from his translucent
green eyes that were far more attractive than in the
photographs Jeff had sent, then Brian released her
hand and moved to flank her other side as they headed away from the gate area toward the green concourse, still talking.

"All except for a couple of stories about our nasty
childhood pranks, like the time you stole a handful
of Grandpa Deering's pipe tobacco and taught me
how to roll it up in those white papers that come with
home permanents, and we both got sick from the
chemicals in the paper when it got in our lungs, and
the time—"

"Jeffrey Brubaker, I did not steal that tobacco.
You did!"

"Well, who found the leftover papers in the bathroom vanity?"

"But who put the idea in my head?"

"I was two years younger. You should have tried
to talk me out of it."

"I did!"

"But that was after we got sick and learned our lesson."

All three of them dissolved into laughter. Jeff squeezed her shoulder once more, looked across the top of her head at Brian and set things straight. "I'll be honest. After we got greener than a pair of garter snakes she'd never let me smoke again. I tried it more than once when I was in junior high, but she squealed on me every time and managed to get me grounded more than once. But in the end, she saved me from myself."

To Theresa's left, Brian's laugh rolled like faraway thunder. She noted its full, mellow tone, and now, when she spoke, that tone became even fuller, richer.

"He did tell me about another incident with home permanents when you gave him one against your mother's orders and forgot to set the timer." While he teased, he studied her hair. Jeff had said it was red, but Brian hadn't expected it to be the hue of a poppy!

"Oh, that," she wailed, hiding a cheek behind a palm. "Jeff, did you have to blab that to him? I could have died when I took those curlers out and saw what I'd done to you."

"*You* could have died? Mother was the one who could have died. That time it was *you* who should've gotten grounded, and I think you would have if you hadn't been eighteen already and going to college."

"Let's finish the story, little brother. In spite of the fact that you looked like an explosion in a silo, it got you that spot in the band, didn't it? They took one look at that ball of frizz and decided you'd fit right in."

"Which also put you beyond mother's good graces for the remainder of the summer, until I could prove

I wasn't going to start sniffing cocaine and popping uppers every night before we played a gig.''

They had reached the escalator to the lower level where the luggage return was located, so were forced to break rank while riding down.

Studying the backs of the two heads below him, Brian Scanlon couldn't help envying the easy camaraderie between sister and brother. They hadn't seen each other for twelve months, yet they fell into a familiar groove of affectionate bantering as if they were good friends who saw each other daily. *They don't know how lucky they are,* he thought.

The revolving luggage carousels were surrounded, for holiday travel was at its heaviest with only a couple days left till Christmas. As they waited, Brian stood back and listened while the two of them filled in each other on family news.

"Mom and dad wanted to come and pick you up, but I got nominated instead because today was the last day of school before vacation. I got out at two, right after the Christmas program was over, but they both have to work till five, as usual.''

"How are they?''

"Do you have to ask? Absolutely giddy. Mom's been baking pies and putting them in the freezer, and worrying about whether pumpkin is still your favorite and dad kept asking her, 'Margaret, did you buy some of those poppy-seed rolls Jeff always liked?' And mom would lose patience and say, 'Willard, that's the third time you've asked me that, and this is the third time I'm answering. Yes, of course I bought poppy-seed rolls.' Yesterday she baked a German chocolate cake, and after all that fussing, came out and found dad had taken a slice from it. Boy, did the fur fly then. When she scolded him and informed him she'd baked the cake for dessert tonight, dad slunk off and took the car to the car wash and filled it up with gas for you. I don't think either one of them slept a wink last night. Mother was absolutely grumpy this morning, but you know how she gets when she's excited—the minute she sees you it'll dissolve like magic. Mostly she was upset because she had to work today when she'd rather have stayed home and gotten things ready, then come to the airport herself.''

It was plain to Brian that this homecoming had taken on premiere proportions in his family's hearts, even before Theresa went on.

"And just guess what dad did?"

Jeff only smiled a query. Theresa tipped him a smile with hidden meaning. "Get ready for this one, Jeff. He took your old Stella up to Viking Music and had new strings put on it and polished it all up and brought it out to the corner of the living room where you always used to leave it."

"You're kidding!"

"God's truth."

"Do you know how many times he threatened to turn both me and my fifteen-dollar Stella out of the house if the two of us didn't quit bruising his eardrums with all our racket?"

Just then a duffel bag came circling toward them, and Jeff shouldered forward to grab it. No sooner had he set it behind him than a guitar case followed. As he leaned to snag it, Theresa exclaimed, "Your guitar! You brought your guitar?"

"Guitars. Both of ours."

She glanced up at Brian Scanlon, remembering he, too, played. She caught him studying her instead of the luggage return, his eyes the hue of rich summer moss, and Theresa quickly dropped her gaze.

"Can't let those calluses get soft," Jeff explained, "and anyway, two weeks without pickin' would be more than we could stand, right, Scan?"

"Right."

"But I promise I'll pick a few on the old Stella, just for dad."

A second guitar case came bumping down the conveyor belt, followed by another duffel bag, and Theresa watched Brian's shoulders stretch his blue uniform jacket taut as he leaned to retrieve them. A young woman just behind Brian was giving him the once-over as he straightened and turned. The end of the guitar case caught her on the hip, and Brian immediately apologized.

The blonde flashed him a smile, and said, "Anytime, soldier boy."

For a moment he paused, then politely murmured, "Excuse me," and shouldered his duffel, glancing up to meet Theresa's eyes, which slid away shyly.

"All set?" She directed her question at her brother, because Brian made her uncomfortably aware of how inordinately pretty his eyes were for a man, and ever aware that they never dropped lower than her coat collar.

"Yup."

"Homeward bound. Let's go."

They stepped beyond the sliding doors of Minneapolis—St. Paul International into the crisp bite of December cold. Theresa walked between them again as they entered the cavernous concrete parking lot. But when they approached the correct row, she announced, "Dad and I traded cars for the day. I have his wagon, he has my Toyota."

"Hand me the keys. I'm dying to get behind a wheel again," her brother declared.

They loaded guitars and duffel bags into the rear and clambered inside. Through the fifteen-minute ride to the nearby suburb of Apple Valley, while Jeff and Theresa exchanged pleasantries, she tried to overcome her resentment of Brian Scanlon. She had nothing against him personally. How could she? She'd never met him before today. It was strangers in general—more particularly *male* strangers—she tried to avoid. Somehow she'd always thought Jeff guessed and understood. But apparently she was wrong, for when he'd called and enthusiastically asked if he could bring his buddy home to spend the Christmas holidays, then explained that Brian Scanlon had no family, there'd been no hesitation from Margaret Brubaker.

"Why, of course. Bring him. It would be just plain unchristian to make a man spend Christmas in some miserable barracks in North Dakota when there are beds to spare and enough food for an army."

Listening on the extension phone, Theresa had felt her heart fall. She'd wanted to interrupt her mother and say, Just a minute! Don't the rest of us have any say about it? It's *our* Christmas, too.

There were frustrations involved with living at home at age twenty-five, and though sometimes Theresa longed to live elsewhere, the certain loneliness she'd suffer if she made that move always gave her second thoughts. Yes, the house belonged to her mother and father. They could invite whom they chose. And even while Brian Scanlon's intrusion rankled, she realized how selfish her thoughts were. What kind of woman would deny the sharing of

Christmas bounty with someone who had no home and family?

But as they drove through the late-afternoon traffic, Theresa's apprehension grew.

They'd be home in less than five minutes, and she'd have to take her coat off, and once she did, it would happen again, as it always did. And she'd want to slink off to her room and cry...as she often did.

Even as the thoughts flashed through her mind, Brian said in his well-modulated voice, "I certainly want to thank you for letting me come along with Jeff and horn in on your holidays."

Theresa felt a flush of guilt working its way past her high gray coat collar, and hoped he wasn't looking at her as she politely lied. "Don't be silly. There's an extra bed in the basement and never a shortage of food. We're all very happy that Jeff thought of inviting you. Since you two started up the band together you're all we hear about when he calls or writes. Brian this and Brian that. Mother's been dying to get an eye on you and make sure her *little boy* has been traveling in good company. But don't pay any attention to her. She used to practically make his girlfriends fill out an application blank with three references."

Just then they drew into the driveway of a very run-of-the mill *L*-shaped rambler on a tree-lined street where the houses were enough alike as to be almost indistinguishable from one another.

"Looks like mom and dad haven't gotten home yet," Theresa noted. A fresh film of snow dusted the driveway. Only one set of tire tracks led from the garage, but a single pair of footprints led up to the back door. "But Amy must be here."

The doors of the station wagon swung open, and Jeff Brubaker stood motionless beside the car for a moment, scanning the house in the way of a man seeking reassurance that none of the familiar things had altered. "God, it's good to be home," he breathed, sucking in a great gulp of the cold, pure Minnesota air. Then he became suddenly effervescent, almost jogging around to the tailgate of the wagon. "Come on you two, let's get this junk unloaded."

Thinking ahead to the next five minutes, Theresa appropriated a guitar case to carry inside. She didn't know how she'd manage it, but if worse came to worst, she might be able to hide behind it.

At the sound of the tailgate slamming, a gangly fourteen-year-old girl came flying out the back door. "Jeffy, you're home!" Smiling with a flash of tooth braces, Amy Brubaker threw her arms wide with an open gesture Theresa envied. Not a day went by that Theresa didn't pray her sister be granted the blessing of growing normally.

"Hey, dumpling, how are ya?"

"I'm too big for you to call me dumpling anymore."

They embraced with sibling exuberance before Jeff plopped a direct kiss on Amy's mouth.

"Ouch!" She jerked back and made a face, then bared her teeth for inspection. "Look out when you do that. It hurts!"

"Oh, I forgot about the new hardware. Let's see." He tipped her chin up while she continued curling her lips back as if not in the least daunted by her unattractive braces. Looking on, Theresa wondered how it was her little sister had managed to remain so uninhibited and charmingly self-assured.

"I tell everybody I got 'em decorated just in time for Christmas," Amy declared. "After all, they do look a little like tinsel."

Jeff leaned back from the waist and laughed, then quirked a smile at his friend. "Brian, it's time you met the rambunctious part of the Brubaker family. This is Amy. Amy, here he is at last—Brian Scanlon. And as you can see, I've talked him into bringing his guitar so we can play a couple hot ones for you and your friends, just as ordered."

For the first time, Amy lost her loquaciousness. She jammed her hands as far as they'd go into the tight front pockets of her blue jeans and carefully kept her lips covering the new braces as she smiled and said almost shyly, "Hi."

"Hi, Amy. Whaddya say?" He extended his hand and smiled at Amy with as charming a grin as any of the rock stars beaming from the postered walls of her bedroom. Amy glanced at Brian's hand, made an embarrassed half shrug and finally dragged one hand from the blue denim and let Brian shake it. When he released it, the hand hung in the air between them for a full fifteen seconds while her smile grew and grew, until a reflection flashed from the bars of metal spanning her teeth.

Watching, Theresa thought, *oh, to be fourteen again, with a shape like Amy's, and the total lack of guile that allows her to gaze point-blank in unconcealed admiration, just as she's doing now.*

"Hey, it's cold out here!" Jeff gave an exaggerated shiver. "Let's go in and dig into mom's cake."

They carried duffel bags and guitar cases into the cheery front-facing kitchen of the simple house. The room was papered in an orange- and gold-flowered pattern that was repeated in the fabric inserts of the shutters on the windows flanking the eating area, which looked out on the front yard. An ordinary house on a street with others just like it, the Brubaker home had nothing exceptional to set it apart, except a sense of familial love that Brian Scanlon sensed even before the mother and father arrived to complete the circle.

On the kitchen table was a crocheted doily of white, and in the center sat a pedestal plate bearing a mouth-watering German chocolate cake under a domed lid. When Jeff lifted the lid, the gaping hole came into view. In the hollow wedge was a slip of folded paper. He took it out to reveal a recipe card from which he read aloud: "Jeff, it looked too good for me to resist. See you soon. Dad."

The four of them shared a laugh, but all the while Theresa stood with the broad end of Jeff's guitar case resting on the floor at her toes, and the narrow end shielding the front of her coat. She was the delegate hostess. She should ask for Brian's jacket and hat and make a move toward the hall closet.

"Come on, Brian," Jeff invited, "see the rest of the place." They moved to the living room and immediately four raucous, jarring chords sounded from the piano. Theresa grimaced and glanced at Amy who rolled her eyeballs. It was "Jeff's Outer Space Concerto."

They drew deep breaths in unison, signaled with nods and bellowed simultaneously, "Je-e-e-eff, knock it off!" While the sisters giggled, Jeff explained to Brian, "I composed that when I was thirteen...before I became an impressario."

Theresa quickly hung up her coat in the front-hall closet and hustled down the hall to her bedroom. She found a pale blue cardigan sweater and whisked it across her shoulders without slipping her arms into the sleeves, then buttoned the top button at her throat. She glanced critically in the mirror, realigned the button-and-buttonhole panels so the sweater covered as much of her as possible, but found to her dismay it did little to disguise her problem. *Oh God, will I ever learn to live with it?*

Her usual, end-of-the day backache plagued again, and she sighed, straightening her shoulders, but to no avail.

The house tour had stopped in the living room where Jeff had found his Stella. He was twanging out some metallic chords and singing an offbeat melody while Theresa tried to bolster her courage and walk out there. Undoubtedly it would be the same as it always was when she met a man. Brian Scanlon would scarcely glance at her face before his eyes would drop to her breasts and he would become transfixed by them. Since puberty she had relived those awful moments too many times to count, but Theresa had never become inured. That horrifying instant when a man's eyebrows twitched up in surprise, and his lips dropped open while he stared at the outsized mammary glands that had, through some unfortunate freak of nature, grown to proportions resembling volleyballs. They rode out before Theresa like a flagship before a fleet, their double-D circumference made the more pronounced by her delicately boned size-nine frame.

The last time she'd been introduced to a strange man he was the father of one of her second-grade pupils. Even as a parent, the poor man hadn't been able to remember protocol in his shock at glimpsing her enormous breasts. His eyes had riveted on them even while he was shaking Theresa's hand, and after that there'd been such awful tension between them the conference had been a disaster.

If she had carved a notch on her bedroom dresser every time that had happened down through the years, there'd be nothing before her now but a pile of wood chips. Now meeting the apprehensive eyes of the woman reflected in the mirror, Theresa quailed with all the familiar misgivings. Red hair and freckles! As if it wasn't enough that she'd been cursed with these mountainous breasts, she'd landed hair the color of paprika and skin that refused to tan. Instead it broke out in brilliant orange heat spots, as if she had an incurable rash, each time the sun grazed her skin. And this hair—oh, how she hated it! Coarse, springy ringlets that clung to her scalp like a Brillo pad if cut short, or if allowed to grow long, developed untamable waves reminiscent of those disastrous messes fried onto women's heads in the early days of the century before hot permanents had been perfected. Detesting it either way, she'd chosen a middle-of-the road length and as innocuous a style as she could manage, brushing it straight back from her face and clasping it at her nape with a wide barrette, below which the "tail" erupted like a ball of fire from a volcano.

And what about eyelashes? Didn't every woman deserve to have eyelashes that could at least be seen? Theresa's were the same hue as her hair—pale threads that made the rims of her eyelids look pink and sickly while framing eyes that were almost the identical color of her freckles, a pale tea-brown. She thought of the dark spiky lashes and the stunning green of Brian Scanlon's eyes, and her own dropped to check her sweater once again, and tug it close together, as Theresa realized she could no longer avoid confronting him. She must return to the living room. And if he stared at her breasts with lascivious speculation she'd think of the strains of her favorite Chopin Nocture, which always had a calming effect upon her.

Amy and Jeff were sitting on the davenport while Brian faced them from the seat of the piano bench. When Jeff caught sight of her, he thwacked the guitar strings dramatically, and let the chord reverberate in fanfare. "There she is!"

So much for slipping quietly into their midst.

Brian was no more than five feet away, still wearing his formal garrison cap. She was conscious of a wink of silver on the large eagle medallion centered above the black leather visor as his eyes swerved her way, directly on a level with the objects of Theresa's despair. Her pale brown eyes met his of sea green. The certainty of what would happen next seemed to lodge in her throat like a pill taken without water. *Now!* she thought. *Now it will happen!* She steeled herself for the sickening embarrassment that was certain to follow.

But Brian Scanlon relaxedly stretched six feet of blue-clad anatomy to its feet and smiled into Theresa's eyes, his own never wavering downward for even a fraction of a second or giving the impression that it even crossed his mind.

"Jeff's been demonstrating the old Stella. She doesn't sound too bad."

Aren't you going to gawk like everybody else? She felt the blush begin to tint her face because he *hadn't* looked, and to cover her fluster grabbed onto the first words that entered her mind.

"As usual, my brother thinks of nothing but

music.'' Theresa strove to keep her voice steady, for her heart was knocking crazily. "And here you sit with your hat and jacket still on. I'll show you where you'll sleep, since neither one of these two had the courtesy to do it.''

"I hope I'm not putting anybody out of their bed.''

"Not at all. We're putting you on a hideaway bed in the family room downstairs. I just hope nobody puts you out of yours, because it'll be in front of the TV and fireplace, and dad likes to stay up at least until after the ten o'clock news.''

He didn't look! He didn't look! The exaltation pounded through her brain as Theresa led the way back through the kitchen to the basement door that opened into the room just behind the stove wall. Oddly enough, she seemed more aware of Brian Scanlon because of the fact that he'd assiduously remained polite and refrained from dropping his eyes. She took his guitar and he his duffel bag, and she led him downstairs into a large basement area with a set of sliding glass doors facing the rear yard. The room was paneled in warm pecan and carpeted in burnt orange that burst into a glow as Theresa switched on a table lap.

Brian watched her hair light up as she paused above the lamp, then scanned the room, which contained a country pine coffee table, a cushioned davenport and pillowed rockers in the Colonial style. A fireplace was flanked by a television set, and at the end of the room where Brian stood, a thick-legged kitchen set of glossy pine was centered before the sliding glass door.

"Mmm...I like this room. Very homey.'' His eyes came back to settle upon Theresa as he spoke.

He seemed the type who'd prefer art deco or chrome and glass, but an appreciative reaction riffled through Theresa, for her mother had largely let her choose the colors and textures of the furnishings when they'd redecorated two years ago. It wasn't her own house, but it gave Theresa a taste of home planning, making her eager for the day when she could exercise her own tastes throughout an entire house.

Brian noted her tightly crossed arms beneath the baby blue sweater and the nervousness that was absent only while her sister and brother were close by.

"I'm sorry it has no closet, but you can hang your things up here." She opened a door leading to an unfinished portion of the basement where the laundry facilities were housed.

He crossed toward her, and she stepped well back as he popped his head around the laundry-room doorway, one foot off the floor behind him. There was a rolling laundry rack with empty hangers tinging in the air currents from the opening of the door. "There's no bath down here, but feel free to use the upstairs tub or shower any time you want."

When he turned to her, his eyes again rested directly on hers as he noted, "It sures beats the BOQ on base, especially at Christmas time." She was conscious of how crisp and correctly knotted his formal navy blue tie was, how smoothly the dark blue military "blouse" contoured his chest and shoulders over the paler blue of his shirt, of how flattering the square-set cap was to the equally square-cut lines of his jaw.

"BOQ?" she questioned.

"Bachelor's Officers' Quarters."

"Oh." She waited for his eyes to rove downward, but they didn't. Instead, he began freeing the four

silver buttons bearing the eagle-and-shield U.S. Air
Force insignia, turning his back on her and taking a
stroll around the room while freeing the "blouse"
and shrugging out of it. He slipped his hat off the
back of his head with a slow, relaxed movement, and
she saw his hair for the first time. It was a rich
chestnut color, trimmed—according to military regu-
lations—far too short for her taste, and bearing a
ridge across the back from the band of his cap. He
turned toward Theresa again, and she noted that
around his face the chestnut hair held the suggestion
of waves, but was cut too short to allow them free
rein. It would be much more attractive an inch and a
half longer, she decided.

"It feels good to get out of these things."

"Oh, here! Let me hang them up."

"Just the blouse—I mean the jacket. We get in
trouble if we hang up our caps."

As she came forward to take his jacket, he extended his cap, too, and its inner band was still warm
from his head. As she scuttled away around the
laundry-room doorway again, that warmth seemed
to singe her palm. When she tipped the cap upside
down to lay it on the rack above the clothes bar, a
spicy scent of some hair preparation found its way to
her nostrils. It seemed to cling to the jacket, too, as
she threaded its shoulders over a hanger and hooked
it on the rack.

When she returned to the family room, Brian was
standing in front of the sliding glass doors with his
hands in his trousers pockets, feet widespread, gazing
out at the snowy yard where twilight was falling. For
a long moment Theresa studied the back of his sky
blue shirt where three crisp laundry creases gave him
that clean-cut appearance of a model on a recruiting

poster. The creases rose up out of the belted waistline of his trousers but disappeared across his shoulders where the blue fabric stretched taut as the head of a drum.

She crossed the room silently and flipped on an outside spotlight that flooded her father's bird feeder. Brian started at the snap of the light, glancing aside at her as she crossed her arms beneath the sweater and joined him at the wide window, studying the scene beyond.

"Every winter dad tries to entice cardinals, but so far this year we haven't had any. This is his favorite spot in the house. He brings his coffee down here in the mornings and sits at the table with his binoculars close at hand. He spends hours here."

"I can see why." Scanlon's eyes moved once more to the view outside where sparrows, caught in the beam of light that lit the snow to glimmering crystals, twittered and searched for fallen seed at the base of the feeder pole. The far edge of the property was delineated by a line of evergreens that appeared almost black in the waning light. Their limbs were laden with white. Suddenly a blue jay darted from them, squawking in the crass, impertinent note of superiority only a blue jay can muster, scattering the sparrows as he landed among them, then cocking his head and disdaining the seeds he jealously guarded.

"I wasn't sure if I should come with Jeff. I felt a little like I was horning in, you know?"

His hands were still buried in his trousers pockets, but she felt his eyes turn her way and hoped she wouldn't blush while attempting to lie convincingly. "Don't be silly, you're not horning in."

"Any stranger in the house at this time of the year is like a fifth wheel. I know that, but I couldn't resist

Jeff's invitation when I thought about spending two weeks with nothing to do but stare at the bare walls of the quarters and talk to myself.''

"I'm glad you didn't. Why, mother didn't hesitate a minute when Jeff called and suggested bringing you home. Besides, we've all heard so much about you in Jeff's letters, you hardly seem like a stranger. As a matter of fact, I believe *one* of us had a tiny bit of a crush on you even before you stepped out of the car in the driveway.''

He laughed good-naturedly and shook his head at the floor as if slightly embarrassed, then rocked back on his heels. "It's a good thing she isn't six years older. She's going to be a real knockout at twenty.''

"Yes, I know. Everybody says so.''

Brian heard no note of rancor in Theresa's words, only a warm, sisterly pride. And he need not lower his eyes to her chest to see that as she spoke, her forearms unconsciously guarded her breasts more closely.

Thanks for warning me, Brubaker, he thought, recalling all that Jeff had told him about his sister. *But apparently Jeff told his family as much about my background as he told me about them,* he thought, as Theresa went on in a sympathetic note.

"Jeff told us about your mother. I'm sorry. It must have been terrible to get the news about the plane crash.''

He studied the snow again and shrugged. "In a way it was, in a way it wasn't. We were never close after my dad died, and once she'd remarried, we didn't get along at all. Her second husband thought I was a drug addict because I played rock music, and he didn't waste any more time on me than was absolutely necessary.''

She evaluated her own family, so warm, supportive, so full of love, and resisted the urge to lay a comforting hand on Brian's arm. She felt guilty for the many times she'd wished Jeff wouldn't bring him home. It had been thoroughly selfish, she chided herself, guarding her family's Christmas from outsiders just as the jay guarded the seeds he didn't want to eat.

This time when she said the words, Theresa found they were utterly sincere. "We're glad to have you here, Brian."

Chapter Two

"THEY'RE HOME!" shouted Jeff overhead, then he stuck his head around the basement doorway and ordered, "Hey, you two, get up here!"

As an outside observer, Brian couldn't help envying Jeff Brubaker his family, for the greeting his friend received in the arms of his mother and father was an emotional display of honest love. Margaret Brubaker was hiking her rotund body out of the deep bucket seat of the low-slung Celica when Jeff swooped down on her. The grocery bag in her arms was unceremoniously dropped onto the snowy driveway in favor of hugs and kisses interspersed with tears, hellos and general exuberance while Willard Brubaker came around the car and took his turn—albeit with far fewer tears than his wife, but there was an undeniable glitter in his eye as he backed off and assessed Jeff.

"Good to have you home, son."

"I'll say it is," put in his mother, then the trio shared an enormous three-way hug. Margaret stepped back, crushing a loaf of bread. "Land! Would you look at what I've done with these groceries. Willard, help me pick 'em up."

Jeff waylaid them both. "Forget the groceries for now. I'll come back and get 'em in a minute. Come and meet Brian." With an arm around each of his parents' shoulders, Jeff shepherded them into the kitchen where Brian waited with the two girls. "These are the two who had the courage to have a kid like me—my mom and dad. And this is Brian Scanlon."

Willard Brubaker pumped Brian's hand. "Glad to have you with us, Brian."

Margaret's greeting was, "So this is Jeff's Brian."

"I'm afraid so, for all of two weeks. I really appreciate your invitation, Mrs. Brubaker."

"There are two things we have to get settled right now," Margaret stated without prelude, pointing an accusatory finger. "The first is that you don't call me Mrs. Brubaker, like I'm some commanding officer. Call me Margaret. And the other is...you don't smoke pot, do you?"

Amy rolled her eyeballs in undisguised chagrin, but the rest of them shared a good-natured laugh that managed to break the ice even before Brian answered frankly, "No, ma'am. Not anymore." There was a moment of surprised silence, then everyone burst into laughter again. And Theresa looked at Brian in a new light.

To Brian it seemed the Brubaker house was never quiet. Immediately after the introductions, Margaret was flinging orders for "you two boys" to pick up the groceries she'd dropped in the driveway. Supper preparations set up the next clatter as fried potatoes started splattering in a frying pan, and dishes were clinked against silverware at the table. In the living room, Jeff picked up his old guitar, but after a few minutes, shouted, "Amy, will you go shut off your damn stereo! It's thumping through the wall loud enough to drive a man crazy!" The only quiet one of the group appeared to be Willard, who calmly settled himself into a living-room chair and read the evening newspaper as if the chaos around him didn't even register. Within ten minutes it was evident to Brian who ruled the Brubaker roost. Margaret issued orders like a drill sergeant whether she wanted to be called Margaret or not. But she controlled her brood with a sharp tongue that wielded as much humor as hauteur.

"Theresa, now don't fry those potatoes till they're tougher than horsehide the way you like 'em. Don't forget your father's false teeth. Jeff, would you play something else in there? You know how I've always hated that song! What ever happened to the good old standards like 'Moonlight Bay'? Amy, get two folding chairs out of the front closet and keep your fingers off that coconut frosting till dessert time. Willard, keep that dirty newsprint off the arms of the chair!"

To Brian's surprise, Willard Brubaker peered over the top of his glasses, muttered too softly for his wife to hear, "Yes, my little turtledove," then caught Jeff's eye, and the two exchanged grins of amused male tolerance. Willard's gaze caught Brian's next, and the older man gave a quick wink, then buried himself behind his paper again, resting it on the arms of the chair.

Supper was plentiful and plain: Polish sausage, fried potatoes, baked beans and toast—Jeff's favorite meal. Willard sat at the head of the table, Margaret at the foot, the two "girls" on one side and the two "boys" across from them.

While they ate, Brian observed Margaret's buxom proportions and realized from whom Theresa had inherited her shape. Throughout the pleasant meal Theresa kept her blue sweater over her shoulders, though there were times when it plainly got in her way. Occasionally, Brian glanced up to find Amy gazing at him with an expression warning of imminent puppy love, though Theresa never seemed to look at him at all.

Midway through the meal the phone rang, and Amy popped up to get it.

"Hello," she said, then covered the mouthpiece and looked disgusted. "It's for you, Jeffy. It sounds like dumb old Glue Eyes."

"Watch your mouth, little sister, or I'll wire your top braces to your bottom ones." Jeff took the phone and Amy returned to the table.

"Glue Eyes?" Brian glanced at Theresa.

"Patricia Gluek," she answered, "his old girlfriend. Amy never liked the way Patricia used to put on her makeup back in high school, so she started calling her Glue Eyes."

Amy plopped into her chair with a grunt of exasperation. "Well, she plastered it on so thick it looked like her eyelashes were glued together, not to mention how thick she used to plaster Jeff with all those purrs and coos. She makes me sick."

"Amy!" snapped Margaret, and Amy had the grace to desist.

Brian curled an eyebrow at Theresa, and again she enlightened him. "Amy worships Jeff. She'd like to keep him all to herself for two solid weeks."

Just then Jeff dropped the receiver against his thigh and asked, "Hey, you two, want to pick up Patricia after supper and go to a movie or something?"

Brian craned around to look over his shoulder at Jeff.

Theresa gulped. "Who, me?"

Jeff flashed an indulgent smile. "Yeah, you and Bry."

Already Theresa could feel the color creeping up her neck. She never went on dates, and most certainly not with her brother's friends, who were all younger than herself.

Brian turned back to Theresa. "It sounds fine with me, if it's all right with Theresa."

"Whaddya say, Treat?" Jeff was jiggling the phone impatiently, and the eyes of everyone at the table turned to the blushing redhead. A bevy of excuses flashed through her mind, all of them as phony as those she'd dreamed up on the rare occasions when single male teachers from school asked her out. At her elbow she sensed Amy gaping in undisguised envy.

Brian realized the house was totally silent for the first time since he'd entered it and wished the rock music was still throbbing from Amy's room. It was obvious Theresa was caught in a sticky situation where refusal would be rude, yet he could tell she didn't want to say yes.

"Sure, that sounds fun."

She avoided Brian's eyes, but felt them hesitate on her for a minute while Jeff finalized the plans, and she withdrew from center stage by going to get dessert plates for the German chocolate cake.

When the meal was finished and Theresa was helping with dishes, she cornered Jeff for a moment as he passed through the kitchen.

"Jeffrey Brubaker, what on earth were you thinking of, to suggest such a thing?" she whispered angrily. "I'll pick my own dates, thank you."

"Lighten up, sis. Brian's not a date."

"You bet he's not. Why, he must be four years younger than I am!"

"Two."

"Two! That's even worse! Why, it makes it look like—"

"All right, all right! What are you so upset about?"

"I'm not upset. You just put me on the spot, that's all."

"Did you have other plans for tonight?"

"On your first night home?" she asked pointedly. "Of course not."

"Great. Then the least you'll get out of the deal is a free movie."

Oh no! the peeved Theresa vowed. *I'll pay my own way!*

Getting ready to go, Theresa couldn't help but admire how carefully Brian had concealed his reluctance. After all, who'd want to be saddled with a *big* sister? And worse yet, a freckle-head like her? She scowled at the copper dots in the mirror and despised each one with renewed intensity. She tried to yank a brush through her disgusting hair, but it was like a frayed sisal rope, only not nearly as pleasing in color. *Damn you, Jeffrey Brubaker, don't you ever do this to me again.* She drew the hair to the nape of her neck, tied it with a navy blue ribbon and considered makeup. But she owned none except lipstick, which she slashed onto her surly lips as if scrawling graffiti on a rest-room wall. *I'll get you for this, Jeff.* Little thought was given to the clothing she chose, beyond the certainty that she'd put on her gray coat and leave it buttoned until they got back home.

She wasn't, however, planning on running into Brian in the front hall by the coat closet. When she did, she came up short, caught without a sweater or guitar or table to hide behind. Instinctively, one hand went up to finger her blouse collar—it was the best she could do.

"Jeff went out to start the car," Brian announced.

"Oh." The word was barely out of her mouth before Theresa realized Brian had shed military attire in favor of brown tennis shoes, bone-colored corduroys and a polo-style shirt of wide horizontal stripes in red and beige. He'd been carrying a brown leather waist-length jacket, and shrugged it on while she watched, transfixed. If Brian had subjected Theresa to the blatant inspection she gave him, she'd have ended up in her room in tears. She hadn't even realized how pointedly she'd been staring until her eyes traveled back up to his. She felt utterly foolish.

But if he noticed, he gave not the slightest clue beyond the hint of a smile that disappeared as quickly as it had come. "All ready?"

"Yes." She reached for her gray coat, but he took it from her hands without asking and held it for her. Even as Theresa felt the flush coloring her cheek at the unfamiliar gesture of good manners, she could do nothing but slip her arms into the coat, exposing the front of her so there was no hiding her proportions.

They called good-night to her parents and Amy and stepped out into the biting winter night. Theresa had gone on few enough dates in her life that it was difficult not to feel seduced into believing this was one, for he held the door of the station wagon while she slid in next to Jeff, then slipped his arm across the back of the seat as he settled in, too. She caught the drift of the same scent she'd detected when he handed her his cap earlier, and since Theresa wasn't a woman given to using perfumes herself, his faint hint of...sandalwood, that was it, came through all the clearer.

Jeff had the radio on—there was always a radio on—and he turned it louder as the gravelly voice of Bob Seger came on. Jeff's own voice had the grating earthiness of Seger's, and he picked up the refrain and sang along.

"We've got to learn this one, Bry."

"Mmm...it's smooth. Nice harmony on the chorus."

When the chorus came around again, the three sang along with it, their harmony resonant and true. "Ooo, shame on the moon...." Beside her, Theresa heard Brian's voice for the first time—straightforward, mellow, the antithesis of Jeff's. It sent shivers up her arms.

When they reached Patricia Gluek's house, Jeff went inside while Theresa and Brian transferred to the back seat, leaving a respectable distance between them. The radio was still playing and the lights from the dashboard lent an ethereal glow to the space beyond the front seat.

"How long have you and Jeff been playing and singing together?"

"Over three years now. We met when we were stationed at Zweibrücken together and started up a band there, and luckily we both landed at Minot Air Force Base, so we decided to look for a new drummer and bass player and keep a good thing rolling."

"I'd love to hear the band sometime."

"Maybe you will."

"I doubt it. I don't have many chances to swing by Minot, North Dakota."

"We'd like to get a new group started when we get out next summer, and hire an agent and make it a regular thing. Hasn't Jeff mentioned it?"

"Why, no, but I think it's a great idea, at least for

Jeff. He's wanted to be a musician since he spent that first fifteen dollars on his Stella and started picking up chords from anybody who'd teach him."

"Same with me. I've been playing since I was twelve, but I want to do more than just play."

"What else?"

"I'd like to try writing, arranging. And I've always had the urge to be a disc jockey."

"You have the voice for it." He certainly did. She remembered her first appreciative surprise upon hearing it earlier. But it went on now, turning attention away from himself.

"Enough about me. I hear you're into music, too."

"Grades one through six, Sky Oaks Elementary."

"Do you like it?"

"I love it, with the rare exceptions like yesterday during the Christmas program when Keri Helling and Dawn Gafkjen got into a fight over who was going to be the pink ornament and who was going to be the blue one and ended up crying and getting the crepe-paper costumes all soggy." She chuckled. "No, seriously, I love teaching the younger kids. They're guileless, and open, and...." *And they don't gawk.* "And accepting," she finished.

Just then Jeff returned with Patricia, and introductions were made as Brian and Patricia shook hands over the front seat. Theresa had known the girl for years. She was a vivacious brunette, now in her second year at Normandale Community College. She was waiting to step into her former status as Jeff's girlfriend the moment he got out of the service, though they'd agreed to date others during their four years apart. So far, though, the attraction had not faded, for each of the three times Jeff

had been home, he and Patricia had been insepar-
able.

When the pretty brunette turned toward the front,
Theresa was chagrined to see her and Jeff share a
more intimate hello than they'd apparently exchanged inside the house. Jeff's arms went around
Patricia, and her head drifted to his shoulder while
they kissed in a way that sent the blood filling up the
space between Theresa's freckles. Beside her, Brian
sat unmoving, watching the kiss that was taking place
in such a forthright manner it was hard to ignore.

Goodness, would they never stop? The seconds
ticked away while the music from the radio didn't
quite conceal the soft murmurs from the front seat.
Theresa wanted to crawl into a hole and pull the
earth over her head.

Brian laced his fingers over his belly, slumped low
in the seat, dropped his head back lazily and politely
turned to gaze out his side window.

I am twenty-five years old, thought Theresa, *and
I've never known before exactly what was implied by
"double date."* She, too, gazed out her dark window.

There was a faint rustle, and, thankfully, it was
Jeff's arm lifting from around Patricia's shoulders.
The wagon chunked into gear, and they were moving
at last.

At the theater, Theresa made a move toward her
purse, but Brian stepped between her and the counter, announcing unceremoniously, "I'll get it." So,
rather than make an issue of the four-dollar expen-
diture, she politely backed off.

When he turned, she said, "Thank you."

But he made no reply, only tipped his shoulders
aslant while slipping his billfold into a back pocket

where the beige wales of the corduroy were slightly worn in a matching square that captured Theresa's eyes and made her mouth go dry. He turned around, caught her gaze, and she wished she'd never come.

Things got worse when they'd settled into their seats and the movie began, for it had an "R" rating, and exposed enough skin to create sympathetic sexual reactions in a sworn celibate! Halfway through the film the camera zoomed in on a bare spine, curved hips and a naked feminine back over which two masculine hands played, their long, blunt fingers feathered with traces of dark hair. A naked hirsute chest rolled into view, and the side of an apple-sized breast, then—horror of horrors!—an upthrust nipple, controlled by the broad, dark hand. A bearded jaw eased into the frame, and a mouth closed over the distended nipple.

In her seat beside Brian, Theresa wanted more than ever to simply, blessedly, *die.* His elbows rested on the armrests, and his fingers were laced together, the outer edges of his index fingers absently stroking his lips as he slumped rather low in the seat.

Why didn't I consider something like this happening? Why didn't I ask what was playing? Why didn't I wisely stay home in the first place?

Theresa tolerated the remainder of the love scene, and as it progressed a queer reaction threaded through her body. Saliva pooled beneath her tongue. She could feel her pulse throbbing in the place where her purse was pressed tightly against her lap. And a quicksilver liquid sensation trickled through her innards, setting her alive with sensations she'd never experienced before. But outwardly, she sat as if a sorcerer had cast a spell upon her. Not so much as a pale eyelash blinked. Not a muscle twitched. She stared spellbound as the climax was enacted, reflected in the facial expressions of the man and woman on the screen and the animal sounds of fulfillment.

And not until those climaxes ended did Theresa realize Brian's elbow had been skewering hers with pressure that grew, and grew, and grew....

The scene changed, and he wilted, pulling his elbow against his side as if only now realizing what he'd been doing. Her elbow actually hurt from the pressure he'd been applying. He shifted uncomfortably in his seat, crossed an ankle over a knee and negligently dropped his laced fingers over the zipper of his corduroy pants.

Considering what had happened within her own body, Theresa had little doubt the same had happened to Brian. The remainder of the film was lost on her. She was too aware of the man on her right, and she found herself wondering who he'd been thinking of while the pressure on her elbow increased. She found herself wondering things about the male anatomy that the screen had carefully hidden. She recalled pictures she'd seen in the bolder magazines, but they seemed as flat, cold and lifeless as the paper upon which they'd been printed. For the first time in her life, she ached to know what the real thing was like.

When the film ended, she took refuge in chattering with Patricia, making certain she walked far enough ahead of Brian that their elbows didn't touch or their eyes meet.

"Anybody hungry?" Jeff inquired when they were back in the station wagon.

Theresa felt slightly queasy, sitting once again with Brian only a foot away. If she tried eating anything, she wasn't sure it would stay down.

"No!" she exclaimed, before anybody else could agree.

"Yeah, I—" Brian spoke at the same time, then politely changed course. "I've been thinking about a piece of your mother's German chocolate cake all through the movie."

In a pig's eye, thought Theresa.

Oddly enough, nobody talked about the film as they drove back to Patricia's house. Nobody said much of anything. Patricia was snuggled up with her shoulder behind Jeff's. Now and then he'd turn and smile down at her with the dash lights clearly outlining the ardent expression on his face. Patricia's shoulder moved slightly, and Theresa conjured up the possibility of where her hand might be. Theresa gazed out her window and blushed for perhaps the tenth time that day.

When they pulled up in Patricia's driveway, Jeff turned off all the lights and gathered Patricia into his arms without a moment's hesitation. Behind the couple, another man and woman sat like two bumps on a log.

Kisses, Theresa discovered, have more sound than you'd think. From the front seat came the distinct rush of hastened breathing, the faint suggestive sounds of lips parting, positions changing, the rustle of hands moving softly. The rasp of a zipper sizzled through the dark confines of the car, and Theresa jumped, but immediately wished she hadn't, for it was only Jeff's jacket.

"Come on, Theresa, what do you say we go for a little walk?" Brian suggested. The overhead light flashed on, and she hustled out his door, so relieved she wanted to throw her arms around him and kiss him out of sheer gratitude.

When the door slammed behind them, Theresa surprised herself by releasing a pent-up breath and bursting out with the last words she expected to say. *"Thank you."*

He stuck his hands into his jacket pockets and chuckled. "No need to thank me. I was getting a little uncomfortable myself."

His admission surprised her, but the frankness definitely relieved some of the tension.

"I can see I'll have to talk with my little brother about decorum. I wasn't exactly sure what to do!"

"What did you used to do when that happened on double dates?"

She was embarrassed to have to admit, "I've never been on a double date bef—" She stopped herself just in time and amended, "I've never been on one."

"Aw, think nothing of it. They're both adults. He loves her—he's told me so more than once—and he intends to marry her soon after his hitch is done."

"You amaze me. I mean, you take it all in stride." *Heavens,* thought Theresa, *do couples do things like that in the same car with as little compunction as her brother showed and think nothing of it?* She realized suddenly how very, very naive she must seem to Brian Scanlon.

"He's my friend. I don't judge my friends."

"Well, he's my brother, and I'm afraid I do."

"Why? He's twenty-one years old."

"I know, I know." Theresa threw up her hands, exasperated with herself and uncomfortable with the subject.

"How old are you, Theresa? Twenty-five, right?"

"Yes."

"And I take it you haven't done a lot of that sort of thing."

"No." *Because every time I got in a car with a boy, he went after only the most obvious two things, never caring about the person behind them.* "I was busy studying when I was in high school and college, and since then...well, I don't go out much."

They were ambling down a snowy street, feet lifting lazily as the streetlights made the surface snow glitter. Her coat was still buttoned high, and her hands were buried in its pockets. Their breaths created white clouds, and their soles pressed brittle ice that crunched with each step.

"So, what did you think of the movie?" Brian asked.

"It embarrassed me," she admitted.

"I'm sorry."

"It's not your fault, it's Jeff's. He's the one who picked it."

"Next time we'll be sure to ask before we blindly follow him, okay?"

Next time? Theresa glanced up to find Brian smiling down at her with an easy laziness that was meant to put her at ease, but that lifted her heart in a strange, weightless way. She should have answered, "There won't be a next time," but instead smiled in return and concurred. "Agreed."

They turned around and were heading toward the Gluek driveway when Jeff backed the station wagon onto the street and its lights arced around, caught them in the glare, and he pulled up beside them.

"Would you two mind if we took you home?" Jeff asked when Theresa and Brian were settled in the back seat again.

"Not at all," Brian answered for both of them.

"Thanks for understanding, Bry. And Treat, you'll take good care of him, won't you?"

She wanted to smack her brother on the side of the head. Jeffrey Brubaker certainly took a lot for granted!

"Sure." What else could she have answered?

When they pulled up at home, Brian opened his door and the light flashed on. Patricia Gluek turned around and hooked an elbow over the back of the seat.

"Listen, a group of us are getting together at the Rusty Scupper on New Year's Eve, and you're both invited to join us. We plan to have dinner there and stay for the dancing afterward. It'll be a lot of the old gang—you've met them all before, Theresa—so what do you say?"

Damn it, does the whole world think it has to line up escorts for the wimpy little Theresa Brubaker who never gets asked out on dates? But she knew in her heart that Patricia was only being cordial and thinking about Brian, too, who was Jeff's houseguest and couldn't very well be excluded. He had one foot on the driveway, but this time instead of putting Theresa on the spot, he answered, "We'll talk it over and let you know, okay?"

"Some people from school are having a party in their home, and I told them I might go." The manufactured tale came glibly to Theresa's lips while she was still puzzling out where it had come from.

"Oh." Patricia sounded genuinely disappointed. "Well, in that case, you'll come, won't you, Brian? We have to make dinner reservations in advance."

"I'll think it over."

"Fine."

Brian swiveled toward the open door, but Jeff

reached out and caught his arm. "Listen, Scan, thanks. I mean, I guess I ought to come in with you and play the host, but I'll see you in the morning at breakfast."

"Go on. Have a good time and don't worry about me."

When the car pulled away, Theresa and Brian stood on the back step while she dug in her purse for the house keys. When she found them and opened the door, they stepped into a dim kitchen where only a single bulb shone down on top of the white stove. It was silent—no stereo, no guitar, no voices.

They were both excruciatingly aware of what Jeff and Patricia were probably going off to do, and it created a corresponding sexual tension between them.

Seeking a diversion, Theresa whispered, "You said you were hungry for cake. There's plenty of it left."

He wasn't, really, but Brian wasn't at all averse to spending a little more time with Theresa, and the cake offered an excuse.

"I will if you will."

"It sounds good."

She moved toward the front hall, which was in total shadow, and made no move to turn on the light while removing her coat. Again, Brian was behind her to help her out of the garment, then hang it up. She left him there with a murmured thanks and returned to the kitchen to find two plates, forks and glasses of milk, taking them to the table where the cake still sat.

He joined her, choosing a chair at a right angle to hers, and they sat for a long time eating, saying nothing. The rafters of the house creaked in the December cold, and though it was very dark with only the small hood light illuminating the blotch of stove beneath it, she sensed Brian Scanlon studying her while he downed gulps of milk that sounded clearly in the silence.

"So, you're going to a party with someone from school on New Year's Eve?"

"No, I made that up."

His chin came up in surprise. "Oh?"

"Yes. I don't like people arranging dates for me, and furthermore, you don't need to be saddled with *me* on New Year's Eve. You go with Jeff and meet his friends. He's got some really nice—"

"*Saddled* with you?" he interrupted in that smooth, deep, unnerving voice that sent shivers up her nape.

"Yes."

"Did I give you the impression tonight that I resented being with you?"

"You know what I mean. You didn't come home with Jeff to have to haul me around every place you go."

"How do you know?"

She was stunned, she could only stammer. "You... I...."

"Would it surprise you to know that you're a big part of why I wanted to meet Jeff's family?"

"I...." But once again, she was struck dumb.

"He's told me a lot about you, Theresa. A lot."

Oh, Lord, how much? How much? Jeff, who knows my innermost fears. Jeff, who understands. Jeff, who can't keep anything to himself.

"What has he told you?" She tried to control the panic, but it crept into her voice, creating a vibrato that could not be disguised.

He made himself more comfortable, stretching his

long legs somewhere beneath the table to find the seat of a chair as he leaned back to study her shadowed face speculatively. His eyes held points of light as he caught an elbow on the table edge and braced one jaw on his knuckles, tipping his head.

"About how you looked out for him when he was a kid. About your music. The violin and piano. How you used to sing duets for your family reunions and pass the hat for nickels afterward, then, as soon as you had enough, go to the store to buy your favorite forty-fives." His lips lifted in a slow half smile, and his free hand moved the milk glass in circles against the tabletop.

"Oh, is that all?" Her shoulders wilted with relief, but in the dimness she had crossed her elbows on the tabletop and took refuge behind them as best she could.

"You always sounded as if you'd be someone I could get along with. And maybe I liked you even before I met you because he likes you so much, and you're his sister and I also like him very much."

Theresa was unused to being told she was liked. In her lifetime a few of the opposite sex had overtly tried to demonstrate what they "liked" about her, in the groping, insulting way she'd come to despise. But Brian seemed to have come to admire something deeper, her little-exposed self, her musicality, her familial relations. All this before he had ever laid eyes on her.

But those eyes were on her now, and though she could not make out their color in the veiling shadows, she caught the sparkle as he continued perusing her freely, the tip of his little finger now resting in the hollow beneath his full lower lip. She seemed unable to draw her eyes away from it as he went on quietly.

"I'd love to go to that party with you on New Year's Eve."

Their eyes met, hers wide with surprise, his carefully unflirtatious.

"But you're...you're two years younger than I am." Once she'd said it, she wanted to eat the words.

But he asked undauntedly, "Does that bother you?"

"Yes. I. . . ." She blew out a huge breath of air and leaned her forehead on the heel of one hand. "I can't believe this conversation."

"It doesn't bother me in the least. And I sure as hell don't want to go to that kind of a thing alone. Everybody'll be paired off, and I won't have anybody to dance with."

"I don't dance." *That* was the understatement of the night. Dancing was a pleasure she'd abandoned when her breasts grew too large to make fast dancing comfortable, their sway and bob not only hurting, but making Theresa feel sure they must appear obscene from the sidelines. And chest-to-chest dancing was even worse—being that close to men, she'd found, only gave them ideas.

"A musical woman like you?"

"Music and dancing are two different things. I've just never cared for—"

"There's time before New Year's Eve to learn. Maybe we can change your mind."

"Let me think about it, okay?"

"Sure." He got to his feet, and the chair scraped back, then he carried their two plates across the room and set them in the sink with a soft chink.

She opened the basement door and snapped on the light above the steps. "Well, I'm not sure if mother made your bed down here or not."

She heard his steps following her down the carpeted incline, and prayed she'd find his bed all decked out, ready for him, so she could simply wish him good-night and escape to her own room upstairs.

Unfortunately, the davenport wasn't either opened or made up, so Theresa had little choice but to cross the room and begin the chore. She tossed the cushions aside, conscious now that Brian had snapped on the lamp, and it flooded the area with mellow light that revealed her clearly while she tugged on the folded mattress and brought it springing out into the room.

"I'll get the bedding," she explained, and hustled into the laundry room to find clean sheets and blankets on a shelf there. He had turned on the television set when she came back out to the family room, and a late movie was glimmering on the screen in black and white. The volume was only a murmur as she shook out a mattress pad, concentrating fully on it when Brian stepped to the opposite side of the davenport to help her.

His long fingers smoothed the quilted surface with the expertise of a soldier who's been trained to keep his bunk in inspection-ready order. A sheet snapped and billowed in the air between them, and above it their glances met, then dropped. Images of the movie's love scene came back to titillate Theresa, while they tucked the corners of the sheets in, and Brian's hands pulled it far more expertly than hers, for hers were shaking and seemed nearly inept.

"Tight enough to bounce a coin," he approved.

She glanced up to find him looking at her instead of the sheet, and wondered what this man was doing to her. She had never in her life been as sexually aware of a male as she was of him. Men had brought her nothing but shame and intimidation, and she'd avoided them. Yet here she stood, gazing into the green eyes of Brian Scanlon over his half-prepared bed, wondering what it would be like to do with him the things she'd seen on a movie screen.

Redheads look ugly when they blush, she thought.

"The other sheet," he reminded her, and abashed, she turned to find it.

When the bed was finally done, she found her pulses leaping like Mexican jumping beans. But there still remained one duty she, as hostess, must perform.

"If you'll come upstairs, I'll give you clean towels and washcloths, and show you where the bathroom is."

"Jeff showed me after supper."

"Oh. Oh...good. Well, feel free to shower or... or whatever, anytime. You can hang your wet towels over the sink in the laundry room."

"Thank you."

They stood one on either side of the bed, and she suddenly realized she was facing him fully for the first time without shielding her breasts. Not once since she'd met him had she noticed him looking at them. His eyes were fastened on the freckled cheeks, then they moved up to her detestible red hair, and she realized she'd been standing without moving for a full thirty seconds.

"Well...good night then." Her voice was soft and shaky.

"Good night, Theresa." His was deep and quiet.

She scuttled away, racing up the stairs as if he were chasing her with ill intent. When she was settled into bed with the lights out, she heard him come upstairs and use the bathroom.

Put a pillow over your ears, Theresa Brubaker! But she listened to all the sounds coming from beyond her bedroom wall, and two closed doors, and envisioned Brian Scanlon performing his bedtime rituals and wondered for the first time in her life how a husband and wife ever made it through the intimacies of the first week of marriage.

Chapter Three

THE FOLLOWING MORNING, Theresa was awakened by the thump-thump-thump of Amy's stereo reverberating through the floor. Rolling over, she squinted at the alarm clock, then shot out of bed as if it was on fire. Ten o'clock! She should have been up two hours ago to fix breakfast for Brian and Jeff!

Within minutes she was washed, combed, dressed in blue jeans and a loose white blouse with a black cardigan slung across her shoulders and buttoned beneath the blouse collar.

Her parents had gone to work long ago. Jeff's door was closed, and the sound of his snoring came from beyond. It appeared Amy was still in her room, torturing her hair with a curling iron while Theresa tried to tame her springing curls by smoothing a hand over the infamous tail that bounced on her shoulders.

She crept down the hall to the kitchen but found it empty. The basement door was open—it appeared Brian was up. She was filling the coffeepot when he slipped silently to the doorway leading directly to the kitchen from one side of the living room.

"Good morning."

She spun around, sending water flying everywhere, pressing a hand to her heart.

"Oh! I didn't know you were there! I thought you were still downstairs."

"I've been awake for a long time. Routine is hard to break."

"Have you been sitting in there all by yourself?"

"No." He grinned engagingly. "With Stella."

She grinned back. "And how did you two get along?" She put coffee in the percolator basket and set the pot on the stove burner.

"She's a brassy old girl, but I talked sweet to her and she responded like a lady."

It wasn't what he said, but how he said it that made Theresa's cheeks pink. There was an undertone of teasing, though the words were totally polite. She wasn't used to such a tone of voice when speaking with men, but it, combined with his lazy half smile while he leaned one shoulder against the doorway, gave her the feeling she imagined a cat must have when its fur was slowly stroked the wrong way.

"I didn't hear you playing."

"We were whispering to each other."

Again, she couldn't resist smiling.

"I...I'm sorry nobody was up to fix breakfast for you. It's my first day of Christmas vacation, and I guess my body decided to take advantage of it. I never even wiggled at the usual wake-up time. I heard Jeff still snoring. He must have come in late."

"It was around three."

So—he hadn't been able to sleep. Neither had she.

"Three!"

He shrugged, his shoulder still braced on the doorway. He was wearing tight, faded blue jeans and a white football jersey that hugged his ribs just enough to make them tantalizing.

She recalled how long it had taken her to get to sleep after the curious way he'd managed to stir her senses last night, and wondered what had really kept him awake. Had he lain in the dark thinking of the movie as she had? Thinking of Jeff and Patricia in the car? Himself and her having cake and milk in the dusky kitchen?

His slow perusal was beginning to make Theresa's nerves jump, so she shrugged. "Why don't you sit down, and I'll pour you a glass of juice?"

He obliged, though she still wasn't rid of his gaze, even after she gave him a glass of orange juice. His eyes followed her lazily as she turned the bacon, scrambled eggs and dropped bread into the toaster.

"What do you and Jeff have planned for today?"

"I don't know, but whatever it is, I was hoping you could come along."

Her heart skipped, and she was disappointed at what she had to reply. "Oh, no, I have too much to do to help mother for tomorrow night, and I have to get ready for the concert I'm playing in tonight."

"Oh, that's right. Jeff told me. Civic orchestra, isn't it?"

"Uh-huh. I've been in it for three years and I really enjoy—"

"Well, good morning, you two." It was Amy, barely giving her sister a glance, aiming her greeting primarily at Brian. To his credit, he didn't flinch even slightly at the sight of Amy, decked out in crisp blue jeans that fit her like a shadow, a skinny little sweater that fit nearly as close, craftily styled hair with its shoulder-length auburn feather cut blown and curled back from her face in that dewy-fresh style so stunningly right for teenage girls. Her makeup application could have taught "Glue Eyes" a thing or two several years ago.

"I thought teenagers spent their vacations flopping around in baggy overalls these days," Brian noted, managing to compliment Amy without encouraging any excess hope.

"Mmm..." Amy simpered. "That just goes to show what you know."

But Theresa was fully aware that had Brian not been under the roof, that's exactly how Amy would have spent her day, only she wouldn't have poked her nose out of her burrow until one o'clock in the afternoon.

Amy stepped delicately to the stove and lifted a piece of cooling bacon, nibbled it with a provocative daintiness that quite surprised her sister. Where in the world had Amy learned to act this way? When? Just since Brian Scanlon had walked into the house?

"Amy, if you want bacon and eggs, get yourself a plate," Theresa scolded, suddenly annoyed by her sister's flirtatiousness. Even though she realized how small it was to feel a twinge of irritation at this new side Amy was displaying, Theresa was undeniably piqued. Perhaps because the fourteen-year-old had the remarkably freckle-free skin, hair the color of most Kentucky Derby winners and a trim, tiny shape that must be the envy of half the girls in her freshman class at school. Theresa suddenly felt like a gaudy neon sign beside an engraved invitation, in spite of the fact that it was Amy who wore the makeup. Theresa held her sweater over her elbow as she reached to turn off a burner.

From the table, Brian observed it all—the quick flash of irritation the older sister hadn't quite been able to hide, the guarded movements behind the camouflaging sweater and even the guilt that flashed across her face for the twinge of envy she could not quite control in moments such as these.

He rose, moved to her side and smiled down into

her startled eyes. "Here, let me pour the coffee, at least. I feel like a parasite sitting there and doing nothing while you slave over a hot stove." He reached for the pot while she shifted her eyes to the eggs she was removing from the pan.

"The cups are...." She half turned to find Amy watching them from just behind their shoulders. "Amy will show you where the cups are."

They had just begun eating when Jeff came slogging out of his room in bare feet and faded Levi's, scratching his chest and head simultaneously.

"I thought I smelled bacon."

"And I thought I smelled a rat," returned Theresa. "Jeff Brubaker, you should be ashamed of yourself. Bringing Brian here as your houseguest, then abandoning him that way."

Jeff shambled to a chair and strung himself upon it, more lying than sitting. "Aw hell, Brian didn't mind, did you, Bry?"

"Nope. Theresa and I had a nice long talk, and I got to bed early."

"What did you think of old Glue Eyes?" put in Amy.

"She's just as cute as I expected from Jeff's descriptions and the pictures I've seen," replied Brian.

"Humph!"

Jeff leaned his elbows on the table and closely scrutinized his younger sister. "Well, lookee here now," he sing-songed. "If the twerp hasn't taken a few lessons from old Glue Eyes herself."

Amy's mouth puckered up as if it was full of alum. She glared at her brother and snapped, "I'm fourteen years old, Jeffrey, in case you hadn't noticed! And I've been wearing makeup for over a year now."

"Oh." Jeff lounged back in his chair once again. "I beg your pardon, Irma la douce."

She lurched to her feet and would have stormed out of the room, but Jeff caught her by the elbow and swung her around till she landed on his lap, where she sat stiffly with her arms crossed obstinately over her ribs, an expression of strained tolerance on her face.

"Wanna come along with Brian and me to shop for mom and dad today? I'm gonna need some help deciding what to get for them."

Her irritation dissolved like a mist before a wind. "*Reeeally?* You mean it, Jeff?"

"Sure I mean it." He pushed her off his lap, swatted her on the backside and sent her on her way again. "Get your room cleaned up, and we'll go right after we eat." When she was gone he looked at the spot from which she'd disappeared around the hallway wall. "Her jeans are too tight. Mother ought to talk to her about that."

LEFT BEHIND, Theresa recalled the breakfast conversation with something less than good humor. Why was it so irritating that Jeff had noticed Amy's burgeoning maturity? Why did she herself feel lonely and left out and—*oh, admit it, Brubaker!*—jealous, because her sister of fourteen was accompanying Brian Scanlon, age twenty-three, on an innocent Christmas-shopping spree?

With the house to herself, Theresa put on her classical favorites, and spent the remainder of the morning boiling potatoes and eggs for the enormous pot of potato salad they'd take to the family gathering scheduled for the following night, Christmas Eve. In the afternoon she washed her hair, took a bath, filed

her nails and rummaged in Amy's room for some
polish with a little more pizzazz than the colorless
stuff she usually wore. She came up with something
called "Mocha Magic" and grimaced as she painted
the first stripe down a nail. *I'm simply not a "Mocha
Magic" girl,* she thought, but completed the single
nail, held it aloft and assessed it stringently. She fluttered her fingers and watched the light dance across
the pearlescent surface and decided—thinking in
Amy's current teenage vernacular—what the heck,
go for it!

When all ten nails were finished she wasn't sure
she'd done the right thing. She imagined them
glistening, catching the lights while she fingered the
neck of her violin. *I'm a conservative person trapped
inside the body of a Kewpie doll,* she decided, and
left the polish on.

She put on a beef roast for supper and pressed her
long, black gabardine skirt and the collar of the basic
long-sleeved white blouse that completed the orchestra "uniform" worn by its female members. The
blouse was made of a slick knit jersey, and there'd be
no sweaters to hide behind, no bulkiness to disguise
the way the slippery fabric conformed to her frame.

She was at the piano, limbering up her fingers with
chromatic scales, when the shopping trio returned.

Jeff was bellowing her name as he opened the door
and followed his ears to the living room. He reached
over her shoulder and tapped out the melody line to
"Jingle Bells," then sashayed on through the living
room with two crackling sacks on his arm, followed
by Amy, also bearing packages. By the time the pair
exited to hide their booty, Brian stood in the opposite
doorway, his cheeks slightly brightened by the winter
air outside, jacket unzipped and pulling open as he

paused with one hand in his back pocket, the other surrounding a brown paper sack. His eyes were startlingly attractive as the dark lashes dropped, and he glanced at Theresa's hands on the keyboard.

"Play something," he requested.

Immediately she folded her palms between her knees. "Oh, I was only limbering up for tonight."

He moved a step closer. "Limber up some more, then."

"I'm limbered enough."

He crossed behind her toward the davenport, and her eyes followed over her shoulder. "Good, then play a song."

"I don't know rock."

"I know. You're a classy person." He grinned, set his package down on the davenport and drew off his jacket, all the while keeping his eyes on her. She pinched her knees tighter against her palms. "I meant to say, you're a classical person," he amended with a lazy grin. "So play me a classic."

She played without sheet music, at times allowing her eyelids to drift closed while her head tipped back, and he caught glimpses of her enraptured eloquent face. When her eyelids opened she focused on nothing, letting her gaze drift with seeming unawareness. He had little doubt that while she played, Theresa forgot he stood behind her. He dropped his eyes again to her hands—fragile, long-fingered, with delicate bones at wrist and knuckle. How supplely they moved, those wrists arching gracefully, then dropping as she weaved backward, then forward. Once she smiled, and her head tipped to one side as the pianissimo chords tinkled from her fingertips while she inhabited that captivating world he knew and understood so well.

Watching the language of her hands, her body, was like having the song not only put into words but illustrated as well. He sensed that within Theresa the music acted as bellows to embers and saw what passions lay hidden within the woman whose normally shy demeanor never hinted at such smoldering fires.

By the time the song ended and Theresa's hands poised motionless above the keys, he was certain her heart must be pounding as heavily as his own.

He laid a hand on her shoulder and she jerked, as if waking up.

"That's very nice," he praised softly, and she became conscious of that warm hand resting where the strap of her bra cut a deep, painful groove into her flesh. "I seem to remember an old movie that used that as its theme song."

"The Eddy Duchin Story."

The hand slipped away, making her wish it had stayed. "Yes, that was it. Tyrone Power and...." She heard his fingers fillip beside her ear and swung around on the bench to face him, again tucking her palms between her knees.

"Kim Novak."

"That's it. Kim Novak." He noted her pose, the way she rounded her shoulders to minimize the prominence of her breasts, and it took an effort for him to keep his eyes on her face.

"It's Chopin. One of my favorites."

"I'll remember that. Chopin. Do you play Chopin tonight, too?"

He stood very close to her, and Theresa raised her eyes to meet his gaze. From this angle, the shoulder-to-shoulder seam across his white jersey made his torso appear inordinately broad and tapered. His voice was honey smooth and soft. Most of the time he spoke that way, which was a balm to her ears after the affectionate grate of Jeff's clamorousness and her mother's usual bawling forte.

"No, tonight we do all Christmas music. I believe we're starting with 'Joy to the World' and then a little-known French carol. We follow that with...." She realized he probably couldn't care less what they were playing tonight, and buttoned her lip.

"With?"

"Nothing. Just the usual Christmas stuff."

She was becoming rattled by his nearness and the studied way he seemed to be itemizing her features, as if listing them selectively in credit and debit columns within his head. She suddenly wished she knew how to apply makeup as cleverly as Amy, picturing her colorless eyelashes, and her too-colorful cheeks, knowing Brian could detect her many shortcomings altogether too clearly at such close range.

"I have to peel potatoes for supper." Having dredged up that excuse, she slid off the bench and escaped to the kitchen, where she donned a cobbler's apron to protect her white blouse as she worked.

A short time later her mother and father returned from work, and in the suppertime confusion, the quiet moment with Brian slipped to the back of Theresa's mind. But as she prepared to flee the house with violin case under the arm of her gray coat, she came to a halt in the middle of the kitchen. There stood Brian with a dish towel in his hands, and Amy, with her arms buried in suds, having uttered not a word of her usual complaints at having the job foisted on her.

"I'm sorry I had to eat and run, but we have to be in our chairs ready to tune up by six forty-five."

Jeff was on the phone, talking with Patricia. "Just

a minute—'' He broke off, and lowered the receiver. "Hey, sis, do good, okay?''

She gave him a thumbs-up sign with one fat, red mitten and as she headed toward the door, found it held open by Brian, his other hand buried inside a dish towel and glass he'd been wiping.

"Good luck,'' he said softly, his green eyes lingering upon her in a way the resurrected the closeness they'd shared at the piano earlier. The cold air rushed about their ankles, but neither seemed to notice as they gazed at each other, and Theresa felt as if Chopin's music was playing within her heart.

"Thanks,'' she said at last. "And thanks for taking over for me with the dishes.''

"Anytime.'' He smiled, grazed her chin with a touch so light she wondered if she'd imagined it as she turned into the brisk night that cooled her heated cheeks.

THE ANNUAL CHRISTMAS CONCERT of the Burnsville Civic Orchestra was held each year at the Burnsville Senior High School auditorium. The risers were set up and the curtains left open as the musicians made their way to their places amid the metallic premusic of clanking stands and metal folding chairs. The conductor arrived and tuning began. The incessant drone of the A-note filled the vaulted space of the auditorium, and gradually, the room hummed with voices as the seats slowly filled. The footlights were still off, and from her position at first chair Theresa had a clear view of the aisles.

She was running her bow over the honey-colored chunk of resin when her hand stopped sawing, and her lips fell open in surprise. There, filing in, came her whole family, plus Patricia Gluek, and of course,

Brian Scanlon. They shuffled into the fourth row center and began removing jackets and gloves while Theresa's palms went damp. She had played the violin since sixth grade and had stopped having stage fright years ago, but her stomach drew up now into an unexpected coil of apprehension. Amy waggled two fingers in a clandestine hello, and Theresa answered with a barely discernible waggle of her own. Then her eyes scanned the seat next to Amy and found Brian waggling two fingers back at her. *Oh, Lord, did he think I waved at him?* Twenty-five years old and waving like her giggling first graders did when they spotted their mommies and daddies in the audience.

But before she could become any further unnerved by the thought, the footlights came up, and the conductor tapped his baton on the edge of the music stand. She stiffened her spine and pulled away from the backrest of the chair, snapped her violin into place at the lift of the black-clad arms and hit the opening note of "Joy to the World."

Midway through the song Theresa realized she had never played the violin so well in her life, not that she could remember. She attacked the powerful notes of "Joy to the World" with robust precision. She nursed the stunning dissonants of "The Christmas Song" with loving care until the tension eased from the chords with their familiar resolutions. As lead violinist, she performed a solo on the compelling "I Wonder As I Wander," and the instrument seemed to come alive beneath her mocha-colored fingernails.

She began by playing for him. But she ended playing for herself, which is the true essence of the real musician. She forgot Brian sat in the audience and lost the inhibitions that claimed her whenever there was no instrument beneath her fingers or no children to direct.

From the darkened house, he watched her—nobody but her. The red hair and freckles that had been so distracting in their brilliance when he'd first met her took on an appropriateness lent by her fiery zeal as she dissolved into the music. Again, there were times when her eyelids drifted shut. Other times she smiled against the chin rest, and he was somehow certain she had no idea she was smiling. Her sleeves draped as she bowed the instrument, her wrist arched daintily as she occasionally plucked it, and the hem of her black skirt lifted and fell as she tapped her toe to the sprightlier songs.

The concert ended with a reprise of "Joy to the World," and the final thunder of applause brought the orchestra members to their feet for a mass bow.

When the house lights came up, Theresa's eyes scanned the line of familiar faces in row four, but returned to settle and stay on Brian, who had lifted his hands to praise her in the traditional way, and was wearing a smile as proud as any on the other faces. She braved a wide smile in return and hoped he knew it was not for the others but just for him. He stopped clapping and gave her the thumbs-up signal, and she felt a holiday glow such as she'd never known as she sat to tuck her instrument back into its case.

THEY WERE WAITING in the hall when she came from the music room with her coat and mitts on, her case beneath an arm.

Everybody babbled at once, but Theresa finally had a chance to croon appreciatively, "Why didn't you *tell* me you were coming?"

"We wanted to surprise you. Besides, we thought it might make you nervous."

"Well, it did! No, it didn't! Oh, I don't know what I'm saying, except it really made the concert special, knowing you were all out there listening. Thanks, all of you, for coming."

Jeff looped an elbow around Theresa's neck, faked a headlock and a punch to the jaw and grunted, "You did good, sis."

Margaret took command then. "We have a tree to decorate yet tonight, and you know how your father always has trouble with those lights. Let's get this party moving home!"

They headed toward the parking lot, and Theresa invited, "Does anybody want to ride with me?" She could sense Amy reserving her reply until she heard what Brian answered.

"I will," he said, moving to Theresa's side and taking the violin case from her hands.

"I will too—" Amy began, but Margaret cut her off in midsentence.

"Amy, you come with us. I want you to run into the store for a carton of milk on our way home."

"Jeff? Patricia?" Theresa appealed, suddenly feeling as if she'd coerced Brian into saying yes, since nobody else had.

"Patricia left her purse in the station wagon, so we might as well ride with them."

The two groups parted, and as she walked toward her little gray Toyota, Theresa suddenly suspected that Patricia had had her purse with her all along.

In the car she and Brian settled into the low bucket seats and Theresa put a tape in the deck. Rachmaninoff seemed to envelope them. "Sorry," she offered, and immediately pushed the eject button. Without hesitation, he reseated the tape against the heads and the dynamic Concerto in C-sharp Minor returned.

"I get the idea you think I'm some hard-rock freak. Music is music. If it's good, I like it."

They drove through the moonlit night with the power and might of Rachmaninoff ushering them home, followed by the much mellower poignance of Listz's "Liebestraum." As its flowing sweetness touched her ears, Theresa thought of its English translation, "Dream of Love." But she kept her eyes squarely on the road, thinking herself fanciful because of the residual ebullience of the performance and the occasional scarlet, blue and gold lights that glittered from housefronts as they passed. In living-room windows Christmas trees winked cheerfully, but it wasn't just the trees, it wasn't just the lights, it wasn't just the concert and not even Jeff's being home that made this Christmas more special than most. It was Brian Scanlon.

"I saw your foot tapping," he teased now.

"Oh?"

"Sure sign of a dancer."

"I'm still thinking about it."

"Good. Because I never get to dance much anymore. I'm always providing the music."

"Never fear. If I don't go, there'll be plenty of others."

"That's what I'm afraid of. Rhythmless clods who'll abuse my toes and talk, talk, talk in my ear."

"You don't like to talk when you dance?" Somehow she'd always imagined dancers using the close proximity to exchange intimacies.

"Not particularly."

"I've been led to believe that's when men and

women whisper . . . well, what's known as *sweet noth-ings.*''

Brian turned to study her face, smiling at the old-fashioned phrase, wondering if he knew another woman who'd use it. *''Sweet nothings?''*

She heard the grin in his voice, but kept her eyes on the street. "I have no personal knowledge of them myself, you understand." She gave him a quarter glance and lifted one eyebrow.

"I understand. Neither do I."

"But I'll give it some thought."

"I already have. Sounds like not a half-bad idea."

She felt as if her face would light up the interior of the car, for it struck Theresa that while she had no knowledge of sweet nothings, she and Brian were ex-changing them at that very moment.

They made it home before the others, and Theresa excused herself to go to her room and change into jeans, blouse and loose-thrown sweater again. From the living room she heard the soft, exploratory notes of the piano as a melody line from a current Air Sup-ply hit was picked out with one finger. She came down the hall and paused in the living-room door-way. Brian stood before the piano, one thumb hooked in the back pocket of his pants while he lackadaisically pressed the keys with a single forefin-ger. He looked up. She crossed her arms. The piano strings vibrated into silence. She noticed things about him that she liked—the shape of his eyebrows, the way his expression said *smile* when there really was none there, his easy unhurried way of speaking, mov-ing, shifting his eyes, that put her much more at ease the longer she was with him.

"I enjoyed the concert."

"I'm glad."

"My first live orchestra."

"It's nothing compared to the Minneapolis Orchestra. You should hear them."

"Maybe I will sometime. Do they play Chopin?"

"Oh, they play everything! And Orchestra Hall is positively sensational. The acoustics are world acclaimed. The ceiling is made of big white cubes of all sizes that look like they've been thrown up there and stuck at odd angles. The notes come bouncing off the cubes and—" She had looked up, as if expecting the living-room ceiling to be composed of the same cubes she described, not realizing that she looked very girlish and appealing in her animation, or that she had thrown her arms wide.

When her eyes drifted down, she found Brian grinning in amusement.

The kitchen door burst open and the noise began again.

WHEN THE BRUBAKER FAMILY decorated their Christmas tree, the scene was like a three-ring circus, with Margaret its ringmaster. She doled out commands about everything: which side of the tree should face front, who should pick up the trail of needles left scattered across the carpet, who should fill the tree stand with water. Poor Willard had trouble with the tree lights, all right, but his biggest trouble was his wife. "Willard, I want you to move that red light so it's underneath that branch instead of on top of it. There's a big hole here."

Jeff caught his mother by the waist, swung her around playfully and circled her arms so she couldn't move, then plopped a silencing kiss on her mouth. "Yes, his little turtledove. Shut up, his little turtledove,'' Margaret's tall son teased, gaining a smile in return.

"You're not too big to spank yet, Jeffrey. Talking to your mother like that.'' But her grin was as wide as a watermelon slice. "Patricia, get this boy off my back.'' Patricia made a lunge at Jeff and the two ended up in a heap on the sofa, teasing and tickling.

Margaret had turned on the living-room stereo, but while it played Christmas music, Amy's bedroom was thumping with rock, and though the door was closed, the sound came through to confuse the issue. Jeff sang with one or the other in his deep, gravelly voice, and before they got to the tinsel, the phone had rung no less than four times—all for Amy.

Brian might have felt out of place but for Patricia's being an outsider, too. When it was time to distribute the tinsel, she was given a handful, just as he was, and protesting that it was *their* tree would have sounded ungracious, so he found himself beside Theresa, hanging shimmering silver icicles on the high branches while she worked on the lower ones. Jeff and Patricia had taken over the other half of the tree while the two elder Brubakers sat back and watched this part of the decorations, and Amy talked on the phone, interrupting herself to offer some sage bit of direction now and then.

They ended the evening with hot apple cider and cinnamon rolls around the kitchen table. By the time they finished, it was nearing eleven o'clock. Margaret stood up and began stacking the dirty cups and saucers.

"Well, I guess it's time I get Patricia back home,'' Jeff announced. "Do you two want to ride along?''

Brian and Theresa both looked up and spoke simultaneously.

"No, I'll stay here and clean up the mess."

"I don't feel like going out in the cold again."

Theresa took over the task her mother had begun. "You're tired, mom. I'll do that."

Margaret desisted thankfully and went off to bed with Willard, ordering Amy to retire also. When the door closed behind Jeff and Patricia, the kitchen was left to Theresa and Brian. She carried the dishes to the counter and filled the sink with sudsy water and began washing them.

"I'll dry them for you."

"You don't have to. There are just a few."

Overruling her protest, he found the dish towel and stood beside her at the sink. She was conscious that he was comfortable with silence, unlike most people. He could go through long stretches of it without searching for ways to fill it. The stereos were off. Jeff's teasing was gone, and Margaret's incessant orders. Only the swish of water and the clink of glassware could be heard. It took them less than five minutes to wash and dry the cups and saucers and put the room in order. But while five minutes of silence beside the wrong person can be devastating, that same five beside the right man can be totally wonderful.

When she'd hung up the wet cloths and switched out all the lights except the small one over the stove, she found a bottle of lotion beneath the sink and squirted a dollop in her palm, aware of Brian watching silently as she worked the cherry-scented cream into her hands.

"Let's sit in the living room for a while," he suggested.

She led the way and sat down on one end of the davenport while he sat at the other, leaning back and draping his palms across his abdomen, much as he had in the theater. Again silence fell. Again it was sustaining rather than draining. The tree lights made Theresa feel as if she was on the inside of a rainbow looking out.

"You have a wonderful family," he said at last.

"I know."

"But I begin to see why your dad needs to spend some quiet time with the birds."

Theresa chuckled softly. "It gets a little raucous at times. Mostly when Jeff's around."

"I like it though. I don't ever remember any happy noise around my house."

"Don't you have any brothers and sisters?"

"Yeah, one sister, but she's eight years older than me, and she lives in Jamaica. Her husband's in exporting. We were never very close."

"And what about your mom and dad? I mean, your real dad. Were you close to them?"

He stared at the tree lights and ruminated at length. She liked that. No impulsive answers to a question that was important. "A little with my dad, but never with my mother."

"Why?"

He rolled his head and studied her. "I don't know. Why are some families like yours and some like mine? If I knew the answer and could bottle it, I could stop wars."

His answer made her turn to meet his eyes directly— such stunning, spiky-lashed beauties. She was struck again by the fact that such pretty eyes somehow managed to make him even more handsome. In them the tree lights were reflected—dots of red and gold and green and blue shining from beneath chestnut eyebrows and lashes, studying her without a smile.

His steady gaze made Theresa short of breath.

There were things inside this man that spoke of a depth of character she was growing surely to admire. Though he was really Jeff's senior by only two years, he seemed much older than Jeff—much older than her, too, she thought. Perhaps losing one's family does that to a person. It suddenly struck Theresa how awesome it must be to have no place to call home. She herself had clung to home far longer than was advisable. But she was a different matter. Brian would leave the Air Force next summer, and there would be no mother waiting with pumpkin pies in the freezer. No familiar bedroom where he could lie on his back and consider what lay ahead, while the familiar lair secured him to the past. No siblings to tease or go Christmas shopping with. No old girlfriend waiting with open arms. . . .

But how did she know? The thought was sobering. She suddenly wanted to ask if there was a woman somewhere who was special to him, but didn't want to sound forward, so she veiled the question somewhat.

"Isn't there anyone left behind in Chicago?"

The smile was absent, but why did it feel as if he was charming her with the twinkle in his eye? "Since we've already eliminated parents and sisters and brothers, you must mean girlfriends." She dropped her eyes and hoped the red tree lights camouflaged the heat she felt creeping up her neck. "No, there are no girlfriends waiting in Chicago."

"I didn't mean—"

"Whether you did or not doesn't matter. Maybe I just wanted you to know."

The silence that followed was scarcely comfortable, quite unlike that which had passed earlier. It was filled with a new, tingling two-way awareness and a thousand other unasked questions.

"I think I'll say good-night now," he announced quietly, surprising Theresa. She wasn't *totally* naive. She'd sat on living-room davenports with those of the opposite sex before, and after a lead-in like Brian's, the groping always followed.

But he rose, stretched and stood with his fingers in his hip pockets while he studied the tree a minute longer. Then he studied her an equal length of time before raising a palm and murmuring softly, "Good night, Theresa."

Chapter Four

BRIAN SCANLON LAY IN BED, thinking about Theresa Brubaker, considering what it was that attracted him to her. He'd never cared much for redheads. Yet her hair was as orange as that of a Raggedy Ann doll, and her freckles were the color of overripe fruit. When she blushed—and she blushed often—she tended to glow like the Christmas tree.

Brian had been playing in a band since high school. In every dance crowd there were women who couldn't resist a guitar man when he stepped down from the stage at break time. They flocked around like chickens to scattered corn. He'd had his share. But he'd always gone for the blondes and brunettes, the prettiest ones with artful makeup and hair down to the middle of their backs, swinging like silk— women who knew their way around men.

But Theresa Brubaker was totally different from them. Not only did she look different, she acted different. She was honest and interesting, intelligent and loving. And totally naive, Brian was sure.

Yet so much heart lay beneath that naivety. It surfaced whenever she was around her family, particularly Jeff, and whenever she was around music. Brian recalled her voice, when the three of them had been harmonizing in the car, and the verve she radiated when playing the violin and the piano. Why, she even had him listening to classical music with a new, tolerant ear. The poignant strains of the Chopin Nocturne came back to him as he crossed his wrists behind his head in the dark and thought of how she'd looked in the long black skirt and white blouse. The blouse had, for once, been covered by no sweater.

He wondered how a man ever got up the nerve to touch breasts like hers. When they were that big, they weren't really...sexy. Just intimidating. He'd been scared to death the first time he'd felt a girl's breasts, but since then he'd touched countless others, and still the idea of caressing Theresa's breasts gave him serious qualms. There'd been times when he'd managed to study them covertly, but Theresa allowed few such opportunities, covered as she usually was with her cardigans. But when she'd been playing the piano, he'd stood behind her and looked down at the mountainous orbs beneath her blouse, and his mouth had gone dry instead of watering.

Forget it, Scanlon. She's not your type.

THE NEXT MORNING, when Brian arose at his usual wake-up hour and crept barefoot upstairs to the bathroom, he came face to face with Theresa in the hall.

They both stopped short and stared at each other. He wore a pair of blue denim jeans, nothing else. She wore a mint green bathrobe, nothing else. There wasn't a sound in the house. Everyone else was still asleep, for it was Christmas Eve day so neither of her parents had to go to work.

"Good morning," she whispered. The bathroom door was right beside them.

"Good morning," he whispered back. Her feet were bare, and it was obvious even without a glance that her breasts were untethered beneath the velour robe, for they drooped nearly to her waist while she lifted her arms and pretended the zipper needed closing at her throat.

"You can go first," she offered, gesturing toward the doorway.

"No, no, you go ahead. I'll wait."

"No, I . . . really, I was just going to put on a pot of coffee first."

He was about to raise another objection when she swept past him toward the kitchen, so he hurried into the bathroom, taking care of necessities without wasting time, then heading for the kitchen to tell her the room was free. She was standing before the stove waiting for the coffee to start perking when he padded up silently beside her.

The sun wasn't up yet, but it had lightened the sky to an opalescent gray that lifted over the east windowsills of the kitchen, providing enough light for Theresa to see very clearly the dark hair springing from Brian's bare chest and diving into his waistline like an arrow. His nipples were like twin raspberries, shriveled up in the centers of squarely defined muscles. The only bare chests she'd ever seen in this house had been Jeff's and her father's. But this one was nothing like either of theirs, and the sight of him brought to mind vivid scenes from the movie they'd seen two nights ago. She dropped her eyes after the briefest glance, but down below she encountered more hair—dark wisps on his big toes. And suddenly she couldn't stand there beside him a moment longer, with him only half dressed and herself coming totally unstrung inside her mint green robe.

"Would you mind watching the coffee till it starts perking, then turn it down to low?"

In the bathroom she switched on the light above

the vanity and checked her reflection in the mirror. Sure enough, beet red! That horribly unflattering red that made her look as if she was going to go off like a Fourth of July rocket. She pressed her palms to her cheeks, closed her eyes and wondered how it felt to be *normal* and come up against a half-naked man like Brian Scanlon in your kitchen.

Lordy, he flustered her so.

What do other women do? How do they handle the first attraction they feel? It must be so much easier when you're fourteen, like Amy, and you go at the natural pace: a first exchange of glances, a first touch of hands, a first kiss, then nubility taking over as boy and girl together begin exploring their awakening sexuality.

But I was thwarted at square one, Theresa thought miserably, looking at her awful freckles and hair, which by themselves would have been enough to overcome without the other even greater obstacles. *I was cheated by nature out of those first kittenish glances that might have led to all the rest, because all the first glances I ever received contained no more than shock or lasciviousness. And now here I am, midway through my twenties, and I don't know how to handle my very first sexual attraction to a man.*

She took a bath, washed her hair and didn't reenter the kitchen until she was properly dressed in a color she wore defiantly—cranberry. She loved it, but when it got anywhere near her hair, the two hues went to war and made her look like beets and carrots mixed in the same bowl. She had to keep the cranberry corduroy slacks separated from her flaming-hair by a band of neutral color across her torso. When she explored her closet, she came upon a wonderful white sweat shirt Amy had given her for

Christmas last year, which Theresa had never worn, no matter how many times she'd been tempted. To the average woman the sweat shirt would have been absolutely dishwater plain. It had hand-warmer pockets on the belly, zipper up the front and two sport stripes running down the sleeves: one of navy, the other of cranberry.

She took it from the hanger, slipped her arms into it and stepped before her mirror while she zipped it up. But the reflection that met her eyes made her want to cry. It looked like two dirigibles had been inflated beneath the garment. There was no power on earth that could make her wear this thing out to the kitchen and face Brian.

Angrily, she jerked it off and tossed it aside, replacing it with a prim oxford-cloth shirt in off-white with long sleeves and a button-down collar, over which she draped the everlasting, hated cardigan.

She was saved from encountering Brian's bare chest again when she heard him take over the bathroom while she was arranging her hair in a round mound just above her collar. When it was confined, at least it didn't look as if it was going to carry her away into the wild blue yonder if a stiff wind came up.

In the bathroom, Brian, too, assessed himself in the mirror. *She's scared of you, Scanlon, so the issue is settled. You don't have to think about the possibility of falling for her.*

But the room was scented with feminine things— the flowery essence of soap left behind in the damp air. There was a wet washcloth over the shower-curtain rod, and when he grabbed it down to close the curtains, he found himself staring at it for a long moment while he rubbed a thumb across the cold, damp terry cloth. With an effort, he put her from his mind and folded the cloth very carefully, then laid it on a corner of the tub. But while he stood beneath the hot spray, soaping his body, he thought of her again, and of the movie, and couldn't help wondering what it would be like in bed with that freckled body, the generous breasts and red hair.

Scanlon, it's Christmas, you pervert! What the hell are you doing standing here thinking about your best friend's sister like some practiced lecher?

But that's not the only reason I can't get her off my mind, his other self argued honestly. *She's a beautiful person. Inside, where it counts.*

He intentionally kept things light and breezy when he met Theresa in the kitchen again. But it was easier, for the rest of her family was beginning to rouse, and one by one they padded out to have coffee or juice. By the time they all sat down to breakfast together, the day had changed mood.

It was set aside for preparations. There was a family gathering planned at Grandma and Grandpa Deering's house, and everybody would take something for the supper buffet. Then tomorrow, the pack would descend upon the Brubaker house for Christmas dinner, so Margaret, Theresa and Amy were busy all day in the kitchen.

Margaret was at her dictatorial best, issuing orders like a drill-team sergeant again while her daughters carried them out. Willard spent part of the day watching for cardinals, while Jeff and Brian broke out their guitars at last, and from the kitchen Theresa heard her first of Brian's guitar playing. She dropped what she was doing and moved to the living-room doorway, pausing there to observe him tuning, then fingering an augmented chord of quietly vibrating quality, bending his head low over the instrument, listening intently as the six notes shimmered into silence. He sat at the piano bench, but had swung to face the davenport where Jeff sat, and didn't know Theresa stood behind him.

Jeff, too, strummed random chords, the two guitars quietly clashing in that presong dissonance that can be as musical in its own off-harmonic way as cleanly arranged songs.

Jeff played lead, Brian rhythm, and from the moment the discordant warmup crystalized into the intro to a song, Theresa recognized a marvelous communion of kindred musicians. No signal had been spoken, none exchanged by eye, hand or tongue. The inharmonious gibberish of tuning had simply resolved into the concord of one single silently agreed-upon song.

Between musicians there can be a connection, just as between friends who somehow single each other out, recognizing empathy from the moment of introduction, just as a man and woman sometimes attract each other at first glimpse. It's something that cannot be prompted or dictated. Among members of a band this connection makes the difference between simply playing notes at the same time and creating an affinity of sound.

They had it, these two. There was almost a mystical quality about it, and as Theresa looked on and listened from the kitchen doorway, shivers ran up her arms and down her legs. They had picked up on "Georgia on My Mind." Where was the clashing rock? Where were the occasional sour chords she used to hear from Jeff's guitar? When had he gotten so *good*?

Neither Brian nor Jeff looked at each other while

they played. Their heads were cocked lazily, eyes blankly turned to the waists of their guitars in that indolent, concentrative pose Theresa recognized well. How many times had she stood before Jeff and asked him a question when he was in such a trance, only to be separated from him by the wall of music until the song finished and he looked startled to find her standing there?

Jeff began to sing, his softly grating voice evocative of Ray Charles's immortal rendition of this song. A lump formed in Theresa's throat. Amy had come up silently behind her, and they stood as motionless as the hands of a sundial. Jeff ''took a ride'' at the break, and Theresa stared at his supple fingers running along the frets with an agility she'd never seen before. Pride blossomed in her heart. *Oh, Jeff, Jeff, my little brother, who started on that fifteen-dollar Stella in the corner, just listen to you now.* He vocalized the last verse, then together he and Brian ''rode it home,'' and as the last poignant notes ebbed to fade-out, Theresa looked back over her shoulder into Amy's wide, amazed eyes. The room was silent.

Jeff's eyes met Brian's, and they exchanged smiles before they concurred, in their two deep voices, ''All ri-i-ight.''

''Jeffrey,'' Theresa said softly at last.

He glanced up in surprise. ''Hey, Treat, how long have you been standing there?''

Brian swung around on the piano seat, and she gave him a passing smile of approval but moved to her brother, bending across his guitar to give him a hug. ''When did you get so good?''

''You haven't heard me for over a year, closer to a year and a half. Brian and I have been hittin' it hard.''

"Obviously."

She turned back to Brian. "Don't take me wrong, but I think you two were made for each other."

They all laughed, then Brian agreed, "Yeah, we kind of thought so the first time we picked a song together. It just happened, you know?"

"I know. And it shows."

Amy, with her hands jammed in her jeans pockets, inched closer to Brian's shoulders. "Gol, wait'll the kids hear this!"

Theresa couldn't resist the temptation to tease. "Is this Amy Brubaker speaking? The same Amy Brubaker who inundates us with AC/DC and scorns anything mellower than Rod Stewart?"

Amy shrugged, showed a flash of braces behind a half-sheepish grin, and returned, "Yeah, but these guys are really *excellent*, I mean, *wow*. And anyway, Jeff promised they'd do some rock, too. Didn't you, Jeffy?"

Instead of answering, Jeff struck a straight D chord, hard and heavy, with a dramatic flourish, and after letting it sizzle for a prolonged moment he met Brian's eye, and the next chord bit the air with the brashness of unvarnished rock. How they both knew the chosen song was a mystery. But one minute only Jeff's chord hung in the air, and the next they were hammering away at the song as if by divine design. Amy stood between them, getting into the beat with her hips. "Yeah..." she half growled, and Brian gave her a nonchalant quasi smile, then turned that same smile on Theresa, who shrugged in reply, a proud smile on her face while she enjoyed every note, rock or not, and each sideward thrust of Amy's hips.

When the song ended, Margaret and Willard were standing in the doorway, applauding. Amy rushed for the telephone, undoubtedly to rave on about the good tidings to as many friends as possible, and Theresa reluctantly returned to the kitchen to listen from there while she worked.

In the late afternoon, they all went to their respective rooms to change and get ready for the trip across town to Grandpa and Grandma Deerings'. When they rendezvoused in the kitchen to load the car, it was Margaret who suggested, "Why don't you bring your guitars? We'll do some caroling. You know how your grandparents enjoy it."

So the station wagon was packed with potato salad and cranberry jello, a vintage Gibson hollow-body 335 and a classic Epiphone Riviera, a rented amp, a stack of Christmas presents and six bodies.

Willard drove. Theresa found herself in the back seat sandwiched between Jeff and Brian. His hip was warm, even through her bulky coat, and when he and Jeff exchanged comments, she was served up tantalizing whiffs of his sandalwoody after-shave, for he'd slung an arm across the back of the seat and repeatedly leaned forward to peer around her.

If Brian thought he'd feel out of place at the family gathering, the delusion was put to rout within minutes of arriving. The tiny house of mid-forties' vintage was popping at the seams with relatives of all ages and sizes. Grandpa Deering was deaf, and when Jeff took Brian over to introduce him to the shriveled little man, he shouted for his grandfather's benefit. "Grandpa, this is my friend, Brian, the one who's in the Air Force with me."

The old man nodded.

"I brought him home to spend Christmas with us," Brian bawled at the top of his lungs.

Mr. Deering nodded again.

"We play in a band together, and we brought our guitars along tonight to do a few carols."

The bald head nodded still once more. Grandpa Deering raised a crooked forefinger in the air as if in approval, but said not a word until the two were turning away. Then he questioned in his reedy old quake, "This y'r friend who fiddles with you?"

It was all Brian could do to keep a straight face. Jeff turned back to his grandfather, leaning closer. "Guitar, grandpa, guitar."

The old man nodded and said no more, replaced his arthritic palms one on top of the other atop a black, rubber-tipped cane and seemed to drift into a reverie.

When Brian and Jeff turned away, Brian whispered in his friend's ear. "Doesn't his hearing aid work?"

"He turns it down whenever it's convenient. When the music starts he'll hear every note."

The thirty-odd aunts, uncles and cousins ate from a table containing more food than Brian had ever seen in one place, and after the buffet supper, opened gifts, having exchanged names at Thanksgiving. When it was time for the music, everyone found a spot as best he could on the floor, the kitchen cabinets, end tables, arms of furniture, and the entire group sang the old standard carols while Theresa was cajoled into playing along with the guitars on an ancient oak organ whose bellows were filled by foot pedals. She complied good-naturedly and pulled out the old stops from whose faces the mother-of-pearl inserts had long ago fallen. For the benefit of the small children in the group, Brian and Jeff were enticed into doing a run-through of "Here Comes Santa Claus," which evolved into a jazz rendition that would have shocked its composer, Gene Autry. Jeff took an impromptu ride, taking outrageous liberties with the melody line, ad-libbing arpeggios while Brian modified the chords to smooth, fluid jazz. When it was over, the house burst into whistles and clapping, and the youngsters called for "Jingle Bells." When that was finished, someone called, "Where's Margaret? Margaret, it's your turn. Get up there."

To Brian's surprise, the hefty-chested dictatorial Margaret stepped center front, and while her daughter played an accompaniment on the wheezy organ, she belted out a stunning "Oh Holy Night." When the song ended, and Theresa spun around on the seat of the claw-foot organ stool to face Brian's eyebrows raised in surprise, she leaned near his ear and whispered, "Mother was a mezzo-soprano with a touring opera company before she married daddy."

"That leaves only Amy. What about her?"

From his far side, Amy spoke up. "I only got the beat, I didn't get the voice, so I play drums in the school band."

Brian smiled. "And dance, I'll bet."

"Yeah. Just wait and see."

Theresa knew a kind of keen envy. Amy could dance the socks off any three partners who tried to keep up with her. The sample she'd given earlier today in the living room had been only a hint of the rhythm contained in her svelte, teenage limbs. Theresa had always been extremely proud of Amy's dancing ability, and moreso, her sister's lack of inhibition whenever any music started. While Theresa herself had felt a lifelong urge to dance, she'd never yielded to it.

She should have grown inured to giving up enjoyments such as dancing. By now, she shouldn't miss them, but she did. She transferred all her emotions into her music and took from it the satisfaction she was denied in other modes of self-expression, as she did now on this Christmas Eve.

She shunned the petty envy that she'd come to hate in herself and lauded, "Amy is the best dancer I know. It's too bad she isn't old enough to go with you on New Year's Eve."

Brian only smiled from one sister to the other, hoping the older of the two would agree to go with him, after all.

On the way home they dropped Jeff off at Patricia's house, where another family celebration was winding down. Jeff would get in on the end of it. When the remainder of the group reached the Brubaker house, the two older ones toddled off to bed while the remaining three turned on the tree lights and sat in the cozy living room exchanging anecdotes about past Christmases, music, the Air Force, school dances, Grandpa Deering and a myriad of subjects that kept them up well past midnight. Jeff joined them then, announcing that he'd just flown in on his jet-propelled sleigh and was looking for a plate of cookies and glass of milk before he filled any stockings.

When Theresa went to sleep that night, it was not to visions of sugar plums dancing in her head, but to visions of Brian Scanlon's long, dexterous fingers moving along the fingerboard of an Epiphone Riviera, picking out the chords to a love song whose words she strove to catch.

ON CHRISTMAS MORNING Theresa was awakened by Amy, pouncing on her bed, giggling. "Hey, come on! Let's make it to those prezzies!"

"Amy, it's blacker than the ace of spades outside."

"It's seven o'clock already!"

"Ohh!" Theresa groaned and rolled over.

"Come on, get your buns out of here and let's go get the boys and mom and dad."

From down the hall came a hoarse call, "Who's doin' all that giggling out there?" Jeff. "Come in here and try that!"

Amy sprang off Theresa's bed and went to wage an attack on her brother, and the squealing that followed told clearly of a bout of tickling which soon awakened Margaret and Willard. The thumping on the floor aroused their houseguest downstairs, and within ten minutes they had all gathered in the living room and snuggled around the Christmas tree, dressed in hastily thrown-on robes, jeans, half-buttoned shirts, bare feet and bedroom slippers, sipping juice and coffee while gifts were distributed.

Brian was sharing a Christmas unlike any he'd ever experienced. This boisterous, loving family was showing him depths he'd never known. The gifts exchanged among them underscored that love again, for they were not many but well chosen.

For Willard, his children had decided on a telescope that would take its place before the sliding glass door downstairs; for Margaret, a mother's ring that would take its place proudly on her right hand, and which prompted a listing of the three birthdays. Brian carefully marked in his memory the date of Theresa's. To Margaret and Willard together the children gave a gift certificate for a weekend at the quiet, quaint Schumaker's Country Inn in the tiny town of New Prague, an hours' ride from the Twin Cities.

From their parents, Jeff, Amy and Theresa received, respectively, a plane ticket home for Easter, a pair of tickets to an upcoming rock concert by Journey and a season ticket to Orchestra Hall.

To Brian's surprise, each of the Brubakers had bought a gift for him. From Margaret and Willard, a billfold; from Amy, blank tapes—obviously she knew he and the other band members learned new songs by taping cuts from the radio; from Jeff, a Hohner harmonica—they'd been fooling around on one at a music store, and Brian had said he'd always wanted to play one; and from Theresa, an LP of classical music, including Chopin's Nocturne in E-flat.

When he opened the last gift, he looked up in surprise. "How did you have time to find it on such short notice?"

"Secret." But her eyes danced to her father's, and Brian remembered Willard's leaving the house for "last-minute items" yesterday.

To Brian's relief, he, too, had brought gifts. For Mr. and Mrs. Brubaker, a selection of cheese and bottle of Chianti wine; for Amy, a pair of headphones, which brought a round of good-natured applause from the rest of the group; for Jeff, a wide leather guitar strap tooled with his name; and for Theresa, a tiny pewter figurine—a smiling frog on a lily pad, playing the violin.

She smiled, placed it on her palm and met Brian's irresistible green eyes across the living room.

"How did you know I collect pewter instruments?"

"Secret."

"My darling brother, who can't keep anything to himself. And for once, I'm happy he can't. Thank you, Brian."

"Thank you, too. You'll make a silk purse of this sow's ear yet." Which was ironic, for Brian was far, far from a sow's ear.

She studied the frog with its bulging pewter eyes and self-satisfied smile and lifted a similiar smile to Brian. "I'll call him 'The Maestro.'"

The fiddling frog became one of Theresa's most cherished possessions, and took his place at the forefront of the collection shelved on a wall in her bedroom. It was the first gift she'd ever received from any male other than a family member.

THAT CHRISTMAS DAY, filled with noise, food and family, passed in a blur for both Brian and Theresa. They were more conscious of each other than of any of the others in the house. The family ate and got lazy, ate again, and eventually their numbers began thinning. That lazy wind-down prompted dozing and eventually, an evening revival of energy. As most days did in this house where music reigned supreme, this one would have seemed incomplete without it. It was eight o'clock in the evening, and the crowd had dwindled to a mere dozen or so when out came the instruments, and it became apparent the family had their favorites, which they asked Jeff and Theresa to play. Margaret and Willard were nestled like a pair of teenagers on the davenport, and applauded and chose another and another song. Eventually, Brian and Jeff branched off into a rousing medley of rock songs, during which Theresa joined in, Elton John-style, on the piano. Then Jeff had the sudden inspiration, "Hey, Theresa, go get your fiddle!"

"Fiddle!" she spouted. "Jeffrey Brubaker, how dare you call great-grandmother's expensive Storioni a *fiddle*. Why, it's probably cringing in its case!"

Jeff explained to Brian, "She inherited her fiddle from one of our more talented progenitors, who bought it in 1906. It's modeled after a Faratti, so Theresa is rather overzealous about the piece."

"Fiddle!" Theresa teased with a saucy twitch of the hip as she left the room. "I'll show you *fiddle*, Brian Scanlon!"

When the beautiful classic violin came back with Theresa, Brian was amazed to hear the sister and brother strike into an engaging, foot-stomping rendition of "Lou'siana Saturday Night," along with which he himself provided background rhythm, while he wondered in bewilderment how Theresa happened to know the song, so different from her classics. After that, the hayseed in all of them seemed to have stuck to their overalls, and Jeff tried a little flat picking on "Wildwood Flower," and by that time, the entire group had gotten rather punchy. The usually reserved Willard captured Margaret and executed an impromptu hoe-down step in the middle of the room, which brought laughter and applause, to say nothing of the sweat to Margaret's brow as she plopped into a chair, breathless and fanning her red face but totally exhilarated.

"Give us 'Turkey In The Straw'!" someone shouted.

Again Brian was shown a new facet of Theresa Brubaker, a first-chair violinist of the Burnsville Civic Orchestra, as she sawed away on her 1906 classic Storioni, scraping out a raucous version of the old barn-dance tune, in the middle of which she lowered the violin and tapped the air with the bow, the carpet with her toe and watched her mother and father circling and clapping in the small space provided, while in a voice as clear as daybreak, Theresa sang out:

Oh, I had a little chicken
And it wouldn't lay an egg
So I poured hot water up and down her leg
Then the little chicken hollered
And the little chicken begged
And the damn little chicken
Laid a hard-boiled egg.

She was joined by the entire entourage as they finished by bellowing in unison, "Boom-tee-dee-a-da... *slick chick*!"

Brian joined in the rousing round of applause and shrill whistles that followed. As he laughed with the others, he saw again the hidden Theresa who seemed able to escape only when wooed by music and those she loved most. She covered her pink-tinged cheeks with both hands, while the "fiddle" and bow still hung from her fingers and her laughter flowed, sweet and fresh as spring water.

She was unique. She was untainted. She was as refreshing as the unexpected burst of hayseed music that had just erupted from her grandmother's invaluable 1906 Storioni.

He watched Theresa bestowing hugs of goodbye on her aunts and uncles. She had forgotten herself and impulsively lifted her arms in farewell embraces. Already Brian knew how rare these moments of forgetfulness were with Theresa. Music made the difference. It took her to a plane of unselfconsciousness nothing else could quite achieve.

He turned away, wandered back to the deserted living room, wondering what it would take to make her feel such ease with him. He sat down on the piano bench and picked out a haunting melody, one of his favorites, with a single finger, then softly began adding harmony notes. Soon he was engrossed in the quiet melody as his hands moved over the keyboard.

The house quieted. Amy was in her room with the new headphones glued to her ears. Willard was downstairs setting up his new microscope. Margaret had gone to bed, exhausted.

There were only three left in the room where the tree lights glowed.

"What are you playing?" Theresa asked, pausing behind Brian's shoulder, watching his long fingers on the piano.

"An old favorite, 'Sweet Memories.'"

"I don't think I know it."

Jeff wandered in. "Play it for her." He swung the old Stella up by its neck, extending it toward Brian, who looked back over his shoulder, with a noncommittal smile. "Do old Stella a favor," Jeff requested whimsically.

Brian seemed to consider for a long moment, then nodded once, turned on the bench to face the room and reached for the scarred, old guitar. The first soft note sent a shudder up Theresa's spine.

Jeff sat on the edge of the davenport, leaning forward, elbows to knees, for one of those rare times when he didn't have a guitar in his hands. He simply sat and paid homage. To the song. His friend. And a voice that turned Theresa's nerve-endings to satin.

She realized she had not heard Brian sing before. Not alone. Not . . . not . . . .

It was a song whose eloquent simplicity brought tears to her eyes and a knot to her throat, tremors to her stomach and goose bumps to the undersides of her thighs as she sat on the floor before him.

> My world is like a river
> As dark as it is deep.

Night after night the past slips in
And gathers all my sleep.
My days are just an endless string
Of emptiness to me.
Filled only by the fleeting moments
Of her memory.

Sweet memories...
Sweet memories...

He hummed a compelling melody line at the end of
the verse, and she watched his beautiful fingers, the
tendons of his left thumb grown powerful from years
of barring chords, the square-cut nails of his right
hand plucking or strumming the steel strings.

She watched his eyes, which had somehow come to
rest on her own as the words of the last verse came
somberly from his sensitive lips.

She slipped into the darkness
Of my dreams last night.
Wandering from room to room
She's turning on each light.
Her laughter spills like water
From the river to the sea
Lord, I'm swept away from sadness
Clinging to her memory.

The haunting notes of the chorus came again, and
Theresa softly hummed in harmony.

Sweet memories...
Sweet memories...

She had crossed her calves, hooked them with her
forearms and drawn her knees up, raising her eyes to

his. And as he looked deeply into the brown depths, grown limpid with emotion, Brian realized she was not some soulful groupie, gazing up in adulation. She was something more, much more. And as the song quietly ended, he realized he'd found the way to break down Theresa's barriers.

The room rang with silence.

There were tears on Theresa's face.

Neither she nor Brian seemed to remember her brother was there beside them.

"Who wrote it?" she asked in a reverent whisper.

"Mickey Newbury."

She was stricken to think there existed a man named Mickey Newbury whose poignant music she had missed, whose words and melodies spoke to the soul and whispered to the heart.

Since she could not thank the composer, she thanked the performer who had gifted her with an offering superseding any that could be found wrapped in gay ribbons beneath a Christmas tree.

"Thank you, Brian."

He nodded and handed the Stella back to Jeff. But Jeff had quietly slipped from the room. Brian's gaze returned to Theresa, still curled up at his feet. Her hair picked up the holiday colors from the lights behind her, and only the rim of her lips and nose was visible in the semidarkened room.

He slipped from the piano bench onto one knee, bracing the guitar on the carpet, his hand sliding down to curl around its neck. He could not make out the expression in her eyes, though he sensed the time was right... for both of them. Her breathing was fast and shallow, and the scent he'd detected in the steamy bathroom seemed to drift from her skin and hair—a clean, fresh essence so different from the girls in smoky night spots. Bracing elbow to knee, he bent to touch her soft, unspoiled lips with his own. Her face was uplifted as their breaths mingled, then he heard her catch her own and hold it. The kiss was as innocent and uncomplicated as the Chopin Prelude, but the instant Brian withdrew, Theresa shyly inclined her head. He wanted a fuller kiss, yet this one of green, untutored innocence was oddly satisfying. And she wasn't the kind of woman a man rushed. She seemed scarcely woman at all, but girl, far less accomplished at the art of kissing than at the art of playing the violin and the piano. Her unpracticed kiss was suddenly more refreshing than any he'd ever shared.

He pushed back, straightened and intoned quietly, "Merry Christmas, Theresa."

Her eyes lifted to his face. Her voice trembled. "Merry Christmas, Brian."

Chapter Five

THE WEEK THAT FOLLOWED was one of the happiest of Theresa's life. They had few scheduled duties, the city at their feet and money with which to enjoy it. She and Brian enjoyed being together, though they were rarely alone. Everywhere they went the group numbered four, with Jeff and Patricia along, or five, if Amy came, too, which she often did.

They spent an entire day at the new zoo, which was practically at their doorstep, located less than two miles away, on the east side of Burnsville. There they enjoyed the animals in their natural winter habitat, rode the monorail part of the time, then walked, ate hot dogs and drank hot coffee.

It was a sunless day, but bright, glittery with hoar-frost upon the surface of the snow. The world was a study in black and white. The oak branches startled the eye, so onyx-black against the backdrop of pristine landscape. The animals were sluggish, posed against the winter setting, their breaths rising in nebulous vapors, white on white. But the polar bears were up and about, looking like great shaggy pears with legs. Before their den, Theresa and Brian paused, arms on the rail, side by side. The bears lumbered about, coats pure and as colorless as the day. A giant male lifted his nose to the air, a single black blot against all that white.

"Look at him," Brian said, pointing. "The only

things that are black are his eyes, lips, nose and toe-nails. On an arctic icefloe he becomes practically in-visible. But he's smart enough to know how that nose shows. I once saw a film of a polar bear sneaking up on an unsuspecting seal with one paw over his nose and mouth.''

It was a new side of Brian Scanlon: nature lover. She was intrigued and turned to study his profile. "Did it work?"

His eyes left the bears and settled on her. "Of course it worked. The poor seal never knew what hit her." Their eyes clung. Theresa grew conscious of the contact of Brian's elbow on the rail beside hers—warm, even through their jackets. His eyes made a quick check across her shoulder where the others stood, then returned to her lips before he began to close the space between them. But Theresa was too shy to kiss in public and quickly turned to study the bears. Her cheeks felt hot against the crisp air as Brian's gaze lingered for a moment before he straightened and said softly, "Another time."

It happened before the habitat of another animal whose coat had turned winter white. They were watching the ermine coats of the minks when Theresa turned toward Brian, saying, "I don't think I could wear—"

He was only three inches away, encroaching, with a hand covering his nose and mouth, eyes gleaming with amused intent.

She smiled and pulled back. "What in the world are you doing?"

From underneath his glove came a muffled voice. "I'm trying the polar bear's sneaky tactics."

She was laughing when his glove slipped aside and swept around her, his two hands now holding her captive against a black railing. The quick kiss fell on her open lips. It was a failure of a kiss, as far as contact goes, for two cold noses bumped, and laughter mingled between their mouths. After the brief contact, he remained as he was, arms and body forming a welcome prison while she leaned backward from the waist, the rail pressed against her back and her hands resting on the front of his jacket.

"There, you see," she claimed breathily, "It didn't work. I saw you coming anyway."

"Next time you won't," he promised.

And she hoped he was right.

PATRICIA TOOK THEM on a guided tour of Normandale College campus, beaming with pride at its rolling, wooded acres. They were walking along a curving sidewalk between two buildings with Patricia and Jeff in the lead, when Jeff's elbow hooked Patricia's neck and he hauled her close, kissing her as they continued ambling. Brian's eyes swerved to Theresa's, questioning. But Amy walked with them, and the moment went unfulfilled.

THE FOLLOWING NIGHT they went to St. Paul's famed Science Omnitheater and lay back in steeply tilted seats, surrounded by an entire hemisphere of projected images that took them soaring through outer space, whizzing past stars and planets with tummy-tickling reality. But the dizzying sense of vertigo caused by the 180-degree curved screen seemed nothing compared to that created by Brian when he found Theresa's hand in the dark, eased close and reached his free hand to the far side of her jaw, turning her face toward his. The angle of the seats was severe, as if they were at a carnival, riding the bullet on its ascent before the spinning downward plunge. For a moment he didn't move, but lay back against his seat with the lights from the screen lining his face in flickering silver. His eyes appeared deep black, like those of the polar bear, and Theresa was conscious of the vast force of gravity pressing her into her chair and of the fact that Brian could not lift his head without extreme effort.

His forehead touched hers. Again their noses met. But their eyes remained open as warm lips touched, brushed, then gently explored this newfound anxiety within them both. There was a queer elation to the sense of helplessness caused by their positions. She wished they were upright so she could turn fully into his arms. But instead she settled for the straining of their bodies toward each other, and again, the unfulfilled wishes that grew stronger with each foray he initiated.

The elementary kiss ended with three teasing nibbles that caught, caught, caught her mouth and tugged sensuously before he lay back in his seat again, watching her face for reaction.

"No fair making me dizzy," she whispered.

They were still holding hands. His thumb made forceful circles against her palm. "You sure it's not the movie?"

"I thought it was at first, but I'm much dizzier now."

He smiled, kept his eyes locked with hers as he lifted her hand and placed its palm against his mouth, wetting it with his tongue as he kissed it.

"Me too," he breathed, then carried the hand to his lap and held it against his stomach, folded between his palms before he began stroking its soft skin with the tips of his callused fingers while he turned his attention back to the broad screen. She tried to do likewise, but with little success. For the interstellar space flight happening on the screen was vapid when compared to the nova created by Brian Scanlon's simplest kiss.

ONE EVENING Brian and Jeff provided the music for the promised rock session, to which Amy invited a mob of her friends. The house was inundated with noisy teenagers who gave their approval by way of prompt, rapt silence the moment the music began.

Theresa was cajoled into joining the two on piano, and before ten minutes were up, the boys and girls were dancing on the hard kitchen floor, after Margaret came through the living room decreeing, "No dancing on my carpet!" She seemed to forget she and her husband had danced a hoedown on it within the past week.

Still, the evening was an unqualified success, and at its end, Amy was basking in the reflected glow of "stardom," for all her friends went away assured that Jeff and Brian would be cutting a record in Nashville soon.

THE DAY FOLLOWING THE PARTY there were no plans made. All five of them were together in the living room, lounging and visiting. The stereo was tuned to a radio station, and when a familiar song come on, Brian unexpectedly lunged to his feet, announcing, "The perfect song to learn to dance to!" He exaggerated a courtly bow before Theresa and extended his hand. "We've got to teach this woman before Saturday night."

"What's Saturday night?" Amy asked.

"New Year's Eve," answered Patricia. "I've invited these two to join Jeff and me and a group of our friends."

Jeff added, "But your sister claims ignorance and has declined to go."

Theresa dropped her eyes from the hand Brian still held out in invitation. "Oh no, please, I can't...." She felt utterly foolish, not knowing how to dance at age twenty-five.

"No excuses. It's time you learned."

She replied with the most convenient red herring she could dream up on short notice. "No dancing on the carpet!"

"Oh, go ahead," Amy said, then admitted, "the girls and I dance on the carpet all the time when mother's at work. I won't tell."

"There!" Theresa looked up at Brian, feeling her face had grown red. "Dance with Amy."

To Theresa's relief, Brian willingly complied. "All right." He directed his courtly gesture to the younger girl. "Amy, may I have this dance? We'll demonstrate for your reluctant sibling."

Amy's braces caught a flash of afternoon sun from the window as she beamed in unabashed delight. "I thought you'd never ask," she replied cheekily.

Looking on, Theresa felt years younger than Amy, who, at fourteen, could bound to her feet, come back with a coquettish response, then present her slim body for leading. Theresa wished she could be as uninhibited and self-confident as her younger sister. Jeff and Patricia joined in the demonstration, Jeff holding his partner stiffly and frowning. "Watch carefully now...a-one...a-two...."

As he always could, Jeff made Theresa laugh with his proficient clowning, for he held Patricia in a prim, stiff-backed, wide-apart mime of the traditional dance position, until the girl threw up her hands and declared laughingly, "You're a hopeless case, Brubaker. Find yourself another partner."

Jeff didn't ask, he commandeered. One minute Theresa was watching from the piano bench, the next she was on her feet, being sashayed around in Jeff's arms. Askance, she saw Brian watching her progress. In all honesty, Theresa had no delusions about being able to dance and dance gracefully. Now, with her brother, her natural rhythm couldn't be denied. Theresa's feet took over where her self-consciousness left off. Within a dozen bars, she was moving smoothly to the music.

She's been hoodwinked—she realized it later—by Jeff and Brian, who'd probably been in cahoots the entire time—for she'd been following Jeff's lead no more than a minute when her hand was captured by Brian's. "I'm cutting in, Brubaker. Snowball time."

After that there seemed no question about New Year's Eve. And when Theresa surreptitiously took Patricia aside to ask what she was wearing, the issue seemed settled.

On Friday, Theresa knocked on Amy's door, but when she got no answer, she peeped inside to find her sister lying in a trancelike state, arms thrown wide, ankle draped over updrawn knee, eyes shut, with the black vinyl headset clamped around her skull.

Theresa went in, closed the door behind herself and touched Amy's knee.

Amy's eyes came open, and she lifted one earpiece from her head. "Hm?"

"Would you take that thing off for a minute?"

"Sure." Amy flung it aside, braced up on both elbows. "What's up?"

"Hon, I have a really big favor to ask you."

"Anything—name it."

"I need you to come shopping with me."

Amy mused for a minute, then rolled to one hip, reaching for the controls of the stereo to stop the music that was still filtering through the headphones. Then she sat up. "Shopping for what?"

Even before she asked, Theresa realized how ironic it was that she, the older, should be seeking the advice of a sister eleven years her junior. "Something to wear tomorrow night."

"You goin' to the dance?"

For a moment Theresa feared Amy might display an adolescent jealousy and wasn't sure how she'd deal with it. But when Theresa nodded, Amy bounded off the bed exuberantly. "Great! It's about time! When we goin'?"

AN HOUR LATER the sisters found themselves in the Burnsville Shopping Center, scouring three levels of stores. In the first dressing room, Theresa slipped on a black crepe evening dress that gave her shivers of longing. But it was scarcely over her head before her perennial problem became all too evident: her bottom half was a size nine, but her top half would have required a size sixteen to girth her circumference.

Theresa looked up and met Amy's eyes in the mirror. They'd never before exchanged a single word about Theresa's problem. But, distraught, the older sister suddenly became glum and depressed. Her gaiety evaporated, and her expression wilted. "Oh, Amy, I'll never find a dress. Not with these damn, disgusting...*dirigibles* of mine!"

Amy's expression became sympathetic. "They make it tough, huh?"

Theresa's shoulders slumped. "Tough isn't the

word. Do you know that I haven't been able to buy one single dress without altering it since I was the age you are now?"

"Yeah, I know. I...well, I asked mom about it one time...I mean, if it's hard for you and stuff, and if...well, if I might get as big as you."

Theresa turned and placed her hands on Amy's shoulders. "Oh, Amy, I hope you never do. I worry about it, too. I wouldn't wish a shape like mine on a pregnant elephant. It's horrible—not being able to buy clothes and being scared to dance with a man and—"

"You mean, *that's* why you wouldn't dance with Brian?"

"That's the only reason. I just....." Theresa considered a moment, then went on. "You're old enough to understand, Amy. You're fourteen. You've been growing. You know how the boys look at you funny as soon as you have a pair of goose bumps on your chest. Only when mine started growing they just kept right on until they got to the size of watermelons, and the boys were merciless. And when the boys were no longer boys, but men, well...." Theresa shrugged.

"I figured that was why you wear those ugly sweaters all the time."

"Oh, Amy, are they ugly?"

Amy looked penitent. "Gol, Theresa, I didn't mean it that way, I just meant...well, I know you never wore that neat sweat shirt I gave you last Christmas. It was way more *in* than anything you had—that's why I bought it for you."

"I've tried it on at least a dozen times, but I'm always scared to step out of my bedroom in it."

"Gol...." The word was a breathy lament as Amy stood pondering the everyday dilemmas her sister had to face. "Well, we could pick out something nice for tomorrow night if we got separate pieces, like a skirt and sweater or something."

"Not a sweater, Amy. I wouldn't be comfortable."

"Well, you can't go out for New Year's Eve in corduroy slacks and a white blouse with an old granny cardigan over your shoulders!"

"Do you think I *want* to?"

"Well...." Amy threw up her palms in the air. "*Horse poop*, there's got to be something in this entire shopping center that's better than *that*." She cast a scathing look at the fashionless shirt Theresa had discarded.

Theresa found her sense of humor again. "Horse *poop*? I suppose mother doesn't know you say things like that, just like she doesn't suspect you dance on the living-room carpet?" Theresa knew perfectly well that at fourteen, Amy experimented with a gamut of profanity much worse than what she'd just uttered— she was at the age where such experiments were to be expected.

Suddenly the gleam in Amy's eyes duplicated the one from her dental hardware. "Listen, what about the sweater? Don't say no until you try, okay?" She splayed her fingers in the air and gazed toward heaven, theatrically. "I have *theee* perfect one. *Theee* most *excellent* sweater ever created by sheep or test tube! I've had my eye on it since before Christmas, but I was outa bucks, so I couldn't get it for myself. But if they have one left in large, you're gonna love it!"

A quarter hour later, Theresa stood before a different mirror, in a different shop, in a different garment that solved all her problems while remaining perfectly in vogue.

It was a lightweight bulky acrylic of rich, deep plum. The neckline sported a generous cowl collar that seemed to become one with wide dolman sleeves. Because it draped rather than clung, it seemed to partially conceal Theresa's overly generous silhouette.

"Oh, Amy, it's perfect!"

"I told you!"

"But what about slacks?"

Amy nabbed a pair of finely tailored gabardine trousers of indefinable color: soft, subtle, as if tinted by the smoke from burning violets. She stood back to assess her older sister and proclaimed in the most overused word of her teenage vernacular, *"Excellent."*

Theresa whirled around and grabbed her sister in a compulsive hug. "It is! It is excellent."

Amy beamed with pride, then took command again. "Shoes next. He's got a good six inches on you, so you could stand a little extra height. Some classy heels. Whaddya say?"

"Shoes. . . right!"

Theresa was pulling her head from beneath the sweater when she thought of the one last thing she'd need help with. "Amy, do you think I'd look too conspicuous if I tried a little bit of makeup?"

Amy's lips were covering her braces as Theresa asked, but her smile grew crooked, and wide, then winked in the glow of the dressing-room's overhead light fixture. "Well, it's about time!" she declared.

"Now, just a minute, Amy," Theresa said as she noted the gleam in her sister's eye. "I haven't decided for sure. . . ."

But that evening, something happened that crystallized the decision. She was in her room, the door open as she was examining the new sweater, when she felt someone's eyes on her. She looked up to find Brian in the doorway, studying her. It was the first time he'd seen her bedroom, and his eyes made a lazy circle, pausing on the shelf holding her pewter figurine collection, then dropping to the bed, neatly made, and finally returning to Theresa, who had quickly replaced the sweater in the closet.

"Have I managed to change your mind about the dance yet?" He crossed his arms and nonchalantly leaned one shoulder against the doorframe.

Theresa had never been honorably pursued before; it took some getting used to. It was disconcerting, having him peruse her bedroom, which seemed an intimate place to come face to face with a man. She'd turned toward him, and he remained very still, one hip cocked as he lounged comfortably and kept his eye on her. *Do I look him in the eye? Or in the middle of his chest? Or at some spot beyond his shoulder? Twenty-five years old and acting less self-confident than I'm sure Amy would act in this situation.* She chose the middle of his chest.

"Yes, you have, but don't expect me to dance as well as Amy."

"All I'll expect is that at some point during the evening, you'll at least look me in the eye."

Her unsettled gaze flew up to his, caught a teasing grin there and dropped again, flustered.

"So this is where you hide away." As he moved farther into the room, he nodded toward the shelf. "I see The Maestro had joined the others. I envy him his spot, looking down on your pillow." He stopped close before her.

She searched but could find not a single reply and swallowed hard, feeling the blush creep up.

"Jeff was right, you know?" Brian teased softly.

She raised questioning eyes to his teasing brown ones.

"R. . .right? About what?"

"The blush camouflages the freckles. But don't ever stop." With a gentle fingertip he brushed her right cheek. "It's completely irresistible." Then he turned and sauntered off down the hall, leaving Theresa with her fingertips grazing the spot of skin he'd so lightly touched. It seemed to tingle yet. The touch had been petal light, but she'd felt the calluses on his fingertips. Both the sensation and his teasing had left her with a light head and a fluttering heart.

That night, late, Theresa tapped softly at Amy's door, then went in to announce, "I'm going to need your help learning how to put on makeup, and I'll have to borrow some of yours, if you don't mind."

Amy's only answer was a beam of approval as she dragged Theresa farther into the room and shut the door with a decisive click.

They did a trial run that lasted till the wee hours. Sitting before a lighted makeup mirror in Amy's room, Theresa experienced the full range of giddy adolescent give-and-take she'd missed out on when she'd been at the age of puberty. The makeup session brought a twofold benefit: not only did it free the butterfly from the chrysalis, it also brought the two sisters closer. Given the disparity in their ages, they'd had little chance to share experiences of this kind.

Amy began by experimenting with foundation colors, trying a rainbow of skin tones on various sections of Theresa's face until the redhead declared, "I look like a Grandma Moses painting!"

Assessing, Amy corrected, "No, more like her palette, I think." They shared a laugh, then went to work finding the right hue that skillfully camouflaged the freckles and gave Theresa a new, subdued radiance.

Next came the eyes, but as Amy bent over Theresa's shoulder and peered critically in the mirror at the blue grease they'd smeared on one freckled eyelid, they burst out laughing once more.

"Yukk! Get if off! It feels like lard and looks like I took a beating."

"Agreed!"

Next they tried a green powder-base eyeshadow, but it made Theresa look like a stop-and-go light, so off it went, too. They settled on an almost translucent mauve that had so little color it couldn't clash with the skin and hair tones that needed to be catered to.

The first time Theresa tried to use the eyelash curler, she pinched her eyelid and yelped in pain.

"This is like trying to curl the hair on a caterpillar's back!" she despaired. "There's nothing there. I hate my eyelashes anyway. They have as much color as a glass of water."

"We'll fix that."

But the tears rolled from beneath her abused lids, and it took several long, painful minutes before Theresa got the hang of the curler, then learned how to brush her lashes with a mascara wand. The results, however, surprised even herself.

"Why, I never knew my lashes were so long!"

"That's cause you never saw the ends of 'em before."

They were a total wonder—quite spiky and alluring and made her whole face look bright and. . .and sexy!

The powdered blush proved an absolute disaster. They swabbed it off faster than they'd brushed it on, deciding Theresa's natural coloring couldn't compete with added highlighting, and decided to stick with the foundation hue only.

Theresa had always worn lipgloss, but now they tried several new shades, and Amy demonstrated how to skillfully blend two colors and accent the pretty bowed shape of her sister's upper lip with a highlighter stick.

With the makeup complete, Theresa appeared transformed. It was a drastic change but one that made her smile at Amy in the mirror.

Yet, Amy wasn't totally pleased. "That hair," Amy grunted in disgust.

"Well, I can't change the color, and I can't keep it from pinging all over like it was shot out of a frosting decorator."

"No, but you could go to the beauty shop and let somebody else figure out what to do with it."

"The beauty shop?"

"Why not?"

"But I'm going to look conspicuous enough with all this makeup on. What would he think if I showed up with a different hairdo, too?"

"Oh, horse poop!" Amy pronounced belligerently, jamming her hands onto her trim hips. "He'll think it's super."

"But I don't want to look like. . . well, it's a date."

"But it *is* a date!"

"No, it's not. He's two years younger than I am. I'm just filling in, that's all."

But in spite of her protests, Theresa recalled Brian's teasing earlier this evening and admitted he'd seemed fully amenable to being her escort.

Several minutes later, standing before the wide mirror at the bathroom vanity, she caught her glistening lower lip between her teeth in an effort to contain the smile of approval that wanted to wing across her features. Then her lip escaped her teeth, and she smiled widely at what she saw. She liked her face! For the first time in her life she genuinely liked it. It seemed a desecration to have to cleanse the skin and remove the radiance from the creature who looked so happy and pleased with herself.

As she forced herself to turn on the water and pick up the bar of soap, it seemed as if tomorrow night would never get there.

BUT NEW YEAR'S EVE DAY arrived at last, and Theresa managed to get an eleventh-hour appointment on this busiest day of the year in the beauty shops. In the late afternoon, she returned home the proud possessor of a new haircut and of the simple tool required to achieve the natural bounce of ringlets on her own: a hairpick.

The beautician's suggestion had been to simply shape the hair and stop trying to subdue it but to soften it with a cream rinse and let it bounce free, with just a few flicks of the wrist and pick to guide it into a halo of color about her head. Even the redness seemed less offensive, for with the light filtering through it, it looked less brash.

While she hung up her coat in the entry closet, Brian called from the living room, "Hi."

But she avoided a direct confrontation with him and hurried down the hall to her room with no more than a "Hi" in return.

And now everyone was scuttling around, getting ready. The bathroom had a steady stream of traffic. Theresa took a quick shower, then went to her room and was applying a new after-bath talc she'd ventured to buy. It had a light, petally fragrance reminiscent of the potpourri used by women in days of old. Subtle, feminine.

She paused with the puff in her hand and cocked her head. On the other side of her bedroom wall was the bathroom, so sounds carried through. She heard a masculine cough and recognized it as Brian's. The shower ran for several minutes during which there were two thumps, like an elbow hitting the wall, while images went skittering through her mind. There followed the whine of a blow dryer, then a long silence—shaving—after which he started humming "Sweet Memories." Theresa smiled and realized she'd been standing naked for some time, dwelling on what was going on in the bathroom.

Crossing to the mirror, she assessed her devastatingly enormous breasts and wished for the thousandth time in as many days that she'd been in the other line when mammary glands were handed out. She turned away in disgust and found a clean brassiere. Donning it, she had to lean forward to let the pendulous weights drop into the cups before straightening to hook the back clasp of the hideous garment. It had all the feminine allure of a hernia truss! The wide straps had shoulder guards, meant to keep the weight from cutting into her flesh, but the deep grooves dented her shoulders just the same. The bra's utilitarian white fabric was styled for "extra support." How she hated the words! And how she hated the lingerie industry. They owed an apology to thousands of women across America for offering not a single large-size brassiere in any of the feminine pastels of orchid, peach or powder blue. Apparently women of her proportions weren't supposed to have a sense of color when it came to underwear! No wistful longing to clothe themselves in anything except antiseptic, commonsense, white!

Just once—oh, just once!—how she'd love to browse along the counters of feminine underthings with tiny bikini panties and bras to match and consider buying a foolishly extravagant teddy, only to see what it felt like to have such a piece of feminine frippery against her skin.

But she wasn't given the chance, for a teddy with size double-D cups would look as if it were two lace circus tents.

White undergarments in place, Theresa covered the full-figure white cotton bra with the new sweater and immediately felt more benevolent toward both herself and the clothing industry. The sweater was stylish and attractive and helped restore her excitement. The smoke-hued trousers fit smoothly, flatteringly, over her small hips, and the strappy high-heeled sandals she'd chosen added just the right touch of frivolity. Theresa had never been fond of jewelry, particularly earrings, for they only drew attention to a woman's face. But as she slipped a wristwatch beneath the cuff of the sweater, she decided her new mocha nail treatment deserved setting off, so clipped a delicate gold chain bracelet around her left wrist. Finally, into the draped cowl neck of the sweater, she inserted a tiny gold stick pin shaped like a treble cleff.

Then she went across the hall to Amy's room to reproduce the makeup magic created in last night's secret session. But Theresa's hands were so shaky she couldn't seem to manage the applicators and wands.

Amy noticed and couldn't help teasing, "Considering this is *not* a date, you're in a pretty twittery state."

Theresa's brown eyes widened in dismay. "Oh, does it show?"

"You might want to stop wiping your palms on your thighs every thirty seconds. Pretty soon your new slacks are going to look like a plumber's coveralls."

"It's silly, I know. I wish I could be more like you, Amy. You're always bright and witty, and even around boys you always seem to know the right thing to say and how to act. Oh, this must sound ridiculous coming from a woman my age."

Somehow Amy's next comment was again just the perfect choice to calm Theresa's nerves somewhat. "He's going to love your new hairdo and your make-up and your outfit, too, so quit worrying. Here, give me that eyeshadow and shut your eyes."

But as Theresa tipped her head back and did as ordered, her sister was given the difficult job of applying makeup to trembling lids. Yet, she managed to produce the same magical effect as the night before, and when Theresa looked into Amy's lighted makeup mirror, all complete, dewy and lashy, she unconsciously pressed a palm to her chest in astonishment.

Smiling, Amy encouraged, "See? I told you."

And for that precious moment, Theresa believed it. She swung around to give Amy an impulsive hug, thinking how happy she suddenly was that none of this had ever happened before. It was wonderful experiencing these first Cinderella feelings at age twenty-five.

"Good luck, huh?" Amy's smile was sincere as she stood back and stuck her hands in the pockets of her jeans.

In answer, Theresa blew an affectionate kiss from the doorway. As she turned to leave, Amy added, "Oh, and put on some perfume, huh?"

"Oh, perfume. But I haven't got any. I got some new bath powder, but you must not be able to smell it."

"Here, try this."

They chose a subtle, understated fragrance from the bottles cluttering Amy's dresser top, leaving nothing more for Theresa to do but face Brian Scanlon. That, however, was going to be the most difficult moment of all.

Back in her room, Theresa puttered around, putting away stray pieces of clothing, checking her watch several times. She heard the voices of Jeff and Brian from the other end of the house, joined by Amy's and her parents'. Everyone was waiting for her, and she suddenly wished she'd been ready first so she wouldn't have had to make a grand entrance. But it was too late now. She didn't care if she soiled her new trousers or not, she gave one last swipe of her palms along the gabardine, took a deep breath and went out to face the music.

They were all in the kitchen. Her mother and father were sitting at the table over cups of coffee. Amy stood with her hands in her front pockets telling Jeff she was going babysitting tonight. Brian was at the sink, running himself a glass of water.

Theresa stepped into the room with her heart tripping out sixteenth notes. Jeff caught sight of her, and his smiling response was instantaneous. "Well, would you lookit here...I think I asked the wrong girl to go out with me tonight." He swooped Theresa into his arms and took her on a Ginger Rogers-Fred Astaire swirl while grinning wickedly into her eyes, then affecting a convincing Bogart drawl. "Hiya, doll, whaddya say we get it on tonight?"

Brian looked back over his shoulder, and the water glass stopped half way to his lips.

As Jeff brought his sister to a breathless halt, she was laughing, aware that Brian had spilled out the water without drinking any. He turned away from the sink and crossed to clap a hand on Jeff's shoulder.

"Just your tough luck, Brubaker. I asked her first." His approving gaze settled on Theresa, creating a glow about her heart.

"Isn't her new hairdo great?" piped up Amy. "And she bought the outfit especially for tonight."

Amy Brubaker, I could strangle you. Jeff lightened his hold and settled Theresa against his hip. "She did, huh?"

Brian's eyes made a quick trip down to her knees, then back up to her makeup and hair. To the best of Theresa's recollection, it was the first time his eyes had ever scanned anything below her neck.

Margaret spoke up then. "Jeffrey, turn your sister around. I haven't had a look at what that beauty operator did to her yet."

Does everybody in the house have to blurt out everything? Beneath her fresh, translucent makeup Theresa could feel the pink ruining the entire effect and hoped that for once it didn't show. Jeff swung her around for her mother and father's approval, but at her shoulder she felt Brian's eyes following.

To Theresa's further chagrin, her mother's verdict was, "You should have done that years ago."

"You look pretty as a picture, dear," added Willard.

Unaccustomed to being the center of attention like this, Theresa could think only of escape.

"It's time to leave."

Jeff released her to check his watch. "Yup. You

can head out. Patricia should be here any minute. She's picking me up in her car."

Theresa whirled around in surprise. "Aren't we all going together?"

"No, she's afraid I might overindulge tonight, and since she claims she's always levelheaded, she thought it would be best if she drove her car and dropped me off at home instead of the other way around."

"Oh." Once she grunted the monosyllable, Theresa felt conspicuous, for nobody said anything more. She realized she sounded rather dubious and ill at ease about being left alone with Brian. But he went to get her coat from the front-hall closet, and Jeff nudged her in the back. She followed and let Brian ease the coat over her shoulders, then she found herself doing something she'd never done before: helping Brian with his. He was dressed in form-fitting designer blue jeans, and a corduroy sport coat of cocoa brown under which showed a neutral tweed rag-knit sweater with the collar of a white shirt peeking from under its crew neck. As he struggled to thread his arms into a hip-length wool coat, she reacted as politeness dictated, reaching to assist him when the shoulder of his jacket caught. Theresa experienced an unexpected thrill of pleasure, performing the insignificant service.

"Thanks." He lifted the outer garment and shrugged his shoulders in a peculiarly masculine adjustment that made her knees feel weak. He smelled good, too. And suddenly all she could think of was getting out of the house and into the car where darkness would mask the feelings she was certain were alternately making her blush and blanch.

She kissed her mother and father good-night. "Happy New Year, both of you." They were spending it at home, watching the celebration in Times Square on television. "Amy...." Theresa turned to find her sister's eyes following her wistfully. "Thanks, honey."

"Sure." Amy leaned her hips back against the edge of the kitchen counter and followed their progress as Brian opened the door for Theresa and saw her out. "Hey, you're both knockouts!" she called just before the door closed.

They smiled goodbye, and a moment later were engulfed by the cold silence outside. Theresa's car waited in the driveway where she'd left it as she'd rushed in from the hair appointment. Brian found her elbow while they crossed the icy blacktop, but she suddenly didn't want to drive. It would take some of the magic away. "Would you mind driving, Brian?"

He stopped. They were at the front of the car, heading around toward the driver's side. "Not at all." Instead of leaving her there, he guided her to the passenger side, opened her door and waited while she settled herself inside.

When his door slammed, they found themselves laughing at his knees digging into the dashboard.

"Sorry," Theresa offered, "my legs are shorter than yours."

He fumbled in the dark, found the proper lever, and the seat went sliding back while he let out a whoof of breath. "Whoo! Are they ever!"

She handed him the keys and he fumbled again, groping for the ignition. "Here." In the blackness, their knuckles brushed as she reached to point out the right spot. The brief touch set off a tingle in her hand, then the key clicked home and the engine came to life.

"Thanks for letting me drive. A person misses it." He adjusted the mirror, shifted into reverse, and they were rolling.

The quiet was disarming. The scent she remembered emanated from his hair and clothing and mingled with her own borrowed perfume. The dash lights lit his face from below, and she wanted to turn and study him, but faced front, resisting the urge.

"So that's where you went this afternoon—to the beauty shop. I wondered."

"Amy and her big mouth." But Theresa grinned in the dark.

He laughed indulgently. "I like it. It looks good on you."

She glanced left and found his eyes on her dimly lit hair and quickly looked away.

"Thank you." *What is a woman expected to reply at a time like this?* Theresa wanted to say she loved his hair, too, but she really preferred a man's hair longer than the Air Force allowed, though she loved the smell of his, and the color of it. She heartily approved of the clothing he'd chosen tonight, but before she could decide whether or not to say so, Brian suggested, "Why don't you put on something classical? We'll have our fill of rock before the night is over."

The music filled the uncomfortable transition period while they rode, with Theresa giving occasional directions. Within fifteen minutes they reached the Rusty Scupper, a night spot frequented by a young adult crowd, many of them singles. They helped each other with coats, left them at the coat check and were shown to a long table set up for a large group. Theresa recognized some of Jeff's friends and performed introductions, watching as Brian shook hands with the men and was ogled by some of the women, whose eyes lingered on him with that inquisitive approval of the single female presented with an attractive male novelty. She watched their eyes drop down his torso and realized with a start that some women checked out men in much the same way men checked out women. She was totally abashed when a attractive sable-haired beauty named Felice returned her eyes to Brian's and smiled with a blatant glint of sexual approval. "Keep a dance free for me later, okay, Brian? And make sure it's a slow one."

"I'll do that," he replied politely, withdrawing his hand from the one that had retained his longer than was usual. He returned to Theresa's side, pulled out her chair and settled himself beside her.

In a voice low enough for only her ears, he questioned, "Who's she?"

Theresa felt dreadfully deflated that he should ask. "Felice Durand is one of the crowd. She's hung around with Jeff and his bunch since high school."

"Remind me to be monopolized by you during the slow dances," he returned wryly, filling Theresa with a soaring sense of relief. She herself had little experience on the boy-girl social scene, and Felice's bold assessment of Brian's body, followed by her forward invitation, was unnerving. But apparently not all men were hooked by bait as obvious as that dangled by Felice Durand. Theresa's respect for Brian slid up another notch.

Jeff and Patricia arrived then, and the table filled with lively chatter, laughter and orders for cocktails. Soon thereafter menus arrived, and Theresa was astounded at the inflated New Year's prices that had been substituted but told herself an evening with Brian would be worth it.

Carafes of wine were delivered, glasses filled and toasts proposed. Touching his glass to Jeff's, Brian intoned, "To old friends...." And with a touch of the rim upon Patricia's glass, and finally upon Theresa's, he added, "and to new."

His eyes held a steady green spark of approval as they sought hers and lingered after she self-consciously dropped her gaze to the ruby liquid, then drank.

Dinner was noisy and exuberant, and for the most part Theresa and Brian listened to the banter without taking part. She felt relieved that he, like her, was rather an outsider. She felt drawn to him, in a welcome semiexclusion.

Over tiny stem glasses of crème de menthe, they relaxed, sat back in their chairs and waited for the dancing to begin.

The dancing. Just the thought of it filled Theresa with a mixture of apprehension and eagerness. It hadn't been so difficult turning into Brian's arms that day in the living room. Here, the dance floor would be crowded; nobody would notice them among all the others. It should be easy to submit to the embrace of an attractive man like Brian, yet at the thought, Theresa felt a tremor tumble through her lower belly. *He's been stuck with me.*

Just then the waitress approached and spoke to the group at their general end of the table. "As soon as the dancing starts, it's a cash bar only, so if you wouldn't mind, we'd like to get the dinner bill settled up now."

Automatically, Theresa reached for her purse, just as Brian lifted one hip from the chair, pushed back his sport coat and sought his hip pocket. As he came up with a billfold, she produced the purse and was reaching to unzip it when his fingers closed over hers.

"You're with me," he ordered simply. Her eyes flew to his. They were steady, insistent. His cool fingers still rested upon her tense ones while her heart sent out a crazy stutter step.

Yes, I am, she thought. *I'm really with you.*

"Thank you, Brian."

He squeezed her fingers, then his slipped away, and for the first time she truly felt like his date.

Chapter Six

THE BAND HAD A LOT OF TALENT wrapped up in five members, plus a female singer. They played a mix of mid- to easy rock, ranging from The Eagles to Ronstadt to The Commodores to Stevie Wonder, but all their music had a hard, sure beat to encourage dancers onto the floor, then once they were warmed up, back to the tables to cool down with another round of drinks. When half the group deserted their table in favor of the dance floor, Brian and Theresa remained behind in companionable silence, watching the dancers.

The band slammed into the driving beat of a recent Journey hit, and Theresa found herself mesmerized by the back view of Felice Durand's gyrating hips. She was wearing a fire-engine red dress that slithered on her derriere with so much resistance that Theresa was certain the friction would soon send up a trail of smoke. But she was good. She moved with feline seductiveness, never missing a beat, incorporating hands, arms, shoulders and pelvis in a provocative invitation to naughtiness. Watching, Theresa felt a twinge of jealousy.

Suddenly Felice spun in a half circle, her back now to her partner as she sent an open-mouthed look of innuendo over her shoulder at him. Two more shakes and her eyes spied Brian. His chair was half turned toward the dance floor while one elbow hung on the table edge. A quick glance told Theresa he'd been watching Felice for some time.

Without missing a beat, the woman somehow managed to shift all her attention to Brian. Her hips traced corkscrews, her mouth puckered in a glistening pout, and her hands with their glossy blood-red nails conveyed come-hither messages. Theresa's eyes moved back to Brian, and she saw his gaze drop from Felice's face to her breasts to her hips and stay there.

A moment later, Felice spun adroitly to face her partner, then maneuvered herself into the crowd where she couldn't be seen, as if to say, you want more, boy, come and get it.

Brian glanced at Theresa and caught her watching him. She quickly dropped her eyes to a plastic stir stick she'd been playing with. She felt herself coloring and felt suddenly very much out of place. This young, brash crowd wasn't for her. Jeff fit in here, maybe even Brian, but she didn't.

Just then the music changed. The keyboard player chimed the distinctive intro to "The Rose"—slow, moody, romantic.

From the corner of her eye, Theresa caught a flash of fire-engine red zeroing in on Brian, but before it quite registered, he'd lunged to his feet, captured Theresa's hand and was towing her toward the dance floor. They'd barely left their chairs when they were intercepted by Felice and her partner returning to the table.

The sable-haired beauty looked attractively flushed and sheeny from her exertions as she stopped Brian's progress with a hand on his chest. "I thought this one might be mine."

"Sorry, Felice. This is our song, isn't it, Theresa?" Too astounded to answer, she let herself be pulled through the crowd onto the dance floor, where she was swung loosely into Brian's arms.

"Is it?" She peered up at him with a gamine grin.

"It is now." His own conspiratorial grin eased the discomfiture Theresa had been feeling while watching him observe Felice.

"It occurs to me that in less than two short weeks we've gathered enough of *our songs* to fill a concert program."

"Imagine what a mixed up concert it would be. Chopin's Nocturne and Newbury's 'Sweet Memories.' "

"And 'The Rose,' " Theresa added.

"And don't forget 'Oh, I had a little chicken and he wouldn't lay an egg....' "

"*She* wouldn't lay an egg."

"What's the dif—"

"*He* chickens don't lay eggs, not even when you pour hot water up and down their legs."

Brian laughed, a melodic tenor sound that sent ripples of response through his dance partner. Something wonderful had happened. During their foolishness their feet had been unconsciously moving to the music. Theresa's natural musicality had taken over of its own accord. With her guard down, and distracted by both Felice and their conversation, she'd forgotten to bring her shy reservations along with her onto the dance floor. She was following Brian's graceful, expert lead with a joyous freedom. He was a superb dancer. Moving with him was effortless and fluid, though he kept a respectable distance between their bodies.

When had their laughter died? Brian's green eyes hadn't left Theresa's but gazed down into her uplifted face, while both of them fell silent.

"Brian," she said softly. "I don't care if you dance with Felice."

"I don't want to dance with Felice."

"I saw you watching her."

"It was rather unavoidable." His dark eyebrows drew together with a brief flicker of annoyance. "Listen, Felice is like the countless groupies who hang around at the foot of the stage and shake it for the guitar man, whichever one is playing that night, hoping to score after the dance. They're a dime a dozen, but that's not what I want tonight, okay? Not when I have something so much better."

At his last words his arms tightened and hauled her against him, that place she'd so often wondered about with half dread, half fascination. Her breasts were gently flattened against the corduroy panels of his sport coat, and her thighs felt the soft nudges of his steps. Upon her waist pressed a firm, secure palm, while hers found his solid shoulder muscle, his cool, extended palm. Against her temple his jaw rested.

I'm dancing. Breast to breast and thigh to thigh with a man. And it's wonderful. Theresa felt released and loose and altogether unselfconscious. Perhaps it was because, in spite of the fact that their bodies brushed, Brian retained a hold only possessive enough to guide her. His hips remained a discreet space apart while the other spots where Theresa's body touched his seemed alive and warmed.

He hummed quietly, the notes sure and true. The gentle vibrations of his voice trembled through his chest, and she felt it vaguely through her breasts. He smelled clean and slightly spicy, and she thought, *look at me, world. I'm falling in love with Brian Scanlon, and it's absolutely heavenly.*

The song ended, and he retreated but still held her

lightly. His smile was as miraculous as the revelation she'd just experienced. Her own smile was timorous.

"You're a good dancer, Theresa."

"So are you."

The band eased into "Evergreen" without a pause, and as the notes began, it became understood Brian and Theresa would dance again. He took her against his body, dipping his head down a little lower this time, while she raised hers a fraction higher. And somehow it seemed portentous that the first word of the song, was, "Love. . . ."

"Theresa, you look as pretty tonight as I imagined you when Jeff first told me about you."

"Oh, Brian. . ." she began to protest.

"When I turned around and saw you standing in the kitchen I couldn't believe it."

"Amy helped me. I. . .well, I'm not too experienced at getting ready for dances."

He lifted his head, gazed into her eyes, folded her right palm against his heart and whispered, "I'm glad."

And the next thing she knew, her eyes and nose and forehead were riding within the warm, fragrant curve of his neck. Her cheek felt the textures of corduroy, wool and cotton and freshly shaved masculine skin. She drifted in his spicy scent that grew more pronounced as the heat of their joined skins released it from his jaw and neck. Somehow—some magical somehow—their hips had nestled together, and she felt for the first time the contour of his stomach against hers, of his warm flesh within the tight blue jeans, seeking to find hers as his forearm held her securely about her waist, pressing her and keeping her close.

She tried closing her eyes but found she was already dizzy from the emotions his nearness stirred in her, and the slow turns he executed increased her vertigo. She opened her eyes and saw through her own lacy lashes the outline of his Adam's apple only an inch away. She watched his thumb as it rubbed the backs of her knuckles in rhythm with the music. He had captured her hand by cupping its backside, and her palm lay flat, pressed against his chest. She felt the steady thump of his heart, then became aware of how callused his fingers were as they stroked her hand. She recalled that long-fingered left hand upon the neck of the guitar as he'd been singing to her. Her eyes drifted closed again as she basked in the new feeling of wonder at where she was, who she was with and what kind of man he was.

This time when the song ended, neither of them moved immediately. He squeezed the back of her hand harder and tightened his right arm until his elbow dug into the hollow of her spine.

Brian, she thought. *Brian.*

He eased back, never releasing her hand as he led the way to their table, and the band announced a break.

At their places, Theresa sat in a private cloud with nobody but him. Their chairs were side by side, turned slightly outward from the table, and when Brian sat, he crossed an ankle over a knee in such a way that the knee brushed the side of her thigh. He left it there intentionally, she thought, a thread of contact still binding them together while they had to forgo dancing.

"So, tell me about what it's like to teach music to elementary-school kids."

She told him. More than she'd ever shared with any other man.

And while she talked, Brian studied her face, with its shifting expressions of laughter, thoughtfulness and something utterly pure and wholesome. *Yes, wholesome,* he thought. *This woman is wholesome in a way I've never encountered in another woman. Certainly in none of the Felices whose offers I've taken up whenever the mood struck me.*

Women like Felice, in their siren-red dresses, with their sleek hair and slithery hips—women like that are one-nighters. This woman is a lifetimer. What would she be like in bed? Naive and unsure and very likely a virgin, he thought. *Totally opposite to the practiced felines who could purr deep in their throats and press themselves against a man with skilled teasing, which somehow always managed to repel even as it allured. No, Theresa Brubaker would be as honest and fresh as. . . as the Chopin Nocturne,* he thought.

"So, tell me what it's like to be on a Strategic Air Command base during the day and playing at the officer's club in the evenings."

He told her.

And while he talked, Theresa pictured the Felices, the "townies" who gazed up at the guitar man from the foot of the stage, for his and Jeff's band also played gigs in the canteens where enlisted men were allowed to bring civilian dates. Theresa thought about what he'd said—something about countless groupies hanging around the stage and *shaking it* for the guitar man, hoping to score after the dance. But he'd added, that's not what he wanted tonight. *Tonight?* The implication was clear. Back at the air base there would doubtless be others who'd capture Brian's attention, others in fire-engine red dresses with faces and bodies like Felice Durand's. A man like him wouldn't be content for long with a wallflower like herself.

She imagined Brian stepping off the stage, taking up the offer of some groupie, tumbling into bed with her for the night.

And if Brian had ample opportunity, she supposed her brother did, too. The thought was sobering.

She came from her musing to find Brian's eyes steady on her face as he spoke in a sober voice. "Theresa, next June, when Jeff and I get out, I'm thinking about settling around Minneapolis some place so he and I can get another band going here."

"You are?" Crazy commotion started in the vicinity of her heart. Brian, returning here to live permanently? "But what about Chicago?"

"I've got no ties there anymore. None that matter. The people I knew will practically be strangers after four years."

"Jeff has mentioned that you two talked about staying together, but what about the rest of the band?"

"We'll audition a drummer and a bass player here, and maybe a female singer, too. We'd like to get into private parties, but it'll take a couple of years of playing night spots and bars before we can manage that."

He seemed to be waiting for her approval, but she was speechless. "Well. . . ." She gestured vaguely, smiled brightly into his eyes and tried to comprehend what this could mean to her future relationship with him.

"That's not exactly the reaction I'd hoped for." She dropped her eyes to her lap and needlessly smoothed the gabardine over her left knee as he went on. "I told you before, what I really want to be—ultimately—is a disc jockey. I want to enter Brown Institute and go to school days and play gigs nights. Jeff is all for it. What about you?"

"Me?" She lifted startled brown eyes and felt her heartbeat tripping in gay expectation. "Why do you need my approval?"

Not a muscle moved on Brian for a full fifteen seconds. He skewered Theresa with his dazzling green eyes, but they were filled with unsaid things.

"I think you know why," he told her at last, his voice coming from low in his throat.

A resounding chord announced the beginning of the next set, and Theresa was saved from replying by the booming sound that filled the house. She and Brian were still staring into each other's eyes when the undauntable Felice appeared out of nowhere and commandeered Brian's left arm, hauling him out of his chair while his eyes still lingered on Theresa.

"Come on, Brian, let's see what you've got, honey!"

He seemed to shake himself back to the present. "All right, just one."

But Theresa was subjected to the prolonged torture of watching Felice appropriate her date for three throbbing, upbeat songs. It took no more than sixty seconds of observation for Theresa's mouth to go dry. And in another sixty, wet.

Brian moved his body with the understated liquidity of a professional stage dancer. But he did it with a seemingly total lack of guile. When he rotated his hips, the movement was so subtle, so sexy, Theresa's lips unconsciously dropped open. The supple twisting of his pelvis appeared to come as naturally to Brian as walking. His face wore a pleasant expression of enjoyment as he occasionally maintained eye contact with Felice. She circumnavigated him in a sultry trip that ended when she almost touched him with her breasts, shimmying her shoulders while the suspended offerings swayed, unfettered, within the folds of her halter-style dress. Felice said something, and Brian laughed.

The song ended and he placed a hand at the small of her back as if to guide her off the floor, but she swung to face him, pressing both hands on his chest, looking up into his face. He glanced briefly toward the table, and Theresa looked quickly away. The music gushed out in another jungle rhythm, and when Theresa's eyes returned to the dance floor she was stung with jealousy. Watching the lurch and roll, the toss and pitch of Brian's lean, oscillating body set up queer yearnings in her own, and it occurred to Theresa that she was as human as some of the men who ogled her when she walked into a room.

Felice managed to link her arm with Brian's at the end of the song and introduce him to somebody on the floor, thereby commandeering him for a third dance. But as Theresa looked on, she saw him put up no resistance.

When the pair arrived at the table, Felice cooed to Theresa, "Ooo, if I were you, I'd hang onto this one. He's a live one." Then, to Brian, "Thanks for the dance, honey."

Jealousy was something new for Theresa. So was the feeling of sexual attraction. Although Theresa no longer spoke in the teenage vernacular, a phrase of Amy's came to her now: *strung out.* She suddenly knew what it meant to be strung out on a man. It had to be this hollow, gutless, wonderful awareness of his masculinity and her own femininity; this sensation that your pulses had somehow found their way to the surface of your skin and hovered there just beneath the outermost layer, as if ready to explode; this supersensitivity to each shift of muscle, each facial expression, even each movement of his clothing upon his body. She watched in a new acute fascination as Brian shrugged out of his corduroy jacket and hung it on the back of his chair. It seemed each of his motions was peculiar to him alone, as if no other man had ever performed this incidental task in as attractive a way. Was this common? Did others who found themselves falling in love feel such out-of-proportion pride and possessiveness? Did they all find their chosen one flawless, superlative and sexy while performing the most mundane movements, such as sitting on a chair and crossing his ankle over a knee?

"I'm sorry," Brian muttered, taking his full attention back to Theresa.

"You didn't look very sorry. You looked like you were enjoying every minute of it."

"She's a good dancer."

Theresa's lips thinned in disapproval.

"Listen, I said I was sorry I left you sitting here for three dances."

She glanced away, finding it difficult to deal with her new found feelings. Brian wiped his brow on the sleeve of his sweater, reached for a glass with some partially melted ice cubes and slipped one into his mouth. Theresa watched his lips purse around it as he turned to study the dance floor. The ice cube made his cheek pop out, then she watched his attractive jaw as he chewed and swallowed it.

When his eyes roved back to hers, she quickly glanced away. Her forearm rested on the table, and his warm palm fell across the sleeve of her sweater.

Their eyes met. He squeezed her arm once, gently. Her heart lifted. Though not another word was said about Felice, the issue was set aside.

A powerful force, this jealousy, thought Theresa, loving the feel of his hand on her arm.

When the tempo of the music slowed, Brian rose without asking her and reached for her hand. On the dance floor, wrapped close to his rag-knit sweater, she could feel how the exertion had released both heat and scent from his skin. The moist warmth radiated onto her breasts. His palm, too, was warmer than before. The keen scent of his after-shave and deodorant was stronger than ever since he'd danced with Felice, and with a secret smile against his shoulder, Theresa thanked the bold temptress for warming Brian up.

Jeff and Patricia danced past, and Jeff leaned toward Brian to ask, "Hey, man, wanna change partners on the next dance?"

"No offense, Patricia, but not a chance."

He resumed his intimate hold on Theresa, who peered over Brian's shoulder at her brother to receive a lopsided smile and a broad wink.

Several times during the remainder of the evening Felice tried to snare Brian for a slow dance, but he refused to be appropriated again. He and Theresa sat out the up-tempo songs together and danced only the slow ones. She was growing increasingly aware of the approach of midnight. When they were at their table she surreptitiously checked her watch as Brian slipped his jacket back on. The discreet time check proved that she'd been consulting her watch at the rate of once every two minutes or less.

They were on the dance floor when a song ended, and Theresa turned toward their table to be waylaid by Brian's hand on her forearm. "Not so fast there, young lady." When she turned back to him, he lifted a wrist, tugged his corduroy sleeve up over his watch.

"Only five minutes to go. Let's stay out here until the big moment, okay?"

A flush of sexual awareness radiated through Theresa. Without realizing where her eyes were headed, they centered on Brian's lips. His mouth was very beautiful, very sensual, the lower lip slightly fuller than the upper, those lips slightly parted now, glistening enticingly as if he'd just passed his tongue along them. She remembered the brief times they'd touched her own, and the maelstrom of emotions his fleeting kisses had created within her heart. The same reaction began again, just from her gazing at his lips.

Her eyes raised to find his upon her own mouth. The lingering gaze held sensual promise she'd never dreamed of finding in a man. She had kissed relatively few men in her life, and all of them in private. The idea of doing so in public heightened Theresa's inhibitions. She glanced around the dance floor: there was a certain amount of anonymity when so many people were pressed almost shoulder to shoulder in a throng of this size and density.

Just then someone nudged Theresa from behind. She turned to find a waitress elbowing through the dancers, passing out hats and noisemakers, confetti and streamers. Brian got a green foil top hat that would have done Fred Astaire proud. He perched it on his head, then adjusted its brim to a rakish angle and pulled it low over the left side of his forehead. He touched the brim, looking as though he wished his hands were encased in formal white gloves, and cocked an eyebrow at Theresa. "How do I look?"

"Like Abraham Lincoln gone Irish."

He laughed. "A little respectable and a little roguish?"

"Exactly." The green hat set off his dark, handsome face and hair in a way that made it difficult for Theresa to draw her eyes away.

"Aren't you going to put yours on?"

"Oh!" She lifted the tiara and turned up her nose in disgust. It was covered with horrible, shocking pink glitter that would clash abominably with her red hair. But she lifted her hands and gamely settled the circlet atop her head. As she felt with her fingertips to determine if it was on straight, Brian took over.

"Here, let me."

He brushed her fingertips aside, then adjusted the gaudy headpiece on Theresa's bouncy curls. His touch seemed to send fire straight down each hair follicle into her scalp. Just being near the man did the most devilish things to her senses.

"How do *I* look?" she asked, trying to get command of herself, keeping spirits light.

"Like the angels sprinkled you with stardust." He touched a fingertip to her left eyebrow. It felt as if she'd received a 110-volt shock. "But there's nothing wrong with a little stardust. Guess I'll put it back." Again he touched her, replacing the flake of pink glitter, this time on the crest of her left cheek, then running the finger slowly down to her chin before dropping his hand between them and capturing both of her hands without looking away from her astounded eyes. His own were penetrating, admiring and seemed to be radiating messages much like those she was unable to hide.

"You'd better close your eyes, Brian, or all this color will give you a headache," Theresa warned, realizing how garish she must look in the gaudy vermilion tiara, with hot pink glitter highlighting her freckle-splattered cheeks.

The drummer began a drum roll. It seemed to both

Brian and Theresa the sound came from the opposite side of the universe, so wrapped up in each other had they become.

"Gladly," Brian agreed, "but not because anything gives me a headache." He was clutching her hands so tightly she completely forgot about everything except his eyes, reaching toward hers with a deep, probing knowledge of something she'd yearned to see in the eyes of one special man, a man just like the one before her now. Around them the crowd bellowed the countdown to midnight. "Five...four... three...two...one!" The band hit the opening chord of "Auld Lang Syne," and neither Theresa nor Brian moved for the duration of several heartbeats.

Then she was being enfolded in strong, warm arms and dragged against his hard chest, against his belly, against his hips and his warm, seeking mouth.

A coil of pink paper came flying through the air and drifted across the brim of Brian's green top hat, trailing down over his ear and jaw, but he was totally unaware of it. A shower of confetti settled onto Theresa's hair and shoulders and drifted down the bridge of Brian's nose, but they were lost in each other, aware only of the closeness they'd at last achieved. Their eyes were closed as they kissed with a full, lush introduction of tongues that sent shock waves skittering down Theresa's spine. Her arms were threaded beneath his, and her palms rested on the center of his back while one of his pressed between her shoulder blades, and the other slipped up into the warm secret place at her nape, under the cloud of soft hair.

The interior of his mouth was warm, wet and compelling. The shifting exploration of his tongue brought hers against it in answer, as a river of longing coursed through Theresa's body.

Brian started moving as if unable to be drawn from a deep spell—slowly, seductively—carrying her with him to the nostalgic rhythm and words of the song. Their hips joined, pressed and swayed together, but their feet scarcely shuffled on the crowded floor. He moved his head in a sensuous invitation to deepen the kiss and opened his mouth wider over hers. Her response was as natural as the evocative dance movements they shared: her own mouth opened more fully. She felt the sensuous drawing of his lips and tongue, and the moist heat of his mouth seemed to burn its way down the length of her body.

In her entire life, nothing like this had ever happened to Theresa. The kisses of her past had been accompanied either by timidity or groping, and sometimes by both in rapid succession. She let Brian rub her hips with his own, lightly at first, then with growing pressure until the side-to-side motion evoked images of further intimacies. Finally, he drew her against him with a possessiveness that made her ribs ache sweetly. And still the kiss continued. . . .

He began humming into her open mouth, and auld acquaintances were indeed forgotten by both of them while she answered by humming too. Before the song was half through, before the new year had been completely ushered in, before she could quite capture the realization that it was really happening to her, Theresa felt Brian's body go hard within the blue jeans. But she remained against him, marveling that someone at last had unlocked her to the wondrous side of physical contact.

"Auld Lang Syne" drifted to an end, and somewhere in the reaches of her consciousness Theresa knew the song had changed into another as Brian lifted his head but not his hands. He held her in a warm embrace while they rocked, remaining hip to hip, breast to chest, gazing into each other's eyes.

"Theresa." He lifted his eyes to her hair, let them skim back to her enraptured face, which reflected amazement, arousal and perhaps a touch of apprehension. "This started before I ever met you. You know that, don't you?" His voice was rich with passion. Her lips dropped open, and she found it very difficult to breathe.

"B...before you met me?"

"Jeff told me things that used to make me lie in bed at night and wonder what you'd be like when I met you. I would have been the most disappointed man in the world if you hadn't turned out to be exactly as you are."

She dropped her eyes to the dusting of confetti on his shoulders. "But, I'm—"

"You're perfect," he murmured, lowering his head until his mouth cut off further words. Then, to her astonishment, he did something utterly provocative, and distractingly sexy. He loosened his hold momentarily and opened his corduroy jacket so that its bulk no longer disguised the state of his body— not in the least. Then he took her back where she belonged, inside the open jacket, with her hands between it and her sweater while they danced the remainder of the song.

When it ended, he backed away, but kept his arms looped behind her waist as their hips rested tightly together.

"Let's get out of here," he suggested in a low, throaty voice.

"B...but it's only midnight," she stammered, awed by the suddenness of the sexual urgings she felt. He lifted his eyes to her hair. It was peppered with confetti. The glittered crown had tipped awry, and he plucked it from her hair, then smiled down at her open lips.

"Let's go home."

"What about Jeff and—"

"Are you scared, Theresa?"

She felt the press of blood staining her neck and pushing upward, but he lifted her chin and forced her to meet his eyes. "Theresa, are you scared of me? Don't be. I want to be alone with you, just once before I leave."

But, Brian, I don't do things like that. I'm not like your groupies. The words crossed her mind, but not her lips. She'd look like a complete idiot if she said them and his intentions were honorable all along. Yet he'd opened his jacket and made his sexual state unquestionably clear! And she was a twenty-five-year-old virgin who was both tormented and compelled by the traumatic first that might very well happen if she agreed to leave early with him.

Instead of waiting for her answer, he turned her toward the edge of the dance floor, his palm riding the hollow of her spine while she led the way to the table, found her purse and couldn't quite meet Jeff's eyes as she and Brian said good-night.

He drove again, by tacit agreement. Inside her warm woolen coat, Theresa was shuddering throughout most of the ride home, even after the heater was blowing warm air. In the familiar driveway, he pulled the car to a stop, killed the engine and handed her the keys in the dark. She began pivoting toward her door when his strong grip on her wrist brought her up short.

"Come here." His command was soft-spoken, but tinged with gruff emotion. "It's been a long time since I kissed a girl in a car. I'd like to take the memory back to Minot Air Force Base with me.''

It had been easier on the crowded dance floor when proximity took care of logistics. Now Theresa had to willingly lean her half of the way across the console that separated them. She hesitated, wondering how women ever learned to perform their part in these rites that seemed to inhibit her at every turn.

He exerted a light pressure on her wrist, pulling her slowly toward him, and tipped his head aside to meet her lips with a new kind of kiss that, though lacking in demand, was no less sensitizing. It was a tease of a kiss, a falling rose petal of a kiss. And it made her long for more.

''Your nose is cold. Let's go in and warm it up.''

Chapter Seven

INSIDE, THE HOUSE WAS QUIET. The light above the stove was on again, and she hurried past its cone of brightness to the shadows of the hallway, knowing that if Brian got a look at her face, he'd see how uncertain and scared she'd suddenly become. She felt his hands taking the coat from her shoulders, though she hadn't known he'd followed her so closely. A myriad of conversational subjects jumped into her mind, but scattered into pieces like the colors in a kaleidoscope. Unable to believe she'd sound anything less than petrified if she introduced any of them, she was preparing to wish him a fast good-night and skitter off to bed, when he turned from the closet and lazily took her hand in one of his.

"It sounds like your mom and dad are in bed already."

"Yes. . . yes, it's awfully quiet."

"Come downstairs with me."

Trepidation stiffened her spine. She tried to dredge up a reply, but both yes and no stuck in her throat. He threaded his fingers through hers as if they were setting out to stroll hand in hand through a meadow and turned them both toward the basement stairs.

She allowed herself to be led, for it was the only way she could approach the seduction she knew was in the offing.

At the top of the basement stairs she snapped on

the light, but once downstairs, he released her hand, crossed to the ruffled lamp and substituted its mellower glow, then unconcernedly switched off the garish overhead beacon.

Theresa hovered by the sliding glass door, staring out at the black rectangle of night, while she chafed her upper arms.

Behind her, Brian noted, "It looks like your folks had a fire. The coals are still hot."

"Oh," she squeaked, knowing what he wanted, but unwilling to abet it.

"Do you mind if I add a log?"

"No."

She heard the glass doors of the fireplace being opened, then the metallic tinkle of the wire-mesh curtains being pushed aside. The charcoal broke with a crunching sound as he settled a new log, and the metal fire screen slid closed again. And still Theresa cowered by the door, hugging herself while her knees trembled.

She was staring out so intently that she jumped and spun to face Brian when he reappeared beside her and began closing the draperies. He was watching her instead of the drapery pulls while he worked the cord, hand over hand. She licked her lips and swallowed. Behind him, the fresh log flared with a *whoosh* and she jumped again as if the puff had announced the leaping arrival of Lucifer.

The draperies drew to a close. Silence bore down. Brian kept his disconcerting gaze riveted on Theresa as he came two steps closer, then extended his hand in invitation.

She stared at it but only hugged herself tighter.

The hand remained, palm up, steady. "Why are you so scared of me?" His deep, flawlessly modulated voice delivered the question in the softest of tones.

"I...I...." She felt her jaw working but seemed unable to close it, to answer, or to go to him.

He leaned forward, balancing on one foot while capturing one of her hands and tugging her along after him toward the far side of the room where the sofa faced the hearth. The fire glowed brightly now; passing the lamp he switched it off, leaving the room dressed in soft, flickering orange. He sat, gently towed her down beside him, and resolutely kept his right arm around her shoulders while he himself slunk rather low, catching the nape of his neck on the cushion, and crossing his calves on the shiny maple coffee table before them.

Beneath his arms, Brian could feel Theresa's shoulders tensed and curled. Everything had changed during their ride home. She'd had time to consider what she was getting into. Her withdrawal gave him a corresponding sense of hesitation, which he hoped he was hiding well. One skittish partner in such a situation was enough. He had misgivings about kissing her again in an effort to break down her reserve. She was pinched up as tightly as a newly wound watch, and he knew she hadn't done anything like this very often in her life. Jeff had told him she was spooked by men, that she turned down most invitations or advances that came her way. And Jeff had told Brian, too, the reason why. That knowledge hovered above him like a wall of water about to curl in upon his head. He felt as if he was savoring his last lungful of air in anticipation of being sucked under when the tidal wave hit.

Brian Scanlon was scared.

But Theresa Brubaker didn't know it.

She rested against the side of his ribs, with her head cradled on his shoulder and the crown of her hair against his cheek. But her arms remained crossed as tightly as if she wore a straitjacket.

With the hand that circled her shoulders, he gently rubbed her resilient upper arm. Her hair smelled flowery and created a warm patch of closeness where it pressed beneath his cheek. He pinched the knit sleeve of her sweater between thumb and forefinger and drew it away from her flesh.

"Is it true that you bought this whole new outfit just for tonight?"

"Amy's worse than Jeff. She can't keep *any* secrets."

His hand fell lightly upon her arm again. "I like the new clothes. The color goes great with your hair."

"Don't mention the color of my hair, please." She clasped an open hand over the top of her head, burying her face against his chest.

He smiled. "Why? What's the matter with it?"

"I hate it. I've always hated it."

The arm that had been circling her shoulders lifted, and what he'd done with the sweater, he did with her hair, lifting a single strand, rubbing, testing it between his fingers while studying it lazily. "It's the color of sunrise."

"It's the color of vegetables."

"It's the color of flowers—lots of different kinds of flowers."

"It's the color of a chicken's eye."

Beneath her cheek she felt his chest heave as he laughed silently, but when he spoke, it was seriously. "It's the color of the Grand Canyon as the sun slips down beyond the purple side of the mountains."

"It's the color of my freckles. You can hardly tell where one stops and the others start."

His index finger curled beneath her chin and forced her to lift her face. "I can." The way he lounged, his chin was tucked against his chest, and she gazed up across his corduroy lapel, feeling its raised wales digging into her cheek as she met his slumberous green eyes. "And anyway, what's wrong with freckles?" he teased, running the callused tip of his left index finger across the bridge of her nose and the crest of one cheek. "Angel kisses," he whispered, while the finger moved down the tip-tilted nose and the rim of her lips, over the pointed chin and on to her soft throat where a pulse thrummed in rapid tempo.

She tried to say, "Heat spots," but nothing came out except shaky breath and a tiny croak.

His nape came away from the back of the sofa in slow motion while his sea-green eyes locked with hers. "Angel kisses," he whispered, closing her eyes with his warm lips—first touching the left, then the right eyelid. "Have you been kissed by angels, Theresa?" he murmured. The tip of his tongue touched and wet the high curve of her left cheek, and the end of her nose, then her right cheek.

"Nobody but you, Brian."

"I know," came his final murmur before his soft mouth possessed hers. His kiss plucked at her reserve, encouraging a foray into the unknowns of sensuality, but her crossed arms still maintained a barrier between them. His tongue sought nooks and crannies of her mouth that it seemed her own tongue had never discovered before. It swept across warm, moist valleys from where tiny explosions of sensation burst upon her senses. He eased the pressure, catching her upper lip between his teeth, sucking it, releasing it, sensitizing the lower one next in the same seductive way.

Framing the contours of her open lips with his, he eased her back firmly against the sofa, twisting at the waist until his chest pressed her crossed wrists.

"Put your arms around me like you did when you were dancing."

He waited with his lips near her ear, measuring her hesitation by the number of thundering heartbeats that issued the pounding blood through her body and raised a delicate pulsepoint at her temple, just beside her hairline. Just when he thought it was hopeless, she at last moved the first hesitant hand, and he lingered above her until finally her arms curved about his shoulders.

"Theresa, don't be afraid. I'd never hurt you."

She began to say, "Brian, don't!" just as his mouth stopped the words from forming, and she felt herself flipping sideways beneath the force of his chest and hands. He shifted and adjusted her without moving his mouth from hers, until she lay beneath him, stretched out on the long sofa, with one foot clinging to the floor for security. Panic and sexuality seemed to be pulling her in opposite directions. *Let him kiss me, let him lie on me, but please, please, don't let him touch my breasts.*

His body was warm and hard, and when he'd tucked her beneath him, Brian opened his knees wide, lifting one to press it over her left thigh, while the other flanked the outside of her right leg all the way to the floor. His belt buckle and zipper pressed hard into her thigh, biting through the thin gabardine of her slacks and bringing to mind images from the movie that was her chief frame of reference to a man's physique. This was more than she had ever willingly let a man do with her. She remembered watching Brian on the dance floor, and his hips took up the same rhythmic tempo that had stirred her earlier. It worked an identical magic on her now, releasing a flood of inner enticement that answered the dance of his body on hers.

"Theresa, I've thought of you for months and months, long before I ever met you." His eyes, as he pulled away only far enough to look into hers, held neither smile nor twinkle. To Theresa's awe-struck wonder, they held what seemed to be a look of near reverence.

"But why?" she whispered.

His left hand contoured her neck underneath her hair, while his right meandered across her brow as he traced her bone structure with two fingertips. "I knew more about you than any man has a right to know about a woman he's never met. Sometimes I felt almost guilty about it, but at the same time it drew me to you as if I'd been hypnotized."

"So Jeff told you more than you let on before."

His parted lips pressed against the side of her nose, then he looked into her eyes again. "Jeff loves you as much as any brother could love a sister. He understands what makes you tick...and what doesn't. I had a picture of you as a sweet-natured little music teacher, directing freckle-faced kids for their mommies and daddies, but until I met you, I had no idea you'd look quite so much like one of them yourself."

She tried to turn aside.

"No." He captured her chin, rubbed his index finger along her jawbone. "Don't turn away from me. I told you, I like your freckles, and your hair, and... and everything about you, just because they're you."

She stiffened involuntarily as his hand left her nape and slid between her shoulder blade and the cushion of the sofa. He felt her rigidity, so instead of slipping the hand around to the front of her ribs, he moved it to her shoulder, then down the length of her arm to entwine Theresa's fingers with his. He forced their joined hands up between his chest and her breasts, his forearm now pressing against one of the warm, generous orbs.

Brian thought of the hours he and Jeff had lain in their bunks and talked about this woman. He knew about the times she'd come home in tears over the teasing of some boy, as long ago as when she was only fourteen years old. He knew about the time Jeff had beaten one of her persecutors and been kicked out of school on probation. He knew about the time she'd gone to the high-school prom but came home in tears after her date had proved he was only after two handfuls of the most obvious thing. He knew why she hid in an elementary school where she had to deal mostly with children who were too young and innocent to care about her accursed size; and why she hid inside dark, unattractive clothes; and behind sweaters; and beneath the chin rest of a violin. He knew he was in a spot where, to the best of Jeff's knowledge, no man had ever been allowed before. And he understood that by making the wrong move, he could cause her interminable hurt, and himself as well.

He sought to relax her with soothing endearments, all of them genuinely from the heart. "You smell better than any girl I've ever danced with." He nuzzled her neck, stringing kisses along her jaw like pearls upon a waxed thread. "And you dance just the way I like a girl to dance." He dropped a kiss on the corner of her mouth. "I love your music. . ." On her nose.

"And your innocence..." On her eye. "Your Nocturnes..." On her temple. "And your long, beautiful fingers on the piano keys...." He kissed five knuckles in turn. "And being with you at midnight on New Year's Eve." At last he kissed her mouth, lingering there to dip his tongue between her soft, innocent lips, to join her in a celebration of a new year, a new discovery, a new awareness of how right they seemed for each other.

Theresa felt lifted, transported above herself, as if this must certainly be someone other than herself in Brian Scanlon's arms, hearing his murmured words of admiration. Perhaps she was an understudy having stepped in at curtain time when the star performer fell ill. Perhaps these words were meant for that other woman, the one with the silhouette of a sylph, with mink-brown hair and golden, flawless skin. That other woman had performed this part so many times she knew instinctively how to react to this man's voice and movements.

But Theresa was not that practiced artiste. She was a hesitant ingenue to whom the part did not come naturally. She wanted to lift her arms around Brian's shoulders and return the string of kisses he'd just bestowed upon her, but relinquishing the guard she'd maintained for years was no easy thing. Experience had taught her only too clearly that to believe she could attract someone because of her hidden attributes was a pipe dream. Each time she had done so, the man upon whom she'd pinned her hopes had proved himself no more honorable than the boy who'd made one blossom-kissed May prom night eight years earlier not a memorable celebration of the end of a school year but an ugly memory of shame and disgust she'd made sure had never been repeated since.

Brian's forearm rested across her right breast, depressing it in an almost lackadaisical fashion that felt natural and acceptable to Theresa, until he began moving his wrist back and forth as if something had tickled it and he was relieving the itch by rubbing the skin across her sweater. His fingers were still interlaced with Theresa's, and he carried her own hand atop his, turning it now so that the back of only his hand came into contact with her breasts.

Don't panic. Don't resist. Let him. Let him touch you and see if it makes you react like the woman reacted in the movie. Theresa swallowed, and Brian's tongue did sensuous things to the inside of her mouth.

He pulled back, teased the rim of her mouth with a butterfly's touch of his lips. "Theresa, don't be scared." She tried not to be, telling her muscles to relax as he released her tense fingers and rested his warm palm upon the ribbed waist of her sweater. *No. Don't let him be like all the others. Don't let him want me for only that. Not Brian, who's been so careful not to even look at me there during all these wonderful days while he grew dearer.*

Beside them the fire danced, sending warmth radiating against the sides of their faces and bodies. But she pinched her eyelids shut, unaware of the troubled expression on Brian's face as he gazed down at her. She lay beneath him with the stillness of fallen snow, pale and motionless, and breathing with great difficulty. But her breath was not drawn through lips fallen open in passion, rather through nostrils distended in apprehension.

Her flesh was warm beneath the sweater, and her ribs surprisingly fine-boned, the skin over them taut and toned. Her frame, Brian now realized, was built for bearing much smaller breasts than those with which she'd been endowed. *Trust me, Theresa. It's you, your heart, your uncomplicated simple soul that I'm learning to love. But loving the soul of you means loving the body of you as well. And we must start with that. Sometime, we must start.*

He moved his hand up her ribs, his warm palm molding itself to the arch of her rib cage, finally placing four fingertips in the warm hollow just beneath one breast. Gently he brushed back and forth, giving her time to accept the idea of his imminent intrusion. Beneath the heel of his hand he felt an unnatural tremor, as if she were holding her breath to keep from crying. Against his belly her midsection was arched up off the cushions, not in enthusiastic acquiescence, but in fortification as if steeling herself to defend at a second's notice.

He covered her lips with his in forewarning, then rolled aside just enough to allow freedom to access to the warm, soft globe of flesh that brushed his fingernails and moved toward it with as much gentleness as he could muster. Seeking not to violate or to trespass, he breached the remaining space, playing her the first time with as fluttering a touch as he might have used to chime the strings of a guitar instead of strumming them. Beneath his mouth, hers quivered. *Easy, love, easy,* he thought.

His first touch brushed scarcely more than the seam of the stiff cotton garment that covered her, as he ran his fingertips along its deep curve, from the center of her chest across her breast to the warm, secret place beneath her arm.

She shuddered and tensed further.

He lightened his hold on her lips until their kiss became more of a commingling of breath than of flesh, a foretoken of the gentleness he was preparing for her. *Trust me, Theresa.* Once more he nudged her lips with a blandishment so weightless it might have been the gossamer approach of nothing more than the shadow cast by his head bending over hers.

But caution cracked through Theresa's nerves and kept her from mellowing and melting beneath him. She waited, instead, like a martyr at the stake, until at last he enfolded her breast, firmly, fully, running his thumb along the horizontal seam of her bra. She acquiesced for the moment, allowing him to discover the breadth, resilience and warmth of her breast.

As his hand caressed and explored, Theresa waited in agony, wanting so much more than what she was able to allow herself to feel in the way of response. She wanted to stretch and loll, to utter some thick sound in her throat as the woman had in the movie. She wanted to know the pleasure other women seemed to derive from having their breasts caressed and petted. But her breasts had never been objects of pleasure, only of pain, and she found herself recalling the hurt of countless callous insults, feeling diminished by those recollections, even while Brian bestowed a touch of utmost honor and respect. But as he pushed her sweater up to her breastbone, she was like a hummingbird poised for flight.

He sensed it, yet steeled himself and moved the next step further along the road toward mutuality, inching down until his hips rested on the sofa between her open legs, and his head dipped down, his open mouth replacing his hand, kissing her through the cotton fabric that separated her flesh from his.

Brian's breath was warm, then hot, and it sent waves of sensation shimmying up her ribs and along

the outer perimeter of her breasts, cresting in a tightening sensation that drew her nipples up into a pair
of hard knots, shriveling them like rosebuds that
refuse to open. Through her bra he gently bit, and the
sweet ache it caused made her hands fly into the air
behind him, palms pushing at nothing.

He lifted his head. She heard him whisper,
"Shh. . ." but she could not open her eyes and meet
his gaze, for behind her lids was the vivid image of
her nipples. She saw again the tiny, demure nipples
of other girls in shower scenes from years ago, envying them their delicacy, their femininity, and her ter-
ror grew. If she could be assured he'd go no further,
she might have relaxed and enjoyed the shivering sensation his kiss sent through her. But she knew, as
surely as she knew the shape of her own bovine proportions, that the next step was one she could not suffer. She could not bare herself to the eyes of any
man. Her breasts were freckled, unattractive and
when released fell aside like two obscene mounds of
dough.

*Oh, please, Brian, I don't want you to see me that
way. You'll never want to look at me again.*

The fireplay illuminated their bodies, and she
knew if she opened her eyes she would see too clearly
how visible she was by its light. His mouth bestowed
a breath-stealing warmth to her opposite breast, and,
as with the first, it was a seductive nip through stiff
cotton whose very scratch seemed to beguile her flesh
to succumb.

But when Brian braced himself above her and
slipped his hands behind her back to free the catch of
her brassiere, no power on earth could allow Theresa
to let him see her naked.

"Don't!" she whispered fiercely.

"Theresa, I—"

"Don't!" She pushed against the hollows of his elbows, her eyes wide with trepidation. "I... please...."

"All I'm going to do—"

"No! You're not going to do anything!" She flattened her shoulder blades to prevent his captured hands from doing what they'd been reaching behind her to do. "Please, just get off."

"You haven't given me a ch—"

"I'm not that kind of woman, Brian!"

"What kind?" Relentlessly he held her where she was.

"Loose, and...and easy." She struggled, unable to free her writhing limbs from the weight of his.

"Do you really believe I could ever think of you that way?"

Tears of mortification stung her eyes. "Isn't that what all men think?"

She saw the hurt flash across his green eyes, the line of his jaw harden momentarily. "I'm not *all men*. I thought maybe you'd come to realize that since I've been here. I didn't start this to see how much I could get out of you."

"Oh, no? Considering where your hands are right now, I'd say I have cause to doubt that."

He closed his eyes, let his head droop forward and shook it in a slow gesture of exasperation while emitting an annoyed puff of breath. He withdrew his hands and dragged himself away, rolling to sit on the edge of the sofa. But their limbs were still half tangled, and she was caught in a vulnerable, splayed pose, with one knee hooked beneath his, the other updrawn behind his back.

She arched up and tugged her sweater down to her

waist while he heaved a frustrated sigh and ran a hand through his hair, then slouched forward, elbows to knees, letting his hands dangle limply while he stared absently into the fire, a deep frown upon his face.

"Let me up," she whispered.

He moved as if only now realizing he had her pinned in a less than modest sprawl. She disentangled herself and curled into the corner of the sofa, not quite cowering, but withdrawn behind her familiar shield of crossed arms.

"You really are an uptight woman, you know?" he said angrily. "Just what the hell did you think I was going to do?"

"Exactly what you tried!"·

"So what does that make me?" He flung up both palms. "A pervert? Theresa, for God's sake, we're adults. It's hardly considered perverted to do a little petting."

She found the word distasteful. Her expression soured. "I don't want to be gawked at like some freak in a sideshow."

"Oh, come on, aren't you being a little dramatic?"

"To you it's dramatic, to me it's. . .it's traumatic."

"Are you saying you've never let a guy take off your bra before?"

She only puckered her mouth and refused to look at him.

He pondered her silently for several seconds before asking, "Had you considered that's not exactly normal—or healthy—for a twenty-five-year-old woman?"

Now her eyes met his, but they shot sparks. "Oh, and I suppose you're volunteering to break me in for my own good, is that it?"

"You'll have to admit, it might be good for you."

She snorted quietly and cast her eyes aside while he grew increasingly upset with her. "You know, I'm getting awfully damn tired of you crossing your arms like I'm Jack the Ripper...*and* of having my motives questioned when the way I look at it, I'm the one with the normal impulses here."

"Well, I've had plenty of lessons on the *normal impulses* of the American male!" she shot back.

They sat stonily for several long, strained minutes, staring straight ahead, disappointed that this night that had started so magically was ending this way.

Finally Brian sighed and turned to study her. "Theresa, I'm sorry, all right? But I feel something for you, and I thought you felt the same about me. Everything between us was right tonight, and I thought it led to this quite naturally."

"Not every woman in the world agrees with you!" she shot back.

"Would you look at me...please?" His voice was low, caring, hurt. She pulled her gaze away from the fire, feeling as if its hue had been drawn to the skin of her face, which was flooded with a heat of a very different kind. Theresa confronted his eyes to find a wounded expression there that disconcerted her. He rested an elbow along the back of the davenport, his fingertips very near her shoulder. "I don't have much time, Theresa. Two more days and I'll be gone. If I had weeks, or months to woo you, things would be different, but I don't have. So I used the accepted approach, because I didn't want to go back to Minot and wonder for the next six months about your feelings." His fingertips brushed the shoulder of her sweater very lightly, sending a shudder down her spine.

"I like you Theresa, do you believe that?" She bit the soft inside of her lip and stared at him, becoming undone by his words, his sincerity. "*You*. You, the person. The sister of my friend, the musician who shares a love of music with me, the girl who kept her brother straight, and who laughs while she fiddles a hayseed hoedown on her classic 1906 Faretti and understands what I feel when I play Newbury's songs. I like the you that never knew how to put on makeup before tonight and had to learn how from her fourteen-year-old sister, and the you that walked into the kitchen with the refreshing shyness of a fawn. I like the fact that you wouldn't know the first thing about dancing the way Felice does. As a matter of fact, there's not much about you I don't like. I thought you understood all that. I thought you understood the reason why I tried to express my feelings the way I just did."

Her heart felt swollen, her throat thick, and her eyes and nose stung. Words like these, she'd always thought, were always spoken only in love stories, to the other girls, the pretty ones with miniature figures and silken hair.

"I do." She wanted very much to reach out and touch his cheek, but her inhibitions were long nurtured and would take time to crumble. So she attempted to tell Brian with the wistful, downturned corners of her lips, with the aching expression in her tear-bright eyes how remorseful she was at that moment. "Oh, Brian, I'm sorry I said that. And it wasn't true. I said it because I was scared, and I... I just got panicky at the last minute. I said the first thing I could think of to stop you, but I didn't mean it. Not about you."

His fingertips still brushed her shoulder. "Did you think I didn't know you were scared?"

"I . . . ." She swallowed and dropped her eyes.

"I've known it since before I met you. I've watched you hiding behind sweaters and purses and even your violin ever since I first got here, but I thought if I took it slow, if I showed you that other things came first with me, you'd. . . ." He made a gesture with his palms, then his hands went limp. She felt her face heating up again, radiating with the embarrassment she felt at confronting this issue. It seemed impossible that she was actually talking about it . . . and with a *man*.

"Theresa, don't look away from me, damn it. I'm not some pervert who took a bead on you and came here to see if he could make another score, and you know it."

Her tears grew plump and then spilled over, and at the moment of her discomposure, she drew her knees up tightly, circled them with her arms, dropped her forehead and emitted a single sob.

"B. . . but you don't know wh. . . what it's like."

"I understand that when you feel something as strong as I feel for you, it's natural to express it like I tried to."

"Maybe for you it's n. . . natural, but for me it's awful."

"*Awful?* You find being touched by me *awful?*"

"No, not by *you*, just. . . *there*. On my breasts, I. . . kn. . . knew you were going to and I was so. . . so. . . ." She couldn't finish but kept her face hidden from him.

"My God, Theresa, do you think I don't know that? The village idiot couldn't miss seeing how you hide them. So what should I have done? Bypassed them and touched you someplace else? What would you have thought of me then? I told you, I wanted—" he stopped abruptly, glowered at the fire, ran his hands down the length of his face and grunted, almost as if to himself, "Oh, damn." He seemed to gather his thoughts for a minute, then faced her again and gripped her shoulder to force her to meet his eyes. Her own were still streaming, and his were angry. Or perhaps frustrated. "Listen, I knew about your hangup before I stepped off that plane. I've been trying to come to grips with it myself ever since I've been here, but I like you, damn it! And part of it is physical, but that's how it is. Your breasts are part of you, and you like me, too, but if you're going to shy away every time I try to touch you, we've got a real problem."

She was surprised with his directness in stating the issue. Even the word *breasts* had inhibited her all her life. Now here he was, pronouncing it with the candor of a health teacher. But she could see he didn't understand how difficult it was for her to cast off her mantle of self-consciousness. It was seated in too many painful memories from her teenage years. And he, Brian Scanlon, long lean, perfect, the target of admiration of countless enamored females, could hardly be expected to fathom what it was like to be shaped the way she was.

"You just don't understand," she said expressionlessly.

"You keep saying that. Give me a chance, will you?"

"Well, it's true. You're...you're one of the lucky ones. Look at you, all lean and trim and handsome and... well, you take for granted being... being *normal* and shaped like everyone else."

"Normal?" he frowned. "You don't think you're normal, just because you're built like you are?"

"No!" She glared at him defiantly, then dashed away a tear with an angry lash of her hand. "You couldn't possibly understand what it's like to be...to be gawked at like a...a freak in a sideshow. They started growing when I was thirteen, and at first the girls were jealous that I was the first one to need a bra. But by the time I was fourteen the girls stopped being jealous and were only...amazed."

Oddly Brian had never considered how girls had treated her. This was a secret hurt even Jeff hadn't known. He felt Theresa's remembered pain keenly as she went on.

"In school when we had to take showers the girls gaped at me as if I was the ninth wonder of the world. Gym class was one of the greatest horrors of my life." A faraway look stole over her face, and her eyes closed wearily. "Running." She laughed ruefully, the sound seeming to stick in her throat as her lids lifted again. "Running wasn't only embarrassing, it hurt. So I...I gave up running at an age when it's a natural part of a teenager's life." She blinked once, slowly, staring at a distant point while wrapping her arms around her knees. Brian gently closed a hand over her forearm, urging her to meet his gaze.

"And you resent it? You feel cheated?"

He understood! He understood! The knowledge freed her to admit it at last. "Yes! I couldn't...." She choked and tears came to her eyes. "I gave up so many th...things I wanted. Trading clothes w...with my friends. B...bathing suits. Sports. Dancing." She took a deeper gulp. "Boys," she finished softly.

He rubbed her arm. "Tell me," he encouraged.

Her gaze shifted to his face. "Boys," she repeated, and again stared at the patterns in the fire. "Boys came in two categories then. The gawkers and the gropers. The gawkers were the ones who went into a near catatonic state just being in the same room with me. The gropers were... well...." Her voice trailed away and she looked aside.

Brian understood how difficult this was for her. But it had to be said to clear the air between them. He touched her jaw. "The gropers were...."

She turned and met his eyes, then hers dropped as she went on. "The gropers were the ones who ogled and leered and liked to talk dirty."

A shaft of heat and anger speared through Brian, and he wondered guiltily if there were times in his youth when he might have tormented a girl like Theresa. Again she continued.

"I went on a couple of dates, but that was enough. Their side of the front seat hardly got warm before they were over on my side to see if they could get a feel of the... the notorious Theresa Brubaker." She turned and asked sadly, "Do you know what they called me, Brian?"

He did, but he let her admit it so the catharsis might be complete.

"Theresa Boob-Acres. Acres of boobs, that's what they said I had." She laughed ruefully, but tears like sad diamonds shot with orange from the fireglow dropped down her cheeks. She seemed unaware they had fallen. "Or sometimes they called me Tits Boobaker. Jugs. Udders—oh, there are a hundred insulting words for them and I know every one."

Brian's heart hurt for her. So much of this he'd learned from Jeff, but it was far more wrenching, hearing it from Theresa herself.

"The gropers..." she repeated, as if steeling herself to face one memory worse than the rest. Brian sat without moving, one hand along the back of the sofa, the other still lightly resting on her arm. Her voice was thick and uneven. "When I was in the ninth grade a bunch of boys caught me in the hall after school one day. I can remember exactly what I was wearing b...because I came home and b...buried it in the bottom of the g...garbage can." Her eyelids slid closed, and he watched her throat working. He'd heard it before and wished he could prevent her from going on, but if she shared it all it meant she trusted him, and this he wanted very badly. "It was a white blouse with little pearl buttons down the front and a tiny round collar edged with pink lace. I'd always I...loved it because it was a C...Christmas present from Grandma Deering." A tear plunged over her eyelid and she dashed it away, then gripped her own sleeves again. "Anyway, I had an armful of books when they...they caught me. I re...remember the books skittering along the floor when they... p...pushed me back against the lockers, and how... c...cold the lockers were." She shivered and rubbed her arms. "Two of the boys held my arms straight out while the other two f...felt me up." Her eyes closed, lips and chin quivered. Brian's hand squeezed the back of her neck, but she was lost to all but the memory and the hurt it revived. She drew a deep, shaking breath and her lips dropped open. "I was too sc...scared to tell mother, but they'd torn the b...buttonholes of my blouse, and I d...." She shrugged helplessly. "I didn't know how I'd answer questions about it, so I...I threw the blouse away where I was sure she wouldn't find it." A sob erupted at last, but she immediately firmed her lips and lifted her chin.

He could bear it no longer and gently forced her close, circling her neck with one arm, urging her into the curve of his body until her updrawn knees pressed his chest and her feet slipped beneath his thigh. She was trembling terribly. He rested his cheek against her hair and felt a devastating sting at the back of his eyes. He closed them and uttered, "Theresa, I'm sorry," and kissed her hair and made futile wishes that he could change her memories to happier ones. She remained tightly curled in the circle of his arms. Again her voice went on tremulously, and she unconsciously plucked at the fibres of his sweater.

"In eleventh grade there was a boy I liked a lot. He was nothing like those other boys. He was quiet and musical and he...he liked me a lot. I could tell. Prom time came, and I'd catch him staring at me across the orchestra room—not at my breasts, but at my face. I knew he wanted to ask me to the prom, but in the end he chickened out. I knew he was scared of my...my enormous proportions.

"But s...somebody else asked me. A boy named Greg Palovich. He seemed nice enough, and he was handsome and really polite...until...until the end of the evening when we were in the c...car." All was silent for a long, tense moment. Her voice was sorrowful as she finished. "He didn't t...tear my dress. He was very careful not to." She turned her face sharply against Brian's chest. "Oh, B...Brian, it was so humiliating, s...so degrading. I still cringe every t...time I hear the word prom."

Brian's hand found her head and smoothed her hair, holding her face protectively against the aching thud of his heart. Again he experienced the deep wish to be sixteen, to be able to invite her to the prom himself and give her a glowing memory to carry away with her. He tipped her face up and ran a thumb beneath her eye, wiping the wetness aside. "If we were in school now, I'd see to it you had some happy memories."

Her heart swelled with gratitude. She watched the fire light the planes and curves of his face. "Oh, Brian," she said softly, "I believe you would." She sat up regretfully and resumed her former pose, feeling his eyes on the side of her face as she again stared at the fire and hugged her knees. "But nobody can change what's past. And neither can you change the nature of man."

"It's still happening?" he questioned quietly. When she only gazed ahead absently without answering, he caught her chin with a finger and forced her to look at him. "Look at me Theresa. Tell me the rest so we can put it behind us. It's still happening?"

She lifted her chin aside and dropped her eyes to her crossed arms. "It happens each time I walk into a room where there's a strange man I've never met before. I tell myself this time it won't happen. This time it'll be different. When we're introduced, his eyes will stay on my face." Theresa's voice was nearly a whisper now, filled with chagrin and an edge of shame. "But no man ever meets my eyes when he meets me. Their eyes always drop straight down to my chest." She fell silent, sensing his frowning scrutiny. His hand was gone from the back of her neck. Only his gaze touched her. When he spoke, his voice was firm.

"Mine didn't."

No, his didn't. And that was why she'd begun liking him almost immediately. But she knew why.

"You were forewarned."

He couldn't deny it, or the fact that if he hadn't

been, his eyes very likely would have widened and dropped. "Yes, I'll admit it. I was."

She stared at a spurting blue flame that gathered a sudden surge of life, even as the fire dwindled. The shadows in the room were deep fingers of gray.

"I've never talked about this with anyone else before in my life."

"What about your mother?"

She turned her troubled eyes to his, and each of them saw the glint of the dying flames reflected beneath unsmiling eyebrows. "My mother?" Theresa gave a soft, rueful chuckle deep in her throat, closed her eyes and dropped her head back against the sofa cushion. Brian watched the curved line of her throat as she spoke. "My mother's answer to the problem was to tell me all I needed was a heavy-duty bra. Oh God, how I hate them. Wearing pretty underclothes is just another one of the things I had to give up. They don't make pretty ones for girls like me, and when you tried to...." She lifted her head but wouldn't meet his eyes. "Well, *before*, I couldn't bear the thought of you seeing me either with my bra or without it. I'm not a very pretty sight either way."

"Theresa, don't say that." He eased closer and laid a hand on the top of her head and stroked her hair, then let his palm lie lightly on her bright, airy curls.

"Well, it's true. But it was never anything I could talk about with my mother. She's generously endowed herself, and once when I was around fourteen and came to her crying over how big I was getting, she treated the problem like it was something I'd get over when I got older. After all, she said, *she did*. When I asked if I could talk to somebody else about it, like our doctor or a counselor, she said, 'Don't be foolish, Theresa. There's nothing you can do about it but accept it.' I don't think she ever realized she's got a totally different personality than mine. She's... well, brazen and domineering. A person like that *can* overcome their hangups more easily than someone like me.''

They sat in silence for several long minutes. She heard Brian draw a deep breath and let it out slowly. "So how do you feel about it now, now that you've talked about it with me?"

"I...." She glanced up to find him watching her closely. His hand had fallen from her head, but those knowing eyes held her prisoner. "Surprised that I really managed to tell you everything like I did."

"I'm glad you confided in me, Theresa. Somehow I think it'll help you in more ways than just... well, letting go."

She studied him now as carefully as he studied her. "Brian, tell me something." Her forearms were crossed atop her updrawn knees, and she picked at a thread of her knit sleeve, thoughtful for a moment, before turning to catch his eyes again. "Tonight at the dance you said that Felice reminded you of the groupies who hang around the stage and hope to... to score with the guitar man after the dance. You said...." She swallowed, amazed at her own temerity, but somehow finding herself unleashed in a new way. "Well, you said they were a dime a dozen, but that wasn't what you wanted... *tonight*." Again she swallowed, but he refused to help her along. He was going to make her voice her question if she wanted an answer. "Does that mean you've... indulged with lots of girls like that... on other nights?"

"Some." The word was quiet, truthful.

"Then why... I mean, I'm not... experienced like

those girls. Why would you want to be with me instead of them?"

He moved closer, his right elbow hooked on the back of the sofa, his hand gently stroking her arm. "Because bodies are not what love is about. Souls are."

"Love?" Her eyes widened and met his in surprise.

"You don't have to look so threatened by the word."

"I'm not threatened by it."

"Yes you are."

"No I'm not."

"If you fell in love, you'd have to face the inevitable sooner or later."

"But I haven't fallen in love, so I'm not threatened." She'd had to deny it—after all, he hadn't actually said he loved her.

"Fair enough. I answered your question, now you answer one of mine. And I want an honest answer."

But she refused to agree until she knew what he was going to ask.

"Why did you go through all the trouble of buying new clothes, learning how to put on makeup and fingernail polish and going to the beauty shop before our date tonight?"

"I . . . I thought it was time I learned."

He smiled, a slow grin that appeared briefly, then was gone, replaced by his too-intense study. He moved nearer, until she had to lift her face to meet his eyes above her. "You're a liar, Theresa Brubaker," he stated in a disarmingly quiet tone. "And if you didn't feel threatened, we wouldn't have had the discussion we just had. But you've got nothing to fear from me."

"Brian. . . ." Her breath caught in her throat as he moved unhesitatingly to encircle her in his arms.

"Put your damn knees down and quit hiding from me. I'm not Greg Palovich, all right?"

But she was too stunned to move. He wouldn't! He wouldn't! Not again. Her muscles were tensing tighter, and she'd just begun to tighten her hold around her knees when with one swift sweep of his hand, Brian knocked her feet off the edge of the davenport. His strong hands closed around her shoulders, and he jerked her forward with deadly accuracy, pulling her up against his chest with their arms around each other. "I'm getting damn sick of seeing you with your arms crossed over your chest. And I'm starting back at the beginning, where you should have started when you were fourteen. Let's pretend that's how old you are, and all I want is a good-night kiss from the girl I took to the dance."

Before Theresa's astonishment could find voice, she was neatly enfolded against the strong, hard chest of the guitar man who'd had plenty of experience at seduction. His warm, moist, open mouth slanted across hers while one warm hand slipped up her neck and got lost in her hair. His tongue tutored hers in the ways of one far beyond fourteen years of age, slipping erotically to points of secrecy that started sensual urges coursing through her limbs and spearing down her belly. He lifted the pressure of his lips only enough to be heard while their tongues still touched. "I'm going to be so damn good for you, Theresa Brubaker. You'll see. Now touch me the way you've been wanting to since we left the dance floor." His tongue returned fully to her mouth, teasing, stroking hers with promises of delight. But he kept one arm around her ribs, the other hooked over the side of her neck, and his hands played only over her back, caressing it slowly but thoroughly while she let hers do the same upon him. Her hand wandered up his neck, to the soft, short hair that still retained the vestige of masculine toiletries she'd first smelled when she'd taken his cap. She thought of a line from the Newbury song: "Wandering from room to room he's turning on each light. . . ." And it felt as if Brian was showing her the light, one small room at a time. Their kiss grew more intimate as he murmured wordless sounds of approval, and she wanted to respond in kind, to give voice to the new explosive feelings she was experiencing. But just at that moment, he pushed her back gently.

"I'll see you tomorrow, okay, sweets? I can only be honorable up to a point."

He got to his feet and tugged her along behind him. Looping a lazy arm around her shoulders, he sauntered with her to the stairway. There he stopped her just as she'd gained the first step. He stood on the floor so their eyes were now on the same level. In the deep shadows, his palms held her hips and he turned her to face him before he enclosed her in a warm embrace once again, found her lips for a last, lingering kiss, then turned her away with a soft, "Good night."

Chapter Eight

THERESA AND BRIAN were not alone long enough during that day to speak of anything that had happened the night before, or to exchange touches or insight as to what the other was thinking of all that had passed between them. It was a lazy day. They'd all been up late and took turns napping, sprawled in chairs, on floors before the New Year's Day football games that flickered on the television screen or tucked into their own rooms. It seemed to take until nearly suppertime for everyone to come fully alive, and even then, it was a subdued group, for with only one more day before Brian and Jeff would be gone, they all felt an impending sense of loss.

The following morning, Theresa awakened shortly after dawn and lay staring at the pewter frog Brian had given her. She recalled everything that had happened between them since the first night when they'd sat side by side with his elbow pressing hers throughout that extremely sensuous love scene.

Who was she trying to fool? It had almost been predestined, this feeling she had for Brian Scanlon. She was falling in love with him, with a man two years her junior who admitted he'd had sexual encounters with any number of admiring fans. The idea that he was fully experienced and worldly made her feel inadequate and puerile. Again she wondered why he'd want an introverted, frightened virgin like her.

She was daunted by his physical beauty, for it seemed to dazzle when compared to her ordinary-to-homely features, making her believe he couldn't possibly be attracted to her, as he'd said he was. How could he possibly be? With women like Felice fawning over him, pursuing him, eager to share more than just a bump-and-grind dance with him, why would Brian Scanlon possibly pursue Theresa Brubaker?

She sighed, closed her eyes and tried to imagine lying naked with him but found it impossible to picture herself in that context. She was too inhibited, too freckled, too redheaded to fit the part. She wished she were shaped like a pencil and had russet skin and sleek, auburn hair. She wished she'd found at least one boy or man sometime during her life who'd have been able to break through the barriers of self-consciousness to give her some sense of what to expect if she allowed Brian more sexual liberties.

The pewter frog sat on the shelf, caught in a still life, fiddling his silent note and smiling. *I'm like that frog. My life is like a silent note; I play, but I haven't felt the music of the heart.*

It was seven-thirty. She heard her parents leave for work, but the rest of the house was silent. She dragged herself from bed, dressed and made coffee, and still nobody else roused. Tomorrow Brian and Jeff would leave, and the house would seem abandoned. The mere thought of it filled her with loneliness. How would she make it from day to day when Brian was gone? How unfair that he should be snatched away just when they discovered their attraction for each other. She wandered to the bathroom, collected the dirty towels from the rack, hung up fresh ones, went to her room and added her own soiled laundry to the pile. She wondered how long she should wait before starting the washing machine to launder Jeff's clothes so he could take them back clean and save a laundry bill.

They had been running free all week, the whole bunch of them, and nobody had bothered much with homemaking chores. The pile of dirty clothes at the bottom of the laundry chute would be mountainous.

She waited until ten o'clock before creeping down the basement stairs like a burglar, sneaking onto each tread, afraid the step would creak and awaken Brian, who lay on his belly with both arms flung up, his ear pressed to one biceps. She halted in her tracks, gazing across the dim room at his bare back, at the outline of his hips and legs beneath the green blanket. His right leg was extended, his left bent with the tip of its knee peeking from under the covers. The only men she'd ever seen in bed were her father and Jeff. But seeing Brian there, listening to the light snuffle of his regular breathing, had a decidedly sensual effect upon Theresa.

She clutched her armload of dirty laundry and tiptoed to the laundry-room door, turned the knob soundlessly and latched it behind her with equally little noise.

She sorted out six piles of colors, dropped the first stack into the machine and grimaced at how loud the selector dial sounded when she spun it to its starting position—the clicks erupted through the silence like a tommy gun. When she pushed the knob to start the water flowing, it sounded like Niagara Falls had just rerouted through the basement. Soap, softener, then she picked her way across the floor between hills of fabric and opened the door to the family room.

She had just managed to get it closed silently again when Brian—still on his belly—lifted his head, emitted a snort and scratched his nose with the back of one hand. She stood transfixed, watching the light from the sliding glass door find its way across the ridges of his shoulder blades and the individual ones of his spinal column to the spot where the sheet divided his body in half. He cleared his throat, lifted his head again and intuitively glanced back over his shoulder.

Theresa stood rooted to the spot, holding onto the doorknob behind her, feeling the blood raddle her cheeks at being discovered there, watching him awaken.

His hair was standing up at odd angles. His cheek and jaw wore the shadow of a night's growth. His eyes were still swollen from sleep. "Good morning," he managed in a voice raspy from disuse. The greeting was accompanied by a slow over-the-shoulder smile that drew up one side of his mouth engagingly. Lazily, he rolled over, crooking one arm behind his head, presenting an armpit shadowed by dark hair and a chest sprinkled with a liberal portion of the same.

"Good morning." Her voice came out a whisper.

"What time is it?"

"After ten." She flapped an apologetic palm at the laundry-room door. "I'm sorry I woke you up with the washer, but I wanted to get the laundry started. Jeff's clothes...are...he...." To Theresa's dismay the words chugged away into silence, and she stood staring at half of a naked man, one who made everything inside her body go as watery as the sounds emanating from the other side of the wall.

"Come here." He didn't move; nothing more than the beguiling lips formed the invitation. His right arm cradled the back of his head. His left lay flat on his belly, the thumb resting in his navel, which was exposed above the blanket. One knee was straight, the other one bent so that its outline formed a triangle beneath the blankets. "Come here, Theresa," he repeated, more softly than before, lifting a hand toward her.

Her startled expression warned him she'd dreamed up an excuse, even before she began to voice it. "I have to—"

"Come." He rolled to one hip, and for a horrifying moment she thought he was going to get up and come to get her. But he only braced up one elbow and extended a hand, palm up.

She wiped her own palms on her thighs and advanced slowly across the room but stopped two feet from the edge of his mattress. His hand remained open, waiting. Upon it she could see the calluses on each of its four fingertips from playing the guitar. He had very, very long fingers. And he slept with his watch on.

It was so still just then she thought she could hear its electronic hum.

He moved himself up just high enough and strained forward across the remaining two feet to capture her hand and drag her toward him. Her kneecaps struck the frame of the bed, and she toppled down, twisting at the last minute to land half on one hip but coming to rest at an awkward angle, half across his bare chest.

"Good morning." His smile was thorough, teasing and warmed places inside Theresa that she'd never realized hadn't known complete warmth before. He slipped one arm between her and the mattress and rolled to his hip facing her, managing to maneuver her stomach flush against his. She recalled in bemused fascination that she'd read that men often wake up fully aroused, but she was too ignorant to know if it was true of Brian this morning. He brushed her cheek with the backs of his knuckles, and his voice was charmingly gruff. "I find it hard to believe there's one woman left in this world who still blushes at age twenty-five." He dipped his head to touch her lips with a nibbling kiss. "And you know what?" He ran the tip of an exploring index finger across the juncture of her lips, causing them to fall open as she caught a breath in her throat. "Some day I'm going to see you wearing only that." He dipped his head again, but when their mouths joined, he rolled her over on her back and lay half across her body. His back was warm, firm, and beneath her palm she felt each taut muscle across his shoulders, then explored his ribs, like a warm, living vibraphone upon which her fingers played.

His naked chest was pressed against her breasts, flattening them in a way that felt wholly wonderful. She was wearing a thick wool hunter's shirt of gold and black squares, buttoned up the front, its deep tails flapping loose about her hips, which were squeezed tightly into a pair of washed-out denim Levi's. The shirt left her totally accessible—she realized that just as his weight bore down on her, and he lifted one knee across her thighs, rubbing up and down repeatedly, slowly inching higher until the inner bend of knee softly chafed the feminine mound at the juncture of her legs. Still kissing her, he found the arm with which she was protecting her breast and forced it up over his shoulder. Then his hand skimmed down the scratchy wool shirt, up under its tails and onto the bare band of skin between her jeans and bra. He drew a valentine on her ribs, then cupped her breast with unyielding authority, pushing on it so hard it caused a queer but welcome ache in the hollow of her throat. She felt the nerves begin to jump deep in her stomach, but controlled the urge to fight him off. The caress was brief, almost as if he was testing her, telling her, get used to it, try it, just this much, a little at a time. But, to Theresa's surprise, when his fingers left her breast, they skimmed straight down the center of her belly, along the hard zipper of her jeans and cupped the very warm, throbbing spot at the base of the zipper. Within the constricting blue denim her flesh immediately responded with a heat so awesome it caught her by surprise. She sucked in a quick, delighted breath, and her eyelids slammed closed. Her back arched up off the mattress and fire shot from the spot he caressed down to her toes. He clutched her with a hard, forceful palm, pushing upward until she was certain he could feel the pulsebeat throbbing through the hard, flat-felled seams of the Levi's. He stroked her through the tight, binding denim—once, twice, almost as if marking her with his stamp of possession.

Before she could decide whether to fight or yield, his hand was gone. She lay looking up at his stormy green eyes while he braced on both elbows, and their labored breathing pounded out the message of mutual arousal.

"Theresa, I'm going to miss you. But six months and I'll be back. Okay?" His voice had gone even huskier with desire. What was he asking? The answer to the ambiguous question stuck in her throat.

"Brian, I...I'm not sure." She didn't think she could make such a promise, if he meant what she thought he did.

"Just think about it then, will you? And when June comes, we'll see."

"A lot can happen between now and June."

"I know. Just don't. . . ." His troubled eyes traveled up to her hair. He soothed it back almost roughly, then returned his gaze to her amazed brown eyes, sending a message of fierce possession as absolute as that he'd delivered in his startling caress of a moment ago. "Don't find somebody else. I want to be first, Theresa, because I understand you, and I'll be good for you. That's a promise."

Just then Jeff's voice boomed from above; the washing machine had brought the house to life at last. "Hey, where is everybody? Brian, you awake?"

"Yeah, just dressing. I'll be right up."

Theresa nudged Brian aside and leaped off the bed. But before she could scamper away he captured her wrist and pulled her back down. She landed with a soft plop, sitting on the edge of the bed. He braced on one elbow, half curling his body around her to look up into her face.

"Theresa, will you kiss me just once, without looking like you're scared to death?"

"I'm not very good at any of this, Brian. I think you'd be a lot happier if you gave up on me," she whispered.

He frowned, released the hand she'd been tugging in an effort to regain her freedom. But when it was released, it lay on the mattress beside her hip with the fingers curled tightly underneath. He studied it, then with a single finger stroked the backs of the freckled knuckles. Looking up onto her uncertain eyes, he said, "Never. I'll never give up on you. I'll be back in June, and we'll see if we can't get you past age fifteen."

How does a person grow to be so self-assured at twenty-three, she wondered, meeting his unsmiling gaze with her own somber eyes.

His weight shifted. He kissed her fleetingly and ordered, "You go on up first. I'll make my bed and wait a few minutes before I follow."

That night they spent quietly at home. Patricia came over to be with Jeff. Margaret and Willard sat side by side on the sofa while Jeff sat Indian fashion on the floor and Brian took the piano bench, and the two played their guitars and sang. Theresa was curled up in one armchair, Amy in another, and Patricia sat just behind Jeff, sometimes resting her forehead on his upper arm, sometimes stroking his shoulder blade, sometimes humming along. But Theresa sat wrapped up with feet beneath her, and palms tucked between her thighs, watching Brian only when his eyes dropped to the fingerboard of his guitar or veered away to some other spot in the room.

She waited for the song she was certain would come sooner or later, and when Jeff suggested it, her heartbeat quickened, and she felt hollow and hot and sad.

Brian was playing his own guitar this time, a classic Epiphone Riviera, with a smooth, mellow sound and a thin body. She stared at the guitar cradled against Brian's belly, and imagined how warm the mahogany must be from his skin.

> My world is like a river
> As dark as it is deep
> Night after night the past slips in
> And gathers all my sleep....

The poignant words affirmed the melody, speaking directly to Theresa's heart. Long before the song reached its second verse, her eyes had locked with Brian's.

> She slipped into the silence
> Of my dreams last night
> Wandering from room to room
> She's turning on each light.
> Her laughter spills like water
> From the river to the sea
> I'm swept away from sadness
> Clinging to her memory.

Theresa's eyes dropped to Brian's lips. They seemed to tremble slightly as they formed the next words.

> Sweet memories. . .
> Sweet memories. . .

His lips closed as he softly hummed the last eight notes of the song, and Theresa didn't realize Jeff's voice had fallen silent, leaving her to hum the harmony notes with Brian.

When the final chord diminished into silence, she became aware that everyone in the room was watching the two of them, adding up what seemed to be passing between them.

Jeff broke the spell. "Well, I've got packing to do." He began settling his guitar into its velvet-lined case. "I'd better get Patricia home. We'll have to get up and rolling by 8:30 in the morning."

The guitar cases were snapped shut. Jeff and Patricia left, and within twenty minutes the rest of the household had all retired to their respective beds.

Theresa lay in the dark, not at all sleepy. The words of the song came back to beguile with their poignant message. . . . "Night after night the past slips in and gathers all my sleep." She knew now what true desire felt like. It was tingling through each cell of her body, made all the more tempting by the fact that he lay in the room directly below hers, probably just as wide awake as she was, and for the same reason. But desire and abandon were two different things, and Theresa Brubaker would no more have gone down those stairs and lain with Brian Scanlon beneath her parents' roof than she would have at age fourteen. Along with desire came an awareness of immorality, and she was a very moral woman who retained the age-old precepts taught her throughout her growing years. Knowing she would be disdained as "Victorian" in this age of promiscuity, she nevertheless had deeply ingrained feelings about right and wrong and realized she would never be able to have a sexual relationship with a man unless there was a full commitment between them first.

But the tingling, pulsing sensations still coursed through her virgin body when she thought of lying on the bed with Brian that morning, of his intimate touches. She groaned, rolled onto her belly and hugged a pillow. But it was hours before sleep overcame her.

THEY HAD A LAST BREAKFAST TOGETHER the next morning, then there were goodbye kisses for Margaret and Willard, who went to work with tears in their eyes, waving even as the car moved off up the street.

Theresa was driving to the airport again, but this time Amy was coming along. All the way, the car had a curious, sad feeling of loneliness, as if the plane had already departed. By unspoken agreement, Brian had taken the front seat with Theresa, and she occasionally felt his eyes resting on her. It was a sunny, snowy morning, its brightness revealing every colorful freckle, every strand of carroty hair she possessed. There was no place to hide, and she wished he wouldn't study her so carefully.

At the airport, they each carried a duffel bag or a guitar case to the baggage check, then entered the green concourse through the security check and walked four abreast down the long, slanting floor that echoed their footsteps. Their gate number loomed ahead, but just before they reached it, Brian grabbed Theresa's hand, tugged her to a halt and told the others, "You two go on ahead. We'll be right there." Without hesitation, he dragged her after him into a deserted gate area where rows of empty blue chairs faced the wall of windows. He took the guitar case from her hand and set it on the floor beside his own duffel bag, then backed her into the only private corner available: wedged beside a tall vending machine. His hands gripped her shoulders and his face looked pained. He studied her eyes as if to memorize every detail.

"I'm going to miss you, Theresa. God, you don't know how much."

"I'll miss you, too. I've loved...I...." To her chagrin, she began to cry.

The next instant she was bound against his hard chest, Brian's arms holding her with a fierce, possessive hug. "Say it, Theresa, say it, so I can remember it for six months." His voice was rough beside her ear.

"I've l-loved being w...with you...."

She clung to him. Tears were streaming everywhere, and she had started to sob. His mouth found hers. Theresa's lips were soft, parted and pliant. She lifted her face to be kissed, knowing a willingness and wonder as fresh and billowing as only first love can be—no matter at what age. She tasted salt from her own eyes and smelled again the masculine scent she'd come to recognize so well during the past two weeks. She clung harder. He rocked her, and their mouths could not end the bittersweet goodbye.

When at last he lifted his head, he circled her neck with both hands, rubbing his thumbs along the bone structure of her chin and jaws, searching her eyes. "Will you write to me?"

"Yes." She grasped one of his hands and held it fast against her face, his fingertips resting upon her closed eyelid before she pulled them down and kissed them, feeling beneath her sensitive lips the tough calluses caused by the music that bound Brian to her, made him someone so very, very right for her.

She raised her eyes at last, to find his etched with as much dread of parting as she herself felt. Oddly she had never thought men to be as affected by sentiment as women, yet Brian looked as if his very soul ached at having to leave her.

"All right. No promises. No commitments. But when June comes...." He let his eyes say the rest, then scooped her close for one last long kiss, during which their bodies knew a renewed craving such as neither had experienced before.

"Brian, I'm twenty-five years old, and I've never felt like this before in my life."

"You can stop reminding me you're two years older, because it doesn't matter in the least. And if I've made you happy, I'm happy. Keep thinking it, and don't change one thing about yourself until June. I want to come back and find you just like you are now."

She raised up on tiptoe, taking a last heart-sweeping kiss she couldn't resist. It was the first time in her life she had ever kissed a man instead of the other way around. She laid a hand on his cheek then, backing away to study him and imprint the memory of his beloved face into her mind.

"Send me your picture."

He nodded. "And you send me yours."

She nodded. "You have to go. They must be boarding by now."

They were. As Brian and Theresa rounded the wall toward their gate area, Jeff was nervously waiting by the ramp. He noted Theresa's tear-stained face and exchanged a knowing glance with Amy, but neither said anything.

Jeff hugged Theresa. And Brian hugged Amy. Then they were gone, swallowed up by the jetway. And Theresa didn't know whether to cry or rejoice. He was gone. But, oh, she had found him. At last!

AT HOME the house seemed as haunted as an empty theater. He was there in each room. Downstairs she found the hideaway bed converted back to a davenport, and his sheets neatly folded atop a stack of blankets and pillows. She picked up the folded, wrinkled white cotton and stared at it disconsolately. She lifted it to her nose, seeking the remembered scent of him, pressing her face against the sheet while she dropped to the sofa and indulged in another bout of tears. *Brian, Brian. You're so good for me. How will I bear six months without you?* She dried her eyes on his sheet, brought his pillow into her arms and hugged it to her belly, burying her face against it, wondering how she would fill 176 days. She experienced the profound feeling that seemed to be the true measure of love—the belief that no one had ever loved so before her, and that no one would ever love in the same way after her.

So this was how it felt.

AND IT FELT THE SAME during the days that followed. School began and she was happy to get out of the house with its memories of him, happy to be back with the children, schedules, the familiar faces of the other faculty members she worked with. It took her mind off Brian.

But never for long. The moment she was idle, he returned. The moment she got into her car or walked into the house, he was there, beckoning. The way in which she missed him was more intense than she'd ever imagined loneliness could be. She cried in her bed that first night he was gone. She found smiling difficult during the first days back at school. Brooding came easily, and dreaminess, once so foreign to her, became constant.

On the first day after he'd left, Theresa returned home from school to find a note pinned to the back door: "Bachman's Florist delivered something to my house when they couldn't find anyone here at home. Ruth."

Ruth Reed, the next-door neighbor, answered Theresa's knock with a cheery greeting and wide smile. "Somebody loves somebody at your house. It's a huge package."

It was encased in orchid-colored paper to which was stapled a small rectangle of paper bearing the terse delivery order: "Brubaker...3234 Johnnycake Lane."

"Thank you, Ruth."

"No need for thanks. This is the kind of delivery I'm happy to take part in."

Carrying the flowers home, Theresa's heart skipped in gay anticipation. *It's from him. It's from him.* She jogged the last ten feet up the driveway and catapulted into the kitchen, not even stopping to take off her coat before ripping aside the crackling lavender paper to find a sumptuous arrangement of multi-colored carnations, daisies, baby's breath and statice, interlaced with fresh ivy, all billowing from a footed green goblet. Theresa's hand shook as she reached for the tiny envelope attached to a heart-shaped card holder among the greenery.

Her smile grew, along with the giddy impatience to see his name on the gift card.

His name was there all right, but hers wasn't. The card read, "To Margaret and Willard. With many thanks for your hospitality. Brian."

Instead of being disappointed, Theresa was more delighted than ever. *So he's thoughtful, too.* She studied the handwriting, realizing it was written not by Brian but by some stranger in a florist shop someplace across town. But it didn't matter; the sentiment was his.

Brian's first letter came on the third day after he'd left. She found it in the mailbox herself, for she was always the first one home. When she flipped through the envelopes and found the one with the blue wings in the upper left-hand corner and the red and blue jets on the lower right, her heart skittered and leaped. She took the letter to her room, got the fiddling frog from his perch on the shelf and held him in her hand while she sat cross-legged on the bed, reading Brian's words.

But his picture was the first thing that fell out of the envelope, and she dropped the pewter frog the moment Brian's face appeared. He was clothed in his dress blues, his tie crisply knotted, the visor of his garrison cap pulled to the proper horizontal level over his brow. He was unsmiling, but the green eyes looked directly into hers from beneath their familiar, sculptured brows. Dear face. Dear man. She turned the picture over. "Love, Brian," he'd written on the back. Theresa's heartbeat accelerated, and warmth stole over her body. She closed her eyes, took a deep breath and pressed the picture against her breast, against the crazy upbeat rhythm his image had invoked, then laid the picture face up on her knee and began reading.

Dear Theresa,
I miss you, I miss you, I miss you. Everything has suddenly changed. I used to be pretty happy here, but now it feels like prison. I used to be able to pick up my guitar and unwind at the end of a day, but now when I touch it I think of you and it makes me blue, so I haven't been playing much. What have you done to me? At night I lie awake, thinking of New Year's Eve and how you looked when you came out into the kitchen dressed in your new sweater and makeup and hairdo, all for me, and then I wish I could get the picture out of my head because it just makes me miserable. God, this is hell. Theresa, I want to apologize for what happened that morning on my bed. I shouldn't have, but I couldn't help it, and now I can't stop thinking about it. Listen, sweets, when I come home I'm not going to put the pressure on for that kind of stuff. After everything we talked about, I shouldn't have done it that day, okay? But I can't stop thinking about it, and that's mostly what makes me miserable. I wish I'd been more patient with you, but on the other hand, I wish I'd gone further. Man, do I sound mixed up. This place is driving me crazy. All I can think about is your house, and you sitting on the piano bench. Last night I

put the Chopin record on but I couldn't stand it, so I shut off the stereo. When I can handle it again I'll make a tape of "Sweet Memories," and send it to you, okay, sweets? It says it all. Just how I'm feeling every minute. You, slipping into the darkness of my dreams at night, and wandering from room to room, turnin' on each light. I don't think I can make it till June without seeing you. I'll probably go AWOL and show up at your door. Do you get Easter vacation? Could you come up here then? Listen, sweets, I gotta go. Jeff and I play a gig this Saturday night, but no girls afterward. That's a promise.

I miss you,
Brian

She read the letter nonstop for half an hour. Though each line thrilled her, Theresa returned time and again to his offhand question about Easter vacation. What would her parents say if she went? The thought rankled and made her chafe against having to tell them at all, at her age. The house seemed restrictive after that, and she felt increasingly hemmed in.

She had put off writing to Brian, feeling that to write too soon would seem...what? Brazen? Overstimulated? Yet his words were thrillingly emotional. His impatience and glumness were a surprise. She'd never dreamed men wrote such letters, holding back nothing of their feelings.

She didn't want to send her picture. But now that she knew what heart's ease there was to be found in having Brian's picture to bring him near, she realized he'd probably feel the same. She got out one of her annual elementary-school pictures, but for a moment wavered. It was a full-color shot: black and white would have pleased her more. The camera had recorded each copper-colored freckle, each terrible red uncontrollable hair and the breadth of her breasts. Yet this was just how she'd looked when he first met her, and still he'd found something that pleased him. Along with the photograph, Theresa sent the first love letter of her life.

Dear Brian,
The house is so lonely since you've been gone. School helps, but as soon as I step into the kitchen, everything sweeps back and I suddenly wish I lived somewhere else so I wouldn't have to see you in every room. The flowers you sent are just beautiful. I wish you could've seen the look on mom's face when she first saw them (and on mine when I opened the package and found they weren't for me.) Naturally, mom got on the phone right away and called everyone in the family to tell them what "that thoughtful boy" had sent.

I really wasn't disappointed to find the flowers weren't for me, because what I got two days later was dearer to me than any of nature's beauties.

Thank you for your picture. It's sitting on the shelf in my room beside The Maestro, who's guarding it carefully. When your letter came I was really surprised to read how you were feeling, because everything you said was just what's happened to me. Playing the piano is just awful. My fingers want to find the notes of the Nocturne, but once I start it, I can't seem to finish. Songs on the radio we listened to together do the same thing to me. I seem to have withdrawn from mom and dad and Amy, even though I'm miserable when I sit in my room alone in the evenings. But if I can't be with you, somehow I just don't want to be with anyone.

It's really hard for me to talk about this subject, but I want to set the record straight. I know I'm really naive and inexperienced, and when I think of how uptight I get about the really quite innocent things we did together, I realized I'm paranoid about...well, you know. I really want to be different for you, so I've decided to talk to the school counselor about my "problem."

Did you really mean it about Easter? I've read that part of your letter a hundred times, and each time my heart goes all sideways and thumpy. If I came I'm afraid you'd expect things I'm not sure I'm prepared for yet. I know I sound mixed up, saying in one breath I'm going to see the counselor and in the next I'm still old-fashioned. I'm sure mother and dad would have a fit if their little Theresa announced she was going up to spend Easter with Brian. Some days mother drives me crazy as it is.

Here's my awful picture, taken in October with the rest of the Sky Oaks Elementary student body and faculty. You say it's the color of flowers. I still say vegetables, but here I am anyway. I miss you so much.

Affectionately,
Theresa

P.S. Hi to Jeff.
P.P.S. I like the name "sweets."

January 10

Dear Sweets,

I can't believe you didn't say no, flat out. Now I'm living on dreams of Easter. If you come, I promise you'll set the rules. Just being with you would be enough to tide me over. You'll probably think I'm speaking out of turn, but I think somebody twenty-five years old shouldn't even be living with their parents anymore, much less having to get their okay to go off for a weekend. Maybe you're still hiding behind your mother's skirts so you won't have to face the world. God, you'll probably think I'm an opinionated sex maniac now, and that all I want is to get you up here so I can act like Greg What's-His-Name. Don't be mad, sweets, okay? Ask the counselor about it and see what she says. Your picture is getting curled at the edges from too much handling. I've been thinking, I wouldn't mind getting away from this place for a while. Instead of coming up here, maybe we could meet halfway in Fargo. Let me know what you think. Please decide to come. I miss you.

Love,
Brian

THE COUNSELOR'S NAME was Catherine McDonald. She was in her mid-thirties, always dressed in casual yet extremely up-to-date clothes and always wore a smile. Although they hadn't had many occasions to work together, Theresa and Catherine had shared many friendly visits in the teachers' lunch room, and Theresa had come to respect the woman's inherent poise, objectivity and deep understanding of the human psyche. There were school counselors whom Theresa thought more qualified to be truck drivers. But Catherine McDonald suited her role and was immensely respected by those with whom she worked.

Rather than meet in school, Theresa requested that they get together over cups of tea at the Good Earth Restaurant at four o'clock one Thursday afternoon. Potted greenery and bright carpeting gave the place a cheerful atmosphere. Theresa was led past the Danish tables and chairs on the main floor to a raised tier of booths overlooking it. Each booth was situated beside a tall window, and it was in one of these where Catherine was already waiting. The older woman immediately stood and extended a hand with a firm grip. Perhaps the thing Theresa had first admired about Catherine was the way the woman's eyes met those of the person to whom she spoke, giving an undivided attention that prompted one to confide in her and believe she cared deeply about the problems others unloaded upon her. Catherine's intelligent, wide-set blue eyes remained unwaveringly on Theresa's as the two greeted each other, settled down and ordered herbal tea and pita-bread sandwiches, then got down to the crux of the meeting.

"Catherine, thank you for taking time to meet me," Theresa opened, as soon as their waitress left them alone. Catherine waved a hand dismissively.

"I'm happy to do it. Anytime. I only hope I can help with whatever it is."

"It's personal. Nothing to do with school. That's why I asked you to meet me here instead of in the office."

"Herbal tea has a mellowing influence anyway. This is much much nicer than school. I'm glad you chose it."

Catherine stirred unrefined sugar into her tea, laid down the spoon and looked up with a laserlike attention in her blue eyes. "Shoot," she ordered tersely.

"My problem, Catherine, is sexual." Theresa had rehearsed that opening line for two weeks, thinking once the last word fell from her mouth the barriers might be broken, and it would be easier to talk about the subject that so easily made her blush and feel adolescent.

"Go ahead, tell me." Again the blue eyes held, while Catherine leaned her head with prematurely silver hair against the tall back of the booth in a relaxed attitude that somehow encouraged Theresa to relax, too.

"It has to do mostly with my breasts."

Amazingly, this woman still kept her eyes on Theresa's. "Am I correct in assuming it's because of their size?"

"Yes, they're...I've...." Theresa swallowed and was suddenly overcome by embarrassment. She braced her forehead on the heel of a hand. Catherine McDonald reached across the table and circled Theresa's wrist with cool, competent fingers, letting her thumb stroke the soft skin in reassurance before gently lowering the hand and continuing to hold it for a full thirty seconds. The contact was something strange and new to Theresa. She had not held a woman's hand before. But the firm squeeze of the counselor's fingers again inspired confidence, and soon Theresa went on speaking.

"I've been this size since I was fifteen years or so. I suffered all the usual persecution, the kind you might expect during adolescent years...the teasing from the boys, the awed stares from the girls, the labels males somehow can't help putting on that part of a woman's anatomy, and even the misplaced jealousy of certain other girls. I asked my mother at the time if I could talk to a doctor or counselor about it, but she's almost as big as I am, and her answer was that there was nothing that could be done about it, so I'd better learn to live with it...and start buying heavy-duty bras—"

Here Catherine interrupted with a single brief question. "You still live with your mother and father, don't you, Theresa?"

"Yes."

"I'm sorry. Go on."

"My normal sexual growth was...impaired by my abnormal size. Every time I found a boy I liked, he was scared by the size of them. And every time I settled for a date with somebody else, he was out for nothing but a groping session. I heard rumors at one time in high school that there was a bet among the boys that anybody who could produce my bra would win a pot worth twenty-five dollars." Theresa looked into her teacup, reliving the painful memory. Then she swept it from her mind and squared herself in her booth. "Well, you don't want to hear all the sordid details, and they're not really as important anymore as they once were." Theresa's eyes grew softly expressive, and she tipped her head slightly to one side. "You see, I've met a man who...who seems to...to look beyond the exterior and find something else that attracts him to me." Theresa sipped her almond tea.

"And?" Catherine encouraged quietly. This was the hard part.

"And...and...." Theresa looked up pleadingly. "And I'm a virgin at twenty-five, and scared to death to do anything with him!"

To Theresa's amazement, Catherine's response was a softly exclaimed, "Wonderful!"

"Wonderful?"

"That you've come right out and unloaded it at last. It was hard to say, I could tell."

"Yes, it was." But already Theresa found herself smiling, loosening up and feeling more and more eager to talk.

"All right, now let's get down to specifics. Tell me why."

"Oh, Catherine, I've been living with this oversize pair of pumpkins for so many years, and they've caused me so much pain, I hate them. The last thing on earth I want to do is let a man I think I love see them naked. To me they're ugly. I thought when he...if he saw them, he'd never want to look at me without my clothes on again. So I...I...."

"You held him off." Catherine's eyes were steady as Theresa nodded. "And you denied your own sexuality."

"I...I hadn't thought about it that way."

"Well, start."

"Start?" Theresa was astounded by the advice.

"Exactly. Work up a good healthy anger at what you've been robbed of. It's the best way to realize what you deserve. But first, let me back up a square and ask about this man."

"Brian."

"Brian. Did his reaction to your size offend you?"

"Oh no! Just the opposite! Brian was the first man I've ever met who *didn't* stare at my breasts when we were introduced. He looked me straight in the eye, and if you knew how rare that was, you'd understand what it meant to me."

"And when he tried to make sexual contact and you put him off, was he angry?"

"No, not really. He told me he'd come to like other things about me that went deeper than superficialities."

"He sounds like a wonderful man."

"I think he is, but I have such an odd feeling about... well, he's two years younger than I am—"

"Maturity has nothing to do with chronological age."

"I know. It's silly of me to bring it up."

"Not at all. If it's a concern, you're right to introduce it. Now go on, because I interrupted again."

For the next hour and fifteen minutes Theresa expounded on all her secret hurts gathered up, stored through the years. She expressed her dismay over the things she'd had to forgo because of her problem, and the reluctance she'd always felt to discuss it with her mother, once Margaret had expressed her opinion on the subject all those years ago. She admitted she'd gone into elementary music because it allowed her to work with children who were less discerning than adults. She confessed that Brian had accused her of hiding in various ways. It all came out, and when Theresa had spilled every thought she'd harbored for so many years, Catherine pushed her teacup away, crossed her forearms on the table edge and studied Theresa intently.

"I'm going to suggest something, Theresa, but I want you to remember it's only a suggestion, and one you should think about for a while and mull over. There *is* an answer for you that you may never have considered before. I believe in time you and Brian will come to work out your self-consciousness, because he sounds like a man willing to go slowly at building your self-confidence. But even when you achieve sexual ease with this man, the other problems will not go away. You'll still feel angry about the clothes you're forced to wear, about your Rubenesque proportions, about the stares of strange men. What I'm suggesting you inquire about is a surgical procedure called mammoplasty—commonly called breast-reduction surgery.''

Theresa's eyes widened unblinkingly. Her lips fell open in surprise.

''I can see it never entered your mind.''

''No, it...breast-reduction surgery?'' The words came out on a breathy note of suspicion. ''But that's *vanity* surgery.''

''Not anymore. The surgery is becoming an accepted treatment for more than just bruised egos, and the idea that it's prompted only by self-indulgence is antiquated. It's my guess that you have more physical discomfort than you even attribute to breast size, and the surgery is being used to eliminate many physical ailments.''

''I don't know. I'd have to think about it.''

''Of course you would. It's not the kind of thing you jump into on a night's consideration. And it may not be the answer for you, but dammit, Theresa! Why should you live your life with backaches and rashes and without the amenities of a woman of more modest proportions comes to take as her due? Don't you deserve them, too?''

Yes, came the immediate, silent answer. *Yes, I do. But what would people think? Mother, dad, the people I work with.*

Brian.

''The yellow pages still list the surgeons under Surgeons—Cosmetic. The term has come to have negative connotations in some circles, but don't let it deter you if you decide to look into the possibility. Better yet, I know a woman who's had the surgery, and I know she'd give you the name of her surgeon and be willing to share her feelings with you. She spent her life suffering all the same ignominies as you, and the surgery has made a profound change not only in her self-image but in her general health. Let me give you her name." Catherine extracted a note pad and pencil from her purse and wrote down the name, then reached out to touch the back of Theresa's hand. "For now, just consider it, let the idea settle in, with all its constituent possibilities. And if you're worried about facing people, don't be. It's your life, not theirs. Not your mother's or your father's or those you work with." The sharp blue eyes brightened further. "Aha! I can see I've struck a nerve already. People be damned, Theresa. This decision is one you make for yourself, not for anyone else."

As they left the restaurant, the silver-haired woman turned toward the redhead. "Whenever you want to talk again, let me know. I'm always available."

That night in bed, Theresa considered the rather stupendous possibilities of "Life After Surgery." She thought of what it would be like to walk proudly, with shoulders back, wearing a slim size-nine sundress. She considered how it would feel to lift her arms and direct the children without the drogueish weights pulling at her shoulders. She dreamed of having no more painful shoulder grooves from the slicing bra straps that marred her flesh. She thought of summer without rash beneath her breasts where the two surfaces rubbed together constantly now. She imagined the sheer joy of buying the sexiest underwear on the rack, and of having Brian see her in it, then without it.

Brian. What would he think if she did such a thing?

In the dark, beneath the covers, Theresa ran her hands over her breasts, feeling their enormity, hating them afresh, but suddenly smitten by a hundred unasked questions about what it would entail to have them reduced in size. It was heady simply knowing she had the option!

She tried to imagine the freedom of having only half as much where all this flesh was now, and it seemed almost unbelievable that it could happen for her. But it was too important a decision to make on one night's consideration, and without all the facts, as Catherine had pointed out.

And there was her mother to consider. Somehow, she knew her mother would disapprove—her fatalistic attitudes already having been voiced. And the people at work—what would they think? How many times in her life had women—ignorant of the attendant miseries of having massive breasts—told her she should be happy she was endowed as she was? Their attitude was programmed by a cultural bias toward large breast size, so she shouldn't blame them for their uninformed opinions.

But with the new seed of suggestion planted, those countless comments and hurts from the past had already ceased to hurt as much.

But what if Brian objected? Always her thoughts went back to Brian, Brian, Brian. What would it feel like to have him see her naked if she was proud of her body instead of ashamed of it?

Chapter Nine

THERESA DIDN'T MENTION IT in any of her letters to Brian, though their correspondence continued weekly, and more often semiweekly. He sent the tape of "Sweet Memories," and the first time she played it Theresa knew an aching loneliness. She closed her eyes and pictured Brian playing his guitar and singing the poignant song, felt again his kisses, yearned to see him, touch him. She still hadn't given him her answer about meeting him in Fargo. She wanted to—oh, how she wanted to—but she trembled to think of telling her parents about her plan. And no matter what Brian had said in his letters, she was sure if she went he'd expect a sexual commitment before the weekend was over.

In early March, Theresa was crossing the parking lot at school, picking her way across the ice-encrusted blacktop when one of her two-inch heels went skittering sideways and dumped her flat onto her back. Books flew, scattering across the pitted ice while she lay looking at the leaden sky with the wind knocked out of her.

Joanne Kerny, a fellow teacher, saw Theresa go down and hurried to help her sit up, a worried frown on her pretty face. "Theresa, what happened? Are you hurt? Should I get help?"

"N...no." But Theresa felt shaky. "No, I think I'm all right. My heel slipped, and I went down so fast I didn't realize I was falling until my head hit the ice."

"Listen, stay right here and I'll go get somebody to help you inside, right away."

The fall had made Theresa's head hurt, but she managed to stay on the job through the remainder of the day. She worked the following day, also, but by the third day she was forced to call for a substitute teacher: her back was in spasm. She went to the doctor, and his examination turned up no broken bones, but some very painfully bruised muscles, for which he prescribed a relaxant. But in the course of his examination and questioning, Dr. Delancy asked some questions he'd never asked before.

"Tell me, Theresa, do you have back pain regularly?"

"Not exactly regularly. Rather *ir*regularly and more so in my shoulders than my back."

He probed further. How often? Where? What seems to bring it on? Does it bother you to wear high heels? Are you on your feet all day? At what age did the back irritation start? And when he stopped at the door on his way out, his next order sounded dire enough to strike a bolt of fear through Theresa: "When you're dressed I'd like to talk to you in my office."

Five minutes later Dr. Delancy informed her without preamble, "I believe, young lady, that you're in for increasing back problems unless something is done about the cause of these aches, which, if I diagnose them correctly, are happening with increasing frequency the older you get. They can only be expected to get worse if untreated." At her startled expression he rushed on. "Oh no, this fall is only a temporary inconvenience. It'll heal and cause nothing permanent. What I'm speaking of is the strain on your back, knees and chest by the extreme weight of your breasts. The back and shoulder aches you've had, which started in your teen years, are undoubtedly being caused by a bone structure too small to support all that weight. I'm going to recommend a good specialist for you to talk to about it, because there is a solution to the problem, one that's far less critical, less risky, and less painful than the back surgery you may eventually have to undergo if you ignore the problem.''

She knew what Dr. Delancy was talking about even before she put the question to him. "Are you talking about breast-reduction surgery?''

"Oh, so someone's suggested it to you before?''

She left the doctor's office with an odd feeling of predestination, as if the fall in the parking lot had happened to lend her a further and more valid reason for considering the surgery. Certainly if she were to bring up the subject to her mother and tell Margaret what Dr. Delancy's prognosis was, her mother would accept the idea of breast reduction far more readily than if Theresa suggested having it only to relieve herself of sexual hangups, and so she could wear the clothing of her choice.

Dear Brian,
I've done the most foolish thing. I slipped and fell down in the parking lot at school. We'd had rain on top of ice and I was wearing shoes with little heels, and down I went. I'm staying home for a couple of days, on doctor's orders, but he says it's just bruised muscles and they'll fix themselves. But meanwhile, I have another vacation (sort of), but I wish you were here to spend it with me.

The pen fell still. Theresa's gaze wandered off to the dismal gray day beyond the window. The clouds scuttled low while sleet pelted down to run in rivulets along the pane.

What would he think if she wrote, I've been thinking about having my breasts made smaller?

She hadn't realized, up to that point, she *was* considering it. But there were many questions yet to be answered before she could make her decision. And somehow, it seemed too intimate a revelation to make to Brian yet.

She pulled herself from her musing and touched the pen to the paper again.

I've been thinking a lot about Easter. I want to come, but you're right. I'm afraid to tell my folks....

TWO DAYS LATER the phone rang at four in the afternoon.

"Hello?"

"Hello, sweets."

It seemed the winds and rain of March dissolved, and the world erupted in flowers of spring. Theresa's free hand clutched the receiver and joy spiraled up through her limbs.

"B...Brian?"

"Do any other men call you sweets?"

"Oh, Brian," she wailed, and the tears suddenly burned her eyes. Her back still hurt. She was depressed. She missed him. Hearing his voice was the sweetest medicine of all. "Oh, Brian, it's really you."

He laughed, a brief dissatisfied sound ending with a gulp. His voice sounded shaky. "How are you? How's your back?"

"Suddenly it's much better." Through her tears she smiled at the phone cord, picturing his face. "Much, much better."

"Your letter just came."

"And yours just came."

"But I didn't know about your accident when I wrote. Oh, babe, I got so worried, I—"

"I'm fine, Brian, really. All except...." All except her life was none of the things she wanted it to be. She was afraid to have the surgery. Afraid not to have it. Afraid to tell her parents about it. Afraid to meet Brian in Fargo. Afraid her parents would disapprove. Angry that she had to seek their approval at all.

"Except what?"

"Oh, I d...don't know. It's s...silly. I...I just...."

"Theresa, are you crying?"

"N...no. Yes!" She placed a hand over both eyes, squeezing. "Oh, Brian, I don't know why. What's wrong with me?" She tried to hold back the sobs so he couldn't hear.

"Sweetheart, don't cry," he pleaded. His voice sounded muffled, as if his lips were touching the phone. But his plea brought the tears on in force.

"No one's ever c...called me sweetheart bef...before."

"You'd better get used to it."

The tender note in his voice reverberated through her pounding heart. She dashed the tears from beneath her eyes with the back of a hand and clung to the phone. So much to say, yet neither of them spoke. Their trembling feelings seemed to sing along the wire. She was unused to having emotions of this magnitude. Voicing them the first time was terrifying. Essential. She could not live with the sweet pain in her chest.

"I've m...missed you more than I ever th... thought human beings missed one another."

A throaty sound, much like a groan, touched her ear. Then his breath was indrawn with a half hiss and expelled in a way that made her picture him with eyelids clenched tightly. Silence swam between them again, rife with unsaid things. Her body was warm and liquid with sudden need of him.

When he spoke again his words sounded tortured, almost guttural. "You're all I think of." Tears were trailing freely over her cheeks, and she felt weighted and sick. Scintillating, silent moments slipped by, while the unspoken took on greater meaning than the spoken. If the house had not been totally silent she might have missed his next throaty words. "You and Easter."

Still he did not ask. Still she did not answer. Her heart trembled. "Brian, nothing like this...." She stopped to swallow a sob that threatened.

"What? I can't hear you, Theresa." In her entire life of painful shyness, no teasing, no taunts had ever hurt like this shattering longing.

"N...nothing like this has ever hap...happened to me before."

"To me either," he said thickly. "It's awful, isn't it?"

At last she released a sniffly laugh that was much sadder than tears, meant to allay the tension, but failing miserably. "Yes, it's awful. I don't know what to do with myself anymore. I walk around unaware."

"I forget what I'm supposed to be doing."

"I h...hate this house."

"I think about going AWOL."

"Oh, no, Brian, you mustn't!"

"I know...I know." She listened to the sound of his labored breathing. Was he running a hand through his hair? Again stillness fell. "Theresa?" he said very, very softly. Her eyes slid closed. She touched the phone with parted lips. "I think I'm falling."

Her soul soared. Her body was outreaching, yearning, denied.

Again came his ragged breath, seeking control. "Listen, kiddo, I've got to go, all right?" The gaiety was decidedly forced. "Now you go rest and take care of your back for me, okay? There'll be a letter from me day after tomorrow or so. And I promise I won't go AWOL. Tell everybody there hello." At last he fell quiet. His voice dropped to a husky timbre. "I can't take this anymore. I have to go. But I won't say goodbye. Only...sweet memories."

Don't go! Don't hang up! Brian...wait! I love you! I want to meet you at Easter. We'll....

The phone clicked dead in her ear. She wilted against the wall, sobbing. *Why didn't you tell him you'd come? What are you afraid of? A man as gentle and caring as Brian? Do all who love suffer this way?*

PERHAPS IT WAS THE BLEAKNESS and unhappiness that finally prompted Theresa to call the woman whose name had been given her by Catherine McDonald. She desperately needed to talk with somebody who understood what she was going through.

As she dialed the number several days later, her stomach went taut, and she wasn't sure she could voice the questions she'd rehearsed so often during the days she'd lain in bed under doctor's orders.

But from the moment Diane DeFreize answered the phone and greeted warmly, "Oh yes, Catherine told me you might call," the outlook in Theresa's life began to change. Their conversation was encouraging. Diane DeFreize radiated praise for the change wrought upon her life by the surgery she'd had. In little time at all she'd made Theresa eager to take the first step.

It was a day in the third week of March when she met Dr. Armand Schaum. He was a lean, lanky surgeon, one of the growing number of people she'd met lately who maintained eye contact on introduction. Dr. Schaum had the blackest hair she'd ever seen and a piercing look of intelligence in his nut-brown eyes. She liked him immediately. Obviously, Dr. Schaum was used to skittish women coming in with diffident attitudes and uncertain body language, as well as with the slumped shoulders caused by their condition. Theresa, like most, huddled in her chair at first, as if she'd come to his pleasant office asking him to perform some perverted act upon her.

Within five minutes, her attitude changed drastically, and she was struck by a sense of how very ignorant and misinformed she'd been all these years. She'd maintained the same outdated viewpoint as the rest of society: that breast-reduction surgery was vain and unnecessary.

Dr. Schaum explained the probable physical ailments Theresa could expect in the future if her breasts remained as they were now: not only backaches but also a bent spine; leg and knee troubles as well as varicose veins; breathing problems later in life when the chest wall responded to the excessive weight; recurrent rashes on the undersides of her breasts; an increase in breast size and its related discomforts if and when she chose the pill, pregnancy or nursing.

Vanity surgery? How few people understood.

But there were two negative factors Dr. Schaum was careful to point out. His long, angular face took on an expression of somber, businesslike concern.

"In mammoplasty, an incision is made around the entire areola—the brightly colored circle surrounding the nipple. The past method of surgery was to remove the nipple completely before replacing it in a higher position. But with a new method we called the inferior pedicle technique, we can now perform the surgery without severing the nerve connection completely. Now, the nipple remains attached by a slender stalk of tissue called the pedicle. With this technique we aren't able to reduce the breast size quite as radically, but the chance of retaining nipple sensitivity is greatly increased. With *all* breast surgery, that sensitivity is lost at least temporarily. And though we can never guarantee it will return, if the nerve connection is preserved, it's very likely. But it's important that you understand there's always the remote possibility of losing the erogenous zone permanently."

Dr. Schaum leaned forward in his chair. "The other consideration you have to make is whether or not you ever want to breast-feed a baby. Although there have been rare cases in which the pedicle technique was used, where mothers *were* able to nurse afterward, the possibility is highly unlikely.

"So having the surgery means accepting the fact that two important things are at stake: the breast's ability to produce milk and to respond to sexual stimulation. It means that you'll almost certainly have to give up the one, and there's the remote possibility of having to give up the other."

So THAT WAS THE RISK. Theresa was devastated. She lay in bed that night wide-eyed, more uncertain than ever. The idea of having all sensation irreversibly numbed was terribly frightening and very disheartening. Suppose the feeling never returned? She recalled those tingles, the feminine prickles of sexuality brought to her breasts by Brian's briefest touch, by nothing more than dancing close enough to lightly rub the front of his corduroy jacket, and she wondered what he'd think if she robbed *him* of the ability to arouse her in that particular way and herself of the ability to respond.

She cupped her breasts in her palms. They remained unstimulated. She moved her pajamas flutteringly across the nipples. Little happened. She thought of Brian's mouth . . . and it began.

Sweet yearning filled her, made her curl, wanting, wondering. What if this powerful feminine reaction was severed before she'd ever known the sweet evocative tug of a man's lips here? He had said, "You'll set the rules." Would he think her a tease if she asked for that much and then pulled back? Could she ask for that, then pull back herself?

She only knew that once . . . just once she must know the wonder before she wagered it.

HE ANSWERED THE PHONE in a crisp, military fashion. "Lieutenant Scanlon here."

"Brian, it's Theresa."

All was silent while she sensed his great surprise. She wasn't sure she should have called him in the middle of the day.

"Yes, can I help you?"

His brusqueness was a dash of cold water. Then she understood—there was someone nearby.

"Yes, you can help me by telling me you haven't given up on me yet, and that it's not too late for me to say yes to your invitation."

"I . . . ." He cleared his throat roughly. "We can proceed with those plans, as discussed."

Her heart was going wild. She imagined how difficult it was for him to remain stern and unemotional-sounding. "Good Friday?"

"Right."

"The Doublewood Inn in Fargo?"

"Affirmative. At 1200 hours."

"D . . . does that mean noon, Brian?"

"Yessir. Have the proper people been notified?"

"I plan to tell them tonight. Wish me luck, Brian."

"You have it."

"Whoever's with you, turn your face away from him because I think you're going to smile." She paused, taking a deep breath, picturing him as he'd been that first day, with his back to her while he looked out the sliding glass door at the snowy yard, wearing dress blues, his too-short hair showing only slightly beneath the stern visor of his garrison cap. She clearly recalled the warmth and scent lingering in that cap when he'd handed it to her. "Lieutenant Scanlon, I think I'm falling in love with you." Silence. Shocked silence. "And I think it's time I did something about it."

After a short pause, he cleared his throat. "Affirmative. Leave it all to me."

"Not quite all. It's time I took my life into my own hands. Thank you for being so patient while I grew up."

"If there's anything we can do at this end to implement matters—"

"I'll see you in two and a half weeks."

"Agreed."

"Goodbye, dear Lieutenant Scanlon."

Again he cleared his throat. But still the last word came out brokenly. "Good. . .goodbye."

THERESA TACKLED HER MOTHER AND FATHER that night, before she could lose her nerve. As it happened, Margaret provided the perfect lead-in.

"Easter dinner will be at Aunt Nora's this year," Margaret informed them at the supper table. The meal was over. Amy had zipped off to do homework with a friend. "Arthur and his family will be coming from California on vacation. Land sakes, it must be seven years since we've all been together. Grandpa Deering will be celebrating his sixty-ninth birthday that Saturday, too, so I promised I'd make the cake and you'd play the organ, Theresa, while we—"

"I won't be here at Easter," Theresa interrupted quietly.

Margaret's expression said, don't be ridiculous, dear, where else could you possibly be. "Won't be here? Why, of course you'll—"

"I'm spending Easter in Fargo. . .with Brian."

Margaret's mouth dropped open. Then it pursed as a chalky line appeared around it. Her eyes darted to Willard's, then snapped back to her daughter. "With Brian?" she repeated tartly. "What do you mean, *with* Brian?"

"I mean exactly that. We've agreed to meet in Fargo and spend three days together."

"Oh, you have, have you?" Margaret bit out.

"Just like that. Off to Fargo without benefit of a wedding license!"

Theresa felt herself blushing, and along with it rose indignation. "Mother, I'm twenty-five years old."

"And unmarried!"

"Had you stopped to think you might be assuming things?" Theresa accused angrily.

But Margaret had ruled her roost too long to be deterred by any one of them when *she knew she was right*! Her face was pink as a peony by this time, the double chin quivering as she claimed distastefully, "When a man and woman go off, *overnight*, alone, what else is to be done but *assume*?"

Theresa glanced to her father, but his face, too, was slightly red, and he was studying his knuckles. Suddenly she was angered by his spinelessness. She wished he'd say something one way or the other instead of being bulldozed by his outspoken wife all the time. Theresa faced her mother again. Though her stomach was churning, her voice remained relatively calm. "You might have asked, mother."

Margaret snorted and looked aside disdainfully.

"If you're going to assume, there's nothing I can do about it. And at my age I don't feel I have to justify myself to you. I'm going and that's all—"

"Over my dead body, you're going!" Margaret lurched from her chair, but at that moment, unbelievably, Willard intervened.

"Sit down, Margaret," he ordered, gripping her arm. Margaret turned her fury on him.

"If she lives in our house, she lives by rules of decency!"

Tears stung Theresa's eyes. It was as she'd known it would be. With her mother there was no discussing things. There hadn't been when Theresa was fourteen and sought consolation over her changing body, and there wasn't now.

"Margaret, she's twenty-five years old," Willard reasoned, "Closer to twenty-six."

Margaret pushed his hand off her arm. "And some sterling example for Amy to follow."

The words sliced deeply in their unfairness. "I've always been—"

But again, Willard interceded. "Amy's values are pretty much in place, don't you think, Margaret? Just like Theresa's were when she was that age."

Margaret's eyes were rapiers as she glared at her husband. It was the first time in Theresa's life she'd ever seen him stand up to her. And certainly, she'd never seen or heard them fight.

"Willard, how can you say such a thing? Why, when you and I were—"

"When you and I were her age it was 1955, and we'd already been married for a couple of years and had a house of our own without your mother telling you or me what to do."

Theresa could have kissed her father's flushed cheeks. It was like discovering some hidden person, much like herself, who'd been hiding inside Willard Brubaker all these years. What a revelation to see that person assert himself at last.

"Willard, how in the world can you as much as give permission to your own daughter to go off—"

"That's enough, Margaret!" He rose to his feet and turned her quite forcefully toward the doorway. "I've let you steamroll me for a lot of years, but now I think it's time we discussed this in the bedroom!"

"Willard, if you...she can't...."

He led her, sputtering, down the hall until the sound of his voice drifted back. "I think it's time you rememb—'' Then the closing bedroom door cut off his words.

THERESA DIDN'T KNOW they were in the kitchen later that night when she roamed restlessly from her room thinking, she'd get something to drink, then maybe she'd be able to fall asleep.

They were standing in the shadows of the sparsely lit room when Theresa came up short in the dark entry, realizing she was intruding. She could see little of her mother, who stood in front of Willard. Their backs were to Theresa, their feet bare, and they wore tired old robes she'd seen around the house for years. But from the movement of her father's elbows, she suspected his hands were pleasantly occupied. A soft moan came from the throat of the woman who was so glib at issuing orders. "Will...oh, Will..." she whispered.

As Theresa unobtrusively dissolved into the shadow of the hall and crept back to her room, she heard the murmur of her father's very young-sounding chuckle.

IN THE MORNING the word Fargo didn't come up, nor did the name Brian Scanlon. Margaret was as mellow as a softly plucked harp, wishing Theresa good morning before humming her way toward the bathroom with a cup of coffee. The sound of Willard's shaver buzzed louder as the door opened. Then, from far way, she heard laughter.

It was Willard who sought out Theresa in her bedroom at the end of that day and questioned quietly from the doorway, "Are you planning to drive up to Fargo?"

Theresa looked up in surprise. "Yes, I am."

He scratched his chin contemplatively. "Well, then I'd better take a look at that car of yours, in case anything needs tunin' up." He began to turn away.

"Daddy?"

He stopped and turned. Her arms opened as she came across the soft pink carpet on bare feet. "Oh, daddy, I love you," she said against his less-than-firm jowl as his arms tightened around her. A hand came up to pet her head with heavy, loving strokes. Rough, then gentling a bit. "But I think I love him, too."

"I know, pet. I know."

And so it was, from Willard, the quiet one, the unassertive one, Theresa learned a lesson about the power of love.

Chapter Ten

THE FIVE-HOUR DRIVE from Minneapolis to Fargo
was the longest Theresa had ever made alone. She'd
worried about getting drowsy while driving but
found her mind too active to get sleepy behind the
wheel. Pictures of Brian, memories of last Christmas
and anticipation of the next three days filled her
thoughts. At times she'd find herself smiling widely,
realizing a rich appreciation for the rolling farmland
through which she drove, as if her newly expanded
emotions had opened her senses to things she'd never
noticed before: how truly beautiful tilled black soil
can be, how vibrant the green of new grass. She
passed a pasture where newborn calves suckled their
mothers, and for a moment her thoughts turned
dour, but she wouldn't allow herself to think of
anything except the thrill of seeing Brian again.

The sapphire lakes of the Alexandria area gave
way to the undulating farmland of Fergus Falls, then
the earth gradually flattened as the vast deltaland of
the Red River of the North spread as far as the eye
could see: wheat and potato fields stretching endless-
ly on either side of the highway. Moorhead, Minnesota, appeared on the horizon, and as Theresa
crossed the Red River that divided it from its sister
city, Fargo, on the Dakota side, her hands were clam-
my, clutching the wheel.

She pulled the car into the parking space before the

Doublewood Inn, then sat staring at the place for a full minute. It was the first time in her life that Theresa was checking in to a motel by herself.

You're only having last-minute jitters, Theresa. Just because the sign says Motel doesn't mean you're doing anything prurient by checking in to the place.

The lobby was beautiful, carpeted in deep, rich green, decorated with Scandinavian furniture of butcher-block coloring and a plethora of live green plants that seemed to bring the golden spring day inside.

"Good morning," greeted the desk clerk.

"Good morning. I have a reservation." She felt conspicuous and suddenly wished the clerk were a woman instead of a man—a woman would sense her honorable intentions, she thought irrationally. "My name is Theresa Brubaker."

"Brubaker," he repeated checking his records, handing her a card to sign. In no time at all she had a key in her hand, and to her surprise the clerk told her brightly, "Oh, Miss Brubaker, your other party has already arrived. Mr. Scanlon is in Room 108, right next to yours." She glanced at her key: 106. Suddenly it was all real. She felt her face coloring and thanked the clerk, then turned away before he could see her discomposure.

She drove around to the back of the motel, wondering if their rooms faced this side, if Brian was watching her from one of the windows above. She found herself unable to glance up and peruse the spaces on which the draperies were drawn back. If he was watching her, she didn't want to know it. Inside, she stopped before room 108. Staring at the number on his door, her heart thudded. The suitcases grew heavy and threatened to slip from her sweating palms. *He's in there. I'm standing no more than twenty feet from him right now.* It was odd, but now that she was here she was suddenly reluctant to face him. What if either of them had changed in some way since Christmas? What if the attraction had somehow faded? *What will I say to him? What if it's awkward? What if... what if....*

Her own door was only one foot away from his. She opened it and stepped into a room carpeted in tarnished gold with a queen-size bed, a dresser, console, mirror and television. Nothing extraordinary but to Theresa, experiencing independence for the first time, the room seemed sumptuous. She set her luggage down, sat on the end of the bed, bounced once, walked into the tiled bathroom, turned on the light, switched it off, crossed the long main room to open the draperies, switched on the TV, then switched it off again at the first hint of sound and color, unzipped her suitcase, hung up some garments near the door, then looked around uncertainly.

You're only delaying the inevitable, Theresa Brubaker. She stared at the wall, wondering what he was doing on the other side of it. *Just a minute more and my nerves will calm. I'd better check my makeup.* The mirror revealed everything fresh and unsmudged except her lips, which needed color. She dug out her lipstick and applied it with a shaking hand. It tasted faintly peachy and contained flecks of gold that glistened beneath the light when she moved. *You don't put on fresh lipstick when you want a man to kiss you, Brubaker, you dolt.* She jerked a white tissue from the dispenser on the wall and swiped it swiftly across her lips, removing all but a faint smudge of remaining color. The tissues was rough and left her lips looking faintly red and chapped.

around the edge. Nervously she uncapped the silver tube and reapplied the peachy gloss. She met her own eyes in the mirror. They were wide and bright with anticipation. But they were not smiling. She glanced at her breasts beneath the baby blue blouse she'd bought new for this occasion. She wore no sweater today, but felt naked without it, though the tiny blue heart-shaped buttons went from the waist of her white skirt up to the tight mandarin collar that was edged with a blue ruffle. The short gathered sleeves of the blouse had a matching miniature ruffle around their cuffs. Suddenly the puffy sleeves seemed to accentuate the size of her breasts but she forced herself to look instead at her very tiny waistband into which the blouse was securely tucked.

All it takes is a knock on his door, and this uncertainty will be over.

A minute later she rapped on 108 twice, but at the third flick of her wrist her knuckles struck air, for the door was already being flung open.

He stood motionless for a long moment, one hand on the doorknob. She, with her knuckles in the air, stared at him wordlessly. Theresa saw nothing but Brian's face, the searching green eyes with their dark spiky lashes, the lips open slightly, the familiar nose, short hair, cheeks shaven so recently they still shone. Then she became aware of how accentuated his breathing was. The form-fitting baby blue knit shirt fit his chest like liquid, hiding no trace of the swiftly rising and falling muscle beneath it.

Her body felt warm, thrumming, yet uncertain. She wanted to smile but stood immobile, staring at the face before her as if he were an apparition.

"Theresa," was all he said, then he reached out a hand and caught hers, drawing her into the room with firm certainty. And still he didn't smile, but only found her free hand, gripping both palms with viselike tenacity while gazing unwaveringly into her eyes. He swung her around, then turned his back to the door and closed it with his hips. "You're really here," he said hoarsely.

"I'm really here." What had happened to all the charming greetings she'd rehearsed for days? What had happened to the smooth entrance with all its urbane chic, meant to put them both on a strictly friendly basis from the first moment? Why wouldn't her lips smile? Her voice work? Her knees stop trembling?

Suddenly she was catapulted into his arms as he thrust forward, hugging her body full against his and taking her mouth with a slanting, wide, possessive kiss. Nothing gentle. Nothing hinting at easing into old familiarities, but the familiarity arising magically between them with all its stomach-lifting force. She found her arms around his trunk, hands pressed against his warm back. And, wonder of wonders, his heart was slamming against her so vibrantly she could feel the very difference between its beats. Her own heart seemed to lift each cell of her skin, sealing off her throat with its solid hammering. His hands at first forced her close, as if he couldn't get close enough, but then as their tongues joined in sleek reunion, Brian's palms roved in wide circles on her back, and as if it were the most natural thing in the world, he drew them up both her sides simultaneously, pressing her breasts, reaching inward with two long thumbs to seek her nipples briefly. His left arm returned to her back and he angled away from her slightly, cupping one breast fully, then exploring it through her blouse and brassiere while his tongue gentled within her mouth. Shudders climbed her vertebrae and raised the hairs along the back of her thighs while the pressure on her nipples continued in faint, sensuous, circular movements. It was so natural. So right. Theresa had no thoughts of stopping his explorations. They seemed as much a valid part of this reunion as the looks of reaffirmation they'd exchanged when she first stood before him.

The kiss went on unbrokenly as his hands clasped her narrow hipbones and pulled her pelvis securely against his. He rocked against her, undulating, weaving from side to side, pressing his most masculine muscles against her acquiescent stomach. Without realizing it, she found herself meeting each stroke of his hips, pressing against him, lifting up on tiptoe because he was so much taller and she yearned to feel his hardness closer to her point of desire.

Still clasping her hips, Brian ended the kiss. His warm palms pushed downward until her heels again touched the floor, then he held her firmly, so she couldn't move. He rested his forehead against hers while their strident breaths mingled, and their moist lips hovered close, swollen and still open.

Her hands were still on his back. She felt the muscles grow taut with resolution as he pressed firmly on her hipbones. It suddenly struck her how easily these things happen, how readily she had lifted against him, how opportune was the hand of Nature in making a body thrust and ebb when the circumstances called for it.

She was chagrined to think that now he might believe she'd come here with sex in mind. She hadn't, not at all. But how fast her body had dictated its wishes.

"I was so scared to knock on that door," she admitted. He lifted his forehead from hers, bracketed her cheeks with his palms and studied her at close range.

"Why?"

"Because I thought...." His eyes were as stunning as she remembered. They wore an expression of ardency that surprised her. "I thought, what if things aren't the same between us? What if we imagined... this?"

His thumbs brushed the corners of her mouth. His lips were parted and glittered with fragments of gloss from her lipstick. "Silly girl," he whispered, before pulling her face upward to meet his descending one. Again she raised on tiptoe, but this time their bodies barely brushed. The peach-flavored kiss was bestowed by his tongue and lips in a testing circle around her mouth, tugging, wetting once again while his hands drew upon her jaws, first lifting her, then letting her recede as if she were drifting in the surf, mastered by its rush and release. "Oh, Theresa," he murmured while her eyes fell closed, "Nothing's changed for me. Nothing at all." He pressed her away only far enough to gaze into her eyes. "Has it for you?"

How incredible that he should ask. He, who emerged so flawless in her loving eyes. When she studied him again, reality seemed to buckle her lungs and knees. The expression in his eyes said he'd been as uncertain as she had. Theresa ran her hands from his elbows along his hard arms to the wrists. "Nothing," she whispered, allowing her eyelids to close once more while pulling first his left hand from her jaw to kiss its palm, then doing likewise with his right. "Nothing." She looked into his somber eyes and watched them change, grow light, relieved. Her gaze dropped to his mouth. "You have more of my lipstick on than I do."

He smiled and hauled her close, speaking against her mouth so that she could scarcely discern the words. "So clean me up." Her tongue seemed drawn to his by some magical attraction, and she learned a new delight in taking command during a kiss.

"Mmm...you taste good," she ventured, backing away only slightly. She ran her nose along his jaw. "And you smell good, just like I remember, only stronger." She backed away and ran a fingertip over his jaw. "You just shaved."

He grinned, his hands now on her back, holding her against him, but undemandingly. "Just like a teenager getting ready for his first date."

"How long have you been here?"

"Twenty minutes or so. How long have you?"

"About ten minutes. I was in my room, putting on fresh lipstick, then wiping it off, then putting it on again and wondering which was the right thing to do. I was so nervous."

Suddenly it struck them how funny it was that they'd been so apprehensive. They laughed together, then gazed into each other's eyes, and without warning simultaneously answered the compulsion to hug. Their arms went about each other—tight, tight—reaffirming. His hands roved her back. Hers touched his hair. When he backed away, he looped his hands around her hips until she rested against his again.

"What do you want to do first?" he asked.

"I don't know. Just...." Her heart pulsed crazily. "Just look at you some more." She shrugged shyly. "I don't know."

He moved not a muscle for a long, silent moment. Then he nudged her backward with his thighs, directing her shoulders with his hands. "Come here then. Let's indulge ourselves for a while." He lifted a knee to the bed, then fell, tugging her along till they lay on their sides, each with an elbow folded beneath an ear. He rested a hand on her hip. Their eyes locked, their feet trailed off the end of the mattress.

Incredible. She had been in his room less than five minutes and already she was lying on the bed with him. But she had no desire to get up or to protest at his taking her there. His head lifted slowly. His mouth covered hers, urging her lips open once again, his tongue delving into the soft recesses, tickling the skin of her inner cheeks then threading its tip along her teeth, as if counting each. Her body came alive with desire, and her breathing grew fast and harsh, as did his. But when he'd explored to his satisfaction, he lay as before, head upon elbow, his hand still resting on her hip, but undemandingly.

It seemed best to set things straight immediately. Timidity brought color rushing to Theresa's face and made her voice unnatural. "Brian, I...." His eyes were so close, so intense, burning into hers. "I didn't come here because I was ready to go all the way with you."

His hand left her hip and fell to the hollow of her waist. "I know. And I didn't come here to force you to. But I want to. You know that, don't you?"

"I'm not ready for that, Brian, no matter what I...well, I might have led you to believe something else when we first kissed."

"I think we're both in for a hell of a weekend then. It's not going to be easy. Obviously your conscience and your libido are at odds." His hands left her waist, squeezed her upper arm gently, then caressed its length until his hand rested on the back of hers.

"And my libido...well, there's no hiding it, is there?" Then, unceremoniously, he carried her hand to the zipper placket of his white brushed cotton slacks. It happened so unexpectedly she had neither the time nor inclination to pull away. One moment her hand rested on his hip, the next it was flattened along his zipper, and he'd raised his upper knee as he gently forced her fingers to conform to the ridge of hot, hard flesh within. His hand disappeared from atop hers and he rolled closer, letting his eyes drift closed as he spoke gruffly against the hollow of her throat. "I'm sorry if I'm too direct, but I want you to know...whatever you choose is what we'll do, as much or as little as you want. I'd be a damned liar if I said I wasn't thinking about making love to you ever since last January when I left you crying in that airport."

While he spoke, his body undulated against her palm, then she reluctantly slipped her hand up his shirtfront and pressed it against his chest. Beneath her palm his heart thudded crazily.

"Shh...Brian, don't say that."

He backed away, pinning her with a distracting, direct gaze. "Why? Because it's true of you, too?"

"Shh." She rested an index finger on his lips. He stared at her silently until at last the fires in his eyes seemed to subside. He clasped the back of the hand at his mouth, kissed its palm, then threaded its fingers through his own. "All right. Are you hungry?"

She smiled. "Ravenous."

"Should we go and find something to eat, then hit all the highlights of Fargo, North Dakota?"

"Let's."

With one lithe motion he was at the foot of the bed, one foot on the floor, the other knee on the mattress. He hauled her up against him and she landed on her knees with her arms around his neck, and his hands on her buttocks. He kissed her fleetingly, then rubbed the end of her nose with his own. "God, it's good to be with you again. Let's get out of here before I change my mind." With a squeeze and a pat he turned her loose.

They were walking hand in hand along the Broadway Mall in downtown Fargo when they suddenly stopped and stared each other up and down, then burst out laughing.

"You're wearing—"

"Do you realize—" they said in unison, then laughed again, standing back, assessing each other's clothing. They were both wearing white slacks, and the baby blue of her ruffle-necked blouse closely matched that of his knit pullover. She wore white tennis shoes on her feet and he white leather sport shoes with a Velcro-closed strap across the arch of his foot.

"If we dressed to please each other, I think we both did a good job," he said with a smile. "I like your blouse."

"And I like your shirt." Again they laughed, then caught hands as they moved on, exploring the entire three-block length of the mall from Main to Second Avenues. At its south end they studied the Luis Jimenez sculpture depicting a prairie farmer behind a pair of oxen, breaking sod for the first time. Sauntering northward they discovered that the curving mall was designed to represent the pathway of the Red River, and that carved granite markers of red, gray and brown had been set into the concrete on either side of the street to represent the cities flanking the great river as it coursed the length of North Dakota from Wahpeton to Pembina. As they sauntered, they read the names of the towns on the North Dakota side and the dates of their founding: Hunter, 1881; Grandin, 1881; Arthur, 1880. The stones were set varying distances from the street to depict the setback between the actual towns and the great life-giving river that fed the area.

The sun was warm on their backs, the sky overhead flawless cerulean. They had a sense of calm and an ever greater one of delight in being together, swinging hands, watching their white-clad legs matching strides. The mall was dotted with redwood planters in which geraniums and petunias had been set out, and all along the mall's length ash trees were beginning to break into first leaf. At the Old Broadway Café, they peered into the twin oval windows on the front doors and decided to give the old landmark a try. Inside, the booths were the high private cubicles of another era, dark-varnished and set with stained-glass panels. The floor was ancient oiled hardwood that creaked and croaked as the waitress delivered their plate dinners of thick-slicked beef, potatoes and gravy and golden, buttered carrots.

"You haven't mentioned your mom and dad," Brian said, studying Theresa across the booth. "What did they say when you told them you were coming up here to meet me?"

She met his serious green eyes and decided to tell him the truth. "Mother assumed the worst. It wasn't a very pleasant scene." She dropped her eyes to her plate, drawing circles on it with a piece of beef.

Beneath the table his calf found hers and rubbed it reassuringly. He closed his ankles around one of hers and stopped the hand that had been pushing her fork in circles. She looked up at him.

"I'm sorry."

She laid her hand atop his. "Don't be. Something quite wonderful came about because of it." Wonder showed in her face. "Daddy. Would you believe he finally stood up to mother?"

"Willard?" Brian asked in surprise.

"Willard," she confirmed, still with the amazed expression on her face. "He shouted 'Margaret, that's enough' and...and...." Theresa had great difficulty not smirking. "And hauled her off to the bedroom, slammed the door, and the next time I saw them she was calling him Will, and the two of them were cooing like mourning doves. That was the end of Mother's resistance."

Brian dropped his fork with a clatter, threw his hands in the air and praised, "Hallelujah!"

They were still chuckling about it when they returned to the mall. They continued their stroll past The Classic Jewelers, stock-brokerage houses, Straus Drugs and so to the far north end where they discovered the Fargo Theater with its vintage art deco marquee announcing that Charlie Chaplin was playing tonight in *The Bank*.

"Do you like the silent movies?" Brian asked hopefully.

"Love 'em." She grinned up at him.

"Whaddya say, should we give old Charlie a try tonight?"

"Oh, I'd love to."

"It's a date." He squeezed her hand, then led her across the street and they started back along the "Minnesota" side of the mall, reading the town names, peering in store windows. In one called Mr. T's, a bridal gown was displayed. Without realizing it, Theresa's feet stopped moving, and she stared at the mannequin. The sight of the white gown and veil, symbols of purity, brought to mind the coming night, the choice she had to make. She thought about other men she might meet in her life, the one she might possibly marry, and what he would think if she did not come to him as a virgin. But she found it impossible to imagine herself being intimate with any man but Brian.

While Theresa gazed at the bridal gown, two young men passed along the sidewalk. Brian watched their eyes assess her breasts—blatantly, neither of them trying to disguise their fascination. Their heads swiveled, gazes lingering as they drew alongside, then passed her. When they moved on, one of them must have made a lewd comment, for he did a little hip-swinging jive step while patting his thighs, then his companion laughed.

Brian was at first angry. Then he found himself assessing her breasts as a stranger would, and found, to his chagrin, that he was slightly embarrassed. Guilt followed immediately. He fought to submerge it, studying the back of Theresa's head as she gazed up innocently at the window display. But as they moved on up the mall, he was conscious of the eyes of each man they met. Without exception, they all dropped to Theresa's breasts, and Brian's discomfort grew.

Scanlon, you're a hypocrite. The thought was distinctly nettlesome, so he hooked an arm around Theresa's neck, settled her against his hip as they ambled back to the car, and when they reached it, he gave her a tender kiss of apology. Her hands rested on his chest. When she opened her eyes they held a dreamy expression, and he felt small and unworthy for a moment, realizing how hurt she'd be if she suspected he'd been embarrassed over her generous endowment. He traced the outline of her lips with a single finger and said softly, "What do you say we get away from people for a while?"

"I thought you'd never ask."

He smiled, kissed her nose, settled her inside, then started the engine. They crossed the river into Moorhead, drove out onto the blacktop highway heading east, then left it behind to wander the back roads between green woods, brown fields and blue ponds where ducks and blackbirds nested. Spring was burgeoning all around them. They felt it in the renewed warmth of the sun, smelled it in the damp earth, heard it as the sound of wildlife lifted through the air.

They discovered the lush wilds of the Buffalo River where it surged under a culvert beneath their gravel road. Brian pulled to the side, turned off the engine and invited, "Let's walk." She slipped her hand into his with a glad heart, letting him lead her down the steep bank to the dappled woods, where they picked their way aimlessly along the surging spring-swelled waters that rumbled southward. The river sang to them. The tangled roots of a long-fallen tree stood silver in their path. Brian led the way along the massive trunk to a spot where he could mount it, then reached down and helped Theresa up beside him. He walked the weathered trunk to its highest point, with her right behind him. Now the river flowed at their feet. A fish leaped. A trio of sparrows darted from the underbrush to the tangled roots of their tree. From far away a crow scolded. Everything smelled fecund, growing, renewed. From behind, Theresa lightly rested her hands on Brian's hips. He remained as before, unmoving, imbibing, gathering sweet memories. His hands covered hers, drew them firmly around his belt, and his arms covered hers while she pressed her cheek and breasts against his firm, warm back. A blue jay carped from a loblolly pine, and the sun shimmered on the forest floor through the partially sprouted leaves of the surrounding trees. Against Brian's back Theresa's heart thrummed steadily. His palms rubbed her arms, which were warm with gathered sunshine.

"Ahh..." he sighed, tilted his head back, said no more.

She kissed the center of his back. It was enough.

In time they moved on through the gold-and-green afternoon. As they ambled, they caught up on the past three months. Brian had stories about Jeff and air-force rigors, the band, the music they'd been working on. Theresa had anecdotes about life with a teenage sister, incidents from school, plans for spring concerts.

But none of it mattered. Only being together had meaning for them.

They found a nest with three speckled eggs, built in the reeds where the river backwashed and bent. They turned back as the afternoon waned and hunger imposed its demands. They kissed in a basswood grove, then climbed the pebbled bank again and settled into the car for the ride back to town. At their doors in the motel Brian said, "I'll pick you up at your place in half an hour." A quick kiss and they parted.

Chapter Eleven

THE KNOCK AT HER DOOR announced a freshly showered and shaved Brian dressed in tight tan jeans, an open-collared shirt of pale tan-blue-white plaid, and a lightweight sport coat the color of an almond shell. She took one look and felt her mouth watering.

"Wow," she breathed.

He smiled guilelessly, looking down at himself and said, "Oh yeah?" Then he closed the door, eased his hips back against it, crossed his arms and grinned. "Come over here and say that, Brubaker."

She felt herself blushing, but swung away teasingly. "I'm not one of your groupies, Scanlon."

She was securing the latch of a trim gold bracelet when his strong hands closed over her wrists, dragging them around his neck. His eyes, ardent and determined, blazed into hers. "God, there are times when I wish you were." His mouth was warm, open and moist as it marauded hers. He swirled his tongue around her freshly applied lipstick, then delved brashly inside to stroke her teeth until they opened at his command. His tongue probed rhythmically in and out of her mouth, suggesting what was on his mind. He tasted of freshly brushed teeth and smelled like chrysanthemums and sage—not flowery, but spicy clean. He pulled back suddenly, leaving no question about the price he was paying for control. His stormy eyes sought and held hers. Then the storm cleared, he relaxed. His thumbs, still at her wrists, stroked lightly. Now it was his turn to declare breathily, "Wow."

Theresa's heart proved what a healthy, red-blooded twenty-five-year-old virgin she was. She was certain he could see it lifting the bodice of her blouse. She whispered thickly, "Let's go see what Charlie's up to."

At the Fargo Theater they were treated to a sensational performance by a local member of the American Theater Organ Society on an immense and wondrous pipe organ that rose out of the floor on a pneumatic lift. They sat in the balcony, because it was a dying species they'd have few more chances to experience. Theresa learned how readily Brian laughed at slapstick. While the organist tickled out an accompaniment, Charlie Chaplin duckwalked down a city street in his oversize shoes and baggy pants, went three times around a revolving door, then spent arduous moments whirling the dials of an imposing-looking vault. Brian snickered, slunk low in his seat. The vault door swung open and the lovable Charlie disappeared inside to return with his precious deposit: a scrub pail, mop and janitor's uniform. Brian rolled his head backward and hooted with full throat while Theresa's heart warmed more to the man beside her than to the one on the screen.

The organ created a musical echo of Charlie's misfortunes in leaving flowers for the black-eyed Edna Purviance, only to have the damsel believe they were a gift from the bank clerk named Charlie. When skulduggery started, the organ rumbled dramatically, creating vibrations through the theater seats. Beside her, Brian slumped low in his seat, trembling melodramatically, tossing his popcorn in the air when the heroine was tied and gagged, stamping and cheering when Chaplin came to her rescue, boo-hooing when the poor unfortunate bank custodian was left awakening from a dream, petting the rags of his floor mop instead of the waves of the damsel's head.

When the film ended and they returned to the street, Brian performed a superb imitation of Chaplin, knees crooked outward, shoulders rolling with his peculiar gait while he scratched his head with stiff fingers and made a vain attempt to open the door of the wrong car. He gave a Chaplinesque flap of the hands, looked around, dismayed, sad-eyed.

How easy it was for Theresa to gasp and clasp her hands before her, distraught at misfortune. She ran jerkily to her car, flung the door open, then stood on the pavement with eyes rolled heavenward in invitation.

Charlie Scanlon duckwalked to her, shyly studied his feet, swept into a clumsy bow, then waved her inside. She interlaced her fingers, simpered, then got in.

Brian made a swipe at the open door, missed, spun in a circle, missed again, spun another circle and finally connected with the difficult door and managed to slam it.

When he climbed in beside her and squeezed the invisible bulb of a horn and made a flatulent-sounding "T-o-o-t" out the side of his mouth, they wilted with laughter. In time they grew too weak to continue. Then they looked at each other in silent discovery.

They ate an Italian supper at a place chosen at random, reminiscing about old movies, but always thinking about the end of the evening ahead. Would it bring *good night* or *good morning?*

Laughter was gone when they walked slowly, slowly down the hall to their doors. They stopped dead center between 106 and 108.

"Can I come in?" he asked quietly at last.

She met his searching eyes, feeling the awesome tugs of carnality and denial warping her heart. She remembered her mother's words, the bridal gown in the window. She touched his chest lightly. "Will you understand how hard it is for me that I have to answer no?"

His hands hung loosely at his sides. He sucked in a huge gulp of air, dropped his head down as his eyes closed, then braced both hands tiredly on his hips and studied the toes of his brown boots.

She felt childish and unworthy. Tears began to burn her eyelids.

He saw and pulled her close, resting his chin against her hair. Though his body rested only lightly against hers, she was close enough to know that her nearness and this compulsion they both controlled so closely had aroused him. "I'm sorry, sweets," he whispered. "You're right and I'm wrong. But that doesn't make it any easier."

"Kiss me, Brian," she begged.

He took her head in both hands and tipped her face up for a deep, hungering kiss. But the pressure of his hands on her jaw and ears told of where he wanted those hands to be. And she clung to his wrists—the safest place—feeling beneath one thumb the surging rhythm of his pulse. They drew apart, troubled eyes clinging.

"Good night," he said raggedly.

"Good night," came her unsure reply.

Neither of them slept well, they confessed over breakfast. The day lolled before them; its hours would be too short, no matter how they were spent.

Yet when considered in the light of their denial, those same hours seemed infinite. They browsed through West Acres Shopping Center, ate lunch in a McDonald's because their stomachs demanded filling, but neither of them cared the least about food. They roamed the green hills of Island Park and sat in its gazebo watching a group of children playing softball across the expanse of green grass. They had supper in the motel dining room, and afterward wandered into the casino where new laws allowed gambling with a two-dollar limit. But while Brian sat at a table playing blackjack, a man with sleek black hair, wearing an expensive silk suit, sidled up to Theresa, gave her a blatant visual assessment, slipped his hands to her hips and whispered in her ear, "You alone, baby?"

It happened so fast Theresa hadn't time to react until the cloying scent of his after-shave seemed to plug her nostrils, and his wandering hands registered their insult.

Suddenly Brian interceded. "Get your hands off her, buddy," he growled, jerking the man's arm, spinning him away from Theresa, whose stunned eyes were wide and alarmed.

The man's eyes narrowed dangerously, then eased as lascivious speculation crossed his features. He pulled free of Brian's hand, shrugged his shoulder to right the expensive suit jacket, and his eyes roved once over Theresa's breasts. "Can't say I blame you, fella. If those were mine for the night, I wouldn't be too quick to share 'em either."

Theresa saw the muscles bunch in Brian's jaw. His fists clenched.

"Don't, Brian!" She stepped between the two men, facing Brian, gripping his arm in an effort to turn him away. "He's not worth it," she pleaded. His arm remained steeled. "Please!" she whispered.

But Brian's livid face scarcely registered if he'd heard. He moved with mechanical deliberation, reaching down without looking to grasp Theresa's hand and remove it from his jacket. Then slowly, menacingly he clutched the man's lapels, lifting until his toes scarcely touched the carpet.

"You will apologize to the lady right now," Brian ground out, "or your teeth will be biting your own ass, from the inside out." Brian's voice was chilling as he held the stranger aloft, nose to nose.

"Okay, okay. Sorry, lady, I didn't know—"

Brian jerked him up another inch. Stitches popped on the expensive jacket. "You call that an apology, sucker? See if you can't do better."

The man's eyes were bugging. Sweat erupted on his sheeny forehead and beneath his lizardlike nose. "I...I'm really sorry, m...miss. I'd like to b...buy you both a drink if you'd let me."

Brian slammed him back down to the floor, released his lapels distastefully while shoving the unpalatable intruder back until he stumbled against a table. "Pour your goddamn drinks in your pants, buddy. Maybe it'll cool you off." He turned. "Let's get out of here, Theresa." His fingers were like brands as he led her by an arm to the casino door, then out into the carpeted hall. She felt his hand trembling on her elbow and had to run to keep up with him. Wordlessly he turned down the hall to their rooms and was fishing in his trousers pocket for the key even before they reached their destination. When he leaned to insert the key into 108, there was no question of where he expected her to go. The door

swung back and he found her hand, leading her inside. There followed a solid thud, then they were
ensconced in a world of unbroken black. His arms
closed convulsively around her, his body pressed
close, sheltering, rocking her as he spoke gruffly
against her hair. "I'm sorry, sweets, God, I'm so
sorry."

"Brian, it's all right." But she was still shaken and
vulnerable and, now that it was over, felt like crying.
But his protection eradicated the sudden need for
tears. His arms had strength she'd never suspected.
They clamped her so hard her back hurt as he bent it
in a bow.

"God, I wanted to kill him!" Brian's fingers dug
into her flesh, just below and behind her armpits,
and she winced, lifting her hands instinctively to
press against his chest.

"Brian, it doesn't matter...please, you're hurting
me."

The pressure fell away. He jerked as if shot. "I'm
sorry...I'm sorry...sorry...." The voice was
pained in the darkness, then his hands were gentle on
her, finding her face in the inkiness, fingertips caressing her temples, then sliding into her hair as his
mouth sought hers. "Theresa...Theresa..." he
muttered, then circled her again with his arms. "I'd
never hurt you, but I want you, you know that. God,
I'm no better than him," Brian finished miserably,
then took her mouth with an abandon that sent
tongues of fire licking down her stomach. His hands
left her back and roamed up her sides, pressing hard,
too hard, as if it were compulsion he was trying to
fight. She clung, unwilling to stop him yet, blessing
the darkness.

His caress trailed down over her small waist, took

measure of her hipbones, then traveled with uniform pressure down her buttocks, cupping them, pulling her up and inward against his tormented body. Along her sides his warm hands moved, compressing the swelling sides of her breasts until all else ceased to matter but that she know more of the treasured warmth of his palms upon them.

In the dense blackness she felt herself swept off the floor. Her arms instinctively encircled Brian's neck. In four steps he reached the bed and set her upon it, then joined her.

"Brian, we should stop. . . ." she whispered against his mouth.

His tongue drove deep once more, then he softly nipped her lips. "We'll stop whenever you say." His kiss made dissent impossible, and then so did his touch. He covered her breasts with both wide palms, pressing down hard and flat and firm, for she lay with her torso precisely aligned with his. He found her hand in the dark, clamped his fingers over the back of it, carried it to his mouth and bit the outer edge, then turned its palm against her own breast. "Feel," he whispered fiercely, rolling aside. The nipple was distended. Even through her bra and summer sweater she could feel it. "Let me touch it too." Again he kissed her hand, then placed it on his ribs. "Let me teach you how good it can feel."

She could see nothing in the infinite darkness, but as she was devoid of sight, her other senses sharpened. His spicy smell, his brandy taste, the slight tremor in his voice were all magnified in their appeal. But above all, her body seemed finely honed to the sense of touch. His breath was like the whisk of a feather upon her face, the dampness his kiss had left felt cool on her lips, the hard contours of his

masculinity took on nearly visible form, the seeking
conviction of his hands moving toward the clasp of
her bra was felt as if from another supremely sensitive dimension.

She whimpered softly, lifting a shoulder. The clasp
parted and her breasts were free. But Brian's elbows
remained at her sides, bracing him above her. Across
her face he took soft, teasing nips with his teeth:
chin, cheek, nostril, lip, jaw, even eyebrow—bone
and all. The bites grew more evocative, tightening the
coil of tension in her stomach. His hands splayed
over her bare back. "Theresa...so soft," he murmured, knowing the full length and width of that
vulnerably soft skin, then kneading it gently. "So innocent." In one smooth motion his hands skimmed
her circumference while his hips pinned hers securely.
Sweater and bra were eased up by his hands. Then the
objects of her long despair became those of her
awakening sexuality as they were enveloped in his
palms—skin on skin, warm on warm, man on
woman.

It was so good, so right, and made her yearn for
the forbidden.

The callused fingers that knew a guitar's strings so
intimately now plucked upon her, as one might sur-
round and pluck the fragile seeds of a dandelion
from its stalk, the span of his fingertips widening,
narrowing, drawing upward, encouraging her nipples
to follow and reach when his touch disappeared. And
they did. Repeatedly her shoulders strained to follow, as if to say, please don't leave me yet.

His hips lay still upon hers, but his flesh was at its
fullest, thick and solid between their bodies. At the
moment she scarcely gave it a thought, so taken was
she by the sweet swellings of these first caresses on

her breasts. He turned his head aside and gently rubbed his hair across the naked nipples. "Ohh..." she sang softly, in delight, entwining her fingers in the hair at the crest of his skull, guiding his head, experiencing the silken texture upon her aroused flesh. A turn of that head, and now it was his cheek where his hair had been. Her hands neither commanded nor discouraged, but rested idly in his hair while she waited...waited....

And then it happened, the first wonder of his mouth upon her breast, a passing kiss of introduction—vague, soft—on her left nipple first, then upon her right. And she thought, *hello at last, my love.* Gradually, as he nuzzled, his lips parted until their sleek inner skin touched her. She felt the texture of teeth, closed yet, making her yearn for them to open, allowing entry. So still she lay, as still as a butterfly poised on a windless day—feeling, feeling, feeling. His silken tongue came to introduce her flesh into his mouth and lead her within where all was wet, warm and slippery soft.

"Ohhh...Bri...." His name drifted into silence, lost to the grander passion now building.

"Mmm..." he murmured, a sound of praise, while the warm breath from his nostrils dampened the swell of skin beyond reach of his mouth. "Mmm...." He was tugging now, sucking more powerfully until she twisted slightly in satisfaction. To each of her breasts he brought adulation, until it felt the threads of femininity seemed drawn from deeper within her...up, up, and into the man whose mouth taught her pleasure.

Combing his hair with limp fingers she charted the movements of his head. "Oh, Brian, it's so good..." she murmured. "All these years I've wasted...."

He lunged up, dragging his hips along her thighs, joining swollen lips to hers. "We'll make up for them," he promised into her open mouth. "Shh... just feel...feel...."

When his mouth took her breast again, it was with acute knowledge of her need, and just how far he could go to send her senses soaring without hurting her. He caressed with his palms while capturing a taut nipple between the sharp edges of his teeth, scissoring until a keen, welcome sting made her gasp. Then there came a point beyond which the arousal of her breasts alone would no longer suffice. It was painful in its yearning. It made her lift to him, made him press to her. He found her mouth in the dark; it had fallen slack in the throes of desire. His was hotter now, and as they kissed he undulated above her until her knees parted of their own accord, creating a lee into which his body arched, rocking against her.

No more difficult words had she ever spoken. "Brian, please...I can't do this."

"I know...I know," came his rough whisper, but his mouth covered hers as he continued the sinuous rhythm along her body, bringing desire knocking upon her heart's door, seeking entry, just as his body sought entry to hers.

"Brian, please don't...or soon I won't be able to stop you." Her hands clenched in his hair, pulling his head back. "But I must, don't you see?"

He stilled. Stiffened.

"Don't move," he ordered gruffly. "Not a muscle." They lay with their breathing falling hard against each other until with a soft curse he rolled from the bed and in the black void she heard him make his way into the bathroom. A line of light spilled, casting his shadow against the wall as he grasped the edge of the sink and leaned against it, his head hanging down.

She lay utterly still. Her pulse throbbed throughout her body. She closed her eyes until Brian returned and sank down on the foot of the bed, leaning his elbows on his knees while running both hands through his hair. Then, with a groan he fell backward, hands flopped palms up.

She laid a hand in his, and at her touch his fingers clasped hers tightly. He rolled toward her, pressing his face against her hip. When he spoke his words were muffled against her.

"I'm sorry."

"And I'm sorry if I led you on and made you expect more."

"You didn't lead me on. You told me from the start that you weren't coming here with sex on your mind. It was me who pushed the issue after promising not to. I thought I had enough control to settle for kisses." He gave a soft, rueful laugh and flung an arm over his eyes.

But she *had* come into his room with sex on her mind, with at least as much as she'd experienced. She had wanted those precious moments because if she decided to have the surgery she might forfeit them forever. She felt a pang of guilt, for it seemed she'd used Brian for her own ends, and now he lay beside her apologizing for his very natural desire. She considered explaining to him, telling him about the surgery. But now that she'd known the rapture to be found beneath his lips, she was doubly unsure about proceeding with it. And furthermore, it was difficult for her to believe that when June came and he was freed to the civilian world, there would not be countless other women he'd find more attractive than her-

self. June was a key word often mentioned in their
letters, but Theresa realized how easy it was for a
lonely man to make plans for the future, but when
that future came, how easily those plans could be
changed. The thought hurt, but it was best to be
honest with herself.

There were no promises made between them. And
until there were, she must avoid situations such as
this.

"Brian, it's late. I should go back to my room."

He rolled onto his back again, but his fingers remained laced with hers. "You could stay if you want
to, and all we'll do is sleep side by side."

"No, I don't think I have that much willpower."
When she sat up to straighten her clothing she felt
him watching and wished the bathroom light was off,
dim though it was. Her hair was tousled, her hand
shaky.

"Theresa...." He reached for her with the plain-
tive word.

Softly she begged, "Let me go now without per-
suasion...please. I'm only one step away from
changing my mind, but if I did I think we'd both be
unhappy with ourselves."

His hand fell. He eased off the bed, helped her up
and they walked silently to the door. It yawned open
and they stood studying the carpet.

He looped an elbow around her neck and drew her
temple to his lips. "I'm not disappointed in you."
The words rattled quietly in his throat.

Relief flooded Theresa and left her weak. She
sagged against him. "You're so honest, Brian. I love
that in you."

His eyes met hers, earnest yet troubled, and still
with a flicker of desire in their depths. "Tomorrow

will be hard enough, saying goodbye after being to-gether like this. It would only have been harder if we'd given in."

She raised up on tiptoe, brushed his lips with hers, then touched them fleetingly with her fingertips.

"I had begun to think I'd never find you in this big old world, Brian Scanlon...." But she could say no more without crying, so slipped into the loneliness of her own room and closed the door between them.

Chapter Twelve

THEIR LAST DAY TOGETHER was bittersweet. The
wasted precious hours silently pondering the lone
someness they'd feel at parting. They suffered re
criminations about the night before. They counte
the weeks of separation ahead. Laughter was rare
and forced, and followed by long gazing silences tha
left them more unfulfilled than ever.

They checked out at eleven and drove aimlessly un
til 1:00 P.M. Brian was flying standby on his retur
flight, so she took him to the airport where they sat i
the coffee shop at a table by the window, unable to b
cheered or consoled.

"You have a long drive ahead of you. I think yo
should go."

She lifted startled eyes to his. "No. I'll wait wit
you."

"But I may not catch a plane until late afternoon."

"But...I...." Her lips started quivering, so sh
clamped them together tightly.

"I know," he said softly. "But will it be any easie
if you stay to watch my plane take off?"

Dismally she shook her head and stared at her cof
fee cup through distorting tears. His hand covere
the back of hers, squeezing it hurting-hard, hi
thumb stroking hers upon the handle of the cup. "
want you to go," he claimed, yet the unsteady word
laced his request with depression. "And I want yo

to do it smiling.'' The tears swelled fuller. He tilted her chin up with a finger. "Promise?"

She nodded, and the motion jarred the tears loose and sent them spilling down her freckled cheeks. Frantically she wiped them away and pasted on the smile he'd requested. "You're right. It's a five-hour drive...." She reached for her purse, babbling inanities, making her hands look busy with important stuff, foolish words pouring from her lips while Brian sat across the table smiling sadly. She fell silent in midsentence, folded her lower lip between her teeth and swallowed an enormous lump in her throat.

"Walk me to the car?" she asked so low he could hardly hear.

Without a word he dropped some change on the table and rose. She moved a step ahead of him, but felt his hand at her elbow then sliding down to capture her fingers and hold them tighter. Then tighter.

At the car they stopped. Both of them stared at the metal strip around the driver's door. A truck pulled up beside them, someone got out and walked toward the terminal. Brian lifted Theresa's hand and studied its palm while scratching at it repeatedly with his thumbnail.

"Thank you for coming, Treece."

She felt as if she were suffocating. "I had a g... good...." But she couldn't finish, and when the sob broke, he jerked her roughly into his arms. A hand clamped the back of her head. Her fingers clenched the back of his shirt. His scent was thick and nostalgic where her nose was pushed flat against his chest.

"Drive safely." His voice rumbled a full octave lower than usual.

"Say h... hi to J... Jeff."

"June will be here before we know it." But she was

afraid to think of June. What if he didn't come back to her after all? He was holding her so close all she could make out through her tears was the soft gray of his shirt. "Now I'm going to kiss you, then you get in that car and drive, do you understand?"

She noded, her cheek rubbing a wide damp spot on the gray cloth.

"Don't think of today. Think of June."

"I . . . w . . . will."

He jerked her up. Their mouths joined for a salty goodbye. His hand clamped the back of her neck as he pressed his warm lips to her wet cheeks, as if to keep something of her—something—within his body.

He put her away from him with a sturdy push, opened the car door, then waited until the engine fired. Resolutely she put the car into reverse, backed from her parking spot, then hung her arm out the window as she pulled forward. Their fingertips brushed as she drove away, and a moment later a turn of the wheel whisked his reflection from her rearview mirror.

THERESA HAD EXPECTED her mother to be inquisitive, but oddly, Margaret only asked the most impersonal questions. How is Brian? Did he mention Jeff? Was there a lot of traffic? Both Margaret and Willard seemed to sympathize with their twenty-five-year-old daughter who mooned around the house as if she were fifteen. Even Amy, sensing Theresa's despondency, steered clear.

On her calendar, Theresa numbered the days backward from June 24 and grew more and more irritable as she remained indecisive about the surgery.

May arrived, and with it hot weather and uncontrollable children at school. The kids were so antsy

hey could hardly be contained in the stuffy school-
oom.

Spring was concert season, and Theresa busily pre-
)ared for the last two weeks of school, when teas
were held for the mothers of the younger children
and a combined evening performance of the choir,
)and and orchestra was scheduled. After-school
neetings were necessary to coordinate the programs
vith the directors of the other two groups. It was a
lectic time of year, but at the same time sad. She was
orry to have to say goodbye to some sixth graders as
hey moved into junior high and a new building and
hree of these managed to find out about Theresa's
wenty-sixth birthday, presenting her with a birthday
:ake in class that day. The tenseness of the past days
led as she felt her heart brimming with special feel-
ngs for the three.

And the glow still lingered when she arrived home
o find flowers and a note from Brian: "With love,
intil June 24th, when I can tell you in person." The
lowers created a stir within the family. Amy was
iwed and perhaps a trifle envious. Margaret insisted
he flowers be left in the center of the supper table,
hough it was impossible to see around the enormous
ong-stemmed red roses. Willard smiled more than
isual, and patted Theresa's shoulder every time their
)aths crossed. "What's all this about June?" he
isked. She gave him a kiss on the jaw, but had no
eply, for she wasn't sure herself what June would
)ring. Especially if she decided to have the surgery.

At nine-thirty that night the phone rang. Amy an-
wered it, as usual. "It's for you, Theresa!" Amy's
:yes were bright with excitement. She anxiously
hoved the receiver into Theresa's hand and mouthed,
'It's him!''

Theresa's heart pattered. Only inadequate letter had passed between them since Fargo. This was the first phone call. Amy stood close, watching with keen interest while Theresa placed the phone to her ear and answered breathlessly, "Hello?"

"Hello, sweets. Happy birthday."

Theresa placed a hand over her heart and said not a word. It felt as if she'd been supping on sweet, sweet rose petals, and they'd all stuck in her throat.

"Are you there, Theresa?"

"Yes...yes! Oh, Brian, the flowers are just beau tiful. Thank you." It was him! It was really him!

"God, it's good to hear your voice."

Amy was still three feet away. "Just a minute Brian." Theresa shifted her weight to one hip lowered the receiver and shot a piercing look o strained patience. Amy made a disgruntled face shrugged, slipped her hands into her jeans pocket and grumbled all the way to her bedroom.

"Brian, I'm back. Had to get rid of a nuisance."

His laugh lilted across the wire, and she pictured him with chin raised, green eyes dancing in delight "The kid, huh?"

"Exactly."

"I'm picturing you in the kitchen, standing beside the cupboard, and Amy beside you, all ears. I've been living on memories just like those ever since left you."

Love talk was foreign to Theresa. She reacted with a blush that seemed to heat her belly and burn its way up to her breasts and neck to her temples. Her heart raced, and her palms grew damp.

"Oh, Brian..." she said softly, and closed her eyes, picturing his face again.

"I've missed you," he said quietly.

"I've missed you, too."

"I wish I could be there. I'd take you to dinner and then out dancing."

The memory of being wrapped in his arms, with her breasts crushed against his corduroy jacket came back in vivid detail and made her body ache with renewed longing to see him again.

"Brian, nobody's ever sent me flowers before."

"That just goes to show the world is filled with fools."

She smiled, closed her eyes and leaned her forehead against the cool kitchen wall. "And nobody's ever plied me with flattery before either. Don't stop now."

"Your teeth are like stars. . . ." He paused expectantly, and her smile grew broader.

"Yes, I know—they come out every night." She could hear his humor blossoming as he went on to the next line of the time-weary joke.

"And your eyes are like limpid pools."

"Yes, I know—cesspools."

"And your hair is like moonbeams."

"Oh-oh! I never heard that one." But by this time they were both laughing. Then his voice became serious once more.

"What were you doing when I called?"

She watched her fingertips absently smoothing the kitchen wall. "I was in my bedroom, writing a thank-you letter to you for the roses."

"Were you really?"

"Yes, really."

It was quiet for a long time. His voice was gruff and slightly pained when he spoke again. "God, I miss you. I wish I was there."

"I wish you were, too, but it won't be long now."

"It seems like six years instead of six weeks."

"I know, but school will be out by then, and we'll be able to spend lots of time together . . . if you want."

"If I want?" After a meaningful pause, he added sexily, "Silly girl."

She thought her heart might very well erupt, for it seemed to fill her ears and head with a wild, sweet thrumming. To her amazement, his next words made it beat even harder.

"I wish you could feel what's happening to my heart right now."

"I think I know. The same thing is going on in mine."

"Put your hand on it."

Only a faraway musical bleep sounded across the telephone line as Theresa digested his order.

"Is it there?" he asked.

"N . . . no."

"Put it there, for me."

Timidly, slowly, she placed her hand upon her throbbing heart.

"Is it there now?"

"Yes," she whispered.

"Tell me what you feel."

"I feel like . . . like I've been running as hard as I can—it's like there's a piston driving in there. My hand seems to be lifting and falling with the force of it."

After a long moment of silence he said rather shakily, "That's where I want to be, in your heart."

"Oh, Brian, you are," she replied breathily.

"Theresa?" She waited, breathlessly. "Now slide your hand down."

Her lips dropped open. Her skin prickled.

"Slide it down," he repeated, more softly. The tremor was gone from his voice now. It was controlled and very certain. Her hand dropped to her breast. "And that's where I want to kiss you... again. And do everything that follows. I'm sorry now that we didn't do it in Fargo. But when I get back, we will. I'm giving you fair warning, Theresa."

The line went positively silent. Theresa's eyes were closed, her breathing labored. Turning, she pressed her shoulder blades and the back of her head to the wall. His face came clearly to mind. She moved her hand back to her breast and riffled her fingers softly up and down. The tiny movements sent shudders of sensation down the backs of her thighs. The thought of the surgery sizzled through her mind, and she opened her mouth to ask him what he would think if he came back and found her with beautifully average breasts, but ones that might not be able to show response.

"Theresa," he almost whispered, again sounding pained. "I have to go. You finish your letter to me, and tell me all the things you're feeling right now, okay, sweets? And I'll see you in six weeks. Till then, here's a kiss. Put it wherever you want it." A pause followed, then his emotional, "Goodbye, Treece."

"Brian, wait!" She clutched the phone almost frantically.

"I'm still here."

"Brian, I...." Her throat worked, but not another sound came out.

"I know, Theresa. I feel the same."

She would have known he'd hang up without warning. He was a man who never said goodbye.

I'M GIVING YOU FAIR WARNING, THERESA."

His words stayed with her during the following days while she continued weighing the possibility of undergoing breast surgery. She had a second talk with Dr. Schaum. He told her the time would be perfect, just when school ended for summer vacation, a time of low stress and less social contact—both desirable. She had learned that her insurance *would* cover the cost of the surgery because of the prognosis for late-life back troubles. She'd received a brochure from Dr. Schaum explaining the surgical procedure, what to expect beforehand and afterward. The discomforts could be expected to be minimal, but they were the least of Theresa's concerns. Neither was she especially bothered by the idea of giving up nursing—babies seemed so far in the future. But the possibility of losing an erogenous zone made her reluctant, and at times depressed, especially when remembering Brian's lips upon her, and the wonder of her own feminine response.

She grew short-tempered with her family and also with her students as the weather warmed. The children's temperaments grew feisty, too. Fights broke out on the playground, and tears were often in need of swabbing. While she performed the duty, Theresa often wished she had someone to swab her own tears, shed in secret at night, as the decision time came closer and closer. If she was going to have the surgery, the choice must be made and made soon. In two weeks summer vacation would start, and three weeks after that, Brian would come home.

She thought of greeting him in a cool, cotton T-shirt—green, maybe—with a new trim profile of her choosing. How amazing to think she could actually choose the contour of breast she preferred! The surgeons didn't even make both breasts the same size anymore, but made the right larger than the left if the woman was right-handed, and vice versa, just as nature would have done. When nipples were replaced, they were lifted to a new, perky, uptilted angle that would remain attractive for the rest of her life.

The idea beguiled.

The idea horrified.

I want to do it.

I can't do it. What would Brian say?

It's your body, not his.

But I want to share it with him. To the fullest.

You still can, even if the sensation doesn't come back.

I should at least discuss it with him.

On the basis of one weekend in Fargo that ended unfulfilled, a bouquet of roses and a seductive phone call?

But he said he wanted me to be exactly the same when he came back!

Supposing you're even better?

Dear God, they'd cut my nipples off.

Not totally.

I'll have scars.

That will disappear almost completely.

But I loved being kissed there—suppose I lose the feeling?

Chances are you won't.

I'm scared.

You're a woman—the choice is yours.

A WEEK BEFORE VACATION she made her decision. When she told her parents, Margaret's face registered immediate shock and disapproval, her father's a gray disappointment that the body he'd bequeathed his daughter had turned out to be less than suitable.

As Theresa had expected, Margaret was the outspoken one. "I don't understand why you'd want to. . .to fool around with the body you've been given, as if it isn't good enough."

"Because it can be better, mother."

"But it's so *unnecessary* and such an expense!"

"Unnecessary!" These were all the arguments she'd been expecting, yet Theresa was deeply disappointed in her mother's lack of understanding. "You think it's unnecessary?"

Margaret colored and pursed her lips slightly. "I should know. I've lived with a shape like yours all my life, and I've gotten along just fine."

Theresa wondered about all the hidden slights her mother had suffered and never disclosed. She knew for a fact there were backaches and shoulder aches. Very quietly the younger woman asked, "Have you, mother?"

Margaret discovered something important needing attention behind her and presented her back. "What a ridiculous question. Movie stars and playgirls tamper with their shapes, not nice girls like you." She swung around again. "What will people say?"

Theresa felt wounded that her mother, with typical lack of tact, could choose such a time to voice the fear uppermost in her mind—which was how it would affect herself. She cared so much about the opinion of outsiders that she let its importance overshadow the reason her daughter had come to this decision. With a sigh, Theresa sank to a chair. "Please, mom, dad, I want to explain. . . ." She did. She went back to age fourteen and described all her disenchantment with her elephantine growth, and explained all that Dr. Schaum had predicted for her future. She omitted the details about her sexual hang-ups, but explained why she'd worn the sweaters, hidden beneath the violin, chosen to work with children and disliked meeting strange men.

When she finished, Margaret's eyes moved to Willard's. She mulled silently for a minute, sighed and shrugged. "I don't know," she said to the tabletop. "I don't know."

But Theresa knew. She had gained confidence by confronting her parents about the trip to Fargo, and she was very certain the surgery was the right thing for her. She sensed her mother softening and realized her own self-assurance was changing Margaret's opinion.

"There's just one more thing," Theresa went on. She met Margaret's questioning eyes directly. "Could you get the day off that Monday of the surgery and be there at the hospital, mother?"

Perhaps it was the realization that the young woman who was slowly but surely snipping the apron strings still needed Margaret's maternal understanding. Perhaps it was because there'd been times in Margaret's life when she'd wished for the courage her daughter now displayed. She squelched her misgivings, forced the squeamishness from her thoughts and answered, "If you're bound to go through with it, yes, I'll be there."

But when she was alone, Margaret leaned weakly against the bathroom door, compressing her own bulbous breasts with her palms, overcome by pangs of empathetic transference. She opened her eyes and dropped her hands, breathing deeply, admitting what courage it took for her daughter to make the decision she had.

ON MEMORIAL DAY, Theresa washed her hair by herself for the last time for at least two weeks; she wouldn't be able to lift her arms for a while after the surgery. She packed a suitcase with one very generously sized nightgown, and three brand-new pairs of pajamas, size medium. She harnessed herself into her size 34DD utilitarian white bra, but packed several of size 34C—not blue, not pink, not even lacy; those would have to wait. She'd be wearing the smaller, sturdy white bra day and night for a month. She dressed in a size extralarge spring top, but packed a brand-new one, again size medium, that looked to Theresa as if it had been made for a doll instead of a woman.

The following morning, Margaret was there when they rolled Theresa into surgery on the gurney. She kissed her daughter's cheek, held her hand in both of her own, and said, "See you in a little while."

THREE AND A HALF HOURS LATER, Theresa was taken to the recovery room, and an hour after that she opened her eyes and lifted a bleary smile to Margaret, who leaned close and brushed the thick, coppery hair back from Theresa's forehead.

"Mom...." The word was an airy whisper. Theresa's eyelids fluttered open twice, but her eyes remained unfocused.

"Baby, everything went just fine. Rest now. I'll be here."

But a limp, freckled hand lifted and dreamily explored the sheets across her breast. "Mom, am... I...beautiful?" came the sleepy question.

Gently restraining Theresa's hand, Margaret felt tears sting her eyes. "Yes, baby, you're beautiful. But you've always been. Shh...." A drugged smile lifted the corner of Theresa's soft lips.

"Brian...doesn't...know...yet...." The lethargic voice hushed into silence, and Theresa drifted away into the webbed world of sleep.

LATER THERESA WAS LUCID and alone in her hospital room for the first time. She'd been warned to limit all arm movement, but could not resist gingerly exploring the mysteries sheathed beneath the white sheets and contained within the new, stiff, confining bra. She stared at the ceiling while moving her hands hesitantly upward. As they came into contact with the greatly reduced mounds of flesh, Theresa's eyelids drifted closed. She explored as a sightless person reads braille. She knew the exact pattern of the incisions and found them covered with dressing inside the bra, thus she imagined more than felt their outline. The stitches ran beneath the curves of both breasts, contouring them like the arcs of an underwire bra. That incision was bisected on each breast by another leading straight upward to encircle the nipple.

She felt no pain, for she was still under the influence of the anaesthetic. Instead, she knew only a soaring jubilation. There was so little there! She lightly grazed the upper hemispheres of both breasts, to find them unbelievably reduced in breadth. And from what she could tell, blind this way, it seemed her nipples were going to be as tip-tilted as the end of a water ski. She felt a surge of overwhelming impatience to see the revised, improved shape she'd been given.

I want to see. I want to see.

But beneath her armpits tiny tubes were inserted to drain the pleural cavity and prevent internal bleeding and pneumonia. For now, Theresa had to be content with imagination.

AMY CAME TO VISIT that night, filled with smiles and flip teenage acceptance of the momentous move Theresa had made. She produced a letter bearing familiar handwriting, but teased her sister by holding it beyond reach. "Mmm. . .just a piece of junk mail, I think."

"Gimme!"

"Gimme?" Amy looked disgusted. "Is that the kind of manners you teach your students? *Gimme?"*

"Hand it over, snot. I'm incapacitated and can't indulge in mortal combat until these tubes are removed and the stiches dissolve."

Truthfully, as the day wore on, Theresa's discomfort had been growing, but the letter from Brian made her forget them temporarily.

Dear Theresa,
Less than four weeks and we're out. And guess how we'll be coming home? I bought a van! A class act, for sure. It's a Chevy, kind of the color of your eyes, not brown and not hazel, with smoked windows, white pinstriping and enough room to carry all the guitars, amps and speakers for an entire band. You're gonna love it! I'll take you out for a spin the minute I get there, and maybe you can help me look for an apartment, huh? God, sweets, I can't wait. For any of it—civilian life, school, the new band—and you.

Most of all *you*. (Theresa smiled at the three slashes underlining the last word.) Jeff and I leave here on the morning of the 24th. Should be pulling in there by suppertime. Jeff says to tell your mother he wants pigs in the blanket for supper, whatever that is. And me? I want Theresa-in-the-blankets after supper. Just teasing, darlin'. . . or am I?

Love,
Brian

Theresa refolded the letter, but instead of putting it on her bedside table, tucked it beneath the covers by her hip. She looked up to find Amy sprawled, unladylike, in the visitor's chair.

"Brian bought a van. He and Jeff are going to be driving it home."

"A van!" Amy's eyes lit up like flashing strobes, and she sat up straighter in the chair. "All ri-i-ight."

"And Jeff says to tell mom he wants pigs-in-the-blanket for supper when they get here."

"Boy, I can't wait!"

"*You* can't wait? Every day seems like an eternity to me."

"Yeah." Amy glanced at the sheet beneath which the letter was concealed. "You and Brian, well. . . looks like you two got a thing goin', I mean, since you went up and met him and everything, you two must really be gettin' it on."

"Not exactly. But. . ." Theresa mused with a winsome smile. Beneath the covers she touched the envelope hopefully.

"But you've been writing to each other for five months, and he sent you the roses and called and everything. I guess things are startin' to torque between you two, huh?''

Theresa laughed unexpectedly. It hurt terribly, and she pressed a hand to her rib cage. "Oh, don't do that, Amy. It hurts like heck.''

"Oh, gol...sorry. Didn't mean to blow your seams.''

Theresa laughed again, but this time when she pressed the sheets against herself, she caught Amy's eyes assessing her new shape inquisitively.

"Have you...well, I mean...have you seen yourself yet?'' Amy's eyes were wide, her voice hesitant.

"No, but I've felt.''

"Well...how....'' Amy shrugged, grinned sheepishly. "Oh, you know what I mean.''

"They feel like I'm wearing somebody else's body. Somebody who's shaped like I always wished I could be shaped.''

"They look a lot smaller, even under the blankets.''

Theresa turned the top of the sheet down to her waist. "They are. I'll show you when we're both back home.''

Amy jumped up suddenly, pushed her palms into her rear jeans pockets, flat against her backside. She looked ill at ease, but after taking a turn around the bed, stopped beside her older sister and asked directly, "Have you told him?''

"Brian?''

Amy nodded.

"No, I haven't.''

"Gol, I probably shouldn't have asked.'' Amy colored to a becoming shade of pink.

"It's okay, Amy. Brian and I...really like each other, but I didn't feel our relationship had gone far enough for me to consult him about having the surgery. And I'm scared of facing him again because he doesn't know.''

"Yeah...." Amy's voice trailed away uncertainly. She grew morose, then speculative and glanced at Theresa askance. "You could still tell him. I mean before he comes home.''

"I know. I've been considering it, but I'm kind of dreading it. I...oh, I don't know what to do.''

Amy suddenly brightened, putting on a jack-in-the-box smile and bubbling, ''Well, one things's for sure. As soon as we spring you from this joint, you and I are going shopping for all those sexy, cute, *tiny* size nines you've been dying to shimmy into, okay?''

"Okay. You've got a date. Soon as I can put my arms up over my head to get into them.''

THE FOLLOWING DAY on his rounds, Dr. Schaum breezed around the corner into Theresa's room, the tails of his lab coat flaring out behind his knees. "So how is our miniaturized Theresa today? Have you seen yourself in a mirror yet?''

"No...." Theresa was taken by surprise at his abrupt, swooping entry and his first question.

"No! Well, why not? You haven't gone through all this to lie there wondering what the new Theresa Brubaker looks like. Come on, young lady, we'll change that right now.''

And so Theresa saw her reshaped breasts for the first time, with Dr. Schaum holding a wide mirror against his belly, studying her over the top of it, awaiting her verdict.

The stitches were still red and raw looking, but the shape was delightful, the perky angle of the upturned nipples an utter surprise. Somehow, she was not prepared for the reality of it. She was... *normal.* And in time, when the stitches healed and the scars faded, there would undoubtedly be times when she'd wonder if she'd ever been shaped any differently.

But for now, a wide-eyed Theresa stared at herself in the mirror and beamed, speechless.

Dr. Schaum tipped his head to one side. "Do I take that charming smile to mean you approve?"

"Oh..." was all Theresa breathed while continuing to stare and beam at her reflection. But when she reached to touch, Dr. Schaum warned, "Uh-uh! Don't investigate just yet. Leave that until the tubes and sutures are removed." Only the internal stitches were the dissolving type. The external ones would be removed by Dr. Schaum within a few days.

Theresa returned home on the fourth day, the drainage tubes gone from beneath her arms, but the sutures still in place. Amy washed her sister's hair and waited on her hand and foot with a solicitude that warmed Theresa's heart. Forbidden to even reach above her to get a coffee cup from the kitchen shelf, Theresa found herself often in need of Amy's helping hand, and during the next few days the bond between the sisters grew.

They were given the go-ahead for the long-awaited shopping spree at the end of the second week, when Theresa saw Dr. Schaum for a postop checkup.

That golden day in mid-June was like a fairy tale come true for the woman who surveyed the realm of ladies' fashions with eyes as excited as those of a child who spies the lights of a carnival on the horizon. "T-shirts! T-shirts! T-shirts!" Theresa sang exuberantly. "I feel like I want to wear them for at least one solid year!"

Amy giggled and hauled Theresa to a Shirt Shack and picked out a hot pink item that boasted the words, "Knockers Up!" across the chest. They laughed exuberantly and hung the ugly garment back with its mates and went off to get serious.

Standing before the full-length mirror in the first item she tried on—a darling sleeveless V-neck knit shirt of fresh summer green, held up by ties on each shoulder—Theresa wondered if she'd ever been this happy. The sporty top was nothing extraordinary, not expensive, not even sexy really, only feminine, tiny, attractive—and utterly flattering. It was the kind of garment she'd never been able to even consider before. Theresa couldn't resist preening just a little. "Oh, Amy, look!"

Amy did, standing back, smiling at her sister's happy expression in the mirror. Suddenly Amy's shoulders straightened as she made a remarkable discovery. "Hey, Theresa, you look taller!"

"I do?" Theresa turned to the left, appraised herself. "You know, that was something Diane DeFreize told me people would say afterward. And you're the second one who has." Theresa realized it was partly because her posture was straighter since her self-image had improved so heartily. Also, the absence of bulk up front carried the eyes upward rather than horizontally, creating the illusion of added height. She stood square to the mirror again, gave her reflection a self-satisfied look of approval and seconded, "Yes, I do."

"Wait'll Brian sees you in that."

Theresa's eyes widened and glittered at the thought. She ran a hand over her bustline, wondering what he'd say. She still hadn't told him.

"Do you think he'll like it?"

"You're a knockout in green."

"You can't see my strap marks, can you?" Th
wide, ugly indentations in Theresa's shoulders hadn
been erased yet, but Dr. Schaum said they would di:
appear in time. The shoulder ties of the top wer
fairly narrow, but wide enough to conceal the depres
sions in her skin.

"No, the ties cover them up. I think you shoul
make it your first purchase. *And* be wearing it whe
Brian gets here."

The thought was so dizzying, Theresa pressed
hand to her tummy. *When Brian gets here. Only or
more week.*

"I'll take it. And next I want to look for a dress—
no, eight dresses! The last time I bought one tha
didn't need alteration was when I was younger tha
you are now. Dr. Schaum says I should be a perfe
size nine."

And she was. A swirly-skirted summer sundress (
pink was followed by another of navy, red-and-whi
flowers, then by a classic off-white sheath wit
jewelry neckline and belt of burnished brown leathe
They bought tube tops and *V*-neck T-shirts (no cre
necks for Theresa Brubaker this trip!) and even on
blouse that tied just beneath the bustline and left h
midriff bare. Jewelry, something Theresa had nev
wanted to hang around her neck before for fear
would draw attention to her breast size, was as e:
citing to buy as her first pair of panty hose had bee
years ago. She chose a delicate gold chain with a tir
puffed heart, and it looked delectable, even again
the red freckles on her chest. But somehow eve
those freckles seemed less brash to Theresa. H
choice of garment colors was no longer limited b

available size, thus she could select hues that minimized her redness.

When the day ended, Theresa sat in her room among mountains of crackling sacks and marvelous clothes. She felt like a bride with a new trousseau. Holding up her favorite—the green shoulder-tie top—she fitted it against her front, danced a swirling pattern across the floor, then closed her eyes and breathed deeply.

Hurry, Brian, hurry. I'm ready for you at last.

Chapter Thirteen

IT WAS A STUNNING JUNE DAY, with the temperature
in the low eighties and Minnesota's faultless sky the
perfect, clear blue of the delphiniums that bloomed
in gardens along Johnnycake Lane. Across the street
a group of teenagers were waxing a four-year-old
Trans Am. Next door, Ruth Reed was standing beside her garden, checking to see if there were blos-
soms on her green beans yet. Two houses down, the
neighborhood four- and five-year-olds were churning
their chubby legs on the pedals of low-slung plastic
motorcycles, making engine noises with their lips. Up
and down the street the smells of cooking supper
drifted out to mingle with that of fresh-cut grass as
men just home from work tried to get a start on the
mowing before mealtime. In the Brubakers' front
yard, an oscillating sprinkler swayed and sprayed
twinkling in the sun like the sequined ostrich fan of a
Busby Berkeley girl.

It was a scene of everyday Americana, a slice of ordinary life, on an ordinary street, at the end of an ordinary workday.

But in the Brubaker house, excitement pulsated.
Cabbage rolls stuffed with hamburger-rice filling
were cooking in a roaster. The bathroom fixtures
gleamed and fresh towels hung on the racks. In the
freshly cleaned living room a bouquet of garden
flowers sat on the piano—marigolds, cosmos, zinnias

and snapdragons. The kitchen table was set for six, and centered upon it waited a slightly lopsided two-layer cake, rather ineptly decorated with some quite flat-looking pink frosting sweetpeas and the words, "Welcome home, Jeff and Brian." Amy adjusted the cake plate one more time and turned it just a little in an effort to make it appear more balanced than it was, then stood back, shrugged and muttered, "Oh, horse poop. It's good enough."

"Amy, watch your mouth!" warned Margaret, then added, "There's not a thing wrong with that cake, so I want you to stop fussing about it."

Outside, Willard had a hedge trimmer in his hands as he moved along the precision-trimmed alpine current hedge, taking a nip here, a nip there, though not a leaf was out of place. Periodically, he shaded his eyes and scanned the street to the west, gazing into the spray of diamond droplets that lifted and fell, lifted and fell across the emerald carpet of lawn—his pride and joy. The kitchen windows were cranked open above his head, and he checked his wrist, then called inside, "What time is it, Margaret? I think my watch stopped."

"It's five forty-five, and there's not a thing wrong with your watch, Willard. It was working seven minutes ago when you asked."

In her bedroom at the end of the hall, Theresa put the final touches on the makeup that by now she was adept at applying. She buckled a pair of flat, strappy white sandals onto her feet, inspecting the coral polish on her toenails—they'd never been painted before this summer. Next, she slipped into a brand-new pair of sleek white jeans, snapped and zipped them up, ran a smoothing palm down her thighs, and watched herself in the mirror as she worked the kelly green top over her head, covering her white bra. She adjusted the knot upon her left shoulder, stood back and assessed her reflection. *You don't look like a Christmas tree, Theresa, but you look like*—she searched her mind for a simile Brian had used—*like a poppy blossom*. She smiled in satisfaction and flicked the lifter through her freshly cut and styled hair, fluffing it around her temples and forehead until it suited perfectly. Around her neck she fastened the new chain with the tiny puffed heart. At her wrist went a simple gold bangle bracelet. She inserted tiny gold studs in her ears and was reaching for the perfume when she heard her father's voice calling through the screened windows at the other end of the house.

"I think it's them. It's a van, but I can't tell what color it is."

Theresa pressed a hand to her heart. The hand wasn't yet used to feeling the diminished contour it encountered in making this gesture. Her wide eyes raked down her torso in the mirror, then back up. *What will he think?*

"Yup, it's them!" she heard in her father's voice before Amy bellowed, "Theresa, come on, they're here!"

A nerve jittered in her stomach, and the buildup of anticipation that had been expanding as each day passed, thickened the thud of her heart and made her knees quake. She turned and ran through the house and slammed out the back door, then waited behind the others as the cinnamon-colored Chevy van purred up the street, with Jeff's arm and head dangling out the window as he waved and hollered hello. But Theresa's eyes were drawn to the opposite side of the van as she tried to make out the face of the driver. But the windshield caught and reflected the bowl of blue sky, and she saw only it and the branches of the elm trees flashing across the glass as the vehicle turned and eased up the drive, then stopped.

Jeff's door flew open, and he scooped up the first body he encountered—Amy—lifting her off her feet and swirling her around before doing likewise with Margaret, who whooped and demanded to be set on her feet, but meant not a word of it. Willard got a rough hug, and Theresa was next. She found herself swept up from the ground before she could issue the warning to her brother not to suspend her. But the slight twinge of discomfort where her stitches had been was worth it.

Yet while all this happened, Theresa was primarily conscious of Brian slipping from the driver's seat, removing a pair of sunglasses, stretching with his elbows in the air and rounding the front of the van to watch the greetings, then be included in them himself. Theresa hung back, observing the faded blue jeans slung low on his lean hips, buckling at the knees from a long day of driving; the loose, off-white gauze shirt with three buttons open; the naked V of skin at his throat; his dark, military-cut hair and eyes the color of summer grasses that smiled while Amy gave him a smack on the cheek, Margaret a motherly hug and Willard a handshake and affectionate pat on the shoulder.

Then there was nobody left but Theresa.

Her heart pounded in her chest, and she felt as if her feet were not on the backtop driveway but levitated an inch above it. The sensuous shock of recognition sent the color sweeping to her face, but she didn't care. He was here. He was as good to look at as she remembered. And his presence made her feel impatient, and nervous, and exhilarated.

They faced each other with six feet of space between them.

"Hello," he greeted simply, and it might have
been a verse from the great love poets of decades ago.

"Hello." Her voice was soft and uncertain and
quavery.

They were the only two who hadn't hugged or
touched. Her tremulous lips were softly opened. The
corners of his mouth lifted in a slow crescent of a
smile. He reached his hands out to her, calluses up,
and as she extended her fingertips and rested them
upon his palms, she watched the summer-green eyes
that last December had so assiduously avoided dropping to her breasts. Those eyes dropped now, directly, unerringly, down to the freckled throat and the
V-neck of her new knit shirt, and then lower, to the
two gentle rises within. Brian's mouth went slightly
lax as he stared in undisguised amazement.

His puzzled gaze darted back up to her eyes, while
Theresa felt her face suffuse with brighter color.

"How are you?" she managed, the question
sounding foolishly mundane, even in her own ears.

"Fine." He released her fingers and stepped back,
replacing the sunglasses on his nose while she felt him
studying her from behind the dark lenses. "And
you?"

They were conversing like robots, both extremely
self-conscious all of a sudden, both trying in vain to
regain calm footing.

"Same as ever." They were scarcely out of Theresa's mouth before she regretted her choice of words.
She wasn't the same at all. "How was your trip?"

"Good, but tiring. We drove straight through."

The others had preceded them up the back steps,
and Theresa and Brian trailed along. Though he

walked just behind her shoulder, she felt his eyes burning into her, questioning, wondering. But she couldn't tell his true reaction yet. Was he pleased? Shocked for sure, and taken aback, but beyond that, Theresa could only guess.

Inside, the Brubaker house was as noisy as ever. Jeff—exultant, roaring, fun loving—stood in the middle of the kitchen with his arms extended wide and gave a jungle call like Tarzan, while from somewhere at the far end of the house The Stray Cats sang rock, and at the near end The Gatlins crooned in three-part harmony. Margaret tended something on the stove, and Jeff surrounded her from behind with both arms, his chin digging into her shoulder, making her wriggle and giggle. "Dammit, ma, but that smells rank! Must be my pigs-in-the-blanket."

"Listen to that boy, calling my cabbage rolls rank." She lifted a lid off a steaming roaster, and Jeff snitched a pinch of something from inside. "Didn't that Air Force teach you any manners?" his mother teased happily. "Wash your hands before you come snitching."

Jeff grinned over his shoulder at Brian. "I thought we were done with C.O.'s when we got our walking papers, but it looks like I was wrong." He patted his mother's bottom. "But this one's all bluff, I think."

Margaret whirled and whacked at his hand with a spoon, but missed. "Oh, get away with you and your teasing, you brat. You're not too old for me to take the yardstick to." But Jeff had leaped safely out of reach. He spied the cake, and gave an undulating whistle of appreciation, like that of a construction worker eyeing a passing woman in high heels. "Wow, would y' look at this, Brian. Somebody's been busy."

"Amy," put in Willard proudly.

Amy beamed, her braces flashing. "The dumb thing is listing to the starboard," Amy despaired, but Jeff wrapped an arm around her shoulders, squeezed and declared, "Well, it won't list for long cause it won't last for long. I'd say about twenty minutes at the outside." Then a thought seemed to occur to him. "Is it chocolate?"

"What else?"

"Then I'd say less than twenty minutes. Shh! Don't tell ma." He picked up a knife from one of the place settings and whacked into the high side of the cake, took a slice out and lifted it to his mouth before anybody could stop him.

Everyone in the room was laughing as Margaret swooped toward the table with the steaming roaster clutched in a pair of pot holders. "Jeffrey Brubaker," she scolded, "put that cake down this minute or you'll ruin your appetite! And for heaven's sake, everybody sit down before that child forces me to get the yardstick out after all!"

Brian took it all in with a sense of homecoming almost as familial as if he were, indeed, part of the Brubaker clan. And it was easy to see Jeff was their mood-setter, the one who stirred them all and generated both gaiety and teasing. It was so easy being with them. Brian felt like a cog slipping into the notches of a gear. Until he sat across from Theresa and was forced to consider the change in her.

"Take your old place," Willard invited Brian, pulling a chair out while they all shuffled and scraped and settled down for the meal. During the next half hour while they gobbled cabbage rolls and crusty buns and whipped potatoes oozing with parsley butter, then during the hour following while they ate cake and leisurely sipped glasses of iced tea and caught up with news of each other, Brian covertly studied Theresa's breasts as often as he could.

Once she looked up unexpectedly while passing him the sugar bowl and caught his gaze on her green shirtfront. Their eyes met, then abruptly shifted apart.

How? Brian wondered. *And when? And why didn't she tell me? Did Jeff know? And if so, why didn't he warn me?*

The kitchen was hot, and Margaret suggested they all take glasses of iced tea and sit on the small concrete patio between the house and the garage. Immediately they all got to their feet and did a cursory scraping of plates but left the stacked dishes on the cupboard, then filed out to the side of the house where webbed lawn chairs waited.

While they relaxed and visited, Theresa was ever aware of Brian's perusal. He had slipped his sunglasses on again, even though the patio was in full shade now as the sun dipped behind the peak of the roof. But occasionally, as he lifted his sweating glass and drank, she felt his gaze riveted on her chest. But when she looked up and smiled at him, she could not be sure, for she saw only the suggestion of dark eyes behind the tinted aviator lenses, and though his lips returned the smile, she sensed it did not reach those inscrutable eyes.

"Oh yeah!" Amy suddenly remembered. "Glue Eyes called and said you should be sure to call her as soon as you got home."

Jeff pointed an accusatory finger at his playful sibling. "Listen, brat, if you don't can it with that Glue Eyes business, I'll have ma take the yardstick to *you.*"

"Aw, Jeff, you know I don't mean it. Not anymore. She's really okay, I guess. I got to like her a lot last Christmas. But I've called her Glue Eyes for so long it kinda falls outa me, ya know?"

"Well, someday it's gonna fall out when you're standing right beside her, then what will you do?"

"Apologize and explain and tell her that when I was learning to wear makeup I tried to put it on exactly like she does."

Jeff gave her a mock punch on the chin, then bounded into the house to make the phone call, and returned a few minutes later, announcing, "I'm going to run over and pick up Patricia and bring her back here. Anybody want to ride along with me?"

Theresa was torn, recalling the ardent reunion embraces she and Brian had witnessed last time, yet not wanting to stay behind if Brian said yes. He seemed to be waiting for her to answer, so she had to make a choice.

"I'll help Amy and mother with the dishes while you're gone," she decided.

"I'll drive you, Jeff," Brian offered, stretching to his feet, adjusting his glasses and turning to follow Jeff to the van. Theresa watched him walk away, studying the back of his too-short hair, the places where the gauze shirt stuck to his back in a tic-tac-toe design from the webs of the lawn chair, his hands moving to his hips to give an unconscious tug at the waistband of his jeans. His back pockets had worn white patches where he carried his billfold, and his backside was so streamlined the sight of it created a hollow longing in the pit of Theresa's stomach.

He's upset. I should have told him.

No, you had no obligation to confide in him. It was your choice.

In the van, the two men rode down the street where evening shadows stretched long tendrils across green lawns. Brian drove deliberately slow. He pondered, wondering how to introduce the subject, and finally attacked it head on.

"Okay, Brubaker, why didn't you tell me?"

Jeff gave a crooked smile. "She looks great, huh?"

"Damn right she looks great, but my eyeballs nearly dropped onto the goddamn driveway when I saw her standing there with her . . . without her . . . aw hell, *they're gone.*"

"Yup," Jeff slouched low in the seat and grinned out the windshield. "I always knew there lurked a proud beauty inside my Treat."

"Quit beatin' around the bush, Brubaker. You knew, didn't you?"

"Yeah, I knew."

"Did she write and tell you and ask you not to tell me?"

"No, Amy did. Amy thought I should know, so I could warn you if I thought that was best."

"Well, why the hell didn't you?"

"Because I didn't think it was any of my business. Your relationship with Theresa's got nothing to do with me, beyond the fact that I'm lucky enough to be her brother. If she'd wanted you to know beforehand, she'd have told you herself. I figured, what business was it of mine to go stickin' my two cents worth in?"

"But. . . ." Brian gripped the steering wheel. "But. . . *how?*"

"Breast-reduction surgery."

Brian's shaded brown lenses flashed toward Jeff. "Breast re—" He sounded flabbergasted. "I never heard of such a thing."

"To tell you the truth, neither had I, but Amy told me all about it in her letter. She had it done three weeks ago, right after school got out for summer vacation. Listen, man—" Jeff turned to watch his friend guide the van onto a broader double-lane avenue "—she's... I don't want to see her get hurt, okay?"

"Hurt?" Brian turned sharply toward Jeff, then back to his driving. "You think I'd hurt her?"

"Well, I don't know. You're kind of... well, you act kind of pissed off or something. I don't know and I'm not asking what went on between you and Theresa, but go easy on her, huh? If you're thinking she should have confided in you for some reason, just understand that she's a pretty timid creature. It'd be pretty damn hard for a girl like Theresa to even have the surgery, much less write and discuss it with a man—I don't care *how* close you'd been."

"All right, I'll remember that. And I'll cool it around her. I guess I backed off pretty suddenlike when we said hello, but Christ, it was a shock."

"Yeah, I imagine it was." They rode in silence for some minutes, then just as they approached Patricia's house, Jeff turned to Brian and asked in a concerned voice, "Could I ask just one question, Bry?"

"Yeah, shoot."

"Just exactly what *do* you think of Theresa?"

Brian pulled the van up at the curb before Patricia's house, killed the engine, removed his sunglasses and half turned toward Jeff, draping his left elbow over the steering wheel. "I love her," he answered point-blank.

Jeff let his smile seep up the muscles of his face, made a fist and socked the air. "Hot damn!" he exclaimed, then opened his door and jumped down to cross the yard on the run.

Brian watched Jeff and Patricia meet in the center of the open stretch of lawn. Jeff flung his arms around the young woman, who lifted her arms around his shoulders, and they kissed, pressed tightly against each other. It was just the way he'd been planning to greet Theresa.

Patricia's parents stepped out the front door and called, "Hi, Jeff. Welcome home. Are you gonna stay this time?"

"Damn right, I am. And I'm gonna steal your daughter!"

"Somehow, I don't think she minds one bit," Mrs. Gluek called back.

Patricia clambered up into the high van, scooted over and gave Brian a peck on the cheek. "Hiya, bud. Long time, no see."

Jeff was right behind Patricia. "Come here, woman, and put your little butt where it belongs, right on my lap." There were only two bucket seats up front. Jeff pulled Patricia down on his lap, and she laughed happily, flung her arms around his neck and kissed him while the van started rolling.

THE DISHES WERE DONE when the van lumbered up the street a second time, pulled into the driveway and began disgorging its passengers. They meandered to the patio, where Margaret, Willard and Amy joined them. When Theresa came out of the kitchen onto the back step, she found Brian standing below her, waiting.

Her heart did a flip-flop, and everything inside her went warm and springing. He reached up a hand to take hers, and she felt a wash of relief that he was touching her at last.

"Come here, I want to talk to you." He pulled her

down the steps to his side, and asked softly, "Do you think your folks would mind if we went for a walk?"

"Not at all."

"Tell them, then. I want to be alone with you, even if it's in the middle of a city street where people are sitting on their doorsteps watching us pass by."

Her heart swelled with joy, and she stepped to the edge of the patio, made their excuses and returned to Brian. He captured her hand, and their joined knuckles brushed between their hips as they ambled down the driveway and onto the blacktop street that was still warm beneath Theresa's sandals after the heat of the summer day. The shadows were falling as evening settled in. The sun rested on the rim of the horizon like a golden, liquid ball. They passed between yards where other sprinklers played the hushed vespers of water droplets spraying greenery.

"Is there someplace we can go?" he asked.

"There's a park about two blocks away."

"Good."

Nothing more was said as they sauntered hand in hand down the center of the street.

"Hi, Theresa," called a woman who was sitting on her front steps.

"Hi, Mrs. Anderson." Theresa raised a hand in greeting, then explained quietly, "I used to babysit for the Andersons when I was Amy's age."

Brian made no reply, lifting a hand in silent greeting, too, then continuing on at Theresa's side, stealing glances at her breasts when she dropped her chin and watched the toes of her white sandals. He wondered what secrets her clothing concealed, what she'd been through, if she hurt, if she was healed. But mostly, he wondered why she hadn't trusted him enough to tell him.

The eastern sky turned a rich periwinkle blue as the sun slipped and plunged into oblivion, leaving the western horizon a blaze of orange that faded to yellow, then violet as they approached a small neighborhood park where a silent baseball diamond was surrounded by a grove of trees. Deserted playground equipment hovered in the stillness of dusk. Great, aged oaks were scattered across the expanse of open recreation area, creating blots of darker shadows beneath their widespread arms, while picnic tables made smaller dots between the trees. Brian led the way from the street onto a crunchy gravel footpath, taking Theresa beneath the shadow of an oak before he finally stopped, squeezed her fingers almost painfully, then turned her to face him.

She looked up into the twin black dots of his sunglasses. "You've still got your glasses on."

Without a word he removed them, and slipped a bow inside the waist of his blue jeans so the glasses hung on his right hip.

"I guess you're a little upset with me, aren't you?" she ventured in a perilously shaky voice.

"Yes, I am," he admitted, "but could we deal with that later?" His long fingers closed over both of her shoulders, drawing her close to his wide-spraddled feet, close to the length of his faded Levi's, close to the naked *V* of skin above his shirt where dark hair sprigged. Her heart was hammering under her newly reshaped breasts. Her body moved willingly against his, then their arms sought to hold, to reaffirm, to answer the question, Is this person all that I remembered?

Brian's lips opened slightly as he lowered them to hers, which waited with warm, breathless expectancy. Tears bit the back of Theresa's eyes, and she was swept with a feeling of relief so overwhelming he body seemed to wilt as the apprehension eased away into the twilight. Then the waiting ended. They clung with the newly revived reassurance that what they'd found in each other twice before was still as appealing and had been magnified by their time apart.

His mouth was June-warm. Indeed, he even seemed to taste of summer, of all things she loved— flowers, music, lazy sprinklers and somewhere, th remembered scent of something he put on his hair But he had ridden nine hours in a warm van, had crossed miles of rolling prairie in the wrinkled cloth ing he wore now, and from that clothing emanated scent she had never quite known before—the scent of Brian Scanlon, male, inviting, a little dusty, a littl soiled, but all man.

The kiss was as lusty as some of the rock song she'd heard him sing, a swift succession of strokes tugs and head movements that seemed to elicit th threads of feelings from the very tips of her toes and send them sizzling up her body. She poured her feel ings into the kiss, meeting his mouth with an equa ardor. With his feet widespread, his midsection wa flush against hers, and it felt good, hard, sexy. The resa was vaguely aware of a difference in the feelin of her breasts pressed against his chest—the small ness, the new tightness, the ability to be closer as hi forearm slipped down across her spine and reeled he even more securely against his hips.

"Theresa...." His lips were at her ear, kissing he temple while his beautiful voice lost its mild note an took on a foreign huskiness. "I had to do that first. just had to."

"First?"

He released a rather shaky breath and backed away from her, searching her upturned face in the deep shadow of the oaks. "It occurs to me we've got some talking to do, wouldn't you say?"

"Yes." She dropped her eyes, blushing already.

"Come on." Capturing her hand, he led her to the nearby area where the swings hung as still as the silence over the park that in daytime rang with children's voices. A steel slide angled down, casting its shadow on the grass as the moon slipped up into the eastern sky and the first stars came out. Brian tugged her along to the side of a large steel merry-go-round and sat down, pulling her to sit beside him, then dropping her hand.

"So..." he began, following the word with a sigh, then leaned his elbows on his thighs. "There've been some changes."

"Yes."

He pondered silently, made an impatient, breathy sound, then burst out, "God, I don't know where to begin, what to say."

"Neither do I."

"Theresa, why didn't you tell me?"

She shrugged very childishly for a twenty-six-year-old woman. "I was afraid to. And...and I didn't know what...well, I mean, we're not...."

"What you're trying to say is that you didn't know my intentions, is that it?"

"Yes, I guess so."

"After what we shared in Fargo, and our letters, you doubted my intentions?"

"No, not *doubted*. I just didn't think we'd had enough time together to get our relationship on its feet." *I wasn't even sure you would come....*

"With me, Theresa, it's not the *amount* of time
but the *quality* of it, and our weekend in Fargo wa:
quality for me. I thought it was for you, too."

"It was, but...but, Brian, we hadn't done much
more than just...well, you know what I'm saying
What we did together didn't really mean a commit
ment or...." Her voice trailed away. This was th•
most difficult conversation she'd ever had.

Brian suddenly sprang to his feet, walked thre•
paces away from the merry-go-around and swung t•
face her. "Couldn't you trust me enough to tell me
Theresa?" he accused.

"I wanted to, but I was scared."

"Of what?"

"I don't know."

"Maybe you thought I was some lecher who wa
only after you because you had big knockers, is tha
it? Did you think if you told me you didn't have then
anymore, I'd brush you off? Is that what you
thought?"

She was horrified. It had never entered her min•
that he might consider such a thing. Tears blurred he
eyes. "No, Brian, I never thought that...never!"

"Then why the hell couldn't you have trusted m•
enough to confide in me and tell me what you wer•
planning, give me time to get accustomed to it befor•
I walked into your yard totally unsuspecting? Christ
do you know what a shock it was?"

"I knew you'd be surprised, but I thought you'd b•
pleasantly surprised."

"I am, I was...." He threw his hands into the ai•
exasperatedly and whirled, presenting his rigid back
"But, God, Theresa, do you know what I've been
thinking about for six months? Do you know how
many nights I've lain awake thinking about your..

problem and figuring out ways to finesse you into losing your inhibitions, telling myself I had to be the world's most patient lover when I took you to bed for the first time, so I didn't put some irreversible phobia into you or make your hangup worse than it already was?" Again he spun on her. "We may not have had time to share much, but what we did share was a pretty damn intimate baring of souls, and I think it gave me the right to be in on your decision with you, to share it. But you didn't even give me the chance."

"Now just a minute!" She leaped to her feet and faced him in the flood of moonlight that was growing brighter by the minute. "You've got no claim on me, no right to—"

"The hell I don't!"

"The hell you do!" Theresa had never fought or sworn in her life and was surprised at herself.

"The hell I don't! I love you, dammit!" he shouted.

"Well, that's some way to tell me, shouting at the top of your lungs! How was I supposed to know?"

"I signed all my letters that way, didn't I?"

"Well yes, but that's just a...a formal closing on a letter."

"Is that all you took it for?"

"No!"

"Well, if you knew I loved you, why couldn't you trust me? Had you ever stopped to think it might have been something I'd have welcomed sharing? Something that might have brought us even closer? Something I would have felt *honored* to share? But you didn't give me a chance, going ahead without a word like you did."

"I resent your attitude, Brian. It's...it's possessive and uninformed."

"Uninformed?" He stood now belligerently, his hands on his hips. "Whose fault is that, mine or yours? If you'd bothered to *inform* me, I wouldn't be so damn mad right now."

"I discussed it with people who didn't lose their tempers, like you're doing. A counselor at school, a woman who'd had the surgery before and a cosmetic surgeon who eventually performed the operation. I got the emotional support I needed from them."

He felt shut out and hurt. During the past six months he'd felt a growing affinity with Theresa. He'd felt they were slowly becoming intimates, and he'd returned here thinking she was ready to pursue not only an emotional relationship but a physical one as well. He found himself intimidated by the changes in her body more than he'd been intimidated by her abundant breasts—they'd been only flesh, after all, and that he could approach and touch the same as he had other women's. The psychological preparation he'd made for approaching her again had been made at no little cost in both sleep and worry. Now that he found it all for naught, he felt cheated. Now that he knew she'd turned to others and implied they'd been more help than he could have been, he felt misunderstood. And now that he wasn't sure how long he'd have to wait to pursue her sexually, he felt angry— dammit, he'd wanted to make love to her, and soon!

"Brian," she said softly, sadly, "I didn't mean that the way it sounded. It wasn't that I didn't think you'd support my decision. But it seemed... presumptuous of me to involve you in something so personal without any commitments made between us." She touched his arm, but he remained stiff and scowling, so she returned to sit on the merry-go-round.

He was very upset. And hurt. And wondering if he had the right to be. He swung back to the merry-go-round, flopped down several feet away from her and fell back, draping his shoulders and outflung arms over the mound-shaped steel heart of the vehicle. As he flopped backward he gave a single nudge with his foot, setting the steel framework into motion. He lay brooding, looking up at the stars that circled slowly above him, getting a grip on his feelings.

Theresa sat with her shoulders slumped despondently, feeling the slight rumbling vibrations rising up through the tubular steel bars.

Oh, misery! She had thought this night of Brian's homecoming would see them close, loving, reveling in being together once again. She felt drained and depleted and unsure of how to deal with his anger. Perhaps he had a right to it; perhaps he didn't. She was no psychologist. She should have discussed it with Catherine McDonald and sought her advice regarding whether or not to tell Brian her intentions.

The merry-go-round was set off kilter, so centrifugal force kept it moving in what seemed a perpetual, lazy twirl. The tears gathered in Theresa's throat and then in her eyes. She brushed them away with the back of her wrist, turning away so he couldn't tell what she was doing.

But somehow he sensed it. A hand closed around her bare elbow and pulled her back and to one side. "Hey. . . ." he cajoled softly. "Come here."

She draped backward across the domed center of the merry-go-round. The steel was icy beneath her bare arms as she angled toward him until only their shoulders touched, and the backs of their heads were pressed against the hard, hard metal as they studied the stars. Around and around. Dots of light on the blue-black sky twinkled like reflections of a revolving mirrored ball above a ballroom floor. Crickets had set up their endless chirping, and the night was growing damp, but it felt good against Theresa's hot face. The incandescent moon lit their draped bodies, the bars of the swing set and the crowns of the oak trees that passed slowly as Brian's foot kept nudging the beaten earth.

"I'm sorry, Theresa. I shouldn't have shouted."

"I am too." She sobbed once, and in an instant, he'd pulled her close.

"Listen, sweets, could I have a couple days to get used to it? Hell, I don't know whether I'm allowed to look at them or not. I do, and I feel guilty. I don't, and I feel guiltier. And your family, all avoiding the issue as if you'd never had any other shape. Anyway, I guess I built my hopes up too high, thinking about tonight and what it was going to be like, seeing you again."

"Me too. I certainly didn't want us to fight this way."

"Then let's not, not anymore. Let's go back and see if everybody else is as tired as I am. I've been awake since two A.M. I was too excited to sleep."

"You too?" She offered a shaky smile.

He smiled down at her in return, brushed a knuckle over the end of her nose and kissed her lightly.

He'd meant to give her only that single light kiss, but in the end, he couldn't let her go with just that. Slowly, deliberately, he returned his mouth to hers, dipping his tongue into the secret warmth of her lips which opened in welcome. His body spurted to life, and his shoulders quivered as he pressed his elbows to the metal surface on either side of her head. God, the things he wanted to do to her, to feel with her, to have her do to him. How long would he have to wait? The kiss lingered and lengthened, growing more dizzying than the slow circling of their perch. The way Theresa lay, sprawled backward over the curved metal, the outline of her breasts was lined by moonlight as they jutted forward. It was as sexy a pose as he'd ever seen her in, and he knew it would take no more than a quick shift of his palm, and he'd feel the relief of touching her intimately. He needn't touch her breast about which he was so unsure—her stomach looked hollow and inviting, and her white slacks were very taut and alluring. He thought about running his hand down her ribs, exploring the warm inviting length of her zipper, and the sheltered spot between her legs as he'd done once before. But one thing might lead to another, and he had no idea if she was allowed to move, twist, thrust, if she had stitches, and where, and how many. . . .

And once he started something, he had no intentions of drawing back.

In the end, Brian pacified himself with the kiss alone. When it ended, he regretfully lurched to his feet, dragging Theresa with him, crossing the shadowy park toward the house where they could mingle with people and wouldn't have to confront the remaining issue. . .at least for a while.

Chapter Fourteen

THE OTHERS HAD GONE INSIDE where they were visit
ing and having second pieces of cake when Brian and
Theresa walked up the driveway. The kitchen light
slanted out across the darkened yard and back step in
oblique slashes of creamy brightness. Mosquitoe
hummed and buzzed against the back screen door
and a June bug threw its crusty shell at the light time
and again. Frogs and crickets competed for firs
chair in the nighttime orchestra. The moon was a
pristine ball of white.

From inside came the voice of the group Theresa
and Brian could see as they walked up the driveway
They were clustered around the kitchen table, bu
outside it was peaceful and private. Just short of the
back step, Brian stopped Theresa with a hand on he
arm.

"Listen, there were a lot of things I wanted to tall
about tonight but...." The thought remained un
finished.

"I know." Theresa recalled the many subjects she
had stored up and was eager to share with him.

"And just because I didn't get into any of them
doesn't mean I'm still mad, okay?"

She was studying the middle button on his shirt
which faced her and the moon. By its light the gauze
appeared brilliant white while her own face was cas
in shadow. He touched her beneath the chin with a

single finger, forcing her to tilt her head up. "Okay?" he asked softly.

"Okay."

"And I probably won't see you for a while after tonight, because Jeff and I have a lot of running to do. I have to find an apartment and buy some furniture, and we want to start working on getting a band together right away. We have to renew our union cards and try to find a decent agent and audition the new drummer and bass guitarist and maybe a keyboard man, too. Anyway, I'm going to be jumping for a while. I just wanted you to know."

"Thanks for telling me." But her heart felt heavy with disappointment. Now that he was back, she wanted to be with him as much as possible. In his letters he'd suggested she could come along with him and help pick out furniture, but now he was eliminating her from that excursion. She could understand that he had a lot of mundane arrangements to make, just to get settled into an apartment, and that she'd only be in the way when they were auditioning new players, but somehow she'd thought they'd find time each day to see each other. But she smiled and hid the fact that she was crushed by his advance warning. Was this how fellows turned girls down gently. *No, she reprimanded herself, you're being unfair to Brian. He's not like that. He's honest and honorable. That's why he's warning you in the first place.*

The finger beneath her chin curled, and he brushed her jaw with his knuckles. "I'll call as soon as I've got my feet planted."

"Fine." She began turning toward the back step, but his hand detained her a second time.

"Wait a minute. You're not getting away without one more kiss."

She was swung around and encircled in warm, hard arms and pulled against his moonlit gauze shirt. While his lips closed over hers, the picture of the naked V of skin at his neck came into Theresa's mind, and she suddenly wanted to touch it. Hesitantly, she slipped her hand to find it, resting her palm on the sleek hair and warm flesh, then sliding it upward to rest at the side of his neck while her thumb touched the hollow of his throat. The thudding of his pulse there surprised her. Lightly, lightly, she stroked the warm, pliant depression. He made a soft, throaty sound, and his mouth moved over hers more hungrily. He clasped the back of her head and swept the interior of her mouth with lusty, intimate strokes of his tongue that sent liquid fire racing across her skin.

Some queer surge of latent feminine knowledge pulsed through Theresa. In her entire life, she'd never actively provoked a sexual response from a man. Instead, she'd always been too busy fighting off the bombardment of unwanted physical advances her partners seemed always too eager to display. Now, for the first time, *she* touched—a hesitant touch at best. But the response it kindled in Brian was at once surprising and telling. All she had done was stroke the hollow of his throat with her thumb, yet he reacted as if she'd done far more. The tenor of his kiss changed with a swift, swirling suddenness, and became totally sexual, not the insipid good-night gesture that it had begun to be.

It came as a surprise to think she, Theresa Brubaker, elementary music teacher, freckled redhead, inexperienced paramour, could generate such an immediate and passionate response by only the briefest of encouragements. Especially when she considered that he was a guitar man, a performer who had, admittedly, enjoyed all the adulation that went with his career. He must have known a great many very experienced women, far more experienced than her. Yet, he thrilled to her very inexperienced touch, and this in turn thrilled Theresa.

Realizing the power she possessed to stimulate this man, she suddenly grew impatient to test it further.

But she hadn't the chance, for as quickly as his ardor grew, he controlled it, lifting his head to suck in a great gulp of damp night air and push her gently away. "Lord, woman, do you know how good you are at that?"

"Me?" she asked, surprised.

"You."

"I'm not good at that at all. I've barely had any practice."

"Well, we'll remedy that when the time is right. But if practice makes perfect, I think you'll end up being more than I can handle."

She smiled and in the dark felt herself flush with pleasure at his words. "Hasn't anybody ever told you it's not nice to start things like that when you don't intend to finish them?" came Brian's husky teasing.

"I didn't start it. You did. I was heading into the house when you stopped me. But if you're done now, let's go in." Smiling, she turned toward the step again.

"Not so fast." Once more she was brought up short. "I can't go in just now."

"You can't?" She turned back to face him.

"Uh-uh. I'll need a couple of minutes."

"Oh!" Suddenly she understood and whirled around, presenting her shoulder blades. As she pressed her palms to embarrassed cheeks, he chuckled softly behind her shoulder, audaciously kissed the side of her neck and captured her hand. "Come on, let's go for a little walk through the backyard. That should cool me down. You can talk about school, and I'll talk about the Air Force. Those are two nice, safe, deflating subjects."

Brian treated sexuality with such frankness. Theresa wondered if she'd ever be as open about it as he was. Her body felt flushed with awareness, equally as charged as his. Thank heavens it didn't show on women!

They entered the kitchen five minutes later and pulled up chairs to join the others around the table, while Margaret sliced cake for them, and the conversation continued. When ten-thirty arrived, Jeff pushed his chair back, lifted his elbows toward the ceiling and gave a broad, shivering stretch while twisting at the waist.

"Well, I guess it's time I get Patricia home."

"Want to take the van?"

"Thanks, I'd love to."

Brian tossed Jeff the keys. "We'd better unload our suitcases first, cause I'm ready for the sack. I'll need my stuff."

While the unloading was being done, Theresa escaped to the lower level of the house to put out clean sheets and blankets for Brian's bed. She experienced a feeling of déjà vu, recalling the intimacies she and Brian had exchanged on this davenport, both on New Year's Eve and the following morning. Somehow, she realized it would be best not to have Brian encounter her here, with the mattress opened up and the bed between them, ready for use. So she left the bedding and the light on and said her good-night to him along with the rest of her family in the kitchen, before they each retired to their respective beds.

IN THE MORNING, Theresa was disappointed to discover both Brian and Jeff gone when she woke up. It was only a little before nine, so they must have been up early. The day stretched before her with an emptiness she hadn't anticipated. Many times she paused to wonder at how the absence of a single person could create a void this distracting. But it was true: knowing Brian was in town made it all the harder to be apart from him. It seemed he was never absent from her thoughts for more than an hour before his image popped up again, speaking, gesturing, sharing intimate caresses and kisses. And, too, angry.

It was the first time she'd seen his anger, and in the way of most lovers, Theresa found it now stimulating to remember how he'd looked and sounded when he was upset. Knowing this new facet of him seemed almost a relief. Everybody has his angry moments, and the way she was feeling about Brian, she thought it imperative to see both his best and worst sides, and the sooner the better. She had fallen totally in love with the man. If he asked her to make a commitment today, she'd do it without hesitation.

But the first day passed, and a second, and a third, and still she hadn't seen Brian again. Jeff reported he'd found a one-bedroom apartment in the nearby suburb of Bloomington. It was vacant, so Brian had paid his money and taken immediate occupancy. The two men had wasted no time going off to a furniture store to buy the single item that was essential: a bed. A water bed, Jeff said. The news brought Theresa's glance sharply up to her brother, but Jeff rambled on, relating the story of how the two of them had hauled the bed to Brian's apartment in the van, then borrowed a hose from the apartment caretaker to fill the thing. The heater hadn't had time to get the water warmed up the first night, so Brian had ended up spreading his new bedding on the carpeted living-room floor to sleep.

Theresa pictured him there, alone, while she lay in her bed alone, wondering if he thought of her as strongly as she thought of him each time she slipped between the sheets for the night. It was late June, the nights hot and muggy, and she blamed her restless-ness on that. It seemed she never managed to sleep straight through a night anymore, but awakened several times and spent long, sleepless hours staring at the streetlight outside her window, thinking of Brian, and wondering when she'd see him again.

He called on the fourth day. Theresa could tell who it was by Amy's part of the conversation.

"Hello?... Oh, *hiiiii*...I hear you found an apartment... Must be kind of creepy without any furniture... Oh, a pool!... All riiiiight!... Can I really!... Can I bring a friend?... Sure she does... Sure she can... Yeah, she's right here, just a sec." Amy handed the receiver to Theresa who'd been lis-tening and waiting in agony.

The smile on Theresa's face put the June sun to shame. Her heart was rapping out an I-missed-you tattoo that made her voice come out rather breathily and unnaturally high.

"Hello?"

"Hiya, sweets," he greeted, as if they'd never had a cross word between them. How absolutely absurd to blush when he was ten miles away, but the way he could pronounce that word always sent shafts of delight through her.

"Who's this?" she asked cheekily.

His laugh vibrated along the wires and made her smile all the more broadly and feel exceedingly clever for one of the first times in her life.

"This is your guitar man, you little redheaded tease. I just got my new phone installed and wanted to give you the number here."

"Oh." Disappointment deflated Theresa with a heavy *whump*. She'd thought he was calling to ask if he could see her. "Just a minute—let me get a pencil."

"It's 555-8732," he dictated. She wrote it down, then found herself tracing it repeatedly while the conversation went on. "I've got a nice apartment, but it's a little empty yet. I did get a bed though." Had he gone on, she might not have become so flustered. But he didn't. He let the silence ooze over her skin suggestively, lifting tiny goose bumps of arousal at the imagery that popped into her mind at the thought of his bed and him in it. Theresa glanced at Amy who stood by listening, and hoped she'd had the receiver plastered hard enough against her ear that Amy hadn't gotten a drift of what Brian said.

"Oh, that's nice!" Theresa replied brightly.

"Yes, it's very nice, but a little cold the first night."

Again, she came up against a blank wall. "Oh, that's too bad."

"I slept on the floor that night, but the water's all warmed up now."

Like a dolt, she went on speaking the most idiotic inanities. "Oh, that's nice."

"Very nice, indeed. Have you ever tried a water bed?"

"No," she attempted, but the word was a croak, hardly discernible. She cleared her throat and repeated, "No."

"I'll let you lie on it sometime and see how you like it."

Theresa was so red by this time that Amy's expression had grown puzzled. Theresa covered the mouthpiece, flapped an exasperated hand at her younger sister and hissed, "Will you go find something to do?"

Amy left, throwing a last inquisitive glance over her shoulder.

"I've got a pool, too," Brian was saying.

"Oh, I love to swim." It was one of the few sports in which she'd ever been able to participate fully.

"Can you?"

For a moment she was puzzled. "Can I?"

"Yes, I mean. . . are you allowed to. . . yet?"

"Oh." The light dawned. Was she healed enough to swim. "Oh, yes, I'm back to full activities. It's been four weeks."

The longest, strangest silence followed while she wondered what prompted it.

"Why didn't you tell me that the other night?"

His question and the tone of his voice told her the reason for his pause. He'd been waiting for the go-ahead! The idea threw her into a semipanic, yet she was anxious to pursue her relationship with him, though she knew beyond a doubt there would be few days of total innocence once they began seeing each other regularly. Considering her old-fashioned sense of propriety, it naturally put Theresa in a vulnerable position, one in which she would soon be forced to make some very critical decisions.

"I. . . I didn't think about it."

"I did."

She realized it now—how lightly he'd held her when they caressed, as if she were breakable. Even when they'd kissed in the driveway near the back door, he'd pulled her head hard against him, but hadn't forced her body in any way.

Neither of them said anything for a full forty-five seconds. They were coming to grips with something unspoken. During that silence he told her his intentions as clearly as if he'd illustrated them by renting a highway billboard with a two-foot-high caption. He was ready for a physical relationship. Was she?

When the silence was broken, it was Brian who spoke. His voice was slightly deeper than usual, but quiet. "Theresa, I'd like us to spend next Saturday together...here. Bring your bathing suit, and I'll pick up some corned beef at the deli, and we'll make a day of it. We'll swim and catch some sun and talk, okay?"

"Yes," she agreed quietly.

"Okay, what time should I come and get you?"

She had missed him terribly. There was only one answer she could give. "Early."

"Ten in the morning?"

No, six in the morning, she thought, but answered, "Fine. I'll be ready."

"See you then. And, honey?"

Being called *honey* by Brian was something so precious it made her chest ache.

"Yes?"

"I miss you."

"I miss you too."

IT WAS FRIDAY. Theresa had spent a restless night, considering the possibilities that lay ahead for her

with Brian. She thought not only of the sexual ten
sion between them, but of the responsibilities i
brought. She had thought herself totally opposed to
sex beyond the framework of marriage, but her brie
experience in Fargo warned that when bodies are
aroused, moral attitudes tend to dissolve and disap
pear in the expanding joy of the moment.

Would I let him? Would I let myself?

The answer to both questions, Theresa found, wa
an unqualified *yes*.

THE FOLLOWING DAY she went to the drugstore to buy
suntan lotion, knowing she'd suffer if she didn't ap
ply an effective sunscreen to her pale, freckled skin
that seemed to get hot and prickly at the mere men
tion of the word *sun*. She chose the one whose labe
said it had ultraguard, then ambled to a revolving
rack of sunglasses and spent an enjoyable twenty
minutes trying on every pair at least twice before
choosing a rather upbeat pair with graduated shading
and large round lenses that seemed to make her
mouth appear feminine and vulnerable when the
oversize frames rested on her nose.

She wandered along the shelves, picking up odd
items she needed: emery boards, deodorant, hair con
ditioner. Suddenly she came up short and stared at
the array of products on an eye-level shelf. *Contra
ceptives.*

Brian's face seemed to emblazon itself across her
subconscious as if projected on a movie screen. It
seemed inevitable that he would become her lover.
Yet why did it seem prurient to consider buying a
contraceptive in advance? It somehow took the warm
glow of love to a cooler temperature and made her
feel cunning and deliberate.

Without realizing she'd done it, she slipped the dark glasses on, hiding behind them, though the price tag still dangled from the bow.

Theresa Brubaker, you're twenty-six years old! You're living in twentieth-century America, where most women face this decision in their midteens. What are you so afraid of?

Commitment? Not at all. Not commitment to Brian, only to the undeniable tug of sexuality, for once she surrendered to it, there was no turning back. It was such an irreversible decision.

Don't be stupid, Theresa. He may keep you out by the pool all afternoon and all this gnashing will have been for nothing.

Fat chance! With my skin? If he keeps me out there all afternoon I'll look like a brick somebody forgot in the kiln. He's already hinted he's going to take me into his bedroom to try out his bed.

So, buy something! At least you'll have it if you need it.

Buy what? I've never paid any attention to the articles about products like these.

So, pick one up and read the label.

But she checked the aisle in both directions first. Even the label instructions made her blush. How on earth could she ever confront the fact that she'd have to use this stuff while she was with a man? She'd die of embarrassment!

It's either that or end up pregnant, her unwanted-companion voice persecuted.

But I'm not that kind of girl. I've always said so.

Everybody's that kind of girl when the right man comes along.

Yes, things have changed so much since Brian came into my life.

She studied the products and finally decided on one. But on her way to the checkout stand, she bought a *Cosmopolitan* magazine and dropped it nonchalantly over her other selections when setting them on the counter. *Cosmopolitan*, she thought, how appropriate. But Helen Gurley Brown would scold me for not placing the contraceptive on top of the magazine instead of vice versa.

On her next stop at the Burnsville Shopping Center, she found it necessary to buy a new purse, one large enough to conceal her new purchase. She chuckled inwardly that it turned out to be her first purchase of a contraceptive that should lead the way to her buying something she'd wanted all her life: a shoulder bag. Her shoulders had carried more than their share of strain in years gone by. She'd never felt willing to hang a purse on them as well, though she'd often wanted to own one. Well, she did now.

But the chief reason she'd come to the clothing store was to shop for a bathing suit, another item that was expanding her clothing horizon, for the suits she'd worn in the past had had to be one-pieces, altered to fit.

Now, however, she tried everything from string bikinis to skirted one-piece jobs in the Hedy Lamarr tradition. She chose a very middle-of-the-road two-piece design that wasn't exactly tawdry, but fell just short of being totally modest. The fabric was the color of her father's well-kept lawn and looked like shiny wet leather when the light caught and reflected from it. The bright kelly green was a hue that in days of old she'd have said contrasted with her coloring too sharply—the old stop-and-go-light look. But somehow, since her surgery, Theresa's confidence had grown. And since the advent of Brian in her sphere, she had felt far less plain than she used to. This gift he'd given her was something Theresa meant to repay in some way someday.

THE FOLLOWING MORNING she awakened shortly after five o'clock. The sun was peeking over the eastern horizon, turning the sky to a lustrous, pearly coral, sending streaks of brighter melon and pink radiating above the rim of the world. Closing her eyes and stretching, Theresa felt as if those shafts of hot pink were penetrating her body. She felt giddy, elated and as if she were on the brink of the most momentous day of her life.

The Maestro grinned down at her from the shelf, and it seemed as if he fiddled a gay, lilting love song to awaken her. She smiled at him, slithered lower in the bed, raised both arms above her head and rolled to her belly, savoring the keen satisfaction a simple act like that now brought into her life. It made her feel diminutive and catlike. Beneath her, the bulk was gone, in its place a body proportioned by a hand that had, in this case, improved upon Nature.

There were times when she still had difficulty realizing the change had happened and was permanent. Sometimes she found herself affecting mannerisms no longer necessary: crossing one arm and resting the opposite elbow on it to give momentary relief by boosting up her breasts, yet at the same time hiding behind her arms. Walking. Ah, but there simply hadn't been a chance to run yet. But she would, someday soon. Just to feel the ebullience and freedom of the act.

She threw herself onto her back, studied the ceiling and checked the clock. Was it broken? Or had only five minutes passed since she'd awakened? Would the rest of the morning go this slowly until Brian came to her?

It did.

In spite of fact that she performed every grooming ritual with the pomp and time-consuming attention of a ceremony. She shaved her legs. . .all the way up, for the first time in her life. She filed her toenails into delicate rounded peaks and polished them with Chocolate Mocha polish. She gave herself a careful and complete manicure, painting her fingernails with three coats. She washed her hair and arranged it with care that was positively silly, considering she was going to leap into a swimming pool within minutes after she got there. But she spared no less care on her makeup. She ironed the aqua blue collar of a white terry beach coverup with matching lounging pants whose ribbed ankles had a matching aqua stripe that continued up the outsides of the legs, and up the arms of the loose sweat-shirt style jacket. She took a bath and put an astringent after-bath splash up her legs and down her arms, and finally, when only a half hour remained, she put her bedroom in order, then hung up her housecoat and picked up the green bathing suit. She slipped into the brief panties, easing them up her legs and turning to present her derriere to the mirror, checking the reflection to find it firm, shapely and nothing she would change, even if she could. The elasticized brief rode across the crest of each hipbone, and just below her navel, exposing both it and the tender hollow of her spine.

As she turned to face the mirror again, with the strappy suit top in her hand, she assessed her reflected breasts. The crescent-shaped scars beneath each had been the fastest to heal, and the circular ones about the nipples had all but vanished. The only ones that were still highly detectable were those running vertically from the bottom up to each nipple. Dr. Schaum had told her to expect them to take a good six months to fade completely, but had assured her they would, for the newer method of surgery allowed the skin to be draped instead of stretched back into place, thus taking stress off the suturing and allowing the tissue to heal almost invisibly. They did, however, itch. Theresa opened the jar of cocoa butter and gently massaged a dollop of the soothing balm along the length of each scar. But as she finished, her fingertips remained on her left breast. But it was not the scar she saw. She saw a woman changed. A woman whose horizons had expanded in thousands of definable and indefinable ways since her surgery. She saw a woman who no longer cared that her freckles ran down her chest and up her legs, a woman who no longer considered her hair carrot-colored, but merely "bright," a woman whose medium, orange-sized breasts appeared almost beautiful to her own eyes. The nipples seemed to have shrunk from the surgery, and their perky position, pointed upward instead of down, never ceased to be a source of amazement.

She raised her arms above her head experimentally. When she did this, her breasts lifted with her arms, as they'd never done before. She pirouetted swiftly to the left, watching, to be rewarded by the sight of her breasts coming right along with her instead of swaying pendulously several inches behind the movement of her trunk.

A marvelous, appreciative smile burst across her face.

I am female. I am as beautiful as I feel. And today I feel utterly beautiful.

She hooked the bathing suit top behind her back, then lifted her arms to tie the strings behind her neck, examining the way the concealing triangles of sheeny green covered her breasts. She ran her fingertips along the deep V, down the freckled skin to the spot where the two triangles met. There was scarcely any cleavage! The wonder of it was almost enough to make her high!

She hated to slip the white terry pants and jacket on and cover herself up. Oh, glorious, glorious liberation! How wonderful you feel!

She packed a drawstring bag with sunscreen, towels, hair lifter, makeup, cocoa butter, shampoo, a pair of jeans and a brand new bra made of scalloped blue lace. Her thirty days of wearing the firm support bra were over. This little wisp of femininity was what she'd long craved. While stuffing her belongings in the bag, she realized even this was a new experience to be savored, for she'd never gone skipping off with boys to the beach when she was a girl. There was so much catching up to do!

By the time ten o'clock arrived, Theresa was not only ready, she was a totally self-satisfied ready.

The van turned into the driveway, and she stepped out onto the back step to await him. Through the windshield she saw him smile and raise a palm, then shut off the ignition, open the door and walk toward her.

He was wearing his aviator sunglasses, white, tight swimming trunks beneath an unbuttoned navy blue shirt with three zippered patch pockets, white buttons and epaulettes. The shirt's long sleeves were rolled up, exposing his arms from the elbow down, and its tails flapped in the light breeze as he approached. He moved around the front of the van in a loose-jointed amble, keeping his eyes on her face until he stood on the apron of the step below her, looking up. Lazily, he reached up to remove the glasses while every cell in her body became energized by his presence.

"Hello, sweets."

"Hello, Brian." She wanted very badly to call him an endearment, but the expressive way she spoke his name actually became an endearment in itself.

Was it she who reached first, or he? All Theresa knew later was that one moment she stood two steps above him, and the next, she was in his arms, sharing a hello kiss beneath the bright June sun at ten o'clock on a Saturday morning. She, the timid introvert who'd often wondered why some women were blessed with lives in which scenes like this were taken for granted, while others could only lie in their lonely beds at night and dream of such bliss.

It wasn't a passionate kiss. It wasn't even very intimate. But it swept her off the step and against his partially exposed chest while she circled his neck with both arms, captured in such a fashion that she was looking down at him. He lifted his lips, brushed them caressingly over hers, then dipped his head to bestow another such accolade to the triangle of freckles that showed above the zippered white terry coverup. "Mmm...you smell good." He released her enough to allow her breasts and belly to go sliding down his body until she stood before him, smiling up at his admiring, stunning, summer eyes.

"Mmm...you do too."

His hands rested on her hipbones. She was piercingly aware of it, even as they gazed, unmoving, into each other's faces and stood in broad daylight, for any of the neighbors to see.

"Are you ready?"

"I've been ready since six A.M."

He laughed, rode his hands up her ribs and turned her toward the door. "Then get your stuff and let's not waste a minute."

Chapter Fifteen

THE VILLAGE GREEN APARTMENTS were tudor-rimmed stucco buildings arranged in a horseshoe shape around a dazzling aqua-and-white swimming pool. The grounds were wooded with old elms whose leafy branches drooped in the still summer morning. Theresa caught a glimpse of the pool as Brian passed it, then pulled around the far side of the second building. Glancing up, she saw small decks flanking the length of the stucco walls, and an occasional splash of crimson from a potted geranium in a red-wood tub.

Inside, the halls were carpeted, papered and silent. Padding along with Brian at her shoulder, Theresa found herself unable to keep from watching his bare toes curl into each step as he walked. There was something undeniably intimate about being with a barefoot man. Brian's feet were medium sized, shaded with hair on his big toes, and it struck her how much more angular a man's foot was than a woman's. His legs were muscular and sprinkled with a modicum of hair on all but the fronts and backs of his knees. He stopped before number 122, unlocked the door and stepped back.

"It's not much yet, but it will be."

She entered a living room with plush, bone-colored carpeting. Directly across from the door by which they'd entered was an eight-foot-wide sliding glass

door decorated with an open-weave drapery that wa
drawn aside to give a view of the pool and surroundin
grassy area. The room held one chocolate brown di
rector's chair, a cork-based lamp sitting beside it or
the floor and nothing else except musical equipment
guitars, amplifiers, speakers as tall as Theresa's shoul
ders, microphones, a reel-to-reel recorder, stereo
radio, tapes and records.

Forming an L in juxtaposition to the living room
was a tiny galley kitchen with a Formica-topped
peninsula counter dividing it from the rest of th
open area. A short hall presumably led to the bath
room and bedroom beyond.

Theresa stopped in the middle of the carpeted ex
panse. It seemed very lonely and barren, and it mad
Theresa somehow sad to walk into the quiet empti
ness and think about Brian here all alone, with n
furniture, none of the comforts of home, nobody t
talk to or to share music with. But she turned an
smiled brightly.

"Home is where the heart is, they say."

He, too, smiled. "So I've heard. Still, you can se
why I invited you over to swim. It's about all I'n
equipped to offer."

Oh, I wouldn't say that, came the sudden impul
sive thought. She shrugged, one thumb hooking th
drawstring of the carryall bag that was slung over he
shoulder. She glanced around his living room again
"Swimming is one of the few active pastimes I've en
joyed ever since I was little. I love it. Is all this equip
ment *yours*?" She ventured across to the impressiv
array of sound equipment, leaning forward to gaz
into the smoked-glass doors of his component cabi
net.

"Yup."

"Wow."

He watched her move from piece to piece, touching nothing until her eye was caught by a three-ring notebook lying open on the floor beside an old, beat-up-looking flat-top guitar. She knelt, examined the handwritten words, and looked up. "Your songbook?"

He nodded.

She turned the pages, riffling through them slowly, stopping here and there to hum a few bars. "It must have taken you years to collect all these."

She found herself drawn to the sheets simply because they contained his handwriting, with which she'd grown so familiar during the past half year. The songs were arranged alphabetically, so she couldn't resist turning to the *Ss. S-A, S-E, S-L, S-O...* and there it was: "Sweet Memories." Without realizing she'd done it, her fingers grazed the sheets feeling the slight indentation made by his ballpoint pen years ago.

Sweet memories of her own came flooding back. And for Brian, standing near, watching her, the same thing happened. He was transported back to New Year's Eve, dancing with her in his arms, then curling her against his chest before a slow, golden fire. But it was shortly after ten o'clock on a June morning, and he'd invited her here to swim. He brought himself back from his concentrated study of the woman kneeling before him to ask, "Would you like to change into your suit?"

Reluctantly she left her musings. "Oh, I have it on. All I have to do is jump out of these." She pinched the stretchy terry cloth and pulled it away from both thighs, while grinning up at him.

"Well, I'm ready if you are."

"Just a minute. I think I'll leave my sandals i
here." She rolled to a sitting position with one kne
updrawn and began unbuckling the ankle strap
While she tugged at it, he moved closer to stan
beside her and study the top of her head. She was te
ribly conscious of his chestnut-colored legs, sprinkle
with hair, just at her elbow, and of his bare toes clos
to her hip.

"I wouldn't have taken you for a woman who'
wear toenail polish." Her hands fell still for a sec
ond, then tugged again and the first sandal cam
free. As she reached for the second one, she raise
her eyes to find him standing with arms akimb
looking down at her, the front panels of his shirt hel
aside by his wrists. His bare chest drew her eye
almost magnetically.

"I'm trying a lot of new things these days that I'v
never had the nerve to try before. Why? Don't yo
like it?"

He suddenly hunkered down, captured her foo
and began removing her sandal. "I love it. You hav
the prettiest toes of any violin player I've ever gon
swimming with." The sandal dropped to the floo
and to Theresa's astonishment, he carried the bar
foot to his lips and kissed the underside of her bi
toe, then the soft, vulnerable skin of her instep. He
eyes flew open, and the blush began creeping up
Brian grinned and unconcernedly retained possessio
of her foot, lazily stroking its arch with a thumb
"Well, you said you were trying new things you'
never tried before, and I thought this might be one t
add to your list." This time, when his teeth gentl
nipped at the sensitive instep, her lips fell open an
her eyes widened.

Theresa stared at him. Her throat had gone dry

and she was unable to move. When he'd lifted her foot, she'd lost her balance and teetered back, so sat now with elbows locked and both hands braced on the carpet behind her. Suddenly she realized her fingers were clutching the fibers. Though her eyes were riveted on Brian's face, she was arousingly aware of his pose. Balancing on the balls of his feet, his knees were widespread, but pointed at her so that it was all she could do to keep her eyes from dropping to the insides of his thighs. She knew by some magical telepathy, though she hadn't looked, that his inner thighs were smoothed of hair, just as his knees were. The muscles of his legs were bulged and taut, his insteps curved like those of Achilles running. His unbuttoned shirt fell loose and wide at his hips. The elasticized fabric of his white bathing trunks was molded to his thighs and conformed to the masculine rises and ridges between his legs.

Swallowing the lump in her throat, Theresa carefully withdrew her foot.

"I think we'd better go out," she advised shakily.

"Right. Grab your bag." Straightening those alarmingly close knees, he reached a hand down and tugged her to her feet. He rolled the sliding screen back and she moved out into the sun ahead of him, her senses so fully awakened by his nearness that even the sound of the vinyl rollers gliding in the track made her feel as if they'd just wheeled smoothly up her spinal column. How odd to be stepping into the intense heat of the late June sun, yet be shivering and experiencing the titillating effect of goose bumps rising up her arms and thighs.

There was nobody else in the pool area this early in the day. Yellow and white striped umbrellas were still closed, and the tubular plastic chairs and recliners

were all pushed neatly under the tables. The concrete
rectangle was surrounded by a broad stretch of thick
green grass on all sides, and as Theresa crossed it, the
cool blades tickled her bare toes.

The pool was stunningly clear, its surface shimmering slightly. In the aqua depths an automatic
cleaning device snaked back and forth, back and
forth, sweeping the pool floor.

Brian dipped one knee and stuck his toe in the
water.

"It's warm. Should we go in right away and work
off our breakfasts?"

"I was too excited to eat breakfast." Realizing
what she'd said, she sucked on her lower lip and
chanced a quick peek at the man beside her to find
him gazing down benignly at her pink cheeks.

"Oh, really?"

"I'll never succeed as a femme fatale, will I? I
don't think I was supposed to admit that."

"A femme fatale would keep a man guessing. But
one of the first things I liked about you was that you
didn't. I could read you as easily as you just read the
words to 'Sweet Memories' in there. That *is* what you
were reading, isn't it?"

"Yes."

"I wonder how many times I played it and thought
of you during the past six months."

He stood so near, Theresa thought she could feel
nothing more than the auburn hairs on his arms entwined with the strawberry blond ones on her own.
His eyes held a sincerity mixed with controlled desire,
and she met it with an expression much the same. On
the cool ceramic coping upon which they stood, his
right foot eased over an inch until his toes covered
hers, and Theresa wondered if a touch that innocent

could release such a wellspring of response within her body, what must the carnal act inspire? His voice was deep and held a note of self-teasing. "There. Now we're even. Whatever the male equivalent of the femme fatale is, I'm not it. I don't want to hold any of my feelings back from you. I never wanted to, not since the first day I met you."

"Brian, let's go swimming. I'm dying of the heat . . . whatever's causing it."

"Good idea. Especially since we have the place to ourselves for now."

He moved to the end of the pool and cranked open one of the umbrellas, then angled its top toward the sun. She flung her tote bag on the tabletop, then unzipped her coverup, shrugged it off and tossed it over the back of a patio chair. With her back to Brian she shimmied the elastic waist of the matching terry pants down past her hips, then flung them, too, onto the chair.

She heard the buttons and zippers of his shirt hit the metal tabletop with a ping, and assumed he was standing behind her, studying her back. This was the moment about which she'd dreamed and fantasized for years. She, Theresa Brubaker, clad in a bathing suit that left just enough to the imagination, was about to turn and face the man she loved. And she didn't have to cross her arms over her chest, nor keep her towel draped around her neck, or hunch her shoulders to disguise the thrust of her feminine attributes.

She turned to find him staring, as she'd known he'd be. Neither of them moved for a long, silent stretch of time. His chest was bare, and the white trunks dipped just below his navel, leaving it surrounded by a thin line of hair leading from the wider dark mat above. His nipples looked like copper pennies in the shade of the umbrella. His ribs were lean. His lips were partially open. His eyes unabashedly scanned her from face to knees, then lingeringly moved back up again with the slow deliberation of an art critic.

"Wow," Brian breathed. And incredible as it seemed, even to herself, Theresa believed him. The airy word was all she needed to reaffirm her desirability. But she could imagine her damn freckles zinging to life on her blushing neck and cheeks, so she turned to open her bag and rummage through it for the sunscreen.

"You'll probably eat your word within an hour. You've never seen what happens to me when the sun hits my skin. I'm a living demonstration of why physicians refer to freckles as heat spots. And I burn to a brilliant neon pink." From the depths of her bag she retrieved the lotion and uncapped it, then squirted a generous curl into her palm. "Want some?"

"Thanks." He took the bottle, and they busied themselves applying the sweet-scented lotion to their arms, necks, faces and legs. When Theresa rubbed it along the edge of the V-neck on her suit, she felt his eyes following the movements of her palm and glanced up to find him putting lotion on his chest. Her eyes dropped to his long fingers that massaged the firm musculature, delving through crisp hair, leaving it glistening with oils. He took another squirt, handed the bottle to her, and they stared at each other's hands—his running across his hard belly and along the elastic waist of his trunks; hers traversing delicate ribs, and the horizontal line along the bottom of her bikini top before curving into the depression of her navel, then around her exposed hipbones.

The lotion was slick and fragrant. It smelled of coconut, citrus and a hint of berry, filling the air around them like ambrosia. Watching his hands gliding over his skin, Theresa conjured up the thought of them gliding over hers. She dropped to the chair and began doing her legs, stretching first one, then the other out before her, sensing his eyes following again as she stroked the tender flesh of her inner thighs. She kept her eyes averted but saw peripherally how he lifted one leg to hook his toes over the edge of a lawn chair and massage fruit-scented magic along the length of his leg. He'd turned to the side, and she had a chance to study him without being studied herself.

Her eyes traversed his curving back, the buttock, the raised thigh and the junction of his legs where secrets waited. It suddenly flashed across Theresa's mind why in Victorian times men and women were never allowed to go ocean bathing together. It was a decidedly sensual thing, studying a man in swim trunks.

She dragged her eyes away, wondering if she was supposed to feel guilty at this new and unexpected curiosity she harbored. She didn't. Not at all. She was twenty-six years old—it occurred to her it was high time this curiosity surfaced and was appeased.

"Will you put some on my back?" he asked.

"Sure, turn around," she answered jauntily. But when she was squeezing the bottle, her outstretched palm trembled. His back was smooth and had several brown moles. He had wide shoulders that tapered to trim hips, the skin taut and healthy. When her hand touched his shoulder he twitched, as if he, too, were keyed up with awareness, and had been awaiting that first touch with as great a sense of anticipation as she. When her fingers curved around his ribs to his sides, he lifted his arms slightly away from his body to allow her access. For a moment, she was tempted to run both hands all the way around his trunks and press her face to the hollow between his shoulder blades. Instead she squirted a coil of white into her palm and worked both hands unilaterally across the crests of his hard shoulders and up the sides and back of his neck, even into the hair at its nape. Already the hair was longer, which pleased her. She had never been crazy about his Air Force haircuts, for she'd imagined that if allowed to grow to collar length, his would curve gently in thick, free swoops. As her fingers massaged his neck, he tipped his head backward and a guttural sound escaped his throat. Her palms, as well as the nerve endings along the rest of her body, felt as if they were instantly on fire.

It grew worse—or better—when he turned and took the bottle from her slippery fingers, ordering quietly, "Turn around."

She spun from the ardor in his eyes, then felt his long palms pressing a cold mound of lotion against her bare flesh, then begin turning it warm with the friction and contact of skin upon skin. His touch made it extremely difficult to breathe, and impossible to control the tempo of her heart, which seemed to rise up and search out the spots his hand grazed, pounding right through the walls of her back. His fingers curved over her shoulder, up beneath her hair, forcing her chin to drop forward, spreading the essence of wondrous exotic delicacies all about her. He massaged the breadth of her shoulder blades, skipped over the elasticized back strip of her suit, and after taking another liberal amount of sunscreen, his fingertips eased up beneath the strap, running left to right beneath it, from just beneath her left armpit to the same spot under her right. Lower they went, down the delicate hollow of her back, and along the elastic of her emerald green briefs, curving upon the sculptured hipbone, teasing at the taut rubberized waistband that cinched tightly against her flesh. The oils made his hands glide sensuously across her skin, and she shuddered beneath them.

His touch disappeared. She heard the faint sound of the cap being replaced on the bottle, then of the bottle meeting the aluminum tabletop. But she didn't move. She couldn't. She felt as if she'd never move again as long as she lived, not unless this fire in her veins was cooled and put out. If it wasn't, she'd stand there and burn into a cinder.

"Last one in's a moldy worm," came the heavy, aroused voice from behind her. Then she was sprinting to the end of the pool—running at last!—hitting the water stretched out full length, just at the instant Brian hit it. The shock was breathtaking. From the heat of a second ago her body dropped what seemed a full fifty degrees. She swam furiously, a powerful, controlled crawl to the far end of the pool, her body temperature stabilizing by the time she reached her goal.

Side by side they swam eight laps, and in the middle of the ninth, Theresa spluttered, waved limply and declared, "Goodbye, I think I'm drowning," then went under. When her head surfaced, he was treading water, waiting.

"Woman, I'm not through with you yet. Sorry, no drowning till I am." And unceremoniously he disappeared, came up in the perfect position to command her body in an exemplary demonstration of a Senior Lifesaving hold, with his left arm angled across her chest while he hauled her to the far end of the pool beneath the overhanging diving board.

She let herself go limp and be pulled along in an unresisting state of breathlessness and sensuality. His elbow clamped down on her left breast, and it felt wonderful.

At the pool wall he released her, and they both crossed their arms on the sleek concrete, resting their cheeks on their wrists while facing each other, both panting, feet flapping lazily on the surface of the blue water behind them.

"You're melting," he announced with a grin, reaching out a fingertip and running it beneath her right eye.

"Oh, my makeup!" She slipped under the water again and scrubbed at her eyelids before emerging sparkly lashed, and asking if she was still discolored.

"Yes, but leave it. It's very Greta Garbo."

"You're a very good swimmer."

"So are you."

"As I said before, it was about the only physical exercise that was easy for me when I was growing up. But I kind of gave it up too, when I was in my late teens, because I was afraid it would...well, build up the muscles all the more, if you know what I mean."

He was studying her wet face carefully. "It seems like there are a lot of things you had to give up that I'd never have suspected."

"Yes, well that's all over now. I'm a new person."

"Theresa, is it...well, are you sure you aren't overdoing it, swimming so hard? It worries me, even though you said you're a hundred percent again."

As if to reaffirm her full recovery, she caught the edge of the pool and boosted herself up, twisting to a sitting position above him with her feet dangling in the water. "One hundred percent, Brian."

He joined her on the edge of the pool. She flung her hair back, feeling his eyes following each movement as she wrung her hair out and sent rivulets running down her back and over her shoulder. Beneath them the concrete was sun-warmed, and the water soon joined their flesh to the sleek surface with a tepid slipperiness.

He ran his hands over his cheeks to clear them of excess water, then wove his fingers through his hair, running them toward the back of his head, and studying the umbrella at the far end of the pool as he asked quietly, "Theresa, would you feel self-conscious answering some questions about your operation?"

"Probably. But ask them anyway. I've been working very hard on my self-image and on trying to overcome self-consciousness. But if you don't mind, I'd better have a little lotion on my face and back. I feel like most of it washed off."

They got to their feet, leaving dark gray footprints along the concrete as they made their way toward the opposite end of the pool. Theresa dried her hair, then spread her towel out on the soft grass and sat down on it while applying lotion to her face once more. When she was done, she flipped over and stretched out full length on her stomach, thinking it would be infinitely easier to answer his questions if she wasn't looking at him.

His hands eased over her skin, spreading it with lotion once more while he asked quietly, "When did you decide to have it done?"

"Remember when I wrote and told you I slipped in the parking lot and fell down?"

"I remember."

"It was right after that. When the doctor examined

my back he told me I should look into having th
problem solved permanently.''

"Your back?''

"There's a lot of back and shoulder discomfor
that goes along with it. People don't know that. Th
shoulders are especially vulnerable. I thought proba
bly you'd noticed the grooves—they still show a littl
bit.''

"These?'' His fingertips massaged one of he
shoulders, and she felt a heavenly thrill rippl
through her body before he went on, "I wasn't exact
ly looking at your shoulders before, but I see th
marks now. What else? Tell me everything about i
Was it hard for you, psychologically, I mean?''

Belly down, on a beach towel, with her cheek o
the back of her hand, with her eyes closed, she tol
Brian everything. All about her misgivings, he
mother's and father's initial reactions to her deci
sion, her fears and uncertainties, omitting the fac
that the feeling had not yet returned to her nipples
She couldn't force herself to share that intimacy wit
him yet. If and when the time came, she'd be honest
but for now she glossed over that and the part abou
being unable to nurse a baby.

When her recital was finished, he was still sittin
beside her with his arm circling one updrawn knee
His voice was soft and disarming.

"Theresa, I'm sorry for getting mad at you m
first night back. I never understood about a lot o
it.''

"I know. And I'm sorry I didn't at least write an
tell Jeff, and let him tell you what my plans were.''

"No, you were right. You didn't owe me anything
That first night when we went for the walk, I'll admi
part of my problem was I was scared. I thought may

be now that you'd taken the big step you'd be out for bigger fish than this underage guitar man whose past isn't quite as pure as you deserve.''

His words brought her head up. Bracing on one elbow she twisted to look back over her shoulder at him. "I long ago stopped placing any importance on the differences in our ages. You're more mature than most of the thirty-year-old men I work with at school. Maybe that's why you were so...I don't know. Understanding, I guess. Right from the first, I sensed that you were different from all the others I'd ever met, that you really did look into me, the person, and judge me by my inner qualities or shortcomings."

"Shortcomings?" He flopped down on his back almost underneath her partially lifted chest and touched the tangled locks above her left ear. "You don't have any shortcomings, sweets."

"Oh, yes I do. Everybody does."

"Where they been hidin'?"

She smiled at his playfulness, glanced down at her forearm, and answered, "Several thousand of them have been lurking just below the surface of my skin and are just now coming out to introduce themselves."

Indeed, her "heat spots" were heating up. The freckles on her arms had already grown so fat their perimeters were dissolving into one another.

He rolled his cheek against the towel, pulled her soft inner arm to his lips, and declared quietly, "Angel kisses." He kissed her again, higher, almost at the bend of elbow. "Have you been kissing any angels lately, Miss Brubaker?"

She studied his green eyes, and let her feelings show in her own. "Not as often as I want to." She smiled and added impulsively, "Gabriel."

"Then what do you say we remedy that?" With swift flexing of muscle, he was on his feet, reachin out a hand to tug her up. He gathered towels, tog and lotion and handed her the bag. She followed will ingly, walking at his side while one light hand guide her shoulders as she crossed the grass toward the slid ing door of his apartment.

She stepped inside where it was cool and shaded She heard him snap the lock on the screen door, the step to the drapery cord and draw the curtain close until the midday light was even more subdue through the open weave of the fabric. It threw gentl checkers across the thick carpet and her bare toes She had the fleeting thought that her hair was proba bly plastered to her head in some places and flying a odd angles in others, and that her makeup was al washed away. Behind her she heard a metallic click then the soft *shhh* of a needle settling onto a disc. Sh was frantically scrambling to find her comb in th bottom of the tote bag when a guitar introductio softly filled the room, and an insistent hand capture the drawstring bag and pulled it from her nervou fingers, as if Brian would brook no delays, no re pairs, no excuses.

My world is like a river
As dark as it is deep. . . .

As the poignant words met her ears, she wa turned around by lean, hard fingers that closed ove the sensitive spot where her neck met her shoulders When his eyes delved into hers, he wordlessly searched out her palms and carried them up around his neck. His body was moving in rhythm to th music but so very slightly she scarcely felt th evocative sway of his shoulders beneath the soft flesh of her inner arms. But some magical force made her body answer the almost imperceptible beckoning as he swayed, drawing nearer and nearer until the fabric of her suit brushed the hair upon his chest. The invitation was wordless at first, as his warm palms found her naked back and pressed her lightly against him. Then he began humming softly, drawing away only far enough to continue searching her uplifted face while his palm gently caressed the hollow between her shoulder blades, then traced the depression down her spine. With only the slightest force he urged her hips closer, closer, until her bare stomach touched his—sleek to rough. He undulated slowly as if bidding her to join him. She responded with a first hesitant movement until she felt his hips and loins, confined by the taut piece of clothing that covered him, pressed firmly against her.

His breath was warm upon her mouth as he touched it first with the tip of his tongue, then lightly with the outermost surfaces of his lips. He was still humming. As her lips dropped open she felt the soft intonation tickling the crests of them. The sound, the feeling and his careful doling out of contact served only to tantalize, then he lifted his head and began singing the refrain that had been in her heart since she'd heard him sing the words with the battered old fifteen-dollar Stella in his lap.

> Sweet memories,
> Sweet memories. . . .

When the voice on the record hummed the final notes and took the song home, she was settled securely against the full, hard length of Brian's body, feel-

ing all its surfaces, ridges and textures as if she were
on an elevated plane of sensory awareness.

In the thundering silence between songs, his hard
body and soft voice combined in a message of latent
passion. "Theresa, I love you, girl...so much...so
much." It seemed too sweeping to take in. Their
bodies no longer moved, but were pressed together
until the naked skin of his thighs and belly seemed
bonded to hers by the slightly oily, very fragrant suntan lotion whose aroma evoked images of tropical
islands, warm sunlit shores and the calls of cocka-
toos. Her senses were filled with the smell of him, his
warmth and firmness, but mostly with the sleek texture of his skin.

"Brian...my guitar man, I think I started loving
you when you stepped off that plane and looked me
square in the eye."

Another song had begun, but its rhythm went un-
heeded, for they were entwined in each other's arms,
hearing only the beats of their hearts pressed together
with nothing but two triangles of thin green material
between them. The kiss lost all tentativeness and
blossomed into a full complementary exchange of
sleek tongues and throaty murmurs. His head moved
sensuously above hers, wooing and winning her slow,
sure acquiescences. Her inhibitions began dissolving
until he felt her hips reaching toward a closer communion with his as she raised up on tiptoe to mold
her curves more securely against his, all the while
clinging to his sleek shoulders.

His palms moved down to learn the shape of her
firm hipbones once more, then the solid flesh of her
rounded buttocks, cupping them in both hands as he
drew close.

He tore his mouth from hers, his eyes glowing with

the fire of a passion too long denied. "Sweets, I promised I wouldn't come back here and force this issue. I said I'd take it slow, and give you time to—"

"I've had twenty-six years, Brian. That's long enough."

When he lifted his head she felt deprived at the loss of his warm lips and reached with her own, as if she suddenly couldn't get her fill of these long-delayed joys.

"Do you mean it, Theresa? Are you sure?"

"I'm sure. Oh, Brian, I'm so sure it hurts. . .right here." She took her palm and pressed it against her heart. "I thought I'd be afraid and uncertain when this moment came, but I'm not. Not at all. Somehow, when you love, you know." She gazed up at him in wonder, touching his lips with her fingertips. "You just know," she breathed.

"Yes, you know, darling."

Slowly he covered her shoulders with his hands and pressed her away from him to gaze into her ardent eyes while he spoke. "I want you to look around at this room." She felt herself turned until her bare back was pressed against his rough-textured chest. From behind he circled her ribs, his forearms resting just below her breasts, touching their undersides. "This room has no furniture because I wanted us to pick it out together. I thought about waiting to ask you until afterward, but I find I want to know first. Will you marry me, Theresa? Just as soon as it can be arranged? And we can fill this place with furniture and your piano and music and maybe a couple of kids, and make sweet memories for the rest of—"

"Yes!" She spun and looped her arms around his neck, cutting off his words with the kiss and muffled word before lifting her mouth from his and singing,

"Yes, yes, yes! I didn't know whether I wanted you to ask me before or after but it's probably best before, 'cause I probably won't do so well...." His eyebrows drew into a puzzled frown. "I'm not experienced at this part," she explained diffidently.

The next minute she was scooped up into his arms and felt his hard belly against her hip while he carried her down the hall to his bedroom.

"Trust me. You will be, as soon as it can be arranged."

From the bedroom doorway where he paused, she saw her marriage bed for the first time. It looked like any other bed, covered with a quilted spread of brown-and-blue geometric design that matched the two sheets haphazardly thrown over the curtain rod to lend the room privacy.

"I never thought to ask you before I bought a waterbed if you like them or not."

"Can a person get seasick on it?"

"I hope not."

With her arms looped around his neck she drew his head down until his mouth joined hers. Muffled against his lips she muttered, "Well, I brought plenty of dramamine pills along, just in case."

Chapter Sixteen

THE TRIP TO THE BED in Brian's arms was like crossing the bridge of a rainbow connecting the earth to heaven. When she was a girl, Theresa had wondered, as all girls do from the time they feel the first stirrings of maturity, what the man would be like when the moment came? And the setting—would it be dark? Winter or summer? Day or night? Inside or outside? And our first intimate encounter—would it be rushed or slow? Silent or vocal? Reckless or poignant? Would it leave me feeling more—or less?

The sheets rippled at the windows. The sun brought the blue-and-brown pattern alive, backlighting it until the entwined diamonds and parallellograms danced upon the shimmering fabric, while from outside came the faraway voices of children who clanged the gate to the pool area, then whooped gleefully as they took their first plunge.

From the living room came the strains of love songs, distant now, unintrusive, but mellow and wooing. Brian's bare feet moved soundlessly across the cocoa-colored carpet. His lips wore a faint smile, and his steady eyes rested upon Theresa's while he sat on the edge of the bed with her legs across his lap. She felt a faint surge of liquid motion lift them momentarily, then subside. Twisting at the hip he placed her the wrong way across the bed, across its width, lying on his side next to her with his knees slightly updrawn.

He braced up on one elbow, smiling down into he
face, running the tip of an index finger along the rin
of her lower lip. The smile had drifted from her face
and her lingering apprehensions were reflected in the
wide brown eyes and the slightly parted lips.

"Are you scared?" he asked softly.

She swallowed and nodded. "A little."

"About anything in particular?"

"My lack of experience, among other things."

"Experience will take care of itself. What are the
other things?" His fingers trailed along her jaw and
began gently freeing the strands of hair from about
her temples, absently arranging them in a brigh
corona about her head.

Already she felt the telltale blush climbing he
chest. "I...." The words stuck, creating a tight kno
in the center of her chest. "I don't...." His eyes lef
the hair he'd been toying with and met hers, but hi
fingers were still threaded through the red strands
resting upon the warm skull just above her left ear
"Oh, Brian," She covered her face with both hands
"This is so hard, and I know I'm blushing terribly
and there's nothing less becoming to a redhead tha
blushing, and I've never—"

"Theresa!" His gentle reprimand cut her off as h
circled her wrists and forced her hands away from
her face. She stared up at him in silence. The repri
mand left his voice, and it became compelling. "
love you. Did you forget that? There's nothing you
can't tell me. Whatever it is, we'll work it out togeth
er, all right? And, just to set the record straight, red
heads look darling when they blush. Now, would you
like to start again?"

The muscles in her stomach were jumping. He
fists were clenched, the tendons tight beneath hi

grasp. She sucked in a huge, fortifying gulp of air and ran the words out so fast she wouldn't have a chance to change her mind. "I-don't-want-to-get-pregnant-and-I-went-to-the-drugstore-yesterday-and-bought-something-to-make-sure-I-wouldn't-but-the-instructions-said-I-had-to-use-it-half-an-hour-before-and-I-don't-know-before-*what*-or-how-long-anything-takes-because-I've-never-done-this-before-and-oh-please-Brian-let-my-hands-go-so-I-can-hide-behind-them!"

To Theresa's amazement, he laughed lovingly and wrapped her in both of his arms, falling to his side and taking her along until they lay almost nose to nose. "Is that all? Ah, sweet Theresa, what a joy you are." He kissed the tip of her very red nose, then lay back, running a finger along the crest of her cheek. His voice was quiet and calm. "I had the same thought myself, so I came prepared, too. That means you have a choice, sweetheart. You or me."

She tried to say me, but the word refused to come out, so she only nodded.

"Well, now's the time." He sat up and tugged her along after him, and she padded to the living room for her purse, then back down the hall toward the bathroom.

When she returned to the bedroom he was lying on his back across the bed, still in his swimtrunks, with his arm folded behind his head.

Through the open doorway he had watched the green bathing suit appear as she opened the bathroom door, crossed the hall and approached the bed. Long before she reached it, he'd extended a palm in invitation.

"Come here, little one."

She lifted one knee to the edge of the bed, placing

her palm in his, and let him tug her down until she
fell into the hollow of his arm, partially across his
chest. The water stirred beneath them, then went still
His right arm remained beneath his head, but ever
one-handed he eased her closer, tighter, until she
hovered above him, and his eyes conveyed the re
mainder of the message. She bent her head to touch
his lips with her own, and the kiss began with a meet
ing no heavier than the morning mist settling upon a
lily. It expanded into the first brief touch of tongue
tips—tentative, introductory, promising. He tasted
slightly sweet, as if some of the tropical sunscreer
still lingered on his lips. His tongue sought the deeper
secrets of her mouth, and hers his. Seek, touch
stroke, chase, devour—they shared each advancing
step of the intimate kiss. Longing sang through her
veins, enlivening each of her senses until she per
ceived each touch, sound, taste, sight and smell with
that new, exultant keenness she'd discovered for the
first time today. His relaxed pose lifted the firm
muscles of his chest and exposed them in a way tha
invited exploration.

She let her hand seek out his neck first, recalling
the throaty sound he'd uttered when she'd stroked
that soft hollow once before. She allowed her thumb
to explore the hard knot of his Adam's apple, and
beneath the soft pad, the masculine point jumped as
he swallowed. When her thumb slid down to the shal
low well at its base, she felt his pulse racing there
pressing against her finger like a knocking engine.

It had happened again, that response she could
kindle so effortlessly in this man. She sensed it and
experimented, a little bit more. Her hand left his neck
and flattened upon the firm rise of his chest, ex
periencing the rough texture of hair, then the tiny

point of his nipple, which she first fanned, then scissored between her fingers while bracing over him, moving her lips downward to touch the warm skin on his chest. She tasted him. Sweet oil and salt and sun and chlorine and coconut and papaya. She had not dreamed he would have taste, yet he did, and it was heady and sensual. Beneath her tongue the rough hairs of his body felt magnified, yet silky. Upon her lips she felt the faint oily residue left behind by the sunscreen. He was warm and resilient and utterly male.

Lifting her head, she felt drugged by senses that had sprung to life from the shield behind which they'd been protected for so many years. Suddenly she was eager to know all, feel all, to glut herself on every texture, hue and scent his body possessed. Her eyes met his, then dropped to travel across the shadowed throat, his ear, his nipples, his jaw where a tiny, tiny scab remained from some incidental nick of razor, perhaps. She touched it with a single fingertip, then pressed the length of her palm along the underside of the biceps of the arm bent beneath his head. She ran the hand down to his armpit, awed that even the wiry hair there could be something she craved to know, simply because it was part of his physical makeup.

"Brian," she breathed, looking into his eyes, "I'm like a child tasting candy for the first time. I never knew all these things before. I have so much to catch up on!"

"Catch then. We have a good seventy years."

A flickering smile passed her features, but was gone again, wiped away by this new rapt interest in his body. He closed his eyes, and like an eager child she twisted onto one hip, bracing a palm on the bed

to get a better overview of this delicacy called Brian
Scanlon. Still it wasn't enough. Finally, she pulled
both legs up beneath her and sat on her haunches at
his hip—looking, touching, familiarizing.

"You're...exquisite!" she marveled. "I never
thought a man could be exquisite, but you are." His
belly was hard, his ribs tapering to the indentation of
his waist, just above the spot where his trunks sliced
his abdomen. Within the white trunks she saw the
mysterious raised contours of his arousal and wondered if it hurt him to be bound up so tightly.

She lifted her eyes to his and found he'd been
watching her. A charming, lopsided grin bent the
corner of his mouth.

"Darling girl." He lazily lifted his hand and ran a
finger along the path of one string of her tie top,
starting at the side of her neck, traveling beside it to
the point where it met the band beneath her breasts.
She shuddered with delight. "I don't think I'm the
one who's exquisite." The finger idled up the opposite strap. Her eyelids felt weighted and a coil of
anticipation wound through her stomach. His four
fingertips traced the line of her collarbone, then
moved downward, drawing a quartet of invisible S's
along the freckled mound of her breast. The faint
tickle lifted the fine hairs on her bare stomach. He
gave the other breast equal attention, fingering her
skin with the brush of a dragonfly's wings. Her eyelids slid closed, and her head dropped slightly backward, listing to one side while his callused fingertip
followed the first strap again, but this time also
moved over the shimmery green triangle of fabric to
graze the hidden, uptilted nipple that gave an unexpected spurt of sensation down her arms, stomach
and straight to the seat of her femininity.

Her eyelids flew open. "Brian!"

A troubled look crossed his features as he misread her exclamation and withdrew his hand.

"Brian! There's feeling there!"

"What?" His fingers poised in midair.

"There's feeling there! It happened, when you touched me just then, something slithery and fiery went...went whooshing down my body, and...oh, Brian, don't you see? The doctor said sometimes the sensation never returns, and I've been scared to death thinking it hadn't come back to me."

He braced up on one elbow and cupped her jaw. "You never told me before."

"I am now, but oh Brian, it doesn't matter anymore, oh please, do it again!" she begged excitedly. "I want to make sure I wasn't just imagining it."

He toppled her over beside him, his lips joining hers to press her onto her back as his hand roamed across her ribs, and up, but stopped just short of her breast.

He lifted his head and she opened her eyes to find him gazing down intently into her eyes, his brows lowered in concern. "I won't hurt you, will I?"

"No," she whispered.

His mouth and hand moved simultaneously, the one to bestow a kiss, the other a caress. He contoured the warm globe of flesh with his palm, gently at first, then with growing pressure, squeezing, fondling, finally seeking out the nipple, which he tenderly explored through the slip of sheeny, damp material.

Her lips went slack and she dropped her shoulders flat to the bed, lolling in the new feelings of arousal. It was slighter than before, but there just the same. She concentrated hard on grasping it, blindly guiding his hand to the exact spot she thought would revive the strong spurt of sensation as before.

Braced above her, he watched the feelings parade
across her face, and at last he reached for the bow a
the nape of her neck. Her eyes opened as she felt i
slipping free, but just before he could lower the green
triangle, she stopped his hand.

"Brian, I have scars, but please don't let them stop
you. They'll be there for several months yet, but then
they'll fade. And they don't hurt, they only itch
sometimes."

Some softening expression around his eyes told her
he understood, and accepted. Then he peeled the first
green tidbit of fabric down and laid it over her ribs
while she watched his eyes. They dropped to the verti
cal red scar, then flew back to her brown gaze. Word
lessly he stripped down the other half of the bathing
suit top.

Where was the shame she had once known? Absent
Evaporated beneath the far greater impact of the lov
ing concern that emanated from Brian's face.

He slipped his hands behind her back and came
away with the suit top, then tossed it onto the pillow
and rolled to give her his full attention again.

"How can it not hurt?" Gently he cupped her right
breast, riding his thumb up the scar, then lightly
lightly circling the nipple. "Did they make an inci
sion here?"

"Yes, but that scar is all healed."

"And here, too." He traced the faded crescent be
neath, to its inception just below her armpit. "O
God, it hurts me to think of them doing that to you."
He lowered his head, trailing his lips along the lower
contour scar.

"Brian, it's all over, and it wasn't nearly as bad a
you'd think. If I hadn't done it, I might not have

been able to overcome all my hangups and be here with you. I feel so different. So. . . ."

He lifted his head and searched her with tortured eyes. "What do you feel? So. . . what?"

"Beautiful," she admitted, with a lingering note of shyness. "Feature that, would you?" She smiled and her voice became soft and accepting. "Theresa Brubaker with her red hair and freckles, feeling beautiful. But it's partly because of you. Because of how you treated me last Christmas. You made me believe I had the right to feel this way. You were all the things I'd ever hoped to find in a man."

"I love you." His voice was strange, throaty and deep, and not wholly steady. He dipped his head and touched the lips to the cinnamon-colored dots between her breasts. "Every freckle of you." He moved his mouth to the gentle swelling mound. "Every red hair of you." And finally to the crest. "Every square inch of you."

He adored her with the gentle strokes of his tongue, and she lay in a blaze of emotions that sprang more from her consummate love for him than from the part of her he tenderly kissed.

"What's happening?" he queried, running his tongue down along the underside of her breast.

She sucked in a breath as a sensual response shuddered down her backbone. "I'm falling in love with my body, and your body, and what they can do to each other. I'm plunging through space. . . freefalling. Only it's so strange. . . I'm falling up."

He ran his tongue up to her nipple again, and closed his lips and tongue around it, murmuring some wordless accolade deep in his throat, while both of his arms reached behind her and his hands slid

down to cup her buttocks and roll her firmly agains
him, both of them now on their sides.

"Mmm...you taste like summer...."

"Tell me," she whispered, threading her finger:
through his hair, knowing an insatiable appetite for
his words, as well as for his arousing touches.

"Sandy beaches and suntan oil that tastes like Pop
sicles and the sweetest fruit in the jungle...." He
lightly nipped the top of a breast with his teeth. "Ber
ries and coconut..." He slipped lower, licking the
sensitive skin on the rib. "Mangos and kiwi...
Mmm...." His mouth pressed moistly upon the
softest part of her abdomen, just above the navel
"There's something else here...wait, let me
see...." He dipped his tongue into her navel and
made several seductive circles around and within it
"Mmm...I think it's passion fruit."

She felt him smile against her belly and smiled in
return.

His mouth was arousingly warm, and his breath
heated the silky triangle of fabric still covering her
His chest weighted her legs, then he lightly bit her
through the bathing suit—fabric, hair and a little
skin. Her ribs lifted off the bedspread, and she
gasped while desire welled and bubbled over in her
feminine depths. His fingers found the sensitive skin
at the back of her knee, then his mouth warmed the
flesh that she'd thought could not possibly know a
heat any greater than it had already experienced. She
trembled and lifted her hips from the bed, offering
herself as fully as he cared to partake. He kissed her
through the silky bikini and worked his chin firmly
against the throbbing flesh within until she found
herself moving against the hardness, seeking some
thing...something....

And when her desire had grown to its fullest, he moved back up to join his mouth to hers, running his palms along the elastic waist of her briefs, then down inside to cup her firm backside while rolling his weight fully on top of hers, his hips undulating against hers while their mouths locked in a bond of mutual desire.

His weight lifted. She felt the wisp of fabric leave the juncture of her legs and inch downward along her thighs, then pass lower still until his mouth was forced to leave hers, and he eased the garment down and off, then tossed it over his shoulder to join its mate on the pillows.

He pressed her back, back, against the bed and caressed her bare stomach with his musician's fingers that were capable, she learned, of much more than adroitly strumming love songs. They raised a kind of music in her flesh as he explored the soft skin of her inner thighs, then the most intimate part of her body.

She was eager, and open, and not in the least abashed by his touch that sought and entered her virgin flesh. Love, that gift of the gods, took away all insecurities, all timidity, all shame, and allowed her the freedom to express her newfound feminity in the way she had so long dreamed.

A soft, passionate sound issued from her throat. She stretched and allowed him total access to explore her as he would, trembling at times, smiling at others, her heart a wild thing in her breast.

But just short of taking her over the edge of bliss, he lay back. And then it was her turn to explore. "Experience will take care of itself," Brian had said. And she believed it as she embarked upon her half of this maiden voyage toward mutuality.

She found the tight waist of his trunks and slipped

her palms inside, against the skin of his lower spine, finding it cool from the slightly damp fabric.

Her caresses were restricted by the taut garment, yet she thrilled at the firmness beneath her palms and the inviting rhythm her touch had set off in his hips. He reached behind his back, found her arm and carried it up out of the elastic and around to his front, pressing it against the flattened, hidden hills between his legs, moving against her palm to initiate it into the ways of sexual contact.

To Theresa's amazement, her own voice begged throatily, "Take it off, Brian, please."

The words were partially muffled by his lips, but when the request had been made, he lifted his head and smiled into her beseeching eyes, his breath beating warmly upon her face.

"Anything you say, love."

He slipped to the edge of the bed, and she rolled onto her side and curled her body up like a lazy caterpillar, watching as he reached inside the garment and found a hidden string against his belly, tugged it, then stood and skinned the trunks down, down, down, before dropping to sit on the edge of the bed again and kicking the suit away across the carpet as he rolled toward her, reaching.

He was beautiful, and somehow it seemed the most natural thing in the world to reach out and caress him.

"Oh, Brian, you're silky... and so hot."

"So are you. But I think that's how we're supposed to be." He reached again for the entrance to her womanhood touching it with a sleek, knowing rhythm until sensation dazzled her nerve endings. She closed her eyes and undulated with the protracted and relentless stroking.

"Brian, something's happening!"

"Let it. Shh...."

"But...but...." It was too late to wonder if it was torture or treasure, for in the next instant the question was answered for Theresa. A burst of sensation lifted her limbs and sent liquid explosions rocketing outward. Then she was shuddering, feeling spasms from the deepest reaches of her body, until she fell back sated, exhausted, gasping.

"Oh, sweet, sweet woman. The first time," he said against her neck after a minute, still holding her tightly. "Do you know how rare that is?"

"No...I thought from the movies that it happens to everyone."

"Not women, not all the time. Usually just men. You must have been storing it all these years, waiting for the right one to come along and set it free."

"And he did."

He smiled lovingly into her eyes, then kissed each lid, then her nose, then her swollen lips. And while he strung the kisses upon her face, he raised his body over hers and pressed it firmly to her entire length.

"I love you, darling—keep remembering that in case it hurts."

"I love you, Br—"

She never finished the word, for in that instant he entered her and she knew the sleek ligature of their two joined bodies, but no pain, only texture and heightened sensations building once again as his hips moved above hers. She felt only pleasure as he began moving, reaching back to teach her how to lift her knees and create a nesting place of warm, firm flesh that buttressed his hips as he shared the consummation of their love.

When he clenched his fists and quivered, she

opened her eyes to find his closed in ecstasy. He rod
the crest of his climax while she watched the reactio
expressed on his beloved features—the closed, trem
bling eyelids, the flaring nostrils and the lips tha
pulled back in a near grimace as sweat broke out o
his back and the muscles rippled for an exhauste
moment. Then he shivered a last interminable tim
called out at the final peak, and relaxed.

*So this is why I was born a woman and Brian Scar
lon was born a man, why we were meant to seek an
find each other in this world of strangers.* She caresse
his shoulder blades, coveting the dead weight of hir
pressing her into the resilient water-filled baffl
beneath her.

"Oh, Brian it was so good. . . so good."

He rolled to his side and opened his eyes, lifting or
hand that appeared too tired to quite succeed in the e
fort of caressing her face. It fell upon her cheek.

He chuckled—a rich, resonant sound from deep i
his chest and closed his eyes and sighed, then lay ur
moving.

She studied him in repose, smoothed the tousle
hair above his temple. His eyes didn't open, and h
palm didn't move. She knew an abiding sense c
completion.

The noon sun lit the ceiling of the room by som
magical twist of physics. The sheets at the windo
riffled lightly, and the sounds of the pool activit
were constant now. From the living room came th
repeated songs of the same record—she smiled, wor
dering how many times it had played.

"Do you know when I first became intrigued wit
you?"

She turned to find his eyes open, watching he
"When?"

They were still entwined, and he pulled her closer o keep possession of her while he went on. "It tarted when Jeff let me read a letter from you. In it ou said you'd gone out on a date with somebody 1amed Lyle, and he turned out to be Jack the Grip->er."

She chuckled, recalling both the letter and the dis- 1strous date.

"That long ago?"

"Uh-huh. Two years or more. Anyway, after we 1ughed about it, and I wondered what kind of voman had written it, I began asking questions .bout you. Little by little I learned everything. About our red hair." He threaded his fingers into it just vhere her widow's peak would have been, had she >ne. "And your freckles." He trailed a finger down 1er nose. "And your endowment." He passed a palm 1own her breast. "And about the time Jeff defended ou and punched out that kid, and about how you 1ught music in an elementary school and played iolin, and how Jeff thought the sun rose and set in ou, and how much he wanted you to be happy, to ind some man who'd treat you honorably and vouldn't ogle and grope and grip."

"Two years ago?" she repeated, stunned.

"Longer than that. Closer to three now. Since Jeff nd I were in Germany together. Anyway, then I saw our picture. It was one of your school pictures, and ou were wearing a gray sweater buttoned around our shoulders, with a little white blouse collar show- ng from beneath. I asked Jeff a lot of questions hen, and pieced together a picture of you and your 1angup even before I knew you. There have been imes when I even suspected that Jeff filled me in on ll the details about you in hopes that when I met you

I'd be the first man to treat you right, and end up d⟨
ing exactly what I just did.''

''Jeff?'' She exclaimed, surprised.

''Jeff. Didn't you ever suspect that he engineere⟨
this whole thing from the start, feeding me tidbi⟨
about his marvelous, straight sister, who'd never ha⟨
boyfriends, but who had so much to offer a man—
the right man.''

She braced up on one elbow and looked though⟨
ful. ''Jeff! You really think so?''

''Yes, I do. As a matter of fact, he all but admitte⟨
it when we were on the plane back after Christma⟨
He suspected things had fired up between us an⟨
came right out and said it'd been on his mind a whi⟨
that he wouldn't mind me as a brother-in-law.''

She smirked and lifted a delicate jaw. ''Remind n⟨
to give old Jeff a gigantic thank-you kiss next time⟨
see him, huh?''

''And what about you? When did you start thin⟨
ing of me as a potential lover?''

''The truth?'' She peered up at him coquettishly.

''The truth.''

''That night in the theater, when the love scene w⟨
on the screen. Your elbow was sharing the armre⟨
with mine, and when the woman climaxed, yo⟨
bones were almost cutting off my blood supply. The⟨
when the man's face came on, showing him in t⟨
throes of rapture, your elbow nearly broke mine, ar⟨
when it was over, *you* wilted.''

''Me?'' he yelped disbelievingly. ''I did not!''

''You did too. I was practically dying of emba⟨
rassment, and then you dropped your hands down ⟨
cover your lap, and I wanted to crawl underneath t⟨
seats.''

''Are you serious? Did I really do that?''

"Of course I'm serious. Would I lie about a thing like that? I was so turned on myself I hardly knew what to do about it. Part of it was the movie, but part of it was you and your arm. After that I couldn't help wondering what it would be like with you. Somehow I knew you'd be good...and gentle...and just what a freckled redhead needed to make her feel like Cinderella."

"Do I make you feel like Cinderella?"

She studied him for a long moment, traced his lips with an index finger and nodded.

He captured the finger, bit it, then as his eyes closed, he lay very still, pressing her four fingertips against his lips.

"What are you thinking?" she whispered.

His eyes opened, but for a moment he didn't answer. Instead he pressed his palm to hers and threaded their fingers together with slow deliberation. His fingers squeezed possessively. Hers answered. "About tomorrow. And the day after that and the day after that, and how we'll never have to be alone again. There'll always be each other...and babies." His fingers gripped more tightly. His eyes probed hers. "Do you want babies, Theresa?"

He felt her grip relax, then tug away. His stomach went light with warning, and he gripped her hand to keep it from escaping. "Theresa?"

She gazed at his face, wide-eyed, and when he saw the color begin to heighten between her freckles, he leaned above her on an elbow, frowning. "Theresa, what is it?"

She brushed his chest with her fingertips, dropping her eyes to follow the movement instead of meeting his frown. "Brian, there's something I haven't told you about my surgery."

In a split second a dozen fledgeling fears spiraled
through him, all dire: the surgery had somehow
taken away more than met the eye, and they'd never
have the babies he was dreaming of.

"Oh no, Brian, not that." She read his trepidation, soothingly bracketed his jaws. "I can have
babies—all I want. And I *do* want them. But...."
Again she dropped her eyes while her fingers rested
against his chest. "But I'll never be able to nurse
them. Not after the surgery."

For a moment he was still, waiting for the worst.
Suddenly he crushed her tightly. "Is that all?" he
sighed, relieved. She hadn't known he was holding
his breath until it rushed out heavily upon her temple. Her lips were on his warm collarbone as he secured her fast and rocked her in his arms.

"It doesn't matter to me, but I thought you should
know. I thought in case you had any feelings about it
we should talk about it now. Some men might consider me only...well, half a woman or something."

He pulled back sharply. "Half a woman?" He
sounded gruff as he squeezed her shoulders. "Never
think it." Their eyes locked, and she read in his total
love and approval. "Think about this." He drew her
into the warm curve of his body as he rolled aside and
snuggled her so near, his heartbeat was like a drum
beneath her ear. "Think about everything we'll have
some day—a house where there'll always be music
and a gang of little redheaded rascals whose—"

"Brown-haired," she interrupted, smiling against
his chest.

He went on with scarcely a missed beat. "Redheaded rascals whose freckles dance when—"

"Oh no! No freckles! If you give me freckled, redheaded babies, Brian Scanlon, I'll—"

The rest was smothered by his kiss before he grinned at her, continuing. "Redheaded rascals whose freckles dance when they play their violins—"

"Guitars. I won't have anybody hiding under any violins!"

"Mrs. Scanlon, will you kindly stop complaining about this family of ours? I said they'll be redheads and I mean it. And they'll play violin in the orchestra and—"

"Guitars," she insisted. "In a band. And their hair will be deep brown like their daddy's."

She threaded her fingers through it and their eyes met, heavy-lidded again with resurgent desire. Their bodies stirred against each other, their lips met, tongues sipped, and hearts clamored.

"Let's compromise," she suggested, scarcely aware of what she was saying, for already his hips were moving against hers.

He began speaking, but his voice was gruff and distracted. "Some redheads, some brown, some with freckles, some with guitars, some with vio—"

Her sweet seeking mouth interrupted. "Mmm-hmm..." she murmured against his lips. "But it'll take lots of practice to make all those babies." Her breasts pressed provocatively against his chest. She writhed once, experimentally, glorying in her newly discovered freedom. "Show me how we'll do it."

Their open mouths clung. His strong arm curved beneath her and rolled her atop him, then he settled her hips upon his, found the soft hollows behind her knees and drew them down until she straddled him in soft, feminine flesh. He pressed her hips away, and ordered thickly against her forehead, "Love me."

Her heart surged with shyness. Then love moved

her hand. Hesitantly she reached, found, then surrounded.

Their smiles met, faltered, dissolved. Eyelids lowered as she settled firmly upon him. A guttural sound
of satisfaction rumbled from his throat, answered by
her softer, wordless reply. Experimentally she lifted,
dropped, warming to his encouraging hands on her
hips.

Drawing back, she found his eyes still shuttered,
the lids trembling.

"Oh, Brian...Brian...I love you so much," she
vowed with tears beginning to sting.

His eyes opened. For a moment his hands calmed
the movement of her hips, then they reached to draw
her face down as he kissed the outer corner of each
eye. "And I love you, sweets...always," he whispered, drawing her mouth to his to complete the
promise within it. "Always...always."

In the living room a forgotten record circled, circled, sending soft music down the hall. To its lazy
rhythm their bodies moved. At the windows, sheets
rippled, and beneath two lovers the soft swell of confined water rose up as an afterbeat to their rhythmic
union. They would build a repertoire of sweet memories throughout their years as man and wife, but as
they moved now, reaffirming their love, it seemed
none would be so sweet as this moment that bound
them in promise.

When their bodies were gifted with the manifest of
that promise, when the sweet swelling peaked and the
shudders ceased, they reaffirmed it once again.

"I love you," spoke the man.

"I love you," answered the woman.

It was enough. Together, they moved on toward
forever.

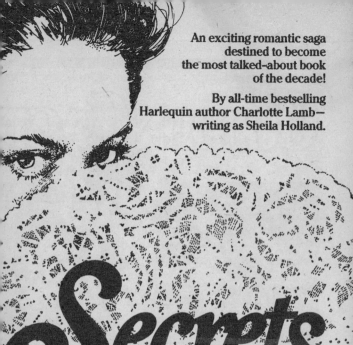

An exciting romantic saga
destined to become
the most talked-about book
of the decade!

By all-time bestselling
Harlequin author Charlotte Lamb—
writing as Sheila Holland.

Secrets
Sheila Holland

Sophia was torn between the love of two men—two
brothers who were part of a great and noble family. As
different as fire and ice, they were rivals whose hatred
for each other was powerful and destructive. Their
legacy to Sophia was a life of passion and regret, and
secrets that must never be told...

THE GOLDEN CAGE

The first Harlequin American Romance Premier Editio
by bestselling author ANDREA DAVIDSON

Harlequin American Romance Premier Editions is an exciting new program of longer–384 pages!–romances. By our most popular **Harlequin American Romance** authors, these contemporary love stories have superb plots and true-to-life characters–trademarks of **Harlequin American Romance.**

The Golden Cage, set in modern-da Chicago, is the exciting and passionate romance about the ver real dilemma of true love versus materialism, a beautifully written story that vividly portrays the contrast between the life-styles o the run-down West Side and the elegant North Shore.

Wherever paperback books are sold, or send your name, address and zip or postal code, along with a check or money order for $3.70 (includes 75¢ for postage and handling) payable to Harlequin Reader Service, to: Harlequin Reader Service

In the U.S.
Box 52040
Phoenix, AZ 85072-2040

In Canada
P.O. Box 2800, Postal Stn. A
5170 Yonge St., Willowdale, Ont. M2N 5T5

Volumes #7 through #12

Once again, Harlequin is pleased to present a specially designed collection of 12 exciting love stories by one of the world's leading romance authors. Each edition contains two of Janet Dailey's most requested titles.

Vol. #7—The Ivory Cane
        Low Country Liar

Vol. #8—Reilly's Woman
        To Tell the Truth

Vol. #9—Strange Bedfellow
        Wild and Wonderful

Vol. #10—Sweet Promise
        Tidewater Lover

Vol. #11—For Mike's Sake
        With a Little Luck

Vol. #12—Sentimental Journey
        A Tradition of Pride

Available now wherever paperback books are sold, or available through Harlequin Reader Service. Simply complete and mail the coupon below.